PENGUIN BOOKS

THE NOWHERE MAN

Gregg Hurwitz is the *Sunday Times* bestselling author of *Orphan X*, the first Evan Smoak novel. He is also the author of *You're Next, The Survivor, Tell No Lies* and *Don't Look Back*. A graduate of Harvard and Oxford universities, he lives with his family in LA, where he also writes for the screen, TV and comics, including Wolverine and Batman.

gregghurwitz.net
facebook.com/gregghurwitzreaders
@GreggHurwitz

By the same author

The Nowhere Man

GREGG HURWITZ

PENGUIN BOOKS

PENGUIN BOOKS

UK | USA | Canada | Ireland | Australia
India | New Zealand | South Africa

Penguin Books is part of the Penguin Random House group of companies
whose addresses can be found at global.penguinrandomhouse.com.

Penguin
Random House
UK

First published in the USA by Minotaur Books 2017
First published in Great Britain by Michael Joseph 2017
Published in Penguin Books 2017

001

Text copyright © Gregg Hurwitz, 2017

The moral right of the author has been asserted

Set in 13.5/16 pt Garamond MT Std
Typeset by Jouve (UK), Milton Keynes
Printed in Great Britain by Clays Ltd, St Ives plc

A CIP catalogue record for this book is available from the British Library

B FORMAT ISBN: 978–1–405–91073–6
EXPORT ISBN: 978–1–405–92989–9

www.greenpenguin.co.uk

MIX
Paper from
responsible sources
FSC® C018179

Penguin Random House is committed to a
sustainable future for our business, our readers
and our planet. This book is made from Forest
Stewardship Council® certified paper.

For Keith Kahla
an old-fashioned editor in all the best ways
and a new-fashioned editor in all the essential ones

How deep do you need to bury the past
before it will stay dead?

— Alan Moore, *Swamp Thing*

The truth will set you free. But not until
it is finished with you.

— David Foster Wallace, *Infinite Jest*

The Nowhere Man

I

What He Needs to Know

A naked selfie.

It starts with that.

Hector Contrell sends a seventeen-year-old kid to troll middle schools in East L.A. The kid, improbably named Addison, makes for fine bait. Seedily handsome, starter mustache, pop-star cheekbones, dirty blond hair flipped just so. He wears a hoodie and rides a skateboard, the better to look like he's fifteen. He says he's a pro skater with a contract. He says he's a rapper with a deal at a major label. He's really a pot-smoking dropout who lives in a rented garage with his older brother and his friends, spends his nights playing Call of Duty and hitting a green glass water bong named Fat Boy.

He hangs out near campuses at lunch, after classes, his skateboard rat-a-tat-tatting across sidewalk cracks just barely past school-ground limits. The girls cluster and giggle, and he chooses one to peel off the herd. He tells her to snap pictures. He tells her to get a secret Facebook account, one her parents don't know about, and upload them there. He tells her that everyone does this in high school, and he's mostly right, but not everyone is hooked into a scheme like this. He targets Title I schools, broke girls, easily impressed, looking for a dream, a romance, a way out. Girls whose parents lack the resources to do much if they disappear.

The secret Facebook page links go to Hector Contrell.

The genius of it is, the girls create the sales catalog themselves.

From Contrell the links go to all sorts of men with unorthodox tastes. Austrian industrialists. Sheikhs. Three brothers in Detroit with a padlocked metal shed. Online they can peruse the merchandise discreetly and, if need be, ask for more product information – different photographic angles, specific poses. They make their selections.

Given immigration confusion, gang influence, and splintered family trees, disappearances aren't rare when you're dealing with broke ethnic girls. They're a renewable resource.

Hector Contrell comes in the black of night, and another girl vanishes off the streets and wakes up in a stupor in Islamabad or Birmingham or São Paulo. Some of the girls are kept. Some are designated for onetime use.

Anna Rezian is the next prospect. Her father is a plumber, works hard, comes home late and tired. Her mother, a cocktail waitress, comes home later and more tired. Only fifteen, Anna takes care of her younger brothers and sisters, tries to remember to look at her textbooks after she gets the kids down. It's a hard routine for a girl her age.

One day after school, Addison's blue eyes peer out from beneath his scraggly bangs and pick her and only her. That night she touches up her eyeliner, sheds the flat-front Dickies with the worn knees, checks the lighting. This choice, this moment, is going to be a portal to a Whole New Her.

But after she uploads the selfie, nothing magical happens. Staring at the image she has released into the world, she feels an unease begin to gnaw at her.

She decides to stop after the one photo. But Addison needs more; they've been requested from a buyer in Serbia. In a ganja haze, he catches her in the alley outside her family's one-bedroom apartment. When his low-rent hipster charms fail him, he tells her what she'd better do. Big-shotting in the Crenshaw night, he lets fly that he works for someone who will hurt her and her family if she turns off the tap.

She stays up all night, trembling in the glow of her ancient laptop, clicking her way through the infinity of Facebook and chasing threads. Friends of friends have heard of friends who have disappeared. Over the top of the screen, she looks at her sleeping siblings and contemplates what it will feel like if harm befalls them because of her stupidity. She looks at her sleeping parents, exhausted after their long workdays. The chasm of guilt inside her widens by the second, pushing her further and further away until she is on an island of her own making, until her family members seem like specks on the horizon. Something awful is coming, either for them or for her. She makes the choice.

She sends new photos.

She stops sleeping. She starts plucking out her hair in patches. She cuts herself at school, hoping the pain will wake her from this nightmare. Maybe it's a cry for help instead, each crimson line across her forearm a smoke signal released in hopes that someone will ride to her rescue.

Someone does see the signal. One of her classmates' fathers, an older man with a cane and a fresh limp, finds her sobbing in the bathroom of a 7-Eleven when she's supposed to be in homeroom. He gives her a phone number: 1-855-2-NOWHERE. A magical fix-it line.

She dials.

Evan Smoak picks up.

'Do you need my help?' he asks.

That's how it works.

*

Fourteen hours later Evan is standing outside Addison's rented garage. The air tastes of car exhaust. The streetlights are broken, the stars smeared by smog, the night dark as tar. Evan is a wraith.

Addison's brother, Carl, and his crew of friends are out scoring black tar at a park in Boyle Heights. Evan knows this. Addison is alone. Evan knows this, too.

He has done his research.

The First Commandment – *Assume nothing* – demands it.

The wraith raises a single knuckle, taps the garage door.

A moment later it creaks upward.

Stooped, Addison emerges from an effluvium of day-old bong water. He rocks on his heels, gauging Evan.

By design, Evan is hard to gauge. Thirty-something. Fit but not muscly. Somewhere around six feet. An average guy, not too handsome.

Addison underestimates him.

This happens a lot, also by design.

The kid's lips twitch to the side. He jerks his head, flips his hair out of the blue eyes that have landed many a young woman on a container ship heading for uncharted waters.

'The fuck you want?' he says.

'Hector Contrell's address,' Evan says.

The pretty-boy lashes flare, but Addison covers quickly. 'No idea who that is. And no fucking way I'd tell you if I did.'

Evan looks through him. This tends to make people uneasy.

Uncertainty washes across Addison's face, but he blinks it away. 'I know people, you tool,' he says. 'People who can make you disappear like that.' The snap of his fingers, sharp in the crisp air. 'Who the fuck you think you are anyways?'

'The Nowhere Man,' Evan says.

The kid's Adam's apple jerks once. Up. Down.

The moniker is not widely known. But dark rumors have spread through certain streets like trash blown down graffitied alleys.

Addison takes a quick step to the side to stabilize himself. His voice comes out husky, pushed through a constricting throat. 'That's just a bullshit story.'

'Then you don't have to be scared, do you?'

Addison doesn't say anything.

'You do know what happens to the girls,' Evan tells him.

It takes a moment for Addison to relocate his voice. 'They disappear.'

'To where?'

'I don't know. Guys.'

'Who use them for . . . ?'

The kid shrugs. Actually muffles a snicker. 'Whatever guys do.'

'The address.'

'I can't tell you. Hector will kill me. *Literally* kill me.'

Evan's gaze is steady.

Addison falters. 'No,' he says, a new realization dawning. 'Oh, no. Look – I'm just a kid, man. I'm seventeen. You're not gonna kill me, are you?'

There is a punch Evan was taught in his early teens by a gruff marine close-quarter-combat instructor.

It is called the palate breaker.

A nonlethal blow that fractures the bridge of the nose, the sinus bones, and both orbital sockets, splitting the skull horizontally temple to temple. It leaves the upper jaw floating, unattached.

Evan's gaze narrows. He picks his spot.

You wouldn't have thought the kid could keep his feet, but there he is, upright on the curb. Something like drool leaks from his lips, the holes of his nose.

'No,' Evan says. 'I won't kill you.'

Addison makes a wheezing noise. With his new face, it will be hard for him to troll for girls anymore.

'The address,' Evan says again.

What is left of the mouth tells him what he needs to know.

2

The Social Contract

Evan slipped through the plastic tarp into a new-construction McMansion, the spoils of Hector Contrell's war on the broke families of East L.A. The house, distanced from its neighbors, topped an inclined driveway at the edge of Chatsworth.

Evan drifted through doorless frames, making silent progress toward the heart of the house. Studs framing the wide halls and exposed ceiling beams gave him the impression that he was walking into a massive rib cage, into Hector Contrell himself. Sawdust chalked the back of Evan's throat. Nails protruded from the floor, poking the soles of his Original S.W.A.T. boots. The aggressively checkered gunner grips of a custom Wilson Combat 1911 pistol bit the flesh of his palm.

He found Contrell in the living room-to-be, ensconced like a pilot within a cockpit of computer monitors and servers from which he ran his flesh empire with impunity. A burly, bearded man wholly unhooked from the social contract, who took what he wanted because he wanted it. The high-tech station with its bluish glow and snaking cables seemed anomalous, sprouting up like a mushroom from the exposed subfloor.

Hector noticed movement in the shadows and stood, revolver quickly in hand. For a time, it seemed, he kept rising.

Standing just past the semicircle of pushed-together desks, Evan looked up at him. A FUCK YOU tattoo on the front of Hector's neck indicated that nuance was not the man's strong suit.

Hector said, 'I don't know who you are or why you're here, but I'm gonna give you five seconds to leave before I aerate your torso.' For emphasis he kicked one of the monitors off the desk, which went to pieces at Evan's feet, sparking impressively.

Both men kept their guns down at their sides.

Evan watched the monitor give off a dying spark. Then he lifted his eyes.

'One of the functions of anger is to convince people of the seriousness of your intentions,' he said. 'To signal that you're out of control. Unpredictable. Willing to do damage. To evoke fear.'

Hector drew himself even taller. No minor feat. Backlit by the monitors, his meaty left earlobe showed a missing slot where an earring had been ripped free.

Evan took a step closer. 'So look at me. Look at me closely. And ask yourself: Do I look scared?'

The big man leaned in, the glow of the computers turning his face into a shadow-ravaged landscape – empty eye sockets, pronounced jowls, the curve of one cheek. His thick lips pulsed, the first show of hesitation.

Evan's gun remained at his side, just like Hector's. They faced each other across the desk.

When Evan was fourteen, Jack had trained him how to fast-draw. It wasn't with *High Noon* theatrics – unholster, lift, and aim. It was a two-millimeter tilt and 3.5 pounds of index-finger pressure.

The shadows shifted across Hector's face. His beefy hand twitched around his gun. He moved first.

The plywood walls gave off a good echo.

Later that night Evan eased into the alley that ran behind the dilapidated apartment that accommodated Anna Rezian's family. A sheen of blood had hardened on his left forearm, cracking like dried mud when he moved. He'd washed his hands and his face but could feel the leftover flecks on the side of his neck.

There'd been backspray.

He lifted his black phone from his pocket. It was a Roam-Zone model, encased in fiberglass and tough black rubber, the screen protected by Gorilla Glass. He kept it on him.

Always.

It was a lifeline. Not to him, but to those who called it.

He sent a text to Anna: OUTSIDE.

As he waited, a concern niggled at the base of his skull. He had seen something in Hector's house – he didn't know what it was, but it was wrong. Was his client in danger? No. He'd been thorough. Not a threat to her. Not a threat to him. Something else. Something important but not immediate.

Anna's backlit silhouette appeared at the mouth of the alley about ten yards away. She wore a nightie, her spine hunched, her dry hair sticking out. The alley formed a wind tunnel, the October air whipping at her brunette tufts, making them wag stiffly.

'You're safe now,' he told her.

Her feet were bare. He could see the tremble in her knees.

'I thought you were one of them coming to get me,' she said. 'I thought walking down here would be the last thing I ever did. But then . . . but then it was you.'

'I'm sorry I scared you,' he said.

'What does it mean? That I'm safe?'

'You don't have to worry anymore,' he said.

'About what?'

'Any of it.'

'Addison?'

'Has other concerns now.'

'And his boss? The guy behind it all?'

'He died.'

Anna trudged forward, her scalp shiny in the spots where she'd plucked out her hair. Her face held the same look he'd seen in his other clients, a worn-through, hollowed-out expression that came from falling out of the slipstream of life.

'Albert is safe?' Her voice cracked. 'And Eduard?'

'Yes.'

Anna came closer yet, her cheeks glinting. 'How about Maria? They won't hurt Maria?'

'There's no one left to hurt Maria.'

Openly sobbing now. *'Mayrig? Hayrig?'*

'Your mother and father will be fine.'

He thought of her family in their beds and wondered at the serenity they might offer her. At her age he hadn't had much, which meant he'd had nothing to leave behind. As a twelve-year-old, he'd stepped off a truck-stop curb into a dark sedan and blipped off the radar. Back then any gamble was worth the taking. This one had gotten him out of East Baltimore. He'd been to Marrakech and St. Petersburg and Cape Town, and he'd left his mark in blood at every stop. But he'd never had what Anna had waiting for her upstairs. The chill breeze brought with it the realization that he'd devoted his life to preserving for others what he couldn't have himself.

'The pictures of me,' she said. 'They'll be so ashamed.'

Before leaving Hector's place, Evan had safed the house, finding little more than construction materials, empty beer bottles, a few hefty dumbbells in the garage. Fast-food wrappers layered a mattress thrown on the floor in one of the bare-bones rooms upstairs where Hector was living during the construction. Evan had gone back down to the comms center and dragged the considerable body out of the way. Once the cockpit was clear, he spent a few stomach-churning minutes navigating the databases, clicking through the files of past 'eligibles' to locate the matching buyers. Client information was sparse and coded, but he forwarded it on to the local FBI field office. But not before wiping all information about Anna Rezian off the servers.

'The pictures are gone,' Evan said. 'No one will have to know anything.'

Anna took an unsteady step to the side and lifted a hand to the cracked stucco wall. 'Eduard. He's safe now. He's safe.' Still working it through, thawing out of denial.

'You're all safe.'

Anna's face wobbled, and for a moment it seemed she might come apart entirely. 'I don't know how I can face them. Knowing what I almost did to us all. I'll never forgive myself.'

'That's up to you.'

She looked stung by his response. Tears clung to her lashes. She bit her lips. Her chest rose, her nostrils flaring. Deep breath. Exhale. The tears did not fall.

'You're not to call me again,' Evan said. 'Do you understand? This is what I do. But it's all that I do.'

'Albert and Maria are okay now.' Her lips barely moved. Her voice, little more than a whisper. '*Mayrig* and *Hayrig*. And Eduard. Eduard.'

'Anna, I need you to focus. Look at me. Look at me. I have one thing to ask of you before I leave.'

Her eyes found a sudden clarity. 'Anything.'

'Find someone who needs me. Like you did. It doesn't matter if it takes a week or a month or a year. You find someone who is desperate and has no way out. Give them my number.'

'Yes, 1-855-2-NOWHERE.'

Every call was digitized and sent over the Internet through a series of encrypted virtual private network tunnels. After pinging through fifteen software virtual telephone switch destinations around the globe, it came through his RoamZone.

'Yes. You tell them about me.'

'Like Nicole Helfrich's dad when he found me in the 7-Eleven?'

'Like that. You find someone. Tell them I'll be there on the other end of the phone.'

That was the final step for his clients. A task, a purpose, an act of empowerment that transitioned them from victim to rescuer. Evan knew all too well that some wounds never healed, not fully. But there were ways to contain the pain, to take ownership over the scars, and this was one of them.

Anna lunged at him and wrapped him in a hug. For a moment his arms floated a few inches above her thin back. He was unaccustomed to this kind of contact. In the moonlight he could see the wine-colored streak on his forearm, the dark half-moons beneath his nails. He didn't want Hector Contrell's blood on her clothes, in her hair. And yet Anna's embrace tightened, her face pressed into his chest.

He lowered his arms. She was warm. He felt the wetness of her cheek through his T-shirt. She clung to him.

Her voice came muffled. 'How do I thank you?'

Evan said, 'Be with your family.'

He'd meant it as the next instruction, but it struck him that it was also the answer to her question.

She stepped back to wipe her eyes, and he took the opportunity to slip away.

3

War Machine

Lurching from stoplight to stoplight, Evan dreamed of vodka. He had a new bottle tucked into the ice drawer of his Sub-Zero, waiting to greet him when he got home. From the outside his Ford F-150 pickup looked like any one of the millions on the roads of America. But with its laminate armor glass, self-seal tires, and built-to-spec push-bumper assembly, it was actually a war machine.

Up ahead, his building came into view. Branded with the inflated title of Castle Heights, the residential tower pinned down the easternmost spot on the Wilshire Corridor, giving his penthouse condo an unbroken view of downtown Los Angeles. Castle Heights was posh but dated, as easily overlooked as Evan's truck. Or Evan himself.

Recruited out of the projects of East Baltimore as a kid, he'd spent seven grueling years training under the tutelage of his handler. To say that Jack Johns had been like a father to him was an understatement. Jack had been the first person to treat Evan like he was human.

Evan had been created by the Orphan Program, a deep-black project buried inside the Department of Defense. It had identified the right kind of boys lost in the system of foster homes, covertly culled them one by one, and trained them to do what the U.S. government could not officially do in places where it could not officially be. A fully deniable, antiseptic program run off a shadow budget. Technically, Orphans did not even exist.

They were expendable weapons.

As Orphan X, Evan had been given bursting bank accounts in nonreporting countries. His assignments spanned more than a decade. Rarely sighted, never captured, he was known only by the dead high-value targets he left in his wake and the alias he'd earned for moving unseen among the shadows.

The Nowhere Man.

At one point, though, he'd wanted out. It had cost him dearly. But it had left him with virtually unlimited money, a rare skill set, and time on his hands. And while he was done being Orphan X, he'd discovered that there was still work he should do as the Nowhere Man.

Pro bono work.

He'd lost the government designation but kept the alias given to him by his enemies.

Evan had heard that the Orphan Program had been dismantled, but last year he'd discovered that it was still operational. The most merciless of the Orphans had taken over. Charles Van Sciver. His new directive: to track down and eliminate former Orphans. According to those holding Van Sciver's leash, Evan's head contained too much sensitive information to remain connected to his body.

One thing had been made clear in their last bloody confrontation – Van Sciver and his Orphans would not stop the hunt until Evan was dead.

In the meantime Evan stayed off the grid and stayed vigilant.

At last he finished the gauntlet crawl through Wilshire Boulevard traffic. Turning in to Castle Heights, he whipped through the porte cochere past the valet and descended to the subterranean parking lot, drifting into his spot between two concrete pillars.

He grabbed a black sweatshirt from the back, tugged it on

to cover the dried blood on his arm, and headed across the floor. He always took a moment outside the lobby door to close his eyes, draw in a breath, and ready himself for the transition into his other persona.

Evan Smoak, importer of industrial cleaning supplies. Another boring tenant.

Given the hour, the lobby was quiet, the air fragrant with the scent of lilies. Evan crossed briskly to the elevator, nodding at the security guard. 'Evening, Joaquin.'

Joaquin looked up from the bank of monitors running live feeds from the building's perimeter and hallways. Castle Heights prided itself on its security, an additional selling point to attract moneyed middle-aged tenants and flush retirees.

'Evening, Mr Smoak. You have a good night?'

'Typical Thursday,' Evan said. 'Burgers with the guys.'

Joaquin controlled the elevators from behind the high counter – another safety measure – and his shoulder dipped as he pressed the button for the car. Evan lifted a hand in thanks, noticed the flecks of dried blood beneath his fingernails, and lowered it quickly. He stepped inside, the button for the twenty-first floor already lit.

The doors were just sliding closed when he heard a familiar voice call out, 'Wait! Hold the elevator, Joaquin – *please.*' The patter of footsteps. 'I meant the "please" to come first so I didn't sound all ordery, but –'

The doors parted again, and Evan came face-to-face with Mia Hall. Her sleeping nine-year-old was slumped in her arms, his chin resting on her shoulder.

Mia's eyes rose to meet Evan's, and she froze.

She was rarely caught off guard, but now her mouth was slightly ajar, a flush coming up beneath the faint scattering of freckles across the bridge of her nose.

They'd had an almost-relationship last year. He'd saved her life, and she'd saved his ass. In the process she'd learned more about him than she should have. Which would have been a problem even if she hadn't been a DA for the City of Los Angeles.

They blinked at each other.

She shifted, straining under Peter's weight.

'Want me to take him?' Evan asked.

There was a time when that would have been normal.

'No,' she said. 'Thanks. I got him.'

They rode up to her floor in silence. Remembering the traces of blood beneath his nails, Evan curled his hands into loose fists. He caught the faintest whiff of lemongrass – the scent of Mia's lotion.

Peter's cheek was smooshed into a half pout, his blond hair stuck up on one side, his lips blue with lollipop residue. When the doors parted with an arthritic rattle, Peter lifted his head sleepily. The smile touched his charcoal eyes first, then his mouth.

'Hi, Evan Smoak.' His voice, even raspier than usual. Before Evan could answer, the boy's lids drooped shut again.

Mia carried him out, and Evan watched them walk up the corridor until the closing elevator doors wiped them from view.

4

Clean as a Scalpel

When Evan turned the key, the lock to Condo 21A unbolted with a clank, various security bars releasing within the steel door concealed behind the homey wood-paneled façade. As Jack used to say, *Ball bearings within ball bearings.*

Evan muted the alarm and walked to the kitchen area. He passed the living wall, a drip-fed vertical garden that sprouted mint and sage, parsley and chamomile. The pleasing scent and splash of green were the sole aspects of the corner penthouse that could be described as cheerful.

The floor plan was largely open, seven thousand square feet of poured concrete split by workout stations, sitting areas, a freestanding fireplace, and a steel staircase that twisted up to a loft. Countless safeguards hid inside the sleek, modern space. The windows and sliding glass doors that turned two walls into a city panorama? Bullet-resistant Lexan armed with shatter-detection software. The periwinkle retractable sunscreens? Woven titanium armor. The quartz-rock-layered balconies cupping the sides of the condo? Secondary alarms rigged to detect the audio signature of an unwelcome guest's boots compressing the stones.

Evan slipped around the island to the Sub-Zero. Nestled among the ice cubes, a fat bottle of Karlsson's Gold beckoned. The handcrafted Swedish vodka, comprising seven kinds of potatoes, was uniquely made, distilled a single time through a copper-lined still. Evan poured a few fingers into a rocks glass over a spherical ice cube and garnished the drink with a single twist of ground pepper from a stainless-steel mill.

Clean as a scalpel up front. Hint of mineral on the finish. Lingering bite of pepper.

Perfect.

Evan walked to the fireplace, fired up the pyre of cedar logs, then peeled off his mission clothes and fed them to the flames. With the rocks glass dangling at his side, he padded naked across the vast space and down the brief hall, passing the spot where his dear departed nineteenth-century katana used to hang. The bare wall hooks reminded him that he'd recently won an online bid for a replacement samurai sword, one that dated back to the Early Edo period. The shipment was due to arrive soon from the Seki auction house.

He stepped through his bedroom into the bathroom and tapped the frosted-glass shower door, which recessed into the wall on silent tracks. Turning the water up as hot as he could stand, he ducked into the stream. He scrubbed. The water ran dark, a crimson swirl circling the drain.

It took a wire brush and some effort to get his fingernails clean.

After drying off he headed into the bedroom and dressed in the same outfit he'd worn before. Dark jeans, gray V-necked T-shirt. Before turning away from the dresser, he hesitated over the bottom drawer.

Emotion came up under his skin, a flush of heat.

He tugged the drawer open and used his thumbnail to lift the false bottom.

Beneath, a blue flannel shirt, blackened with old blood.

Jack's blood.

There wasn't a night in the past eight years that Evan

didn't turn off the light, close his eyes, and watch Jack bleed out in his arms.

Evan shut the drawer and rose, trying to dissipate the tightness in his chest. He sat on his bed, a Maglev that literally floated two feet off the floor, the slab held airborne by neodymium rare-earth magnets. Closing his eyes, suspended between floor and ceiling, he focused on his breathing, dropped inside his body, felt the weight of his bones inside his flesh. It usually helped him find tranquility.

But not tonight.

Images strobed through the darkness behind his eyelids. Hector Contrell's shoulders jerking back as if yanked by strings. Ink pooling in the hollow of his neck, a punctuation mark for the FUCK YOU tattoo. Those mighty legs collapsing, a slow-motion avalanche crumble. The mess on the floor upstairs around the mattress – residue-stained Styrofoam ramen bowls, empty burrito wrappers, crumpled protein packets. The rib cage of the house, bare studs scrolling by as Evan crept inside. The hall telescoping out like some Kubrickian horror, each empty doorframe replaced by another and another.

Evan's eyes flew open.

No doors. Which meant no door handles. That was what had been nagging at him. The house was open to the world, fluttering tarps in place of walls.

No locked area for the kidnapped girls.

The logistics of moving them around the world were complicated. There had to be a holding area somewhere off premises.

Which meant the possibility existed that another young woman remained in it.

Evan hopped off the bed and moved back into the bathroom, stepping into the shower. He squeezed the lever handle for the hot water, and a moment later came a faint click. The lever, keyed to his palm print, doubled as a doorknob. He turned it the wrong way, and a door, disguised by the tile pattern of the shower wall, swung inward.

He stepped into the Vault.

Four hundred asymmetrical square feet crowded by the underbelly of the public stairs to the roof, the walled-off storage space served as Evan's armory and ops center. From the weapon lockers to the sheet-metal desk burdened with monitors, servers, and cables, it contained all the tools of his trade. The screens displayed pirated security feeds of Castle Heights. Every hallway, every stairwell, every access door.

He breathed in the smell of damp concrete, dropped into his chair, and rolled to the L-shaped desk to access the law-enforcement databases. All the major criminal and civil records, forensic files, and ballistics registers – anything that the local police could dig up on the Panasonic Toughbook laptops wired into their patrol cars – Evan could access.

His training had consisted of learning a little bit about everything from people who knew everything about something. He was hardly an expert hacker, but he'd broken into a few cruisers and uploaded a piece of reverse SSH code into their laptops – a back door for him to get into the system anytime he beckoned.

He beckoned now, searching Contrell's known associates, past residences, former cellmates. Nothing raised a red flag. A few hours later, the watered-down vodka sat forgotten beside the mouse pad, pepper grinds floating like ash.

Through the DMV site, Evan grabbed the license-plate number of Contrell's Buick Enclave. Another series of backstage maneuvers got him into the vehicle's GPS records. He printed out the data captures – longitudes and latitudes listed in an endless scroll.

As the LaserJet spit out page after page, he started breaking down the pauses between the Enclave's movements.

Contrell's destinations.

Evan's work was not done.

The Tenth Commandment: *Never let an innocent die.*

5

The Eyes of the Data-Mining Beast

The room could have been anywhere. Midway up a high-rise. At the distal end of a mansion's wing. Underground, even.

It was big.

The size of a movie theater, but without the rows of chairs. There wasn't a screen.

There were *hundreds* of them.

Lining three walls, stacked top to bottom, the most elaborate display of computing power this side of DARPA. Each monitor scrolled an endless stream of code. The screens were the eyes of the data-mining beast; the banks of servers bunkered behind the bomb-resistant fourth wall were the brain.

Guttering light from the monitors strobed across the dim room, living camouflage. It was hard to see anything aside from the screens. Everything melted together – the rugs, the consoles, the sparse furniture. Even the few visitors with clearance to enter – usually a not-fully-read-in engineer making tech adjustments – seemed to disappear, fish blending into rippling water.

Charles Van Sciver liked it in here. Liked it for the darkness, through which he could drift alone and unseen.

There were no windows. No mirrors either, not even in the adjoining bathroom. He'd covered them up. The occasional visitor was made to stand at a distance so Van Sciver could stay bathed in the protective anonymity of the flickering lights.

It was safe and contained in here. Just him and his algorithms.

It wasn't fair to say that *all* the computing power was directed at locating Orphan X.

Only 75 percent.

Or 76.385, to be precise.

After all, as the head of the Program, Van Sciver did have other mission responsibilities.

But none as important as this.

For better than a decade, Evan had been the top asset in the entire Orphan Program. He didn't merely know where the bodies were buried. He had buried most of them.

Though the naked eye couldn't process a sliver of the information whipping across the monitors, Van Sciver liked to watch the large-scale data processing in real time. Though he knew the buzzwords – 'cluster analysis,' 'anomaly detection,' 'predictive analytics' – he couldn't even comprehend what was before him. But he could grasp the output reports, which he checked meticulously on the hour, searching for filaments in the ocean of cyberspace. These threads of the Nowhere Man had to be delicately backtraced. If Van Sciver allowed the slightest quiver showing that he had something on the hook, the line would snap.

Lately his team of engineers had been focused on data warehousing, piecing together bits of information from offshore bank accounts, trying to reconstruct enough of the mosaic to point them in the right direction. They had leads on Evan, of course. A few floating strands on the water. But every time they tugged slack out of the line, they came up with more slack, a money transfer zigzagging off into the depths, a shell corp vanishing behind a mailbox corporation, another trail ending at a disused P.O. box off some dusty Third World dirt road.

Van Sciver paced the perimeter of the room, his ever-paler skin drinking in the antiseptic blue glow of the screens. The lack of human contact ensured that he would never be deterred from his goal. Ultimately it would come down to discipline and abstinence, and so he had cleared out any distracting clutter from his existence. His willingness to deny all pleasure and warmth was why he would win. That was why he would beat his nemesis. Victory would be pleasure enough.

Van Sciver halted. Facing the horseshoe of the rippling walls, he basked in the power represented before him. Time was meaningless in here. The present was spent reconstructing the past and extrapolating the future, a dragon ever swallowing its tail, an infinity of numbers that summed to zero.

But one day they would add up to everything.

One day they would search out the right thread of ones and zeros that would lead to Orphan X.

It was only a matter of time.

6

Struck Oil

Evan noticed everything when he drove. Especially gray Ford Transit Connect vans with no side windows and dealer plates. Like the one that had been hovering in his rearview mirror for the past few blocks.

He threw on his right-hand turn signal. The van did not. Either it wasn't following him or it was driven by a pro unwilling to take the bait. Evan drove straight past the entrance of the Norwalk FedEx office, and the van kept right on behind him. Evan muted the signal, keeping his head down but his eyes nailed to the rearview. He waited a few beats and then abruptly veered off onto a side street. The van coasted by, not even slowing.

He could never be too careful.

He'd spent the morning completing a circuit of the safe houses he kept in the Greater Los Angeles Area, testing his load-out gear, checking the oil on his alternate vehicles, changing up the automated lighting. At his Westchester place, a crappy single-story beneath LAX's flight path, he'd switched out his usual rig for a mud-spattered 4Runner with a scuba flag sticker in the back window.

On the side street now, Evan sat behind the wheel and watched the road for a while. Finally he dropped the transmission back into drive. Backtracking to the FedEx office, he entered, signed a series of customs forms, and left with an elongated cardboard box.

His new katana. This blade had been forged relatively

recently, in 1653, by Heike Norihisa, last smith of the five-layered smelt. The katana was decorative, as Evan had intended the last one to be, and he was eager to mount it on the empty hooks in his hall.

But he had another location to check first. He'd spent hour after excruciating hour parsing the data from Contrell's GPS, checking the man's frequent stops, searching for the location where he stored the girls before shipping them out. With every passing day, more sand trickled through the hourglass.

Evan drove to Fullerton. A sheaf of papers rested in his lap, much of the data on them already crossed out with red pen.

The next place on the list proved to be a humble residence, semi-isolated behind a stretch of soccer fields gone to dirt. Detached garage, new shingles, fresh paint, curtains drawn. A security gate guarded a concrete front walk hemmed in by flower beds. A Stepford house writ small.

Evan parked several blocks away and doubled back. He vaulted the fence, put his ear to the door, heard nothing. The lock gleamed, a shiny Medeco. He raked it with a triple mountain pick, feeling for the rhythm of the wafers inside as they lifted to different heights. At last he felt the pleasing click of the release.

The well-greased door swung in on silent hinges. He drew his Wilson from his Kydex high-guard hip holster and eased inside. The interior, dim from the drawn curtains, stank of cleaning solution and unventilated air. Though he sensed that the place was empty, he moved silently from room to room. It was cheaply constructed and surprisingly clean. Dishes neatly stacked on a spotless counter. Sparkling linoleum floors. IKEA-looking slipcovered couch and chairs, calming taupes, distressed blues. In the living room, he parted the curtains with a hand.

The windows were nailed shut.

He ran his fingers over the heads of the nails, the metal cool against his prints. His heart rate ticked up with anticipation.

He moved on.

The master bedroom featured two double beds, sheets neatly made. Men's clothes in the wardrobe. *Big* men's clothes. One of the jackets looked like it could cover a deck chair.

Evan stopped, breathed, listened.

Then he started down the tiny hall to the rear room. Three door bolts. On the *outside*.

Pistol drawn, Evan stood perfectly still outside the room for a full ten minutes. No sounds of breathing within, no creaking of the floorboards.

Finally he threw one bolt. The muted clank of metal against metal might as well have been a clap of thunder.

Standing to the side of the door, he waited.

Nothing happened, and then more nothing.

The next two locks he unbolted in rapid succession. He bladed his body. Let the door creak inward. Leading with the 1911, he nosed around the jamb. A nicely made bed, lavender comforter, brand-new TV on a stand.

A lovely room, aside from the plate of sheet metal drilled over the window. When Evan shouldered the door to step inside, he felt it to be heavier than the others. Solid core.

The holding pen.

No one inside. The room – bare, pristine, equipped with only the basics – seemed like a diorama. In fact, the whole place had a dollhouse feel.

It had been designed with one purpose in mind: comfortable functionality.

Hector Contrell had to ensure that the merchandise wasn't damaged before delivery.

The bathroom door remained closed. Evan tried the doorknob, but it didn't budge. Seating the pistol in his holster, he took out his tension wrench again. The cheaper lock required only a hook pick and a few jiggles.

As the door swung inward, the smell hit him first.

A smooth leg, mottled blue-purple, hooked over the brim of the bathtub. A mass of tangled black hair covered the face, leaving only a delicate ivory chin exposed. He put the body as older than most of Contrell's 'eligibles.' Late teens, early twenties. Probably designated for a buyer looking for variety.

Until Contrell's operation had been blown and his middlemen decided to liquidate the inventory.

She'd been alive when he killed Contrell. She'd been alive when he went home and poured himself a glass of vodka and drank to a job well done.

Evan lowered the pick set.

That was when he heard the footsteps behind him.

Two men, no doubt the inhabitants of the roomy clothes in the wardrobe of the master bedroom. The one nearest Evan gripped a snub-nosed Smith & Wesson Chief's Special and gripped it well. Firmed wrists, locked elbows. A second pistol hung in a cheap nylon holster under his left armpit, semiauto backup in case five bullets weren't sufficient.

The man behind him carried a healthy gut and a SIG Sauer. His gun was also raised, but he could afford to be less on point given that his buddy had Evan pinned down. Evan couldn't get a clear look around the front man's barrel chest. The man seemed to block everything out. It wasn't just his girth but the way he canted in aerodynamically at Evan. Thrusting chin, ledged brow, chest and biceps tugging him forward on his frame so it seemed that only the balls of his feet were holding him back – a bullet train made incarnate.

'Who's been sleeping in our beds?' he said.

Evan lowered his hands slightly. The S&W followed the motion, stopped level with his heart.

'Goldilocks?' Evan said. 'Really?'

'I gotta agree, Claude,' the man by the door said. 'Not your finest work.'

Claude's features rearranged themselves. His cheeks looked shiny, as if he'd recently shaved, but stubble was already pushing its way through again. His face, the target demographic for five-blade razors.

'I just thought, you know, the whole breaking-and-entering thing,' Claude said. 'Us coming home, catching you. Plus the Goldilocks reference, it's demeaning.'

'Because she's a girl,' Evan said.

Claude nodded.

Evan held his hands in place. 'You know what they say. If you have to explain the joke . . .'

The man in the back flicked his SIG at Evan. 'Gun on the ground.'

Evan complied.

As he squatted, he gauged the distance to the tips of Claude's shoes. Maybe five feet. Evan could close the space in a single lunge. Easy enough, if he didn't have two guns aimed at his critical mass.

Rising, he eyed the barrel of the Chief's Special. Since Claude was muscle-bound and right-handed, Evan's first move would be to juke left, make him swing the gun inward across that barrel chest. The compression of delt and pec might slow his arm, buy Evan a half second.

That would be all he'd need.

His stare dropped to Claude's second gun, the one slung in the loose-fitting underarm holster. A Browning Hi-Power. It was cocked and locked – hammer back, safety engaged. The safety lever peeked out beneath the retention strap of the nylon holster. Good presentation.

The odor wafted from the bathroom over Evan's shoulder,

precipitating on the taste buds at the back of his tongue. Just past the threshold in the hall, he saw the bright red of a few plastic gasoline jugs; the men had set them down quietly. 'You guys cleaning up the operation?'

'Contrell was the CEO,' Claude said. 'We're just workaday guys. Glorified babysitters, really. Sit around, eat pizza, watch the tube. Beats digging ditches.'

Evan flipped the tiny hook pick around his thumb, pinched it again. 'Those were the only options, huh? Sell girls or dig ditches?'

Claude smiled with sudden awareness, his magnificent jaw jutting out all the more. 'You're the guy who put us out of work.'

With a flick of his wrist, Evan flipped the hook pick at Claude's eyes, lunging left just before the gunshot. The bullet cracked past his ear. He dove not so much at Claude as *into* him, using him as a shield, getting inside the range of the revolver. Evan's right hand flew at that Browning in the underarm holster, and then he smacked into the big man, pressing chest to chest, a dance move gone wrong.

It happened very fast.

Evan's thumb shoved the safety lever off as his forefinger curled around the trigger. He rode the gun back in the sling and fired straight through the holster from beneath Claude's armpit. The man behind them took the shot through the cheek, blood welling like struck oil. The pistol in his fist barked twice as he flew back. Evan felt both impacts ripple Claude's flesh, friendly-fire smacks to the spine.

Claude dropped fast and lay still.

The other man had wound up sitting next to the bed, slumped forward over his gut, one hand clutching the lavender comforter. A perfect stillness claimed the room.

The whole thing had gone down in about a second and a half.

Evan picked up his gun and started out. Though the

neighboring houses were far, the noise of a firefight would carry.

As he stepped over Claude, he noticed a yellow slip peeking from the inner lapel pocket of the laid-open jacket. Instinct halted him there above the body, told him to crouch and reach for it. He teased it out.

A customer copy of a shipping bill, rendered on thin yellow carbonless copy paper.

All at once the air felt brittle, as if it might shatter if he moved wrong.

His eyes pulled to the bed. Queen size.

Big enough for roommates.

He looked back at the form, taking in the data.

Origin: Long Beach, CA
Destination: Jacksonville, FL
ETA: Oct 29, 11:37pm
Distance: 5141.11 miles (8273.82 km)

That was not the distance a package would travel by truck or plane. Not even close. That distance would be two thousand miles and change. This package was traveling down around the bottom of the continent and through the Panama Canal.

He scanned farther down the form.

Sure enough, a twenty-foot ISO-standard container had been secured on a midsize bulk carrier called the *Horizon Express*. An additional port fee of $120 was to be paid upon delivery to the Jacksonville Port Authority.

At the bottom of the form, something was written in pen, the blue ink distinct from the black dye pressed through from the other sheets. A name. And an age.

Alison Siegler/17 yrs.

Seeing the casual scrawl fired something at Evan's core.

31

He wondered about the seventeen-year-old girl locked inside Container 78653-B812.

It seemed that Claude and friends had managed to fulfill one last order this morning before shutting down the assembly belt. Which meant that Evan had one last head to sever from the hydra of Contrell's operation to put it down for once and for all.

He had sixteen days until that container ship reached Jacksonville. He would meet the buyer there. But he didn't plan on leaving Alison Siegler alone until then.

Folding the yellow form in his hand, he headed out, stepping past the trio of gasoline jugs in the hall and through the front door. Jogging up the front walk, he vaulted the security gate.

His boots had just hit the sidewalk when he heard the screech of tires.

Two Ford Transits flew in at him, one from either side, a narrowing V. Familiar gray, no side windows. As Evan reached for his hip holster, their doors rolled open, exposing a row of eyes peering out through balaclava masks. Inside each van a line of shotguns raised in concert, like a gun turret.

Neon orange spots floated within the dark vehicle interiors. The shotgun stocks, color-coded for less-lethal.

Evan had a moment to think, *This is gonna hurt,* and then the twelve-gauges let fly. The first beanbag round hit him square in the thigh, knocking him into a 180, a volley of follow-ups peppering his right side. A rib cracked. Another flexible baton round skimmed the side of his head, a glancing blow, but given the lead shot packed inside, it was enough. No pain, not yet, just pressure and the promise of swelling.

He spun with the blow, wheeling to round out the 360, somehow managing to draw his Wilson in the process. The black-clad men had already unassed from the vans in shooting-squad formation. These men were expert assaulters, leagues beyond Hector Contrell and his sorry assemblage of freelancers.

An enormous man in the middle held a bizarre gun, its conical barrel flaring to accommodate a balloonlike plug. It looked like a basketball stuck in a snake's craw.

It discharged with a whoosh. Evan watched it unfurl at him with detached and helpless wonder. Durable nylon mesh, steel clamps weighting the four corners, the whole thing yawning open like the maw of some great beast.

A wildlife-capture net.

It cocooned him, his wrist smashed to his nose, one knee snapped up into his chest, his feet pointed down like an Olympic diver's. This must have been what the Neanderthals felt like when the lava flow caught up, fossilizing them in all their awkward non-glory.

His gun hand, pinned to his left ear, was as useless as the rest of him.

The pavement smashed his cheek. For a split second, a dot of dancing yellow grabbed his focus – the shipping slip catching a gust of wind, riding an air current into the gutter. The last trace of Alison Siegler, whisked away.

Evan pegged his pupil to the corner of his eye, straining to look up. A massive dark form loomed, a needle held vertically in latex-gloved hands.

The form leaned in.

A prick of metal in the side of the neck.

Then searing darkness.

7

The Inevitable Gurgle

Once again Evan is inside that underground parking lot just south of the Jefferson Monument. Parking Level 3 is his personal hell.

Or, more aptly, his purgatory.

It is a humid summer night in 2008, the same night he has been stuck inside for eight years and change.

The elevator sign glows red as always, casting bloody shadows across the slumbering construction equipment. The lot is shut down for improvements. Evan waits behind a concrete pillar, scraping his boots against a bumper curb to dislodge the cherry blossoms from the tread.

He has summoned Jack here for a midnight meet. Evan is supposed to be in Frankfurt right now, lying low after a high-profile job in Yemen, but instead he has flown back to the States, impulsive and agitated and needing to see the face of the only person in the world he can trust.

Evan wants out.

Jack raised him to be the finest assassin in the world. He also raised him to keep his humanity. Two trains on a collision course.

After a decade spent operating as Orphan X, Evan knows he has to jump off before the crash, even if the jump kills him.

He doesn't consider that there might be worse outcomes.

Jack didn't want to meet. He said he was watching his movements. That he didn't want to be drawn out, to break cover. But Evan demanded, and despite his better judgment Jack finally agreed.

It happens as it always does.

Jack appears from nowhere, footsteps ticktocking off the concrete walls, shadow stretched to noirish proportions across the oil-stained floor. He and Evan embrace. It has been more than two years since they've seen each other face-to-face. Jack appraises Evan as if he's a son come home from grad school. A glint of pride touches Jack's eyes. He is baseball-catcher square and rarely permits emotion to leak through the mask.

The words spill from Evan's mouth. 'I'm out.'

Jack answers with the words Evan has heard in a thousand renditions: 'You're never out. You know this. Without me you're just —'

'A war criminal.'

The discussion intensifies as is ordained.

Until.

The roar of an engine and a startling burst of headlights snap their heads around to the black SUV flying down the ramp, careening onto the deserted parking level. Guns fire through the windshield, muzzle flares strobe-lighting the vehicle's advance.

Jack grabs Evan, yanks him behind a pillar. Evan rolls across the back of the rounded concrete, the cool surface kissing the blades of his shoulders, and pops out the other side already shooting. He Swiss-cheeses the front seats and whoever occupies them. The SUV slows to a crawl, rolls forward to brush Evan's thighs. The would-be assassins, tilted over the dashboard, have been made unrecognizable by his well-placed hollow points.

He braces himself for the noise he knows will come next.

The inevitable gurgle from behind him.

Bright arterial blood soaks the shoulder of the blue flannel. Jack's hand, already wearing a glove of crimson, clamps the wound.

Evan rips the flannel off to get a clean look. Needles of blood spray from between Jack's fingers. Lingering beneath the familiar tang of iron, the sickly sweet trace of cherry blossom churns Evan's gut.

Years of training have stripped the panic reaction out of him, have crushed it from his cells.

And yet.

His face hot.

Time moving differently.

35

Grief clawing free of the lockbox in his chest, crowding his throat.

Jack is saying things he never said, things he would never say. He is speaking not from the memory but from Evan's heart of hearts.

I took you in.

Raised you as my own.

And you killed me.

Why?

He raises an arm cloaked in blood, pointing out, away.

Banishing Evan from the intimate sight of his last ragged breaths.

Banishing Evan to a lifetime of atonement.

Banishing Evan from himself.

With the bloody flannel mopped around his fist, Evan runs. He runs for the darkness, because only darkness can cover the nakedness of his shame.

Only in darkness can he be alone.

He came to in silk.

Liquid sheets caressing his skin, a sea of rumpled purple darker than eggplant, a bed fit for a maharaja.

At first he thought he was still in the dream.

And then the pain hit.

8

His Own Dollhouse

When Evan lifted his head from the pillow, his ribs gave a complaint that set his teeth on edge. He took a moment to remember how to breathe. Then he threw back the silk-soft sheets and sat up with a groan. Facts pinged in at him like june bugs hitting a windshield.

He was naked.

Wine-red bruises splotched his right side – thigh, stomach, chest.

His room was as spacious and luxurious as the sleigh bed unfurled beneath him.

Through a groggy haze, he assembled his surroundings in pieces. Vaulted ceiling, exposed beams. Insulated curtains on a wrought-iron rod. Distressed-leather chair and ottoman with whipstitched edges and hammered nailheads. Mahogany counter and built-in desk without a chair. Crackling logs in a travertine-faced fireplace. The design seemed as un-Los Angeles as one could get, Ralph Lauren sprucing up the von Trapp family lodge.

Evan allowed himself one great big moment of What The Fuck.

Then he stood, wincing. His head swam from the drugs or too much time spent horizontal – or, most likely, both. Rustic oak plank floorboards, cool and smooth beneath his soles, brought welcome relief from the toasty hearth. He stretched, taking stock. His hands were fine. Likely a cracked rib – nothing to do there. The bruising, pyrotechnic but harmless, looked to be at least a few days along.

All things considered, the beanbag rounds had lived up to their billing.

He crossed to the walk-in closet. Inside hung five button-up shirts, slotted like dominoes. Jeans, T-shirts, and sweaters, folded and placed neatly in stacks, took up very little space on the long shelves. No belt. Beside the stacks he found underwear, socks, and two new pairs of high-top hiking boots in ten and a half. His size.

What he'd been wearing prior to his collision with the wildlife-capture net was missing, his boxer briefs as long gone as his gun and folding knife.

Well, then. First things first.

He pulled on a pair of jeans, the denim scraping across his bruised thigh. Then he yanked a shirt from the rod, the hanger pulling out of shape. Bizarre. Freeing it, he turned it over in his hands. It was made of pipe cleaner, a pliable chenille stem twisted into the rough shape of a hanger. It took his brain a second to process this oddity.

A normal plastic or wooden hanger could be fashioned into a weapon. And they – whoever *they* were – wanted to make sure he had no weapons.

However lovely the decor, Evan was no guest here.

His gaze traced the length of the nearest laminate shelf. Bolted to the wall. He reached under it, felt the cool of the steel beneath. The hanging rod was welded in place. To get anything loose, he'd need a socket wrench or a plasma torch.

Turning his attention to the shirt, he examined the stitching, the collar, the taper from chest to waist. The fabric slid like velvet across his skin. The fit confirmed what he'd suspected – the shirt was custom-tailored. Which raised further questions.

He'd add them to the list.

In the main room, he took note of the huge screws securing the leather chair and ottoman to the floor, the curtain rod welded to the wall, the drawerless face of the chairless desk. Crouching by the fireplace, he dipped his head and checked the flue. The metal hatch looked wide enough to accommodate his shoulders, but the robust flames would roast him on the way up. Just for the hell of it, he tried the suite's main door, an oversize block of mahogany that matched the counter and desk. It was locked – surprise, surprise – but he was impressed by how little it budged in the frame.

Next he trudged over to the bathroom. The door swung open to a new design ecosystem. Asian grays and soothing cobalts. Big interlocking bamboo tiles, as hard as stone, lined the walls. A rain showerhead protruded from the wall, unencumbered by a stall. Beneath it the floor sloped to a drain. Resting beside the drain, a single bar of unwrapped soap and a fluffy bamboo-shoot-patterned towel with scalloped edges befitting a fine hotel. No cabinets, no drawers. On the floor next to the lidless and tankless metal toilet, a trash-can liner rested in the spot where a bin might go.

A wall mirror floated above two sinks scooped from a single slab of floating granite. Evan drew closer, eyeing not his reflection but the mirror itself. It was recessed, set behind a plate of armored glass.

He took advantage of the mirror to check his bruised ribs more thoroughly. The needle prick at his neck looked to be healed and gone, but a crimson dot in the crook of his elbow showed where a line had been inserted. They'd kept him out, all right, feeding who knew what drugs into his system.

A prison toothbrush rested between the sinks. Prepasted, with a stubby handle made of flexible rubber. The mint tasted chalky but did the trick, scrubbing the medicinal coating from his teeth.

He splashed cold water over his face and then leaned against the jamb, regarding the well-appointed bedroom. His own holding pen in his own dollhouse.

It struck him that this was precisely the kind of situation that other people called *him* for.

The inconvenience of this mystery detour made him angry. It was costing him time better spent tracking down Alison Siegler, who was currently trapped inside Container 78653-B812, as terrified as it was possible for a seventeen-year-old girl to be.

He strode across the room and threw back the heavy curtains. The sight beyond the balcony made the breath snag in his throat. The view, segmented by welded steel bars at the balustrade, showed mountains blanketed with white pines.

It took a moment for the shock to subside. When he twisted the lock and shoved open the sliding glass door, cold air cut straight through his clothes. Rain turned to snow at around thirty-two degrees Fahrenheit, and the temperature was flirting with that now, the flitting drops hard and angry, hungry for transformation.

He wasn't just 'not in L.A.' He was nowhere *near* L.A.

Wherever he was, it was on the floor of a valley. The sun, a blurred splotch of gold, hovered above a ridge to the left. Dusk? Dawn?

He stepped out toward the bars that were celling in his balcony, the view yawning wider. Standing here gave him a vantage, however slight, to see part of the massive building in which he was imprisoned. From what he could make out, it looked to be a rambling stone-and-wood chalet. Above one of the visible A-frames to his right, black smoke poured from a stone chimney. Gauging the distance to the ground and then to the eaves, he guessed he was on the third of four floors.

Movement caught his eye below. Two men wearing night-vision goggles jogged into view, hunched against the cold, Doberman pinschers at their sides. Evan made a mental note of each man's build, posture, and gait before they disappeared into a bright red barn a quarter mile away from the house.

He thought, *Two dogs, two guards, and counting.*

The rolling barn door boomed shut, and then the gray diorama beyond the balcony reclaimed the same desolate quality it had before. Evan swept his gaze up the looming rise of the valley but saw only trees and more trees, not a single other residence in sight.

Who wanted him badly enough to stage such an elaborate snatch? Who had the resources, the operational skill?

Charles Van Sciver and the remaining Orphans, certainly, but this didn't seem to match their modus operandi. Van Sciver would have little interest in keeping Evan comfortable, let alone in luxury.

Over the years Evan had killed a lot of people, disrupted innumerable operations, and left behind countless mourning relatives. Was this the work of a tribal warlord bent on vengeance? A Saudi billionaire with a jihadi son whom Evan had dispatched? Or maybe a foreign agency wanting to come to terms with a lost U. S. asset?

Judging by the accommodations, they planned for him to be *kept.*

For what?

It dawned on him that he was shivering, so he stepped back inside and secured the door. He gave the walls and ceiling beams a quick scan, deciding where he would place security cameras if the equation were flipped. He walked around so he could watch the light strike the surfaces at different angles. A dot-size glint caught his eye in a heating vent out of reach on the sloped ceiling. Okay, then. That gave them a view of roughly half the room, including the door leading to the hallway. He searched for where additional pinpoint cameras might fill out the picture. A crack in the doorframe above the bathroom looked promising. If it were up to him, he'd have sunk something in the caulking between the travertine tiles of the hearth as well.

He was just starting to consider how the bathroom might be wired when he heard the knock at the door.

9

Our Lady of Holy Death

Standing in the middle of the room, Evan squared to the sound of the knock and braced himself. There came a click as the door unlocked.

An honest-to-God room-service cart wheeled in. White linen, stainless-steel dome plate covers, basket of bread, French press. The only thing that didn't match the Ritz-Carlton presentation was the guy pushing it.

Aside from the tattoo high on his neck, a missing incisor, and a general air of menace, he seemed pleasant enough. As the cart rattled into the room, two near-matching gentlemen entered at his heels and fanned out. Each carried an AK-47, a mistake in such tight quarters, though no one had asked Evan's opinion. A pistol or an FN P90 would've been preferable, but both lacked the big-dick factor beloved by *narcotraficantes*, and these boys seemed to be cartel muscle through and through. *Narcos* generally called the Kalashnikovs *cuernos de chivo* — goat's horns — due to the curved magazines. Choosing their spots, they brandished the AKs with a fetishistic air, posing as if Evan were about to snap their portrait.

Two dogs, five guards, and counting.

The tattoo on the side of each man's neck featured Santa Muerte. A folk saint favored by *narcos*, Our Lady of Holy Death resembled Mother Mary, if you ignored the grinning skull. Additional ink classing up eyebrows, cheekbones, and forearms indicated that the men had worked for the Sinaloa

43

Cartel, responsible for at least half the drugs migrating across the border into the U.S. every year.

They'd cleared space at the front door, making way for someone's dramatic entrance. Evan anticipated a cartel leader, strong of jaw and mustache, but the man who appeared defied any expectations.

He was Caucasian, with coffee-colored eyes that sloped down at the outer corners and a face ratcheted taut and shiny from too much plastic surgery. The lids seemed tight across his eyes, as if he were wearing another man's face. Though the surgeries made his age hard to peg, he seemed to be softening into his late fifties, swells bulging the sides of his suit. His tie, vest, and shirt were all patterned, paisleys and plaids orchestrated in a way that eluded Evan's sensibilities and yet conveyed an undeniable elegance. Somehow they clashed and didn't clash at the same time.

At his back hovered a refrigerator of a man, pale as the moon, with a shaved skull and soft, rounded features that made it look as though someone had Photoshopped the head of a newborn onto Lou Ferrigno's body. Evan would have expected him to hum with steroidal rage, and yet he seemed calm, almost placid, as if fully aware that his heft gave him the advantage of not having to get worked up over anything. His enormous form tugged at a memory – was he the one who'd fired the wildlife-capture net? Unlike the *narcos*, he sported no obvious tattoos, though Evan caught flashes of color on the backs of his hands, as if he'd rolled them on a painter's palette.

'Your accommodations are good?' the man with the suit said, flaring a hand. His fingernails were slightly too long, buffed to a high shine. 'I'm a touch OCD, so I wanted everything to be perfect.'

Evan had long thought that people who announced

themselves as OCD should be subjected to death by paper cuts, but this guy, with his elaborate yet understated suit, manicured nails, and done-to-a-turn jail cell-cum-bedroom guest suite, seemed the genuine article.

Evan wondered at the kind of money it took to hire muscle *away* from the cartel.

'Where are your manners, Chuy?' the man said. 'Prepare the tray for our guest.'

The *narco* who'd delivered the cart lifted the stainless-steel domes off the plates to reveal eggs, bacon, and hotcakes, then stood at attention with a mix of aggression and embarrassment, like a pit bull made to wear a dog sweater.

The breakfast offerings provided an answer to one of Evan's questions. Moments before, he'd been looking at the sunrise, not the sunset.

He moved his gaze past Chuy at the well-dressed man. 'Who are you?' he asked.

'René,' the man said. 'I know, a faggot name. I can't help but feel that my parents might have gone with something with a bit more spine to it.'

'Last name?' Evan said.

'Let's not get ahead of ourselves. Now, please . . .' As he gestured for Evan to sit, he smiled, though his face did not fully obey. 'I'd imagine you're starving. You haven't eaten anything not from an IV bag in three days.'

Three days, then.

Evan had been taken on Friday, October 14. Which meant it was Monday, October 17.

Which in turn meant that he still had thirteen days before Alison Siegler was delivered to the Jacksonville Port Authority and whoever had purchased her.

Unless the man was lying about the date.

The First Commandment: *Assume nothing.*

Evan eyed the rifles, then sat on the bed. As René stepped forward into the room, his men floated around him in perfect Secret Service diamond formation. The big guy's round face peered over René's shoulder like a second head. Through a break in the bodies, Evan could see the wide tips of his fingers on the small of René's back, cheated to the side, ready for the hook-and-grab if Evan made a move. The big man's position and body language made clear that he was the right hand, elevated above the cartel stooges.

René shot a look back at him. 'It's fine, Dex.'

Dex removed his arm, and Evan strained to catch a glimpse of what was on the back of his hand, but it was gone too fast.

Chuy pushed the dining cart forward until it bumped lightly against the ledge of Evan's knees. There was no knife or fork, just a flexible rubber spoon. Scents wafted up. A butter patty dissolved into the hotcake stack. Bacon beckoned. A cloth napkin was cinched in a segment of bamboo stem that acted as a ring, the fine linen bloused out on either side like butterfly wings. There was a fucking sprig of parsley.

Evan thought, *You've got to be kidding me.*

'I suppose you're wondering why you're here,' René said.

'You need me.'

René's moist lips pursed with amusement that wasn't really amusement at all. He didn't like being correctly anticipated. 'I'm sorry?'

'A bullet goes for around twenty-five cents. These arrangements cost a touch north of that. So you require me for something. Or you wouldn't go to the trouble.'

René's stare, lasering out from behind that Saran Wrap skin, was as unnerving as it was direct.

'Where am I?' Evan asked.

'Think of this as a private-sector rendition.'

'Where am I?' Evan asked again.

'That's not relevant.'

'What's relevant is relative,' Evan said.

'Good point. It's not relevant to me for the purposes of this conversation. And what's relevant to me is the only thing that matters anymore.'

René's hand dipped behind a lapel and came out with Evan's RoamZone phone. He held it aloft theatrically, then dropped it on the floor and smashed it with the heel of his dress shoe. He stomped on it again until the Gorilla Glass cracked and the innards showed. Then he picked it up and tossed it into the fireplace.

Evan didn't move his head but watched with his eyes.

René turned, a bead of perspiration carving its way down his flushed cheek. 'You are in my hands. On my time. There is no help coming for you.'

'I don't wait for help. I am the help.'

'Well, you're doing a fine job thus far.'

'I haven't started yet.'

'Let's hope you're smart enough to cooperate. If you do, everything will stay precisely this pleasant.'

'Pleasant,' Evan said.

'Pleasant is relative as well,' René said. 'Do you have a name?'

Did he really not know who Evan was, or was this an act? Evan watched him closely for any tells. 'I do.'

'What is it?'

'Evan.'

'Your last name?'

'Let's not get ahead of ourselves.'

René remained several steps back, safely tucked behind Chuy, who was still dumbly holding the stainless-steel domes. The cart, pushed up against Evan's legs, had the added advantage of pinning him to the bed. Evan took a croissant from the tray and set it on the bedspread beside him. He removed the napkin from the slender bamboo ring. Dex watched him carefully, flat eyes peering out from their doughy recesses.

René said, 'I don't know who you are, but we saw the wreckage you left behind at that house in Fullerton. Were you a client of Hector Contrell's?'

His tone, Evan noted, held no judgment.

'No.'

'You had a business conflict with him?' René asked.

'No.'

The steel gaze appraised Evan. 'You're too skilled to be an angry relative or the like,' he said. 'So what were you there for?'

Evan stared at him.

Realization dawned, excitement asserting itself across René's features. 'You just didn't like him. I respect that.' He wet his lips. 'Who are you?'

Evan stared at him some more.

René said, 'Your driver's license appears to be real, but it's not. No other identification on you. Your fingerprints turned up nothing.'

Evan rubbed his thumb across his finger pads, only now noticing the faintest trace of blue ink among the whorls. Another violation.

'We looked at the registration of your 4Runner,' René continued. 'The vehicle is owned by a shell corp in Barbados. We kicked over that rock and found that shell corp held by another in Luxembourg. I have a feeling that the more rocks we kick over, the more rocks we're going to find.'

Evan picked up the bamboo napkin ring, peered through it like it was a telescope. It was about two inches long, which was long enough.

'I think I understand,' René was saying, 'this thing you're playing at.' He circled a hand at Evan.

Evan slipped the bamboo ring over his forefinger and middle finger. The hollow stem fit snugly, locking the knuckles.

Turning the fingers into a weapon.

'I'm not playing,' Evan said.

He leapt to his feet and drove his sheathed fingers through Chuy's eye, straight into his brain. Blood spurted over the white linen. As Chuy tumbled back, quivering in his death throes, René recoiled in horror.

Two dogs, four guards, and counting.

The remaining pair of *narcos* had their AKs raised, but Evan knew damn well they hadn't gone to all this hassle to gun him down on an overpriced bedspread. Hurling the cart aside, he lunged forward. Dex looped an arm around René's midsection, spinning him out into the hall.

Before Evan could close the distance, he heard a hissing behind him. He wheeled around, sourcing the noise to the heating vent, only now grasping that it was –

10

The Strange Language of Intimacy

Blood on his neck, swollen cheek, wrists still scraped raw from hand-cuffs. Evan's small for a twelve-year-old, scrawny, and can't remember the last time he had a full belly.

He has undergone a daunting set of initiation rites to land here, in this passenger seat of this dark sedan, heading God knows where. He doesn't know where he is. He doesn't know what he will be used for. He doesn't know anything aside from the name of the man driving.

Jack Johns.

Maybe this time everything will be different, and —

Evan stops the thought. Hope is dangerous. In his brief life, he's done his best to eradicate it.

Jack clears his throat. 'You no longer exist,' he tells Evan. 'You went away for a felony and disappeared into the system.'

' 'Kay,' Evan says.

Jack bobs his bulldog head.

An hour later they cross the murky green water of the Potomac and forge west into Arlington, Virginia. The commercial district gives way to tree-lined streets, and then there are more trees and fewer streets. Finally they turn off between twin stone pillars onto a dirt road and wend their way back to a two-story farmhouse.

The silence has grown oppressively thick in the car, and it feels risky to break it. Evan waits until they've pulled in to the circular driveway and gotten out by the old-fashioned porch. Then he asks, 'Where are we?' and Jack says, 'Home.'

The house smells damp but pleasant, redolent of burned wood. Evan regards the foyer and the family room with suspicion. He doesn't trust the maroon carpet runner up the stairs, the plush brown corduroy couches, the pots hanging from a brass rack in the kitchen. The spectacle of undeniable domesticity leaves him humming with distrust.

'Would you like to go upstairs, see your room?' Jack asks.

'No.'

'What do you want?'

'I want to know what I'm here for.'

'Later.'

Evan gathers his courage, does his best to summon Van Sciver. 'After everything I did to get here, I think I've earned some respect.'

Jack regards him calmly. 'If you have to ask for respect, you're not gonna get it.'

Evan does his best to digest this. The words feel less like a slap than a solid wall dropped before him from a lofty height.

Jack says, 'Someone smarter than either of us once said, "If you want a quality, act like you already have it." '

Evan stares at Jack, and Jack stares right back at him.

Evan blinks first. ' 'Kay,' he says.

They head up the flight of stairs to a dormer room with a wooden bed. On the mattress the sheets are folded crisply, ironed into neat squares.

Jack's voice floats over his shoulder. 'I get paid for this. To have you here. It's a job. The money is not why I took you or want you here. I don't want you to find out later, for it to be a surprise.'

'Who's paying you?'

'Later.'

Jack walks to the desk, lifts the blotter, and uses a fresh handkerchief to wipe away an invisible speck on the polished wood surface. He folds the handkerchief neatly and inserts it back into his rear pocket. 'Make your bed.'

Jack leaves Evan alone in the room. Evan struggles with the sheets. He pulls and tugs but cannot get them on properly, let alone taut and wrinkle-free.

He goes downstairs and pokes around until he finds Jack in the garage, meticulously cleaning a handgun. Evan stiffens at the sight of the weapon, then swallows down his fear.

'The sheets aren't right,' Evan says.

Jack keeps his gaze on the skinny brush, poking it in and out of the bore. 'The sheets aren't the problem. I've used them to make up that bed many times.'

Evan takes a breath. 'Okay,' he says. 'I can't make the bed right.'

Jack's eyes tick up above the top of the barrel. 'And?'

It takes a moment for Evan to understand what Jack is waiting for him to say. He finds the words: 'Can you help me?'

Jack lays aside the gun. 'Be happy to.'

Back upstairs, Jack regards the sloppy bed as Evan squirms. Jack walks over, inverts the edge of the fitted sheet over his hand, and shows Evan how to flop it neatly over the corner of the mattress. Jack continues straightening the sheets, keeping his body out of the way so Evan can watch and learn.

'I'll never be able to do it that good,' Evan says.

'You don't have to. You just have to make it better than you did last time.' *Jack snaps the top sheet into place, and it responds like something scared into competence.* 'Next time. That's all that matters.' *He finishes and pulls himself upright beside the pristine bed. He passes Evan on his way out.* 'Would you like to go for a walk?'

Outside, Jack gives a whistle, and a moment later a big dog bounds around the corner of the porch and joins them, keeping a few feet off Jack's right thigh. The dog is at least a hundred pounds, with a honey-gold coat and what looks like a racing stripe of reversed fur on his spine.

Evan says, 'Can I pet him?'

'Strider can be touchy. Let him get used to you.'

Their shoes crunch pleasingly in the tall grass. They make their way up a slight hill, and the view is all leafy canopy and fields.

'What are we doing?' *Evan asks.*

'Walking.'

'You know what I mean.'

'We're deciding if we're gonna like each other or not.'

Evan's training begins the next day, a test of will that puts the previous ones to shame. At knifepoint in a dark barn, he learns his destiny. His future is illuminated, each revelation like a burst of fireworks.

To the world and even to his own instructors, he will be known only as Orphan X.

As his handler, Jack accompanies him to every session. There is breaching and shooting and hand-to-hand, spyops and spycraft and espionage technology. Evan generally returns home exhausted and bloodied. Their days are regimented.

In the evenings they set up in the study, just them and a framed photo of a woman, which rests alone on a side table. She has waist-long hair, a slender neck, and thick-framed eyeglasses from another decade. Evan sneaks glances at her now and then when Jack's not looking. They read a lot, mostly biographies and history books. Evan finds them boring until Jack talks about them, and then the stories come to life. They listen to classical-music records, too. One night an opera is playing in the background as Evan tries to decipher a chapter about Thomas Jefferson.

Jack's voice interrupts the music. 'Do you hear that?'

When Evan looks up, he sees that Jack's eyes are closed. The opera singer wails ever louder.

'Nine high C's. When Pavarotti sang this aria at the Met on February seventeenth, 1972, he had seventeen curtain calls. Seventeen.*'*

Evan does not know what an aria is, or the Met, or a curtain call. So he asks, 'Were you there?'

'No.'

Evan hesitates. 'Where were you?'

Jack closes the book around his thumb. The textured skin around his eyes shifts a bit as he seems to decide whether or not to answer. 'Laos,' he says.

With this response Evan senses they have broken through onto new terrain, and this is at once exciting and perilous. He ponders a reply, but even rehearsed in his head the words sound clumsy.

He dares to gesture toward the tarnished silver frame. 'How'd she die? Your wife?'

Jack says, 'An embassy bombing. In Kuwait.'

'Was she a spy?'

'She was a secretary.'

'Oh.' Evan waits until Jack's attention returns to his book. He hesitates, unsure how to proceed in this foreign tongue, the strange language of intimacy. Then he says, 'Her eyes are friendly.'

Jack's gaze stays fixed on the book. 'Thank you, Evan,' he says, in a voice even more gravelly than usual.

The alarm goes off early the next morning. Strider is curled on the rug in the dormer room, where he now sleeps. Evan scratches behind the dog's ears, then makes the bed. Pausing, he realizes that the sheets are tight enough to bounce a dumbbell on.

Next time, *he thinks.* The two best words in the English language.

When he gets downstairs, he expects to find Jack at the stove, readying the omelet pan, but instead he has his keys in hand and is ready to go. They drive to a Veterans Day parade in town. Evan stands at Jack's side, and they watch the open-topped cars drive by. There are fire engines and fried dough and soldiers with empty sleeves pinned up at the elbows. There are crying moms and old men with watery eyes, their hands over their hearts. There are babies in strollers and young wives with firm tanned skin and lush curls and golden sunlight falling across them, turning the tiny hairs of their arms white. Evan feels an odd sense at his core, a blurring of himself into something greater, all these people joined in common emotion, and the fine, fine flags snap overhead, and he breathes the powdered sugar and the scent of sunscreen and feels the pulse of all these hearts beating inside his own chest. That night when he slides into bed and gazes at the slanted ceiling, he feels the pulse still moving through his body, an almost sexual ache in his cells like the swell of an orchestra on Jack's old record player, the sound track of desire, of belonging.

He thinks of Jack sleeping downstairs and how that makes him feel safe. Jack has cracked the world open like a geode, laying its glittering treasures bare. As long as Evan has Jack at his side, he can do anything. A sensation rolls through his body, unfamiliar and warm, and at last he is able to name it.

It is the feeling of being given a place in the world.

11

No Longer the Same Place

Evan came to lying flat on his chest, his mouth open against the floorboards. He shoved himself up and leaned back against the sleigh bed, letting the ache between his temples subside.

The cart was gone. Damp spot on the floorboards where they'd been scrubbed. No sign of Chuy's body.

Serious room service.

Two fingertips of his left hand were crusted. He went into the bathroom and washed his hands. Then he went to the hearth and pretended to warm himself. His busted RoamZone had fallen through the log grate. Careful to keep his back to the hidden surveillance cameras, he managed to poke beneath the flames to knock the phone into reach. The rubber casing was scorched. Smashed-to-shit bits of Gorilla Glass turned the screen into a mosaic. Holding the phone low against his belly, he thumbed it on. Miraculously, the lights flickered as it powered up. The Gorilla Glass had protected the phone from the worst of the stomping and the fire, but he could see bits of the circuit board through the cracks. The smart screen seemed unresponsive to touch.

There'd be no dialing out.

He examined the damage, his excitement quickly fading. He was adroit with electronics, but fixing the phone was beyond his capabilities. When he was sixteen, he'd been taught by a hacker around the same age who could've figured something like this out in a Red Bull-fueled minute, but that's why she'd been the teacher and he the student.

Keeping the phone hidden, he went back to the bed and surreptitiously shoved it between the mattress and box spring.

On the unmade sheets, the croissant waited, cold. His stomach announced itself. He took big bites, chewed thoughtfully, his mouth dry from the sleeping gas. In the course of his training, Evan had endured halothane vapor and methoxypropane, but given the roaring fire he guessed René had gone with something less flammable, probably a halogenated ether. He rubbed his eyes, trying to clear his head, then crossed to the window and noted the sun's position high in the sky. He'd been unconscious for a while. Despite the midday blaze, he knew not to be fooled; it was well-digger-ass cold out there.

Movement caught his eye below, three men jogging past the barn, disappearing into the tree line. Evan hadn't seen them before.

Two dogs, seven guards, and Dex.

His thoughts were scrambled, fragments of plans jabbing him from all angles, opposing directives warring in his mind.

Well, then. As Jack had encoded in the Fifth Commandment, *If you don't know what to do, do nothing.*

Evan went back to the bed and sat cross-legged on the unmade sheets. Closing his eyes, he took a few deep breaths. He slowed each exhalation, counting to four, letting the alpha brain waves kick in and drop him into a meditative state.

After five minutes, or twenty, he opened his eyes and slid off the mattress. Then he made the bed carefully. He stretched and did push-ups, sit-ups, and a quick core workout, favoring his bruised rib. His muscles felt creaky from the days he'd spent unconscious. He kept all thoughts at bay, focused only on breaking a good sweat. Then he showered and changed and returned to the spot by the window. Standing in the same place with a clearer mind meant it was no longer the same place. He reviewed what little he knew.

He now had a grasp on the time: midday.

He'd gleaned the date: October 18.

The next priority was figuring out where he was.

His gaze swept the walls low, just above the baseboards. Nothing. He moved to the built-in mahogany desk. The backing floated an inch or so off the wall, no doubt to leave room for appliance plugs. He put one eye to the dark sliver but could make out only darkness. Then he crawled into the space where a chair should be and flattened his cheek to the wall. The power outlet floated a few inches away in the gap between desk and wall.

It had only two holes, designed to fit round pins.

Clearly not built to receive an American plug.

Evan popped to his feet and headed briskly into the bathroom. After scanning the walls, he dropped onto a knee and found a wet-room outlet tucked beneath the floating granite slab housing the sinks. This one took a three-pin plug – two round, one grounding.

That was helpful, too.

He searched the bathroom for a hidden surveillance camera but found none. With the stark stone and tile, there were scant hiding places. He had to assume that the mirror was a one-way and that a pinhole camera was positioned inside the ceiling vent as in the bedroom, but he couldn't be certain. That still left him a blind spot beneath the sink and in the corner by the toilet.

He needed to create a blind zone in the bedroom as well. Pausing in the doorway, he searched the crack in the frame, careful not to be obvious. There it was, a pencil eraser-size circle of metal nestled back in the wood like a dug-in pinworm. He walked over to the hearth and ran his fingertips across the caulking between the travertine tiles but felt nothing. The vent camera he'd spotted earlier and the bathroom doorframe unit gave them eyes on three-fourths of the bedroom. He looked for a spot that would pick up the remaining quarter.

The corner above the closet where the walls met the ceiling. He flicked a gaze quickly in that direction, noting that the point of blackness there was slightly more pronounced than in the other corners.

Solid tradecraft.

What was the best way to play this?

Evan put himself in René's shoes and thought for a time before settling on the next step. It was a gamble, but everything was a gamble.

Back in the bathroom, he thumbed the remaining paste off the rubber toothbrush where it had been squirted between the bristles. He added a drop of water and worked it between his thumb and forefinger until it gummed up into a gooey mortar.

He smeared it over the crack in the frame outside the bathroom. That knocked out their view of half the bed and the sliding glass door. Then he worked up more paste and went to the corner of the room by the closet. Bracing his bare foot against the closet hinges, he put his back to the wall and squirmed his way up off the ground like a rock climber until he could reach the ceiling. He put his face big in the hidden camera, went for a smug smirk. A few swipes and he'd obscured the tiny lens, eliminating René's visuals on the fireplace.

He dropped back to the floor and wiped his hands on his

jeans, acting satisfied with himself. He'd left them the most essential camera, the one in the heating vent that captured half the room, including the door to the hallway. The one they'd need to discern his position before they entered the room. The one that was filming him right now, acting as though he'd just put one over on them.

If René was smart, he'd hit Evan with sleeping gas again and reposition the cameras he'd knocked out. But if he was *really* smart, he'd concede the ostensible defeat, let Evan believe he was surveillance-free in the room, and use the remaining camera to observe what Evan got up to when he thought no one was looking.

Head lowered, Evan paced the rustic oak planks, doing his best to construct the chessboard mentally, to anticipate René's counter and plan several moves ahead.

A knock came at the door once again.

He was about to find out how well he was playing the game.

12

Magical Machinations

The entourage entered, René flanked by the same *narcos*, now brandishing familiar, less-lethal shotguns. Dex loomed after them, a pipe swinging low behind his leg. With some pleasure, Evan noted that there was a new front man. He looked nervous.

Two dogs, eight guards, and Dex.

René said, 'Shall we try this again?'

Evan looked at him. 'No more croissants?'

René took a few steps toward the bathroom, the men locked in position around him. They moved effortlessly, maintaining a practiced standoff distance. The movement of the air brought a whiff of expensive-smelling cologne. Dex kept a clear route to the door, ready to whisk René to safety the instant something went down.

René regarded the caulked-over crack in the frame above the door. His smile spread his lips flat to the sides, his face slightly off kilter on his skull.

Folding his arms, he drummed his fingers on the fine tweed of his blazer sleeve. 'I'll allow you your temper tantrum,' he said. 'After all, it's not like you're going anywhere.'

Evan said, 'Are we in Switzerland or Liechtenstein?'

René blinked and then blinked again. 'Why not Romania or Russia?'

'The outlets,' Evan said. 'The C plug behind the desk puts us in Europe and knocks out the UK. But the J in the bathroom is only used in Switzerland and Liechtenstein.'

'Well traveled, are you?'

Evan stood by the foot of the bed, tense on his feet. 'Are we gonna keep answering questions with questions?'

René turned to Dex. 'I like him.'

Evan waited, his gaze steady. The front man grimaced, showing a mouthful of gold-capped teeth, the grill both ridiculous and menacing at the same time. He had lush curly hair tamped down by a purple Dorados de Chihuahua cap featuring a mustachioed baseball wearing a sombrero.

At last René pivoted back to face Evan. 'Graubünden,' he conceded.

The easternmost canton of Switzerland.

Evan hadn't been here before but had stayed in neighboring Ticino. After he escaped, he would get across the border to Liechtenstein. He had a papers guy in Triesenberg who lived in the cellar of an eighteenth-century parish church. Once Evan was set up with a new passport, he'd hightail it to Vienna, lie low, make his way back to the States. Then he'd intercept the *Horizon Express* and free Alison Siegler.

René said, 'I hope we can agree that you're helpless here. You're outmanned, outgunned, and overpowered to an extent you're not even aware of yet. Your surrendering to these realities is inevitable.'

Evan considered. Then he feinted at the group, nothing more than a twitch of his shoulders. The front man jerked away so fast he lost his footing and stumbled. The other two *narcos* had their shotguns up instantly.

Evan said, 'Nothing is inevitable.'

The third shotgun rose, trembling, and for a moment Evan thought the front man might just be nervous enough to pull the trigger accidentally. René rested a hand on his shoulder. 'Easy, Manny.'

At this range, aimed at Evan's head, the less-lethal shotgun might prove to be not so less-lethal.

René alone remained unshaken. He continued as if there'd been no interruption. 'You're a very difficult man to track.'

Evan looked past the three shotgun bores at René. Dex stared back from the rear, a head taller than the others, his face as expressionless as ever. Just another casual conversation.

'Why are you interested in me?' Evan asked.

'I'm not interested in people. I'm interested in bank accounts.' René peered out from the stretched mask of his face. '*Your* bank account in particular.'

Account. Singular.

Evan said nothing. René was talking, and there was no advantage in stopping him.

'I know that you hold assets worth twenty-seven million dollars in an account in Zurich.'

Privatbank AG didn't house the lion's share of Evan's money. When Evan was operating as Orphan X, Jack had stocked accounts for him the world over and taught him how to hide behind financial veils, how to wire money invisibly from offshore account to offshore account. The cash was printed by the Treasury and shipped directly to areas of non-reporting. It was as untraceable as Evan himself – at least he'd thought it was. Both he and his bank account seemed to have suffered a sudden bout of visibility.

'We managed to persuade one of the managers there to turn over account information,' René said. 'Your client profile – or *lack* of one – caught our interest. You seem like someone whom no one will miss.'

René's eyes gleamed. Clearly he enjoyed this part of the dance. His nose was ruddy, spider veins clutching the edges of his nostrils. It looked as though he'd dabbed cover-up over them. A vain man.

'As you'd probably guess,' he continued, 'there aren't a lot of people you can steal twenty-seven million dollars from without anyone else caring. But you happen to be one of those people.'

'You assume you have a handle on who you're dealing with,' Evan said.

'A drug or arms dealer,' René said. 'Everything about you fits the profile. No footprint, digital or otherwise. Conversant in violence. Familiar with detention.'

He waited for Evan to confirm or deny.

When it became clear he would get no response, he continued, 'So you worked your illicit trade and made a fortune, if a small one – fortunes not being what they used to be. And then what? You started atoning for your sins? Wiping out the likes of Hector Contrell. Is that what you're interested in now, Evan? Atonement?'

'Actually, lately it's been flower arranging.'

René pretended to smile. 'I'm always curious about the ways people fool themselves. In fact I admire it. I wish everything weren't so *bare* to me. I'm a straightforward man. I like money. More money than one can make honestly. So when my coffers needed replenishing, the question I asked myself was, why deal with drugs or weapons and all the danger that goes with them? Why not go right to the source? So that's what I did. I looked for a bank account like yours, built up over years of sweat and toil but not linked to anything respectable.' His skin quivered, the smile finding its footing. 'Ripe for the taking.'

He seemed to want Evan to compliment him on this ingenious ploy.

Instead Evan asked, 'How did you find me?'

'It wasn't easy. Cooperative bank managers are hard to find in Switzerland, but I have a gift for creating . . . *leverage*.'

He tasted the word and liked it. 'Then came the persistence to even *attempt* to follow your wires. Most of them zigzagged off into the World Wide Web, ping-ponging around the globe, and then – *poof.* We were about to give up when we had a stroke of luck. A data-mining program matched the precise amount of a particular wire made from your account to an online purchase registered by an auction house halfway around the world that same day.'

'The katana.'

'Yes. Your samurai sword. An odd choice of toy. Do you know how many other transactions of $235,887.41 were conducted on September seventeenth?'

'None.'

'Five, actually. But the other four were easily eliminated from consideration. Because we had the starting and ending points of your payment, all your magical machinations in the middle were for naught.'

The smug set of René's face brought to mind a Jack saying: *Someone who thinks he's the smartest guy in the room rarely is.*

Evan made a note to attune his payment procedures by adding a few cents to each transaction in the future.

He pictured that gray Ford Transit van springing up in his rearview mirror as he'd neared the Norfolk FedEx office. The same FedEx to which the Seki auction house had shipped the sword. The van hadn't been tracking him, not yet; it must have been patrolling the block, waiting for a signal from inside that the package had been claimed.

René seemed pleased by the specifics he held in his plump palm, but everything attached to that wire was cut-bait ready. Evan's bank account was as end-stopped as the 4Runner, registered under a false identity nestled inside a confusion of front companies. He just had to keep his head level, follow his training protocols, choose his moment.

Manny must have sensed a shift in Evan's emotions, because he firmed the shotgun to his right shoulder. He was closest to Evan, the barrel no more than four feet away. After the fate of his predecessor, he'd earned the right to be jittery. In the back, Dex remained alertly forward on the balls of his feet, his massive body idling, a Mustang waiting for the light to change. He lifted a pawlike hand to scratch his face, and again Evan caught a glimpse of something on the skin. Red and black Magic Marker? A tattoo? A stitched wound?

Evan looked at René. 'What next?'

'Your money in the account is denominated in various currencies, some fairly exotic. Our cooperative bank manager has instigated the necessary transactions to convert your holdings into Swiss francs, my preferred brand. Three full business days are required for the trades to settle. First thing Friday morning, you will type your codes, send the wire transfer, and go on your merry way.'

Friday would still give Evan nine days to intercept Alison Siegler. Nine days was plenty of time. If he had any faith that René was in fact planning to let him go on his merry way.

René couldn't release Evan. Not after he knew what Evan was capable of. Not after he'd taken $27 mil from him. Not after Evan had seen René's face.

'Until then,' René continued, 'your life can be as pleasant as you choose to make it.'

'And if I opt for unpleasant?' Evan asked.

'I've never sparked to torture,' René said. 'Not like these fellows.' He rested a hand on the shoulder of the *narco* to his left and gave an affectionate squeeze.

Evan let his posture deflate, a show of defeat.

'Then we have an agreement?' René asked.

Evan extended a hand as if to shake.

The cartel men shouted in Spanish. Manny reared up,

readying to fire. Feigning puzzlement, his arm still extended, Evan took a half step forward.

Then he whipped his hand up, knocking the shotgun back over Manny's shoulder. It discharged at point-blank range into the face of the *narco* behind him, putting a hockey-puck-size dent in his forehead. The recoil kicked the shotgun from Manny's grip. The third *narco* fired recklessly in front of Manny's face. The round skimmed across Evan's back, trailing friction heat.

Disoriented, Manny swung at Evan. His punch glanced off Evan's chin and struck him square in the shoulder, and Evan spun with the impact, letting himself drop to the floor. He threw a leg sweep that caught the other *narco* behind the Achilles, launching his feet out from under him. The guy hit the floor flat on his back, his breath leaving him in a seal-like bark an instant before Evan hammered the heel of his foot into the man's throat, crushing his windpipe.

Two dogs, six *guards, and Dex.*

Through Manny's legs Evan could see the first *narco* seizing on the floorboards, saliva webbing from the corner of his mouth. Dex's pillar legs were visible, too, rotating powerfully to the doorway, René clamped beneath his arm in a rag-doll dangle, his high-ticket loafers skimming the floor.

Manny kicked Evan in the stomach, knocking a clump of air from his lungs. Evan fought through the pain and clenched around the boot. Somehow he held on, Manny toppling over, his mouth stretched wide in a grimace, gold teeth flashing. Before Evan could get to him, the room seemed to darken.

Dex, blocking out the light, one massive arm drawn back. As he swung the pipe down, Evan rolled to the side. The metal end splintered the plank next to his cheek. Flipping over, he grabbed the pipe.

Too late he realized it was a cattle prod.

Everything turned a brilliant shade of white. He felt a vague sensation of sliding several feet, the uneven floor sandpapering his ass, his shoulders, the back of his head. The inside of his mouth prickled. His face stuck with a thousand pins. His body was immobilized save for the scorching pain still twitching the nerves of his arm. Somewhere he registered sounds of retreat, the bedroom door slamming shut.

Lying there on his back gave him an excellent view of the gas hissing through the ceiling vent above, wavering the air like a heat mirage.

13

Last Glance Back

For Evan's seventeenth birthday, a former Army Ranger exposes him to a brutal week of sleep deprivation and caloric reduction, then drives him to a desolate stretch of the snowy Allegheny Mountains, gives him a set of coordinates, and leaves him shivering in a T-shirt and jeans. As the four-wheeler pulls away with a cheery toot of the horn, Evan recalls Jack's Third Commandment: Master your surroundings. *Looking around, he wonders how this is possible.*

He has weathered SERE training, which focuses on the four basics of operational up-the-creek-ness — survival, evasion, resistance, and escape. He's been taught woodcraft and wilderness skills, counterinterrogation and camouflage techniques. He can make a fire, build a shelter, and distinguish mushrooms he can eat from mushrooms that will Cuisinart his kidneys or send him on a psychedelic trip on the magic bus, but now, as he faces the reality of the damp earth and empty pockets, it seems like all that knowledge is for shit.

Forty-eight hours later, near hypothermic and bedraggled beneath a paste of mud and leaves, he stumbles upon a long-deserted cabin. The roof is partially torn off, the walls rotted, critters nesting in the walls. In a fallen cabinet, he finds an ancient energy bar still in the wrapper and devours it.

Mistake.

Too late he notes the bitter aftertaste at the back of his tongue. A gentle poison or emetic, probably hydrogen peroxide or syrup of ipecac. Curled up on the dusty floorboards, he vomits the scant contents of his stomach. It seems that the heaving will never end. In hour two he hears an engine approach over the rugged terrain. The door opens, and a shadow falls over him.

'Why the hell would there be an energy bar in a deserted cabin?' Jack asks.

'The First Commandment,' Evan croaks.

'That's right.' Jack crouches, sets down a bottle of water by Evan's face. 'See you at home.'

Four days later, having staggered out of the woods, cleaned up in a gas-station bathroom, stolen clothes from a church coatroom, and hitchhiked dogleggedly back to northern Virginia, Evan passes through the twin stone pillars and begins the painful climb up the dirt slope to the two-story farmhouse. Strider meets him at the porch, nuzzling his palm, wagging his tail so hard his rear end swivels.

Jack is sitting at a dinner table set for two, a steaming turkey in a basting pan set on a trivet before him. He sips a vodka martini, still ice-crystal cloudy from the shaker.

Evan crosses his arms, winces from the pain. He thinks back to Van Sciver, how when they were kids he always seemed to loom overhead, backlit by the sun, the edges of his red hair turned golden, the bearing of a god. He would've done better. He would have faced the wild fearlessly. He would have known to avoid the energy bar. He would have made it out a day quicker. Or two.

Evan feels emotion in the back of his throat, in his nostrils. The words come like broken glass. 'I didn't do so hot.'

Jack is all rough edges and rugged exterior, but his eyes and the etched skin around them convey something much, much softer. 'Next time,' he says. 'Next time.' He rubs his hands, appraises the turkey. 'It still needs to rest before carving. There's a hot bath waiting for you.'

Evan nods and heads upstairs.

Several years later on a bleak gray morning, Evan finds himself riding shotgun east on Route 267, a carry-on bag across his thighs. In his back pocket is a real passport with real stamps and a false name. Jack's hands grip the wheel in the ten-and-two, and he gazes straight ahead as signs for Dulles International float overhead.

'I am the only person who knows who you are,' Jack says. 'What you *do. The only person inside the government or out. The only person in the world.'*

This is not news. Evan wonders what is motivating Jack to break character this dreary East Coast morning by repeating the obvious.

'I am your only connection to anything,' Jack continues. 'Anyone else contacts you, says I told them, do not believe him. I am it.'

'Okay,' Evan says.

'I will always be there. The voice on the other end of the phone.'

Evan realizes he is witnessing something he has never seen before: Jack is anxious.

'Jack? I'm ready.'

The airport cop flicks a gloved hand, and Jack coasts up to Departures. At the curb ahead of them against the backdrop of a minivan, a teary mother and a stoic father hug their son. The teenager wears a college shirt with intersecting lacrosse sticks. He looks impatient.

Evan reaches for the door handle. 'See you when it's clear.' He starts to get out, but Jack's hand grips his forearm firmly, stilling him in the passenger seat.

'Remember, the hard part isn't killing,' he says, not for the first time, or the fiftieth. 'The hard part is staying human.'

A microexpression flickers across Jack's features so fast that Evan might have missed it if he didn't know him the way he does.

Fear.

Evan feels his throat constrict ever so slightly. Neither of them is accustomed to expressing emotion. Not trusting his voice, Evan nods.

The vise grip on his arm relents. Jack waves a hand at the waiting terminal. 'Go on, then,' he says, slightly bothered, as though Evan has been holding him up.

Evan climbs out, the chill whipping around his neck, cooling the flush that has crept up into his face. He blends into the thickening crowd entering the international terminal, walking neither too fast nor too slow, a face among faces, invisible in plain sight. The boarding pass rustles in his hand. When he reaches the printed destination, *there will be additional orders from Jack, directing him to a man he will kill.*

He is nineteen years old and as ready as he'll ever be.

He gives a last glance back through the big glass doors at Jack, his only connection to legitimacy.

He is also Evan's only connection to humanity.

14

Rambo in a Bespoke Shirt

This time when Evan arced up from the depths and broke the surface of consciousness, he sensed a difference in the consistency of the air.

A draft.

Rolling his head to the side, he noticed that the bedroom door was ajar.

He rose, wobbling a bit on his feet. Then made his way toward the door. When he stepped through, he picked up movement far down the hall on either side of him. First he looked left, where Manny waited, shotgun leveled. To Evan's right was another *narco* – one of the guards he'd spotted earlier from his window – with his weapon also at the ready. Evan took a step toward Manny, and both men moved with him, maintaining the twenty-foot buffer.

They had learned.

Manny jerked the end of the shotgun at the other man. *'Dígale, Nando.'*

Santa Muerte, tattooed on the side of Nando's neck, looked like she was melting. He swiped sweat from the ink quickly, his hand slapping back onto the shotgun's barrel. 'Mr René say he invite you to take some air. He say perhaps you can find some perspective.'

René's arch tone, replicated through poor diction and a strong Mexican accent, made Evan smirk.

Nando flicked his head, making clear that the request wasn't really a request.

Evan started down the high-ceilinged hall, Manny back-pedaling and Nando bringing up the rear, the three men moving of a piece. The chalet smelled of dust and sweet rot, all the scents of a time-honored place. The space opened up around Evan, such a contrast to the locked and barred room.

They reached a landing. 'Hold up,' Manny said. He shot a quick glance behind him, finding the top step with his boot, then looked back and ran his tongue across the caps. 'Okay. Slow as shit, *ése*, or you be wearing a round in your face. Then you need golds like me.' He bared his teeth in something resembling a smile. '¿*Comprendes?*'

'*Comprendo.*'

The three men moved awkwardly down a few broad flights of stairs, Manny sliding his hip along the polished wooden banister for balance so he could move backward while keeping the shotgun raised. They reached the ground floor, stepping into the embrace of an expansive parlor. The lush Persian carpet yielded softly underfoot. Evan took in the intricate woodwork, the scattering of billiard tables, the excessively stocked bar. René certainly didn't skimp, particularly when it came to luxury. Two foot soldiers sat on leather couches sipping scotch, Kalashnikovs resting on the cushions at their sides. They barely took notice of the bizarre procession moving past them.

A hostage being moved at double gunpoint didn't warrant a second glance. Business as usual. Evan wondered how many times René had played through this scheme. How much blood had the walls of this chalet seen?

Evan paused, adding the men to the tally – *two dogs, eight guards, Dex* – before Nando prompted him to keep heading down a wide corridor. They passed a library, a sunroom, an empty ballroom with a listing grand piano and a past-its-prime air right out of a Victorian novel.

The grand entrance rose two stories, crowned by a glittering chandelier the size of a Buick. Evan leaned back on his heels, looking up, a country rube visiting Kuala Lumpur. Chalet windows filtered in the burnt orange of the setting sun. Manny halted by a curved Hollywood staircase and gestured for Evan to continue outside.

Evan placed his hand on the doorknob. The metal felt like ice. 'I can just leave?'

Manny smiled. 'You can try.'

And then Evan understood.

His thin tailored shirt and jeans would provide scant protection from the cold. René wanted to show him just how unforgiving the terrain was, to dissuade any thoughts of escape.

But he didn't need to escape. Not yet. He needed to recon, gather intel, get the lay of the land. And René was providing him with a perfect opportunity to do just that.

Evan stepped outside, the breeze sweeping straight through him, biting at his ankles, his neck, his wrists. Clenching his fists, he drove them into his pockets. A light snow fell, so fragile that the flakes dissipated the instant they hit his clothes. For a moment he stood on the vast stone porch, giving his body a chance to acclimate.

René was right to show off the brutal landscape. SERE training aside, without a clear plan Evan would die of exposure. He appreciated the pageantry. Now he had to bear down and gather as much information as he could.

A circular cobblestone driveway received a gravel road that pointed east, the only clear route in or out. The hard earth crunched beneath Evan's hiking boots as he stepped off the edge of the cobblestones, putting the chalet behind him. Pine air whistled in his windpipe, clean as mouthwash. Turning back, he admired the grand exterior. Four stories of stone and wood plunked down on an apron of landscaping carved out of the hard terrain. Boxy shrubs artfully concealed a few sunken basement windows. A tower stretched up from the east wing, manned by a rail-thin guard whose silhouette Evan didn't recognize. He included the man in his mental count.

Evan rotated in a full circle, taking in the sweep of the surrounding range. The valley position was ideal for René. A single lookout could monitor incoming traffic from all directions, the amphitheater effect of the mountains ensuring that a car or a plane would be heard from miles away.

It made even more sense why René had hired *narcos* for his detail. Aside from ISIS bodyguards who were unwooable by money, *narcos* had the most experience conducting illicit and elaborate operations while staying off the radar. Evan had no doubt that these men had cut their teeth hiding powerful drug lords from the *federales*, rival cartel assassins, and DEA drones while doing the legwork to keep the empire running. Procuring these men was ingenious and bold – René's trademarks.

The air was crisp, the view at postcard resolution. Above the ridge a hawk caught a wind current, frozen in place like a fleck of paint on a camera lens. The slope to the north looked to be the most gradual, which suited Evan fine. The border to Liechtenstein lay that way.

The red barn sat a few hundred yards to the east. Two *narcos* perched on wooden crates by the door, smoking and sipping coffee, their AKs dangling from straps. They wore long dark coats, heavy enough to add bulk. One poked a fork into a plate of food. A fire languished between the crates, down to ash and embers, a pot hanging over it like something from a cowboy movie. Evan recognized them as two of the men he'd seen jogging into the barn earlier. The Dobermans lounged at their boots, resting.

Evan started toward the men, and they both rose quickly. The dogs lunged to their paws and issued a rumbling growl in stereo. But still they kept slack in the leash. They were well trained, not junkyard menaces.

The wet air conveyed the scent of cigarettes, onions, and garlic. As Evan drew near, he saw that the plate held a half-eaten tamale smothered in green salsa. His stomach leapt at the sight.

Giving the men a wide berth, Evan passed by. *'Buenas tardes,'* he said.

'Buenas tardes.'

The barn door rumbled open with a metallic rasp. Another *narco*, with grease stains on his hands and shirt, stepped outside as he lit up a cigarette. A tenth guard. His left cheek sported an impressive knife scar, his patchy beard riding the pitted flesh haphazardly. He saw Evan and froze.

Through the rolled-back door, Evan took in the interior. Only now did he realize that the barn, for all its cozy Old World appearance, was built of metal. There were no stables inside, but an open stretch housing a pair of big Mercedes SUVs – Geländewagens with their license plates removed. Beside the G-Wagons, a vintage Rolls-Royce Phantom was parked, jacked up on the left side, its rear tire removed. Gear lockers lined the back wall. A distressed feminine voice carried out, ringing sharply off the metal, echoes making her words unintelligible.

Evan strained to source the sound, catching a flash of movement between the G-Wagons, a woman doubled over, head bent painfully, her mane of straight black hair thrown forward over her face. He couldn't see her features, but the sounds clarified as cries.

She slid bizarrely along the ground like a stop-motion insect, one arm twisted up as if in supplication. It wasn't until just before she skittered behind one of the vehicles that Evan spotted the massive hand clamped over her wrist, wrenching the arm painfully as it dragged her from sight.

It had a streak of color across the back just beneath the knuckles.

Dex.

The man with the grease-stained shirt slammed the door shut quickly behind him, clearly concerned by what Evan had seen. Or was he? Had the whole episode been staged?

At a twenty-yard standoff, the men regarded Evan, blinking. Then they flicked their *cuernos de chivo* at him: *Get moving.*

He kept on toward the edge of the pine forest, half expecting them to herd him back toward the chalet. But they let him roam.

There'd be no going Rambo in a bespoke shirt on an empty stomach with zero planning. Not in this weather.

As Evan hiked through the trees even the muddy patches held firm, frozen in place. Though the branches filtered out most of the snow, a light dusting still fell, melting on impact. He worked his way up the first slope, sticking to the ridge. The trees were less dense here, providing better sight lines to the chalet below and the looming crest. He paused, breathing hard, his sweat clammy and cold across the back of his neck. His hands were going numb.

He spotted a clearing ahead and set up the jagged slope toward it. When he finally reached the break in the trees, he paused, leaning against a boulder. A glasslike puddle at his boots looked like a portal to the underworld, the reflected pines thrusting down to a miasma of subterranean clouds. A loon arced gracefully down to land, kissing its mirrored opposite and shattering the illusion. The sleek black head bobbed, and then a mournful wail drew out and out, warbling the air.

Evan would have to head back soon or risk frostbite. He climbed atop the boulder and peered up the northern face of the range, charting a mental course over the brink.

His thoughts traveled to a midsize carrier that right now was sliding south alongside the Baja Peninsula toward the Panama Canal.

Seventeen years old. Locked in a goddamned twenty-foot ISO-standard container like a piece of break bulk cargo.

For a moment the image of Alison Siegler made him debate going for it. Insulating his skin with a paste of mud. Once he got past the rim, he could build a shelter, search out tinder, forage for food. Maybe it was worth taking the shot now.

The loon's howl cut off abruptly, and it took flight with a graceless flapping, flecks of water raining down on Evan's head. He turned to see what had scared it off.

A ten-point buck had wandered silently to the water's edge. His majestic head was raised, obsidian eyes fixing Evan where he stood. Evan's breath gusted out, wisps riding the air. He could see the buck's breath, too, twinning plumes from the nostrils. The buck lowered his front leg, muscles sheeting beneath the fur.

A frozen moment.

Then the buck jerked.

An instant later the gunshot thundered across the valley.

Evan's head snapped upslope to search out the shooter, but it was too late.

The stag buckled onto bent front legs. He wheezed. His hind legs kicked, propelling him forward onto his neck. The puddle sprayed, dark with churned-up muck. Then the buck collapsed onto his side. Crimson matted his fur, running into the water.

Evan slid down from the boulder and walked over. Breath

fluttered the tattered fur at the wound, air leaking through the punctured lung, the sound like a deep, hoarse sigh. Saliva frothed the mouth. One rolling black pupil looked up at him.

Evan squatted over the buck, rested a hand on the warm neck, stroked it gently until an inner stillness claimed the eye.

He tallied the new count: *Two dogs, ten guards, Dex. And a sniper.*

He understood better what René had wanted him to learn on his little nature hike.

Now that the point had been made, Evan was not surprised to hear heavy footsteps approaching through the underbrush. It was time for him to be returned to his box. A moment later Dex broke through the tree line into the clearing. Still crouched, Evan looked up at him.

Dex was expressionless as always, his gaze absent of life. His face maintained that preternatural blankness as he lifted his right hand and cupped it over his mouth – elbow flagged to the side, palm pressed to his lips, the V of his thumb and forefinger snug against his nose. For the first time, Evan saw the tattoo on the back of his hand clearly. It was a mouth stretched eerily wide, conveying pleasure but no happiness.

A painted smile, slapped monster-mask crooked over Dex's actual mouth.

15

Back-Alley Philosophers

René's sleek steak knife sliced through the cut of venison, juice oozing from the pink center. He skewered the cube of meat on a designer fork and held it out to his side. Dex took it gingerly and deposited it into his mouth. He chewed, swallowed, nodded.

A poison taster to the king.

Of course, the majority of toxins would take much longer to manifest, but Evan was learning more and more how much René indulged his affectations.

With its dark woods, brass sconces, knockoff Monet, and silk rugs overlaying a parquet floor, the formal dining room had a somber ambience, taking itself too seriously. Evan sat at the opposite end of an elegantly set table the size of a small sailboat. He and René were the only two dining. Aside from Dex cast in the role of guinea pig, the sole deviation from the *Citizen Kane* setup was Manny standing ten yards behind Evan with a shotgun aimed at the base of his skull.

René's eyes flicked down the length of the table at Evan. At last, he spoke. 'This is proving to be a protracted conversation.'

He mopped a pink square through the juice pooled on his plate and took the meat off the tines. He closed his eyes as he chewed, then dabbed the corners of his plush lips with a linen napkin.

Evan looked down at his setting. His venison had been cut into bite-size pieces. No utensils. His napkin had no bamboo ring. But the bone-china plate would shatter readily, and he could wrap the napkin around the base of one of the shards.

René interrupted his thoughts. 'You have to stop trying to kill my men.'

Evan said, 'Trying?'

René's laugh seemed to catch him by surprise. When the smile faded, it was as though it had never existed. 'Eat,' he said.

Evan ate with his fingers, the meat delicious and salty, tinged with rosemary. He couldn't remember being this hungry since he was a kid. He'd spent a lot of years half starved, fighting for every mouthful.

René looked genuinely pleased that Evan was enjoying his meal. 'Would you like seconds?' he asked.

'Yes.'

René moved a bejeweled finger to a slender white remote on the table beside him, and a moment later one of the broad kitchen doors swung open. The *narco* from the barn, now wearing a chef's smock in place of a grease-stained shirt, emerged with another plate of meat, also cut as if for a child.

'Careful, Samuel,' René said. 'Right there is fine.' He gestured to a spot several feet up from where Evan sat.

Keeping a wary eye on Evan, Samuel placed the plate down with a thunk and retreated to the kitchen. As the doors fanned wide, Evan peered through, taking in the huge kitchen with its center island, wood-fired oven, and cavernous pantry. He plugged it into the blueprint of the house he was constructing in his head.

He rose, claimed his plate, and returned to his seat. The bore of Manny's shotgun tracked him the entire way.

'Look up,' René said.

Evan did.

'Smile.'

Evan stared at him. René's eyes peered out through the unnaturally smooth skin of his face. He was serious.

'What, René? You want to be friends?'

René pointed the knife at him. 'Given your circumstances, is it wise to make me an enemy?'

'We're well past that already,' Evan said.

He resumed eating, letting his eyes pick across the room. European outlet plugs spotted the wainscoting. The knock-off Monet upon closer examination *was* a Monet. On the east side, the dining area blew open into a cathedral-style living room. Beyond oversize couches and ottomans arrayed like sleeping elephants, floor-to-ceiling windows showed off snow-spotted panes backdropped by the black of night. Evan could see his own ghostly reflection floating in the glass.

Even across the length of the table, René's gaze felt cold on the side of Evan's face.

'You're not a complainer,' René said. 'I appreciate that. It's amazing what people can convince themselves constitutes stress. Most Americans seem to believe that safety assurances are awarded at birth like factory-issued warrantees. So far as I can tell, the only American growth industry is entitlement.' He settled back, folded his hands across his belly. His suit, made of a thick velvetlike fabric, didn't wrinkle. It rippled gracefully, flowing like water. 'For the sheep, moral outrage is the coin of the realm. They *smother* themselves in it.'

Evan ate his meat, one precut bite at a time.

René bristled, his first show of impatience. 'Well?'

'This doesn't interest me,' Evan said.

'Why not?'

'I've dealt with enough tin-pot tyrants and back-alley philosophers for one lifetime.'

Rene drew his head back, just slightly, but Evan could see

that he was stung. His complexion was bloodless, save for tinges of pink rimming his nostrils and eyes. Despite all his efforts, he looked unwell.

His fingers drummed on a BlackBerry that sat next to the clicker. He peeked at the screen, let it darken again. Since BlackBerry was a Canadian company, many believed that it gave better protection from the NSA. Evan guessed that René used a mirror system for his comms, transmitting every text or call through several intermediaries. Only his inner circle would know where he was, keeping him as safe and hidden as a cartel kingpin gone to ground.

René broke in on Evan's thoughts. 'I assumed you would understand,' he said. 'After all, we function outside the rules.'

'No.' Evan thumbed another nugget of venison into his mouth. 'I'm the sum of my rules.'

'*Your* rules, perhaps. Not *the* rules.' René waited for Evan's counter until it was clear that none was forthcoming. 'There aren't many things I do well. But what I *do* do well? I do that better than just about anyone. Discerning financial patterns. The ebbs and flows of accounts. Reading the digital droppings people leave behind. It wasn't the $235,887 you spent on that sword that sank you. It was the forty-one cents.' He leaned forward, searching for a reaction. 'That's my superpower. I see things in numbers others can't. And I know how to . . . rearrange matters to get those numbers in my column rather than in someone else's. My father, he didn't view that as work. No "value add." To him it wasn't a gift. It was just manipulation. He never saw my talent. In another life I could've been a director at Goldman Sachs.' His smile was a memory, cold as a ghost. 'Imagine that. Imagine if there was one thing, one thing you were meant to do. And it wasn't acceptable in the eyes of *anyone*. And yet it was who you are.'

Evan thought of the scattering of freckles across Mia's nose. The way she swayed when she listened to jazz. The fact that they had decided – for her safety and Peter's – that he should stay away from her.

René said, 'Whether you want to admit it or not, I can see that you understand me. People like us, we exist out of time, really. The day-to-day wear and tear that grinds ordinary folks down. Cubicles and carpool lanes. Earning a penny at a time. Why wade through it all when it's so easy to . . . *not*?'

'I suppose,' Evan said, 'that I have an overdeveloped sense of justice.'

'Where do you think it came from?'

'I've been on the other side.'

'Isn't that interesting,' René said. 'So have I. That's what convinced me justice doesn't exist.'

'What *does* exist?'

'Luxury.' René sipped his wine. 'You could take silk sheets and caviar and inject them directly into my veins.'

'So that's what you live for?'

'I want to have everything I want for as long as I want it.'

'At any cost?'

'At any cost to *others*, yes. Look at me. I'm fat. I'm ugly. What do I have? Money and fearlessness. Which equals power. Through power I get my needs met. I value luxury, yes. Youth. And beauty.'

A young man trudged in from the hall, rubbing one eye with a fist. His T-shirt pulled up, exposing the kind of stomach only achieved in one's early twenties, a slight concavity runged with muscle. His dirty blond hair swirled up, bedhead chic. He was either stoned or really tired.

René's son?

René stiffened. 'It's not safe for you here, David.'

David looked around through heavily lidded eyes, taking

in Evan, Dex, Manny with his raised shotgun. 'Looks plenty safe to me.' He plucked a piece of meat off René's plate, chewed it languidly.

Then he leaned over and kissed René full on the mouth.

Oh.

David mussed René's perfectly coiffed hair. 'The steam room is broken.'

'Broken?'

'It takes too long to get, ya know, steamy.'

'I'll have Samuel look at it.'

'Yer a doll.' David cast a bored gaze at Evan, then disappeared back into the hall.

René shared an exasperated look with Evan. 'When you're young, you're never going to be old. Remember?' He forked some green beans into his mouth. More wine. 'I'm not gay,' he said. 'I just sometimes like to sleep with men.'

He pressed the clicker again, and Samuel appeared, scratching at his scar.

'Go look at the steam room,' René said. 'There's nothing wrong with it, but David's fussing again. Pretend to make adjustments to the valve.'

Samuel nodded, exiting swiftly.

'If my interests are aligned with someone else's, I can be quite generous,' René said. 'As with you. I've done my best to acquaint you gently with your circumstances. I hope you've seen that you're free to enjoy certain liberties, that you've been treated well.'

Evan shifted in his chair, bringing Manny and his shotgun into view over his right shoulder. 'It's been lovely.'

'It's a lot of money to lose. I understand that. You have seventy-two hours to come to grips with it. But let me be clear. At the end of that time, if you don't cooperate, you won't like what will happen.'

'What will happen?'

Behind René, Dex stepped forward into the dim light cast by the chandelier. He'd been standing so still and silent in the shadows that until he'd moved, Evan had nearly forgotten he was present. Dex raised his left hand and pressed it across his lips. The tattoo on the back of this one was not a smile but a bared grimace. The incisors were pronounced, not quite vampiric, though they dripped with blood. The kind of mouth that would chew right through your gut. The sight of the inked scowl held up before Dex's otherwise blank features sent a chill corkscrewing up Evan's spine.

Dex had answered his question without having to speak.

'Dex is mute,' René said. 'Dumb, they used to call it, but I promise you that's not the case.' His teeth were tinted from the Bordeaux, the red distinct against his pasty face. He regarded Dex like a prize steer. 'He manages to convey so much without saying a word.'

Evan stood up. Instantly, Manny shouted at him from behind. '*¡Siéntate! Ahora,* motherfucker.'

But Evan didn't sit. Instead he kept his stare fixed on Dex. Holding his painted fangs in place over his mouth, Dex looked back him, his gaze containing no menace or fear. It held almost nothing at all, just the relentless focus of an owl watching a mouse about to scurry from cover.

'I can see you've won some fights,' René said. 'I bet you think about them from time to time. Replay them in your head.'

'Not as much as the ones I've lost.'

René crossed his utensils neatly upon his plate and pushed it away. From inside his lapel, he removed a clear cylindrical spray bottle. He squirted down his place setting and then rose and sprayed the cushion of his chair. He did this as though it were normal postprandial etiquette.

The mysterious bottle vanished inside his jacket. He tugged the front panel, seating the coat properly on his shoulders, then flipped a button into place with an expert twist of his thumb. He nodded at Manny. 'It's okay. It seems we're done.'

He turned to leave.

'So this wire,' Evan said. 'You think it's not traceable?'

'The computer is air-gapped, never been connected to the Internet before. The wire will be encrypted. The receiving account will relay the money out through a series of . . .' René stopped when he saw that Evan was smiling. 'What about this amuses you?'

'That you think it's enough.'

'Enough for what?'

Evan shook his head. 'Trust me. You don't want to do this.'

'Why not?'

'Because,' Evan said. 'You never know who's watching.'

16

Faithful Companions

Except for the swim cap, Candy McClure was naked. She loved being naked, though right now it was for work, not pleasure. That's why she was hunched forward, the corpse flopped atop her back, marble-white arms dangling over her shoulders as she carried it toward the conveyer belt leading to the crematory unit. The dead body pressed against her skin wasn't the most pleasant thing she'd felt this week, but she went to great lengths on disposal operations to avoid leaving fibers or residue at the scene.

It was one of those pet joints. She preferred animal mortuaries to human ones. If you could get around the inevitably cutesy names – they all seemed to be called 'Loving Paws' or 'Puppy Heaven' – they had certain advantages, looser security being foremost.

She'd broken into this outfit, Faithful Companions, in the glam outskirts of Muskego, because it used the Power-Pak II, her cremation unit of choice and the same one used for humans. Nice and roomy. Ideal for a St. Bernard or an investigative reporter from the *Journal Sentinel* who'd decided to start asking questions about black-budget allocations.

She flopped Jon Jordan's body onto the track atop a rigor-mortised, three-legged American Shorthair. She'd preheated the unit before retrieving the body from the stolen van she'd parked by the back loading dock. Ramming the heel of her hand into the button, she engaged the equipment and watched the unlikely twosome rumble into eighteen hundred degrees of obliteration.

Curiosity killed the cats.

Snapping her gum, she stretched out her shoulders, limboed a bit to loosen her lumbar. The flesh of her back itched and burned. Jon Jordan was not a small man. She caught sight of her naked form in the stainless steel of the crematory unit and paused to admire herself.

A knockout body by all accounts. Large, firm breasts that still sat high and proud. Tapered waistline befitting a cello. Wide, feminine hips. Shapely legs.

But.

She turned slowly, bringing her mottled back into view. Since Orphan X had knocked her on top of her own jugs of concentrated hydrofluoric acid, she'd had countless skin grafts and scar-tissue-release surgeries. The pain was intense and unremitting, infections always one shower away.

From the front, a centerfold. From behind, Freddy Krueger.

Though she loathed to admit it to herself, the scarring had eaten away almost imperceptibly at her rock-star confidence. Self-doubt was not her strong suit. In fact, it wasn't a trait she could remember experiencing, and yet there was something familiar in the shadows of doubt that crept beneath the repulsive surface now. Something from her early days in which she'd more or less raised herself, emotion she'd buried out of sight, excavation deep.

The question, like a whisper in her ear: *Are you still good enough?*

After all, the Orphan Program liked its products pristine. Candy had been perfect before. Now she had an incontrovertible flaw. Which made her human.

Orphans were not supposed to be human.

Beneath her swim cap, her cell phone vibrated against her skull. A girl punk band's cover of Whitney Houston's 'I'm Every Woman.'

The melody of employment.

She untucked the phone and answered. 'Yes?'

'Is the package neutralized?'

The voice on the other end wasn't so much a voice as a collection of words and syllables recorded from various TV shows and commercials – male and female, old and young, accented and not – hashed together, the audio equivalent of an old-timey ransom note fashioned from words clipped out of different newspapers.

Charles Van Sciver redefined paranoia. Though the calls were encrypted, he took this added step to dodge voice-recognition software. He was a ghost, a whisper in your ear. She'd met him only once, though she hadn't seen him clearly, not even then. She knew him mostly through secondhand stories.

The upside of Orphan X's efficiency was that he had knocked out the middleman. Now she could communicate with Van Sciver directly. Or at least with whatever software was proxying for his voice. She imagined him clicking away on his keyboard manically, Lon Chaney hunched over the organ in *Phantom of the Opera*.

She flopped down the unit door to gauge the progress of the flames, a housewife checking her pot roast. 'The package is cooking as we speak.'

'I have a POTENTIAL lead on ORPHAN X,' the mosaic of voices informed her.

She rolled her lush lips over her teeth and bit down. Throughout the past year, there had been countless potential leads, all turning up nothing. And yet each time Van Sciver called with a juicy new morsel, her breath quickened. The only thing she found more stimulating than sex was the prospect of revenge.

Orphan X had defaced approximately 40 percent of her

glorious surface area. What got her through the excruciating surgeries, the torturous recovery periods, the needle-stab showers and sleepless nights tossing in sandpaper sheets was one thing and one thing only.

The fantasy of what she was going to do to his body when she got ahold of him.

Van Sciver shared her enthusiasm. For him, too, nailing Orphan X was profoundly personal. She'd heard once that his relationship with X went back to when they were kids, but she knew nothing beyond that.

That's how they had a first name, Evan. His original surname had long been abandoned. Though Evan operated now under his alias, the Nowhere Man, Van Sciver insisted on referring to him by his Program code name.

Van Sciver was Orphan Y.

She was Orphan V.

The code names bound them.

With a stainless-steel brush, Candy swept the remains from the crematory unit into an aluminum hopper to cool. 'What's the lead?' she asked, trying to keep the eagerness from her voice.

'The PHONE service for 1-855-2-NOWHERE was moved RECENTLY, PARKED at a company outside Of Sevastopol.'

Van Sciver's data-mining algorithms cast a wide net, sifting the information superhighway for network ports, VoIP soft switches, bank accounts – any red flag that might mark a trail leading back to Orphan X.

'For OBVIOUS REASONS we can't get ANY information OUT OF CRIMEA withOUT Putin's goons catching WIND,' the voices continued. 'I need YOU to GO THERE. You'll BE paired WITH Orphan M.'

Ben Jaggers. A sullen, sallow little man who looked more

like a door-to-door salesman than a trained assassin. And yet she'd seen surveillance footage of him putting a chopstick through the eye of a wavering informant in a crowded Shanghai marketplace, leaving the man lobotomized over his egg-drop soup.

In the Program's original iteration, Orphans never worked together. But for Orphan X, Van Sciver had proved willing to make exceptions. When Van Sciver had taken over operations, there'd been a shift in focus. The Orphan Program still occasionally carried out the bidding of the secret-handshake men while allowing them full deniability. But since drone assassinations had demonstrated their click-button efficiency, there was less need of human assaulters and the complications that came with them. So a loyal core of Orphans under Van Sciver's direction now devoted themselves to hunting down wayward operatives carrying damning information in their heads. Like sharks in the womb, devouring one another until only the strongest remained. The most elusive and most dangerous of their targets was Orphan X.

She dumped the remains from the hopper into the pulverizer, reducing what was left of Jon Jordan and Mittens to fine powder. 'Why Orphan M?'

'Because he's THE ONLY one who WON'T find you ... DISTRACTING.' The last prerecorded word, spoken by a woman with an Indian accent, held particular emphasis.

'Why not?' Candy asked. 'What's wrong with him?'

No reply. Van Sciver didn't waste words even when they were not his own.

'When am I leaving?' she asked.

'Now,' Van Sciver said through another voice, and disconnected the line.

A knock from the rear echoed through the crematorium.

Tucking the phone back beneath her swim cap, Candy sighed and walked across the Lysol-scented tiles. She opened the back door.

Jaggers stood in the cold, his stringy suit hanging from his bones. He was five foot four, maybe a buck twenty. He kept his eyes on her face, no small feat given what was on display.

'Don't get in my way, don't question my tactics, and I'm not gonna fuck you,' she told him. 'Any questions?'

He coughed into a jaundiced fist. 'What makes you think I want to fuck you?'

She turned, breezing back to the pulverizer, which had just stopped its brittle grinding. 'Everyone wants to fuck me once they've been around me awhile,' she said. 'You'll see.'

If he took note of her burn scars, he didn't show it. In fact, he seemed entirely unaffected by her body. A sexless mole of a man.

'I have our plane tickets,' he said. 'We fly into Kiev and move from there.'

'We're husband and wife?'

'Photojournalists for a Canadian travel magazine,' he said. 'You can memorize the specifics on the flight.'

'Are we backstopped?'

'Yes. Several phone numbers deep, answering machines, our "editor" on standby.'

She swept the ash into a tray and then distributed it into various urns lining a shelf against the wall – Fido, Spot, Max. Ah, Wisconsin, with your stalwart Midwestern values and anachronistic pet names. She loved it here. It gave her a glimpse of what a real life might have been like.

She ran her hands beneath a faucet and dried them across her firm, firm thighs.

'One more thing.' She walked up on Jaggers. Her breasts

were level with his chin. Still he neither stepped back nor lost focus. 'When we catch up to Orphan X, I get him alive first. Understood?'

He gave a faint nod.

'Okay.' She started for the door. 'Let's go.'

He didn't follow.

'What?'

He gestured to the puddle of fabric behind her in the corner. 'You forgot your clothes,' he said.

17

Beautiful Monster

René despised the mirror. It used to be his friend. In his youth he could spend hours preening, admiring the line of his jaw, the strokes of his collarbones, the way his ass arced firmly into leg. He'd never been exactly handsome, but he could strike the right poses in the right lighting to make himself into something worth looking at.

His family never shared his interest in himself.

He turned now in the soft light of the master bathroom, regarding the two-inch deviation of his spinal column.

The slightest lateral curve. And yet it had changed everything.

No matter how hard he worked, no matter what sort of discipline he exhibited, that thumb-size bend meant he would never be acceptable in the eyes of his family. The Cassaroy name carried with it certain obligations, expectations handed down from generation to generation, gathering moss and heft. His great-great-grandfather had fought in the Civil War. And the Cassaroy males made regular appearances in the historical record after that, inevitably linked to combat. Here a first lieutenant in the Spanish-American War, there an artilleryman in the trenches of Château-Thierry. The Cassaroys were represented in the lesser wars as well, wars no one had ever heard of, wars no one would ever remember were it not for the framed battlefield portraits that lined the dark hallways of his childhood manor. The Sheepeater Indian War, the Second Sumatran Expedition, the Red River

War. If two forces spit at each other, there you'd find a Cassaroy, brandishing a rifle and a razor-straight spine, the first to show up, like an overeager party guest. His father had stormed Omaha, a muck- and blood-drenched affair he never hesitated to relive in the flickering light of the hearth, waving around a glass of century-old Grande Champagne cognac for punctuation.

Countless times René had heard that old chestnut about veterans never speaking of their wartime experiences. Would that it were true for the Cassaroys, who trotted out every scrape and scare like campfire tales made better by the retelling.

Were he not the sole Cassaroy heir and the biological end of the line, the pressure might have been less. And the disappointment. Born prematurely, René suffered from asthma and sundry illnesses in his childhood. He wasn't classic Cassaroy stock, but he had a passable build and was willing to give it the college try. None of his ailments mattered until he tried to enlist. His scoliosis was so minor it was missed by his pediatrician, and yet the eagle-eyed army recruiter had picked it up in an instant. As had the navy man. The marines. Even the air force. Despite Papa Cassaroy's considerable connections, René's application to the CIA didn't make it past the first round.

No one wanted him.

René was in his mid-twenties when Father threw a clot and cracked his head open on the claw-foot bathtub. Mother, a long-suffering waif out of a Tennessee Williams play, had succumbed to some vaguely defined ailment a few years prior. Father hadn't seemed to mind – she'd given him only one son of inferior make – and René certainly felt no loss of love when she passed. Yet when Father had gone, he felt not just the lifting of an age-old weight from his shoulders but

97

also an intense loneliness. All the old man's badgering and bullying had at least been a form of attention, an acknowledgment that René Peter Cassaroy did in fact exist.

His existence was called into further question at the reading of the will, an awful three-hour affair in the solemn offices of the family attorney, René squirming in an itchy tweed suit, the lawyer stroking his fulsome mustache. Father parceled out the family estate to countless veteran causes, leaving René with a measly couple hundred grand. He would no longer be able to live in the fashion he was accustomed to.

For six months he withdrew entirely from the world, holed up in a summer home that had yet to fall under the auctioneer's gavel. He knew he was a failure in the eyes of his family and the world, but hearing this fact confirmed so starkly by the walrus-mustachioed attorney was almost too much to bear. René had been deemed not worthy of sharing in a Cassaroy fortune that dated back to the 1600s. A two-inch curve of the spine had been enough to bring four centuries of prestige and affluence to a halt.

His father had unwritten him from history.

Perhaps the only benefit of being made nonexistent was that he was able to write a new story for himself. Play by new rules, ones that favored his strengths.

Using nothing more than a lifetime's education in pitilessness, he had assembled a fortune of his own. He now lived in a manner befitting a Cassaroy, but rather than being bound by convention or tradition, he did exactly what he fucking wanted.

He could control everything. Even – quite possibly – nature and time.

He had received only one noteworthy inheritance from his long, proud lineage of hale forebears, and yet it would prove more valuable than all the family jewels and dusty paintings put together: an AB blood type, present in a mere 4-percent sliver of the population. In this, René was exceptional. No – perhaps not exceptional *yet*. But it would make him so.

It would precipitate his transformation into something worth looking at again.

Standing before the mirror, droplets from the shower clinging dewlike to the hairs that furred his sloped shoulders, he saw his deficiencies on display. The sea-lion bulge of his pale belly. The half-moons of skin sagging beneath his eyes. The fineness of his hair such that the overhead light shone straight through to the dome of his skull.

Now was the hard part. Bracing himself, he thumbed the light switch to high.

There he was in all his starkness, every flaw captured in the unforgiving glare.

He began his evening restorative process.

Cover-up for his crow's-feet. A little concealer applied with a cotton disk to take the dark off the bags beneath his eyes. Color corrector for the sun spot staining his left cheek in front of his ear. He'd tattooed on a hint of eyeliner to make his chocolate brown irises pop, but it had been a few years, the ink fading. He made a note to have it redone.

Bottles lined the counter, diligent sentinels guarding against the ravages of aging. He filled his water glass to the brim. Down went three fish-oil pills, translucent and gold. Zinc for his skin, calcium for his nails, vitamin E for his follicles. Lipitor for cholesterol, Prinivil for blood pressure, Singulair for asthma. Concerta for focus, Klonopin to take the edge off, a second dose of Lexapro to ward off depression. Acidophilus for the gut. He washed down three green-tea capsules in hopes of speeding the fat-burning process and then heard David rustling around in the bedroom behind him and popped a Cialis.

With a dropper he applied Rogaine to the thinning area at the back of his head. It didn't work for the recession at his part, but he sprayed hair filler along the line of exposed scalp, the fibers clinging to his own strands, making them more robust. Propecia would take care of the rest. He wished he could reattain the rich umber shade of his youth, but no matter how often he dyed his hair, it held a fake copper sheen.

It took more and more work and more and more pills, morning and night, to resurrect himself, pull his body into alignment, reassemble his façade. He stared at himself through his father's eyes, through the eyes of generations of Cassaroys, and saw what they saw: someone pathetic and human and frail.

He felt the Need rise in him, clawing its way up his throat, crying out from his cells. His habits, so expensive, had to be supplied with blood.

There was a reason he kept Dr Franklin on premises. It was expensive, retaining a physician of his caliber. The medical equipment was expensive. *Everything* was expensive. René's life was an extravagant machine that required more upkeep every year. A beautiful monster that needed to be fed.

Dropping the towel from around his waist, René entered the bedroom. David lay nude and languorous, draped across the plush pillows. He cast a glance over a muscled shoulder, and René braced himself for the inevitable flash of disgust that flickered through his eyes before submerging beneath the drugged surface.

It cut him to the quick, that flicker. And yet he couldn't blame David one bit.

David threw an arm wide, welcoming him to the bed.

How handsome he was, with his rosebud lips, soulful eyes, and flushed cheeks. Like something from a Pre-Raphaelite painting.

René approached. 'You're going into town later tonight? For some fun?'

'That's right.'

The Need clamored inside René's chest, a trapped bird. 'Bring me a fix,' he said.

David tilted his chin down, a lazy approximation of a nod. 'Male or female?'

'A few of each,' he said. 'Do you think you can manage?'

Of course David could. With his looks and the promise of the chalet, anything was possible.

David rolled over, baring himself. 'I can manage anything,' he said.

18

Flesh and Bone

Locked in his room, Evan paced circles in his boxers, waiting for the fire in the hearth to burn down. It was going at a pretty good clip, the roaring cedar bringing memories of his penthouse perched on the twenty-first floor of Castle Heights. The logs had been restocked while he was at dinner and would likely burn through the night.

He moved to the sliding glass door and peered out at the mountain rims, barely visible, deeper black in the black night. The north slope was most gradual; that was probably why René had parked a sniper there. But were there more long-gunners on the other slopes? Evan gauged the rest of the range. A dip to the west looked promising. He'd have to assess it in the cold light of day.

For now he had to keep his head clear. Mind and body. The Second Commandment: *How you do anything is how you do everything.* Above all else, Jack had taught him to train his focus. To be one thing at a time, one thing and one thing only.

He stretched. The push-ups felt less painful, the bruises dissipating. His ribs still ached – Manny's kick to the gut hadn't hastened healing – but the pain was manageable. He sat on the bed, crossed his legs, aware of the camera charting his every move. Then he closed his eyes and let the hidden lens fade into inconsequentiality, let his focus turn inward, let himself find the breath and only the breath. It moved inside him, a breeze whispering through flesh and bone. The transience of each instant also held its beauty. This one breath, this single moment in time. This one body, impermanent and perishable and gloriously mortal. There would be this breath and then another, and at some point he will have drawn enough breaths to be still. He could control only how he chose to spend each one. And only in choice was there meaning.

A whip-poor-will was at it outside, whistling into the gloom, lonely and haunting. The roar of an engine came audible, drowning it out. Tires crackled across frostbitten ground.

Evan hopped from the bed, stepping out onto the balcony in time to see one of the G-Wagons slalom up the drive. It skidded to a stop, the driver's door popped open, and David spilled out. Two men and two women, also in their early twenties, emerged from various doors, pint glasses in hand. A bottle shattered. Peals of laughter.

Snatches rose to Evan, distorted by distance and the wind:

'Nice house, dude!'

'I hafta pee.'

David dug a slender white remote from an inner jacket pocket, raised it over his head, and clicked. Lights flared from beneath the eaves, flooding the grounds.

The young women tittered, wobbling on high heels.

'Whoa,' one of the guys said. 'That's *so* James Bond.' Gauge earrings the size of silver dollars stretched his lobes to tribal proportions.

David turned a circle, arms raised. A bottle of champagne had appeared in one of his hands. 'Well,' he said. 'You coming?'

He stumbled drunkenly toward the chalet's front door, the partyers following in his wake. Shivering, Evan watched until they vanished from view. Then he turned and stepped back inside.

Standing before the fire was a naked woman.

Her jet-black hair, thick and glossy, was swept up in the back, twisted around a chopstick. Wisps fell forward, framing her cheeks, clutching her neck. Her body demanded his attention, but he returned his focus to her face. Smooth, straight nose, olive skin, large dark eyes with prominent lashes.

The woman he'd seen Dex manhandling in the barn.

Red streaks grasped her wrist where the capillaries had broken. Again Evan wondered if the episode had been staged for his benefit. Her appearance here, like this, made it seem more likely.

She spread her arms, a *ta-da* gesture.

Then a pronounced frown. 'Normally men look happier to see me.' Her accent was strong but musical – Croatian? Greek? Serbian? Her hands clapped to her sides, sending a shudder through her strong hips. 'What's the matter? Don't you like gifts?'

'Not slaves.'

She stepped nearer, taking his hand in hers, drawing him to the warmth of the fireplace. 'Let's make an exception.'

Her mouth was close, her lips full. Heat prickled his skin, not just from the fireplace. She kissed him. It took a good measure of restraint not to kiss her back.

She pulled away, more amused than anything else. Then she pivoted him, tented a hand on his chest, and pushed him gently onto the bed. He sat. She sidled close, her breasts brushing his mouth. He was acutely aware of the camera above.

'Step back or I'll move you back,' he said.

But instead she eased him gently onto the mattress, leaning over him. Her hair fell like a curtain, connecting their faces, caressing his cheek. It was the first time he hadn't seen through a promise, maybe in his entire life.

When she looked at him now, her expression was different, her brow pinched, her dark eyes moist. *Fear.*

He realized that she'd let her hair cover their faces to block them from the camera.

'Then we need to fake it,' she whispered. 'Or it will be bad for me.'

He whispered back, 'He punishes you when someone turns you down?'

'I don't know.' Her teeth pinched her puffy lower lip. 'No one has ever turned me down.'

'What's your name?'

'Despi.'

Greek, then, from *Despina*.

She flicked her hair back over one shoulder. He could feel her against him, all warmth and pressure.

'Please,' she said.

He mostly believed her. And yet it seemed a gambit theatrical enough for René to have dreamed up. He studied the faint pulse in her neck. Thought about the chopstick in her hair.

He gripped her at the waist and rolled her over toward the part of the bed the ceiling-vent camera couldn't reach. He kept the edge of their bodies in view so as not to give away that he knew about the remaining surveillance.

'Here,' he said.

'Okay.' She was breathing hard. 'Okay.'

She sat up on him, tugged free the chopstick, shook her mane of hair. It resettled as if she'd placed it there strand by strand. She let the chopstick clatter to the nightstand, then ran a finger across the yellowed bruise on his shoulder from the beanbag round.

'You are tough,' she said. 'But are you tougher than René?' The name brought a faint shudder.

'I know enough not to underestimate him.'

'That's wise,' she said quietly. 'You've killed some of his workers.'

'How do you know?'

'The men talk.' She was undulating on him, her shoulder blocking the camera above. 'So you did?'

It was taking all sorts of focus and nonfocus for Evan to maintain the ploy. 'Yes.'

'That's what you do? Wait in this little room dreaming up ways to kill your way out of here?'

'Yes.'

Her skin carried the fragrance of jasmine. She leaned forward, pressing the softness of her stomach to his. The tips of their noses nearly touched. Her hips worked and worked some more, her eyes watching him appraisingly the whole time. 'How would you kill *me*?'

'I'd put the chopstick on the nightstand through your carotid artery.'

Her eyes flared. 'What an ugly thing. To know something just like that.'

'Yes,' he said.

She rolled off him, threw an arm across her forehead, ostensibly worn out. He slid the rest of the way out of the lens's purview. She let her head fall to the side so she was facing him. 'That's why they told me I had to take the chopstick when I left. It was an experiment. To see if you'd fuck me or kill me.' Sadness touched her eyes. 'You did neither.'

She waited for him to say something, but he had nothing to say.

'That's what I am now,' she said. 'A lamb staked to the ground to test the predators.'

She got up abruptly, slipping off the bed. She was sure to get the chopstick on her way out. When the door opened, Evan heard multiple sets of footsteps outside. It closed, dead bolts clanking into place, one after the other. He barely had time to consider what had just happened when he heard a familiar hissing from above.

'Fuck,' he said.

Gas flooded down on him.

19

Somewhere Much, Much Worse

A hint of cherry blossom laces the air. In other circumstances it might be lovely.

But beneath it is the earthy stink of damp concrete and the coppery tang of blood.

Jack stands stooped, one hand clutching the ball of his shoulder to no avail. Blood sprays through his fingers. His blue flannel shirt saturated. His eyes accusing.

Darkness prevails. There is the spotlight of Jack and nothing else. Evan watches from somewhere in the gloom, spellbound.

They are in Parking Level 3. Or somewhere much, much worse.

Jack's mouth pulses, his lips locked shut, but Evan can hear his thoughts.

What have you done?

Little boy who I loved as my own, what have you done to me?

Jack's mouth opens, but instead of words there is only blood, black as oil, loosed as if from a faucet. It sheets over his lower teeth, pours across his chin, streams down his legs. It pools on the floor and spreads and spreads, filling the spotlit circle and oozing outward.

Evan is helpless, trapped in the darkness. He tries to open his own mouth, but he cannot. When he reaches to see why, bristling sutures poke his tender palm.

His lips have been stitched shut.

Jack's blood seeps through Evan's shoes, warm and tacky. It waterlogs his socks, claims his ankles, his calves. He tries to cry out, to no avail. He is a mute witness to what he has wrought.

The warmth is at his waist now. His pants sodden. His shirt grows heavy, clings to his flesh. The blood rises past his clavicles, fills the hollow of his neck. And then he is under, his eyes wide and comprehending, the world below vast and empty.

The universe strained through a crimson filter.

20

No End Point

Young voices lit up the parlor. David was being David – making trick shots on the billiard table, mixing drinks behind the bar, licking salt off a young woman's gazelle-like neck before throwing back another amber shot and sinking his immaculate teeth into the embrace of a lime. The other girl slumped on the couch, propping up her forehead with one hand and sloppily texting with a thumb. Her iPhone in its sparkly case slipped from her manicured grip. The young men were doing young men things – pounding pints, warring over the foosball table, enacting elaborate handshakes and high-fives.

There was free-flowing top-shelf booze, and there were Viennese chocolates and Cohiba Robustos. Platters of short-rib sliders and sashimi. Kale salad with bacon-blue cheese vinaigrette and fresh oysters on spoons. Invisible as stagehands, the least sinister of René's rented men circulated and cleared, dressed in servantwear with mandarin collars, the better to hide the menacing tattoos. The more colorful of the men – and certainly Dex – were best kept from view.

Pretending to leaf through a *Wall Street Journal*, René observed from a divan at an avuncular remove. This was his place, the perennial outsider lingering just past the reaches of the social glow. Or as he preferred to think of it, Oz behind the green curtain. Aside from the occasional appreciative nod to their host and benefactor, the kids ignored him.

The boy with the soul patch and the tribal earrings – Joshua – had graduated to drinking Johnnie Walker Blue out of the bottle. That could prove problematic.

René didn't want him too dehydrated.

He was a burly kid, broad-shouldered and thick-thighed, young enough that his muscle propped up the fat, held it firm. He'd already sweated through his guayabera. Inexplicably, he'd decided to plug into a bling-bling set of cushy headphones and was dancing with his reflection in the tall windows, a sort of airplane flight pattern that involved tilting his arms this way and that, a landing approach with no end point.

The laughter reached a manic pitch, warmed with booze and friction. David pressed the girl with the slender neck up against the bar. With an expert flip of his hand, he popped the top buttons of her jeans and wiggled his hand inside. She threw back her head in a manner that suggested more rehearsal than spontaneity. The other boy was on top of the girl on the couch, trying to snap a selfie, and she was cackling, pushing at the balls of his shoulders, her fingers splayed. It was self-conscious without the benefit of shame, as if they were enacting a scene they'd all studied, a commercial for unlimited cell-phone minutes.

That was the problem with young people nowadays. Give them their very own Pleasure Island and they all reach for a script.

Youth is wasted on the young, sure. But it needn't be.

René let the top of the newspaper crinkle down. Across the parlor, low-lidded and clearly bored, David looked back at him over the girl's shoulder. She hooked her arms around his neck, swaying with the action of his hidden hand, whimpering. She had one of those names that didn't use to be a name – Kendall or Cammy.

Her movements grew more sluggish. Her blinks became longer. As her legs buckled, David clasped her around her waist and lowered her to the floor.

Over by the windows, Joshua now lay on the rug where he'd fallen, the Beats headphones shoved down around his neck giving off tinny hip-hop. The tangled couple on the couch had passed out mid-selfie. All that faux youthful abandon, fading down into a Rohypnol stupor.

René rose.

One of his *narco*-butlers had already fetched Dr Franklin, who entered now loose-limbed and unshaven. As he surveyed the tableau, his eyes attained a surgeon's clarity behind round rimless lenses. He straightened out of his slouch. Instant sobriety. Despite his habits he was a man who could find the foundation in a hurry when he had to.

Two of the men rolled the girls onto stretchers. Dex entered. With a faint whistle of breath, he hoisted Joshua up off the floor and flopped him over his shoulder. David took hold of the other boy's biker boots and dragged him along after the others as if pulling a wheelbarrow. René watched them pass, the kid's arms windshield-wipering the floor behind him.

René felt the Need stirring inside him, awakening to the possibility of a meal.

'Ready?' Dr Franklin asked.

René swept an arm magnanimously. 'After you.'

Following the convoy of unconscious bodies down the hall, Dr Franklin snapped on one latex glove and then the other.

21

In Trouble

A buzzing pulled Evan from sleep.

Was it in his body? The sheets? No – under the mattress, vibrating him through the fabric. The princess and the epileptic pea. Groggily, he lifted his ten-ton head from the pillow, trying to regain his bearings.

The buzzing came again.

The RoamZone? It couldn't be.

He rolled off the bed, his knees striking the floor, hands digging the phone out from its hiding place between mattress and box spring.

Sure enough, light leaked through the shattered façade. The caller's number flickered, carved up by dozens of hairline fractures. The TALK icon at the bottom floated in the sole section of unbroken glass. He held his breath, thumbed the icon.

He held the phone to his ear.

It took him a moment to recall the script, to remember the words he was supposed to say when he picked up. He forced them out through the drug-induced grogginess. 'Do you need my help?'

'Yes.' The voice of a boy, high-pitched and scared.

Evan knew he was clear of the hidden camera, but he turned his back anyway, leaning against the bed. He pressed his thumb and forefinger to the bridge of his nose, blinked hard around them.

'Where did you get this number?' Evan asked.

'A girl gave it to me. She said you help people and stuff.' The boy was whispering. He sounded somewhere around ten years old.

'What's her name?'

'Anna something.'

'What's she look like?'

'Dark hair. Patchy, like it's falling out in places.' The whisper grew more hoarse, more urgent. The boy's words were distorted ever so slightly. A speech impediment? 'Look, can you help me or not?'

'I can.'

'I don't know how much time I have till they catch me. I stole the cordless. I'm under the couch. I'm not supposed to make calls.'

'What's your name?'

A hesitation. 'I can't . . . I can't tell you. I'll get in trouble.'

The kid's quick breaths were audible even over the crackle of static.

'If they catch me with the phone, it'll be bad.'

Evan listened to the kid's articulation. Not a lisp. He closed his eyes, his brain still gummy from the sleeping gas. It took a moment, but he put it together. 'Someone beat you up.'

'So what?' the kid said, his words blurry across a swollen lip. 'I get beat up all the time. Please come. Please help me.'

'Where are you?'

'You should see how they keep us here. Like cattle, all lined up.'

'Where are you?' Evan asked again.

'Are you coming to get me?'

Evan looked around, the dead-bolted door, the caged balcony, the gas-breathing vent. He took stock. First: Escape. Second: Rescue Alison Siegler. Third: Help the kid.

'Soon,' Evan said.

'Then I don't . . . Then I can't risk saying yet.'

'Who else is there?'

'Other boys.'

'Where are you from?'

'I don't know. I don't remember.'

'Do you have a family? Parents?'

'I don't . . . I don't know. It's been so long.'

'How long have they kept you?' Evan asked. 'How old were you when you were taken?'

'Oh, shit. I can't – they're coming. I'll try 'n' call back. Will you help me? Will you?'

'Yes. I will get to you.'

'Promise me.'

'I promise.'

The broken phone cut out. Evan stared down at the shattered shards held together loosely in the cracked casing of the RoamZone.

He shoved the phone back into its hiding place and crawled into bed. He imagined Alison Siegler, locked in her container aboard a ship halfway around the globe. Did she have enough food? Enough air? He thought about a little boy also waiting for his help, his words blurred over a swollen mouth: *You should see how they keep us here.*

Evan's blinks grew heavier.

Two dogs, ten guards, one sniper, Dex, and counting.

He'd have to kill a lot more of them tomorrow.

22

Divine Right

Propped on a brace of pillows on a regally upholstered gurney, René drew in a deep lungful of air as the needle sank beneath his flesh. This was his favorite moment, when the fix first flowed into his body and set the world quivering with potency. Everything turned vibrant, the colors saturated even down here in the bowels of the chalet. Every sensation felt enhanced – the oxygen in his lungs, the hum of adrenaline hurtling through his veins, the creamy sheets caressing his bare skin.

The rush hit his arteries, a surge that rocketed him to his feet. The catheter in his arm couldn't slow him. He seized the IV pole and dragged it beside him, one stubborn wheel giving off a squeak.

His finest bequeathment, an AB blood type, served him exquisitely. Having both key antigens and neither constraining antibody made him a universal recipient. Anyone could give to him. Few could receive from him. He was a taker. He hadn't merely resigned himself to this fact; he embraced it as divine right.

Sure of foot, his back ramrod-straight and unaching, he threaded through the youthful bodies lying prone and unconscious on their gurneys. Through the dim light, he moved erect and proud, an ageless sovereign lording over his minions.

All was right in the Great Chain of Being.

He swore he could already feel the pyrotechnics exploding through him. His aging tissue rejuvenating. Tired muscles mending. New neural connections sprouting in his hippocampus. His heart, his brain, even his cartilage reviving. His memory fortifying. Liver cells generating. He felt swollen with vitality, with youth, with timelessness.

Even his sense of smell grew more keen. This was no trick of the mind. From across the basement lab, he picked up a trace of dewy perfume on the slender neck of David's girl.

Kendall was an AB type, too, unlucky dove. She would receive from him tonight, and that would cost her. Each of the guests had to be replenished, and there was no use wasting valuable O neg from the freezer when she could take what had to be drawn out of René to make room for the new.

From time immemorial man had searched for the fountain of youth. From Herodotus's recitations to Ponce de León's hapless wanderings, it had cast a mythological shadow across the ages. Silver chalices and bubbling springs.

Who would have thought it had been right in front of everyone all along?

Someone just required the audacity to take it.

If you considered it, *really* considered it, this was a move befitting a Cassaroy. Rather than forging through enemy fire to claim some godforsaken battle-torn hill, René had fought his way through social mores and human limitations to stake his flag in the virgin terrain of an age-old fantasy.

Passing among his unsuspecting acolytes now, he brushed against dangling bags of blood, as bright and cheerful as Christmas decorations.

That was when he heard a groan behind him. He halted. Turned. There was movement in the bed where there was supposed to be none.

And then Joshua sat up.

The kid was not supposed to come to for another few hours. Dr Franklin rarely got the dosing wrong, but the bigger the fellow, the more unpredictable the anesthesia. All that mass, it seemed, gave the boy the tolerance of a water buffalo.

It was awful when they woke up in the middle.

They got so confused.

It wasn't just the whir of the processing machines, the hum of the medical refrigerators, the white-noise rush of the benchtop centrifuges, all of it amplified off the basement walls. Nor the smells, the sharp tang of rubbing alcohol, the nail-polish reek of iodine, the hospital-room whiff of PVC tubing and dried sweat. The sights weren't what did it either – not the needles plunged into their flesh, the blood piping from their veins, their acquaintances laid out in neighboring beds, dead to the world. Not the scrape of the sanitized pillowcase at their nape. Not the taste, old pennies at the back of the tongue.

It was the vertiginous sense of dislocation.

They were no longer in the world as they knew it. No, this gave them a glimpse of The World As It Really Was.

Might is right. Eat or be eaten. Accrue resources or starve. Repeated again and again and again, because all ten thousand years of civilization had been built upon mankind's desire to deny this fundamental truth.

René tried to protect them from reality. They were supposed to pass out full-bellied, drunk, and happy. Never know the difference. He was greedy, sure, but not inhumane.

No sense spooking the livestock on their way to the abattoir.

And yet now Joshua was certainly spooked.

He reared up from his gurney, tubes snaking around his bulging arms, IV poles crashing over.

René unhooked his own IV bag and dashed away, using Kendall's gurney as a shield. He was too charged to feel fear, but a dark excitement gripped him. Tingling electrified his body – his gums, his arms, the skin of his lower back.

Joshua's head pivoted, fixing on René. Even across the gurney, René registered the wounded rage and stripped-bare terror lurking behind the dilated pupils. It gave him a heady, almost sexual rush. He wondered if this is what his ancestors had felt charging through the fray, shrapnel grazing their cheeks.

Joshua lunged at René, sending the gurney skidding. Dead to the world, Kendall rolled to one side, smashed beneath Joshua's weight. Scrambling toward them, Dr Franklin tried to hit the kid with a syringe full of Versed, but with all the flailing he couldn't get to the port. Joshua clawed across the unconscious girl, his churning legs propelling the gurney until René was backed to the wall, Joshua's straining fingers inches from his face.

That was when Dex stepped in.

However big the boy was, he looked like a puppet in Dex's hands. Dex lifted him in a choke hold. There was a crackling sound, and then Joshua poured limply from Dex's arms onto the floor.

Silence reasserted itself in the basement.

Joshua lay still, one dead palm pressed to the concrete.

This was not a substantial problem. Come morning René would generate some excuse to cover for the boy's absence. He'd peddled such excuses before. If the others showed bruising from the needles, he would instruct David to tell them that in their drunken state they'd played around with heroin one of the kitchen workers had brought. Not to worry – what happened at Chalet Savoir Faire stayed at Chalet Savoir Faire. And that's what would happen. The best way to ensure silence was to bury the truth beneath shame.

From over by the door, David coughed out a note of disbelief, hugging himself around the waist, his arms trembling. Dr Franklin leaned against a cabinet, flushed from the scare.

René, too, was breathing hard, though not from fear. He'd never felt more alive. He looked down at the IV bag compressed in his fist, now depleted. In all the excitement, he had rapid-bolused the final unit into his arm. All that fresh young blood bathing his stem cells, turning back the clock.

With a furrow of his shiny forehead, Dex looked past Joshua's slumped body at René. He seemed unclear which mouth the present circumstances called for.

René pointed to Dex's right hand.

Dex raised the smile, folded it across his mouth.

Yes, that looked appropriate.

It was, after all, a happy occasion.

23

Destroying Angel

When Manny and Nando came to get Evan for his walk, he took some extra time to layer his clothes, donning two shirts and two sweaters. They'd brought both breakfast and lunch on the room-service cart earlier, making Evan stand against the wall with his back turned until they exited. The new procedures were effective. They maintained their spread now as they guided him down the halls and stairs to the foyer, one shotgun aimed at his face, another at his kidneys.

Manny gestured at the front door, his gold caps sparkling. 'You get your yard time now. Just like in the prison.'

Evan said, 'Trade you two cartons of cigarettes for a shiv.'

Manny looked at him, puzzled, then jerked his gun. 'You go.'

The doorknob felt cold enough to stick to Evan's hand. When he stepped onto the porch, the cold flew straight through the layers of clothes and tightened his skin. He stomped his boots, blew a breath that clouded and faded away, a ghost that couldn't be bothered.

Over by the barn, David corralled three of the partyers into one of the G-Wagons. The kid with the gauge earrings must have either left last night or was already in the vehicle behind the tinted windows. The three kids in view looked wan and weak, no doubt atrophied from first-rate hangovers. One of the girls in particular moved creakily, clinging to David, her legs barely strong enough to push her into the back of the Mercedes. Her face was gray, her lips bloodless. She coughed weakly into a sleeve-covered fist. David helped her gingerly into the rear seat, closed the door, then paused for a moment with his back to the van, his head tilted up at the sky, his lips trembling.

He seemed upset. Conflicted.

He lowered his gaze, noticed Evan noticing him. But he didn't look away, not even as he blinked back tears. Finally he walked around to the driver's seat and drove off.

From the porch Evan watched the vehicle head up the gravel road, and then it was just him and the cold. From here on out, the math was simple. He had to mark the position of every one of René's hired men. Then kill them.

The skinny guard in the tower leaned on the railing, eyeing Evan. Evan waved. The guard did not wave back. Across the way, three *narcos* were gathered at their post by the barn. Evan envied their heavy black coats. The scorched pot hung over the fireplace, and their heads were bowed as they shoveled food from bone-china plates. The Dobermans idled beside the men, pointed at him, rumbling.

Evan gestured at the forest inquisitively, and one of the *narcos* waved his fork in response: *Be our guest.*

The guard muttered something to the others, and they laughed. As Evan hiked up to the trees, their amusement became clearer. Despite the sweaters and shirts he was wearing, the cold asserted itself in his joints. Already his feet felt numb in the hiking boots. He could hold out for an hour, maybe two, but without heavier clothes and a fire, hypothermia would set in. However, escaping wasn't today's plan.

From the edge of the woods, he looked back. Two magenta circles winked at him from the tower, the guard's binoculars tracking his movement. The big chimney behind him sighed a tendril of black smoke.

Evan paused to search for that notch in the western rim of the mountains. The silhouette had looked promising last night, but now, seeing the sheer face leading up to it, he felt his hopefulness evaporate. The southern rise was higher but the ascent more gradual. A viable second option if the northern route proved unmanageable.

As Evan turned back, something caught his eye on the distant treetops. A large bird perched in the upper reaches of a pine tree, its white head as pronounced as a golf ball against the dark tones of the forest. He did a double take, focusing his gaze.

A noise from the tower carried to him on the breeze, the guard talking into a radio. A moment later a hidden rifle cracked and the bird disappeared, a few feathers floating in the space where it had been.

Evan's brain was still working on what his eyes had just seen, the imprint of that bird floating in the white space, a visual memory.

A bald eagle.

In Switzerland.

Not likely.

He understood now why the tower guard had relayed word to the sniper to remove it from the picture. René could control a lot, certainly. But not nature.

Not wanting to give away what he'd seen, Evan didn't dwell. Continuing quickly up through the trees, he berated himself for forgetting the First Commandment – *Assume nothing*.

He was in North America somewhere. Vermont, maybe. Alaska or Canada. René wanted him to believe he was halfway around the world on the desolate edge of the Alps, a further disincentive to escape.

But he was closer to home than that.

He remembered hearing that whip-poor-will last night, annoyed that he didn't know what region the damn bird was indigenous to. Jack would've chided him for not paying better attention during wilderness-survival skills.

Really, Evan? It took a bald friggin' eagle *to pin you down on a continent?*

But this was good news, too. Closer to home meant he was closer to Alison Siegler. And closer to the kid who had called.

Evan hiked to the clearing he'd made it to last time. There was no buck at the water's edge, no loon in the half-frozen puddle. Just a porcupine feeding in a treetop, sprinkling down needles, forty pounds of quilled bowling ball.

Evan looked up the ridgeline, hoping to catch a glint from a scope to place the sniper. No such luck. Wind whipped his cheeks raw.

He thought about the perfect shot placement that had dropped the buck, two inches behind the shoulder, slightly below the midline of the body, straight through the lung to the upper heart. The tournament-worthy round to knock the bald eagle from the treetop. Even more impressively, both shots had been made from a cold bore.

He searched the ground, spotting a pinecone. He retrieved it, placed it on the flat of his palm, held out his hand, and faced upslope.

A challenge.

He waited. Waited some more.

A muzzle flashed high on the slope, and the pinecone exploded, seemingly at the same instant. Shrapnel flecked his cheeks as the supersonic crack echoed around the bowl of the valley.

Evan's stomach had leapt into his throat at the impact, but he focused, judging the sound, gauging the distance. A high-power, major-caliber rifle was in play, .30 or bigger. Given that the shooter could take a pinecone off a flattened hand at five hundred meters, he could probably hit critical mass at three times that distance. Committing the sniper's position to memory, Evan nodded respectfully toward him, lowered his hand, and started back toward the house.

Halfway down the slope, he became aware of a stinging in his palm. A closer examination revealed that a few splinters from the pinecone had been embedded in the skin. He picked them out with his teeth and spit them to the wind.

The guards no longer held their spot by the fire outside the barn. The wide door was rolled back slightly, and he could hear them inside. The tower guard remained alert above, watching Evan's every move, the binoculars swiveling with him like a part of his face.

Rather than veering toward the porch, Evan continued past the chalet and into the tree line on the other side. He made his way up the southern slope a short distance, the chill razoring beneath his skin. The sun was low, the sky textured with dusk. He didn't have much more time before the cold would drive him inside.

An outcropping of shale shaved a treeless patch on the mountainside. Evan clambered onto the rock and stood, eyeing the rise, thinking about where he'd tuck in himself if he were behind a sniper scope.

A gulley two-thirds up provided an ideal vantage of the surrounding terrain while guarding the pass. Evan hopped off the rock, found another pinecone, and returned to his position in the open.

He displayed the pinecone on his outstretched hand, held his breath, closed his eyes.

A crack.

The whistle of a round.

A wet thud behind him.

He exhaled, letting the pinecone drop. The sniper to the

south was a weaker shot, a fact that Evan filed away for future use. It was a trial of one, sure, but that was all he was willing to risk. Judging by the miss, he was lucky his hand was still connected to his wrist.

His cheeks and nose felt stiff, his flesh gone to rubber. Time to get indoors. Turning back, he eyed where the bullet had blown a hole through the side of a soggy log, revealing clumps of moss and a white conical cap the size of a quail egg.

Drawing close, he knelt with his back to the sniper and pretended to tie his bootlaces. He studied the mushroom.

It grew singly out of a sack at the base of the stem. A thin skein of moss covered the cap. Evan plucked it and ran a nail across the surface, revealing pure white beneath. *Amanita virosa.*

Destroying angel.

Even a few drops of its juice could shut down a person's kidneys.

He rose, palming the mushroom to hide it from the sniper. As he started down the mountainside, he pinched at the cap with a thumbnail, chopping it into tiny pieces, which he wadded in his hand.

Breaking from cover, he looked up at the tower guard peering down at him through the graying air. Holding the powdered bits in a loose fist, he walked over toward the barn and the deserted fire.

The tower was behind him now, but he could hear the skinny guard chattering into the radio. Evan neared the barn door, the crates where the *narcos* sat, the pot hanging over the fire.

He'd barely arrived when the door rolled open, both Dobermans charging at him. Snapping and snarling, they strained their leashes into straight lines. Two *narcos* spilled out after them, AK-47s raised, barking orders in Spanish.

Evan pointed to the fire, made a shivering gesture. The guards yelled some more, one of them prodding him toward the house with a gun barrel.

He gave no resistance, stumbling from being shoved. Shuddering in his layers of clothes, he hastened his pace toward the porch, dusting off his empty hands.

24

A Complex, Sticky Business

Crimea smelled like sewage, artillery shells, and boiled hot dogs. Candy strolled with Ben Jaggers along a boardwalk overlooking a rocky beach. Holding his arm through his raincoat felt like clutching a stick wrapped in cloth. A head taller than him, she wore leather pants and a bustier top. She'd teased out her blond hair voluminously, hoping to pass for a local girl. Jaggers was playing the role of a rich married guy out for a little fun, though he seemed to have forgotten to tell his face. He slouched along in a plaid button-up and brown slacks.

She felt like a Bentley being taken for a spin by the mechanic's kid.

Girls passed by, laughing and waving lipstick-smeared cigarettes. They were magnificent creatures, as girls from this region of the world were, all fuck-you sneers and aggressive makeup. Tights wrapped their impossibly long legs, and they wore white platform boots capped with fur, trotting along with the graceful force of Clydesdales.

As they wafted by in clouds of hair spray, smoke, and knockoff Chanel No. 5, the sullen little man at Candy's side didn't so much as raise his head to take in the girl-power scenery. His nose twitched, his mouth pursing as if on the verge of hocking a loogie. He smelled vaguely of mothballs. A camera dangled from around his neck, bouncing off what passed for his chest.

He eyed the streets behind the boardwalk, his hand tightening on her forearm. 'Here,' he said.

She posed for him, leaning back against the railing as he snapped photos. Though he pretended to focus on her, he was really zooming in over her shoulder on a building up the hill from the beach.

She blew kisses. Scoop-crossed her arms to shove her tits together. Turned sideways and threw up a Marilyn Monroe leg.

He continued shooting the boulevard behind her. 'Most of them have cleared out, but he's still in the office on the second floor,' he said, his words snatched away by the wind.

They'd spent the day photographing the building from every angle.

The mottled skin of Candy's back complained beneath her fitted top, no doubt angry from the cold breeze and salty air. She put the pain in the bank, a mental account she'd been saving up for Orphan X. She couldn't wait to start taking withdrawals out of *his* flesh.

Willing away the discomfort, she smacked her bubble gum. The gum was neon green, her lipstick orange, both props to help her blend in. A gaggle of girls legged by, giving her competitive glares. God bless these Ukrainian-Russian broads. They oozed so much natural sexuality that they could slap the 1980s all over themselves and still knock the skin right off an American girl.

Except for Candy, of course.

She leaned over, grabbing her knees, gave the knock-'em-dead smile. Jaggers clicked and clicked.

'Everyone else is gone,' he said. 'He's the last one there now.'

'Hey, M,' she said. 'It's not polite to not stare at a lady. Especially when she looks like this.' She straightened up, spreading her stance, arms on her hips, her breasts pushing high – Colossus of Rhodes if he was fucking hot.

Jaggers moved the camera to the side of his cheek. His flat

eyes observed her. Blinked. The zoom lens drifted over her shoulder. More clicking. At least it blocked his face.

She should be thankful for small mercies.

She thought about the kind of fun she could have here if it weren't for Orphan M.

Of course, the mission was primary. Though they'd been in-country for only twelve hours, they'd ascertained a few things.

The phone-service company to which Orphan X had moved his number was located on the second and third floors of the converted cannery that Jaggers was currently lensed in on. Given present conditions in Crimea and the Nowhere Man's proclivities, it was no surprise that TeleFon Star placed a premium on the privacy of their customers.

Van Sciver had identified the target as Refat Setyeyiva, vice president of operations, a thick-bodied man with scruffy good looks. A youthful forty, he had come up as a hammer thrower in the Soviet Olympic program, juiced and primed from the age of eight. He'd blown out his knees in his late teens, and here he was, overseeing operations for the discreet comms company that Candy and Jaggers needed to infiltrate.

Rather than dick around with hacking through firewalls, which neither of them specialized in, they'd been tasked with stealing Setyeyiva's laptop to get the passwords and access the company databases. They were to eliminate him to buy themselves time with the computer before it could be reported as missing.

Given Setyeyiva's sturdiness and physical prowess, this would be challenging. Attaining a gun in this climate would be conspicuous. So they'd come up with another plan.

Jaggers let the camera drop from around his neck. 'He's leaving now.' He checked his watch, jotted down the time in his notepad with a skinny silver pen.

Candy pictured the route Refat Setyeyiva would likely trace on his way out – through the rear door and across the narrow alley to the parking structure next door. There were specifics to lock down, angles to consider, sight lines to account for. It would be a complex, sticky business, and success rested on timing and preparation.

As her junior-high shop teacher used to say, *Measure twice, cut once.*

25

Not Very Nice

Back in his luxurious cell, Evan checked his phone to see if the boy had called back, but the shattered screen showed no missed calls. He slid the RoamZone between mattress and box spring again and went into the bathroom. Getting down on his hands and knees by the sink in the hidden camera's blind spot, he stared at the J-plug outlet placed beneath the floating counter. Then he rolled onto his back and smashed the plastic cover with the heel of his boot. It took only a few kicks for it to chip and fall away.

Beneath it was nothing but an empty hole in the drywall. Wires stubbed out of the socket, connected to nothing. It was a prop, inserted in the space where a functional outlet had been.

He broke the cover into smaller pieces and flushed them down the toilet.

In the bedroom again, he crawled beneath the built-in desk. The Type C outlet was there in the darkness behind the back panel and the wall. He slipped his hand into the gap and managed to slide the edge of his thumbnail into the groove of one of the tiny screws. After five minutes of cramped machinations, the screw pinged loose, the outlet cover swinging down to reveal the blank wall beneath.

Evan sat back on his heels and marveled at René's attention to detail. So many fakes and misdirects. Impeccable tradecraft.

When he crawled out, Despi was once more standing by the fireplace. She wore lipstick and a hair tie.

'Wanna not have sex again?' Her full lips shaped the words, a hoarse whisper to thwart the surveillance.

He drew himself upright. 'Don't you get cold?'

She stepped closer, her hips ticktocking. She ran a finger along his jaw. 'What I feel is irrelevant. There's only what I have to do.' Her flat words and expression were divorced from her body language, which she laid on thick for the hidden camera.

He regretted the joke.

She undressed him, pulling off the layers. Then she slid her hand to the nape of his neck, tugging him toward her. 'Should we get this over with?' The sensuous affect paired with her matter-of-fact declarations made her seem like an actress who'd been given the wrong dialogue.

Evan steered her to the same spot on the bed, keeping them mostly in the camera's blind spot. She pulled him on top of her, putting her mouth to his ear. 'You have very strong willpower.'

'To not rape you?'

'What it would be,' she said, 'is complicated.'

'Not to me.'

'So virtuous.' Her lips tugged to one side, a smirk. 'Have you decided that you trust me?'

'Mostly.'

'Only mostly?' She feigned offense. 'Well, I have no chopstick. So how would you kill me now, Virtuous Man? Right now?'

He ran his fingers through her thick hair. 'I'd rake your head to the side hard enough to fragment your C2 vertebra into your brain stem.'

She took a moment with that one. 'And there is a Hollywood movie crackle, and then I die instantly?'

'No. You'd be a quadriplegic. Maybe you could still speak.

Or scream. But the break would cut off impulses from your brain to your diaphragm, and you'd eventually suffocate.'

Their faces were close, and they spoke in whispers. 'That's not very nice,' she said.

'No.'

'I'm glad you mostly trust me.' She clasped her hands around his ribs and pulled him tighter. She was skilled at selling the performance. He cringed to think of the experiences that had led her to perfect this skill set.

'How did you get here?' he asked. 'Were you taken like me?'

'I was stupid. There was a party on a yacht docked off the coast of Rhodes – that's where I'm from. My girlfriend was going, and she asked me to join. I was recently divorced, so I said what the hell. René was there. I interested him. Not sexually. But as an object. He takes things and people. He doesn't understand the difference.'

'No,' Evan said. 'He doesn't seem to.'

'He thinks I am a Greek goddess. It is the only thing we agree on.'

'How did he take you?'

'I drank the champagne. I woke up very much later out at sea. He showed me pictures of my parents in our little apartment. My younger sister at the Athens School of Fine Arts. She's nineteen. René had her class schedule printed up. He set the pictures and documents before me but said nothing. He didn't have to.'

He studied her liquid brown eyes for a sign that she was lying. 'How long ago was that?'

'Seventeen months, two weeks, and a day.'

'I'm sorry.'

'Me, too.'

'You weren't stupid.'

'Yes. I was. That doesn't mean it was my fault, though.' A

133

pause. 'When people think of human trafficking, they think of Thai virgins kidnapped from villages and shipped overseas. But sometimes it's just drinking the wrong glass of champagne.' She let that one land for a moment, then said, 'But I don't know how to fragment a C2 vertebra into someone's brain stem. So I must do this.' Her grip on his back flagged. 'You're no good at not having sex.'

'Thanks.'

She flipped them over so she was on top. 'Let me be in charge.'

'Gladly.'

Her hips did something magical. 'Is that you getting aroused?' she asked.

'No,' he said.

'Uh-uh,' he said.

'Nope,' he said.

She smiled. 'Maybe I should be less in charge?'

'Maybe so.'

She eased off him a bit.

All of a sudden, outside lights went on, flooding the bedroom through the sliding glass door. There were shouts and sounds of commotion.

Evan got up, pulled on his jeans, and stumbled through the slider, the balcony frosted beneath his bare soles. By the barn four *narcos* were laid out on their backs, making tiny, listless movements. Another was curled on the wet ground beside them, clutching his stomach, vomit drooling from the side of his mouth. The skinny guard was off the tower, radioing frantically. He waved around one of the slender white remotes, clicking on more lights to illuminate the grounds. Samuel staggered out of the barn, veering unevenly toward the fire. He banged into the suspended pot, knocking it to the ground. A sludge of chili spilled out.

Samuel sat heavily on a crate, wiping sweat from his brow. He pointed to the dark glop of chili on the ground.

The skinny guard's posture changed. His rail-thin shoulders lowered. He crouched and picked up one of the bone-china plates resting on a crate. Let it drop from his hand. It shattered. He sat on the crate, lowered his head into his hand.

Then he rose, doubled over, and ran into the barn. No doubt looking for a toilet.

'What?' Despi said, keeping a few steps back from the threshold to the balcony. 'What is it?'

Before Evan could answer, he heard the resonant boom of the chalet's front door opening. A moment later Dex lumbered off the porch into view, his massive back bowed, his shadow elongated before him. He approached the barn and spoke to Samuel.

Hard rain spit at Evan. He squinted through the haze as Samuel slid off the crate, collapsing to the ground.

Two dogs, three guards, two snipers, and Dex.

Dex turned, the lights of the eaves hitting him full in the face, his pale bald head seeming to glow. He stared directly at the balcony, at Evan. For a chilling moment, they locked eyes through the quickening rain.

Dex lifted his left hand and slapped the bloody scowl across his face. The tattoo colors were sharp in the glare, glossy red dripping from pointy incisors.

Evan backed into the room.

'What is it?' Despi asked.

The door flew open. Manny charged in, shotgun raised, firing a beanbag round that hit Evan's center mass. It knocked him into the wall. He slid down lurchingly to sit on the floor.

Nando grabbed Despi's bare shoulder and flung her behind him. She banged into the desk before falling to the floorboards at René's feet.

With a polished loafer, René shooed her toward the door. She staggered a bit, pulling herself upright in time to collide with Dex's chest, now filling the doorway. His rain-wet shirt clung to him, every muscle pronounced. He grabbed her by the wrist, wrenching her arm, and tugged her out of view. A moment later a door opened and slammed up the hall and Dex returned, pocketing a key.

Evan's lungs were locked up. He couldn't breathe.

With the toe of his boot, Manny tipped him over, cuffed his hands, hoisted him onto the bed. Evan leaned forward, his mouth wavering, air still out of reach.

At last his muscles relaxed, and he drew in a screeching breath and then another.

René walked over and leaned casually against the desk, examining his fingernails. 'Let's have a talk,' he said.

26

Man or Nature

Evan sat on the bed, his wrists cuffed painfully behind him. The flexible baton round had left a red mark the size of a fist in the middle of his chest. He was still having trouble finding oxygen.

And yet René wanted to talk. 'My guards seem to have been stricken with an illness. Vomiting, diarrhea, crippling abdominal pain. I don't suppose you know anything about that.'

'I don't.'

René nodded as if Evan had confessed. 'Your skills are fascinating,' he said. 'I want to know more about you.'

Evan managed to get out a few words. '. . . not . . . that interesting.'

'You are to me.' René removed a kerchief, wiped his brow. His face was flushed from all the excitement. 'What are you?'

'A drug kingpin. An arms dealer.'

'No. You're more lethal than that. Something doesn't add up about you. I've been thinking about your hobby, killing Contrell. Who does something like that? Who kills a human trafficker for fun?'

Evan did not respond.

'I'd imagine the same kind of person who would poison my guards,' René said. 'Dr Franklin is seeing to the men now.'

Manny and Nando glared at Evan, looking as though they'd like to beat him to death with their shotguns. Manny took a menacing step toward him, but René held up a hand and he halted.

'Those are our *hermanos*,' Manny snarled.

'No,' René said. 'They were my employees. And they failed at their job. Make sure you don't fail at yours.'

Dex barely had to move for the floorboards to groan beneath him. Manny looked at him, then stepped back into line.

René returned his attention to Evan. 'There are two kinds of people in the world. Those who make messes and those who clean them up.'

The handcuffs forced Evan to hunch forward, but he looked up at René through a tangle of hair. 'Which kind are you?'

'The third kind, who gets to make the categories.' His eyes gleamed from their burrows in his face. 'You made a big mess tonight.'

Evan stared at Manny. 'Or cleaned one up.'

Manny slid his tongue across his gold grill as if Evan were something he'd like to eat.

Someone tapped on the door, and then a man with long white hair came in, wearing a pair of tattered scrubs. The doctor hadn't shaved in a few days; he had the wrecked good looks of an aging surfer who'd lived through one too many tequila sunrises.

'Hi.' Dr Franklin looked across at Evan. 'Oh. Hey.' Then at René. 'Talk to you?'

René stepped out into the hall. Hushed murmurs carried back inside, though the words were unintelligible. Nando and Manny glowered at Evan.

It was an uncomfortable few minutes.

Finally René returned. 'Six of my guards are in bad shape. Internal bleeding, renal failure. Their kidneys seem to be shut down.'

Manny made a noise between a growl and a cry.

'It is Dr Franklin's opinion that they ingested poisonous mushrooms.'

'It's hard to distinguish them sometimes,' Evan said sympathetically.

'None of them claim to have picked any mushrooms, let alone added them to their chili.'

'If I added mushrooms to chili, I wouldn't admit it either,' Evan said.

He watched Manny's jaw tighten and enjoyed it a bit.

René cleared his throat. Evan was surprised to see his brown eyes moisten. 'There's nothing anyone can do,' René said. He added quickly, 'And no major medical facilities nearby.'

'Here in Graubünden,' Evan added.

The chocolate eyes sharpened. 'That's right.' René swept a hand over his hair, though no strands were out of place. 'They'll die within days.'

'In excruciating pain.' Evan directed a look at Manny and Nando. 'You should put them out of their misery. It's the only humane thing to do.'

Manny and Nando studied the floorboards, waiting on their orders.

Evan switched his gaze to René. 'Dying men drain resources quickly,' he added. 'You should consider what's best for everyone.'

After a moment René gave a little nod. 'Do it kindly,' he said.

Manny bared his fourteen-karat teeth at Evan on his way out. And then Evan was alone with René and Dex.

'You're upset,' Evan said.

'Not for them. For me.'

'Why's that?'

'We all get sad when someone dies. It reminds one of one's mortality.'

Jack's blood-drenched hand trying to stem the arterial spray from his shoulder. The crimson soaked blue flannel mopped around Evan's fist. Jack's smile, rare as a rainbow, warming his eyes at the corners.

Evan said, 'That's why you think people get sad?'

'Remember when you first found out about death as a child? I never got over it. I don't think any of us do. It's an awful thing, to die. I don't buy any of the marketing pitches that try to assuage the horror of it. Heroics of war. Drifting off into a blaze of white. The welcoming arms of God.' René's teeth clenched, a sudden intensity. 'I don't want to,' he said. 'And I won't.'

'You'd be the first.'

His lips pursed, pulled taut. 'Remember how long summer used to last when you were a child? An eternity. Everything still in front of you. Life feels . . . *limitless*.' He folded his hands at his waist and studied them. 'And then one day you see a picture. You're in your thirties, getting out of a pool in Santorini. And your hair is thinning, so much so that you can see the scalp beneath. It's been that way for a year, maybe years – how often do you see a photograph of yourself swimming?' His palm rose again, hovering over his thinning hair. He seemed to realize what he was doing and pulled his hand away. 'I don't like limits. Being told what is possible. By man or nature. Just like you.'

'No,' Evan said. 'You want to be everything. I want to be one thing well.'

'Then you suffer from a failure of imagination.' René leaned forward, a fall of light illuminating his meaty features, the dried dabs of cover-up, the augmented hairline. 'We all want to beat death. It just becomes embarrassing to admit. But think if you could. Control time. If you control time, you control *everything*.' When he leaned back against the chairless desk, the thick fabric of his suit rippled like spread butter. 'Imagine being who you were in your twenties.'

'Like the good book says, "You can't repeat the past."'

René smiled, showing a gleaming row of beautiful ivory caps. '"Why of course you can!"'

The cuffs were cutting off the circulation in Evan's hands. He wondered how long René was going to leave them on.

René produced the skinny bottle and sprayed down the surfaces he'd touched. 'Uncuff him and lock him in,' he told Dex. On his way out, he paused before the big man. 'No need to be gentle.'

Dex's softball biceps flexed as he raised his right hand and cupped it over his mouth.

Happy face.

27

Six in Total

Evan lay on his back in the darkness, waiting for the gas to hiss through the vent and knock him out. He was tired enough to sleep without the encouragement, but there was no way René could know that.

He had just drifted off when a distant gunshot woke him. And then another. They kept on at regular intervals, one after another.

Six in total.

The vibration of the final bullet held the air for an extra few moments, unwilling to let go. At last there was complete silence.

Evan stared at the ceiling.

To Alison, to the boy, he sent a simple thought: *I'm coming soon.*

Then he fell asleep on his own.

28

The Grim Reapress

The next morning Evan was roused from sleep with a shotgun pressed into the side of his neck. He opened his eyes, looking up the length of the barrel past the neon orange stock at Manny. Manny grimaced, those teeth flashing – Jaws from James Bond gone rapper. 'Get your *culo* up.'

Evan eased to a sitting position. The metal bore remained shoved into the side of his throat. Nando stood five feet back and to the side, a second shotgun at the ready.

'You're wanted downstairs,' Manny told him. 'But I'm thinking maybe you have a *accidente* right here. You made a move on me. I reacted.'

Evan's eyes slid to Manny's finger on the trigger. His knuckle was white, the trigger partially depressed. Another half pound of pressure and the opposite wall would be wearing Evan's trachea.

'Samuel. Yoenis. Álcides. Memo. Luis. Eddie. I will not forget those names.' Manny's voice shook. 'We took them out to the woods last night. And said good-bye.'

Tears leaked from his eyes, but he kept the shotgun level, making no move to wipe his face. He glided the barrel up Evan's chin, ground it across his cheek, shoved his nose to the side.

Evan didn't meet his eyes. He looked at the far wall. Kept his body language neutral. Hoped he hadn't pushed Manny far enough that he'd contradict René's orders and kill the golden goose. Though Evan had stared down more gun barrels than he'd care to recount, decapitation by beanbag presented new intricacies he didn't want to contemplate.

Santa Muerte's skull head grinned from the side of Manny's neck. The Grim Reapress. She wore a blue cloak bedecked with roses, one skeletal hand clutching a scythe, the other an hourglass. At the moment of death, she was said to sever the silver thread of life.

Evan wondered if now was the moment that the scythe would fall, that his own thread would be cut. He stared ahead. Waited for a one-centimeter movement of Manny's knuckle.

'Manny,' Nando said. '*Manny.*' He stepped forward and tugged at Manny's shoulder. An instant later the pressure relented.

'We won't forget what you made us do,' Manny said. 'Now get your shit downstairs.'

Evan was marched along the ground floor through a moist corridor scented of lavender and rose water. At Nando and Manny's prompting, he pushed through a glass door beaded with condensation and stepped into a sprawling spa area.

They passed a Jacuzzi, a cold-water plunge pool, a teabag stuffed with herbs slung into a freestanding marble tub. Various enclosures were labeled with sleek metal placards: SAUNA, EUCALYPTUS STEAM ROOM, RAIN SHOWER. The Korean mist room featured a concrete bench studded with large smooth pebbles, matching the Zen-Disneyland motif of the rest of the spa.

They came to a small lap pool fringed with artificial grass that crunched pleasingly beneath Evan's bare feet. He was wearing only the boxer shorts he'd slept in.

René waited cocked back in a zero-gravity chair, paperback hoisted overhead, the inverted V like a bird in flight.

An IV tube snaked from one arm to a saline bag dangling off a chrome stand.

Smoking an electronic cigarette, David propped himself against a paisley-shaped bar made of rich polished wood and decorated with a string of fat Christmas lights. A bottle of Bacardi 151 sat beside his rocks glass, which was filled to the brim with square ice cubes and the amber rum. A tray of bar treats waited at his elbow. He munched Doritos from a crinkly bag, puffed vapor, sipped his drink.

René rotated forward in his chair, sinking his feet into a bubbling tank suffused with blue UV lighting. As Evan neared, he noticed dozens of tiny fish inside, swirling about René's feet and ankles.

René flicked his paperback toward the bar. 'Made from sustainably farmed rain-forest wood from Brazil,' he said. 'Can you imagine caring that much?'

'Why do you have it, then?'

'None of this is *mine*.' His gesture encompassed the chalet. 'I rent this life. What is mine is hidden away down a rabbit hole.' A smile. 'Just like you do it.'

Leaning over a side table, he exchanged his book for one of the slender white remotes that seemed to operate the entire chalet and its personnel. He keyed a few buttons and let it rattle back onto the table.

A moment later two huge metal panels in the far wall parted to reveal a narrow elevator with Dr Franklin inside. He trudged over to René, cautiously removed the IV from the crook of his elbow, and scurried back to the elevator. The doors closed, and Evan watched the lit numbers above as the doctor descended to a basement level.

Straightening his pricked arm, René buttoned his shirtsleeve. Even here in the humidity of the spa, his sartorial elegance was on display. 'Would you like a refreshment?'

'Bag of Doritos would be good.'

'Nando, please fetch our guest some chips.'

Before Nando could move, David reached for a bag.

'Don't, David,' René said. 'Let Nando handle it.'

David smiled around his plastic e-smoke filter, the blinking Christmas lights casting his face in different colors. He pushed himself off the bar, walked across to Evan, and held out the bag. Manny and Nando moved closer, aiming at Evan's head.

David shook the bag in front of Evan. 'Go on,' he said.

Evan took the Doritos.

David scanned Evan's body. 'You don't strike me as the junk-food type.'

'You don't strike me as the e-cigarette type.'

'Oh. This. I'm trying to work my way up to real cigarettes, but I hate the taste. I just graduated from nicotine patches.'

'Congratulations.'

David gave a mock curtsy.

'Step away from him,' René said.

'He's not gonna hurt me,' David said.

René tilted his head at Manny, who gently but firmly pulled David back toward the bar while Nando and his raised shotgun eased into Evan's blind spot.

David returned to his overproof rum. 'You're such a dick,' he said into his rocks glass. 'You think you can control *everything*.' He gulped down the rest, slammed the heavy tumbler on the sustainably farmed rain-forest wood, and ambled out.

René smiled indulgently.

He followed Evan's gaze, looking down at his feet. In the tank the fish had clustered around his toes and heels. 'You starve them, you see. Doctor fish. At a certain point of hunger, they develop a taste for human flesh. I suppose anything will. They eat away the dead skin, slough off the calluses and psoriasis patches.' The grin widened. 'Nibble away my imperfections.' He waved a hand. 'You're welcome to have a treatment yourself.'

Evan pictured himself with cucumber slices on his eyes, slathered with mud, Manny and Nando zeroed in on him over shotgun sights.

'No thanks.'

'Maybe have Dr Franklin do some laser treatment on that nasty scar on your stomach.'

Evan stared down at the white line on his abdomen where a woman had once slid his own knife beneath his ribs. He'd stitched it up himself on the floor of his bathroom, a bloody, painful affair during which he'd discovered fresh nuances in an already intimate relationship with pain.

'I like my scars,' he said. 'They remind me of who I am.'

'I don't understand that.'

'You don't need to,' Evan said. 'Why am I here? I assume not just to discuss your grooming habits?'

'Do you have somewhere you need to be?'

Evan thought of the *Horizon Express,* steaming onward. And the boy's voice coming through the wrecked RoamZone: *Will you help me? Will you? Promise me.*

'Yes,' he said.

René said, 'Two more days and you can be on your way.'

'Assuming I send the wire.'

'You haven't resigned yourself to the outcome?'

'Why give up when I'm winning the war?'

Behind him Evan heard Manny curse at him in Spanish.

'About that.' René lifted one dripping foot from the tank and then the other. 'There's something I'd like to show you.'

Pulling on a heavy robe, he knotted the sash. Then he leaned over and sprayed down the zero gravity chair with mist from the clear cylindrical bottle.

'What *is* that?' Evan asked.

'Privacy spray. It removes ninety-nine-point-five percent of DNA from surfaces. And obscures the remaining point-five percent by layering it over with a blend of genetic material.' René stomped his feet into a waiting pair of moon boots. 'You're not the only one who can make himself disappear. When I decide I don't want to be found, no one ever finds me.'

For now Evan let that go.

Manny and Nando got Evan moving back through the gauntlet of steam rooms and up various hallways, René keeping well ahead of them. At last the giant chandelier of the foyer bloomed overhead.

Tightening his thick bathrobe, René stepped out onto the porch, then turned and faced them across the expanse of the foyer. Wind fluttered his hair. Snow had fallen last night. Standing there in the doorway, he was silhouetted against the vivid white backdrop.

He curled a finger. *Come.*

Manny and Nando prompted Evan, and he walked across the frigid marble floor. Already he could feel the bite of the outside air. The minute he stepped out, the air assailed him. His boxers provided scant cover. Manny and Nando put him on the opposite side of the porch, safely away from René, who stood waiting in his cozy robe and moon boots.

Evan tucked the bag of chips into the waistband of his boxers so he could blow into his hands. His cheeks and lips felt raw. He wasn't sure how long he would be made to stand out here.

Before he saw anything, he heard the faint drone of an engine reverberating around the walls of the valley. Then a plume of exhaust came visible, thin as a straw, way up the gravel road at the horizon. Soon he made out the dot of a black vehicle. It resolved as one of the Mercedes Geländewagens.

The autumn chill burrowed beneath his flesh, firing the nerves inside his scrapes and bruises. Muscle throbbed over aching bones. He thought he might freeze solid before the vehicle – and whatever it was carrying – arrived.

He bounced on his bare feet, doing his best to keep warm. He could no longer feel his face. On the far side of the porch, René whistled a chipper tune.

It took an eternity, but at last the G-Wagon pulled in to the circular driveway, the tires clicking over the cobblestones. It stopped. The tinted windows threw back Evan's reflection. His skin was tinged blue.

The driver's door opened first, and Dex unloaded himself from behind the steering wheel. Then the other three doors and tailgate opened in concert.

New *narco* guards emerged from the G-Wagon, one after another, a clown-car stunt carried off with military precision. Ten of them. They formed a neat line in front of the vehicle, awaiting orders from René.

'Good,' Evan said. 'You brought me more people to kill.'

But René just turned to him, his moon boots scraping on the porch, and smiled.

'No limits,' he said.

29

Your Bad Self

According to the intel Candy and Jaggers had gathered over the past day and a half, Setyeyiva was planning to leave his office between six and six-fifteen this evening. They shivered through another faux photo shoot down on the boardwalk, Candy looking fetching as ever in her leather pants and bustier getup, Jaggers zooming in over her head at the converted cannery. Soon enough only Refat Setyeyiva remained at the office once again, toiling away.

Jaggers checked his watch. 'It's time.'

They hustled back to their rental, a Škoda Fabia Combi, which, with low standards and some squinting, could be considered a car. As Jaggers pulled out of the parking space he'd shoehorned into, Candy bought a berry Popsicle from a vendor.

They zipped up the hill in the hatchback supermini. She hopped out behind the building in the alley that ran between TeleFon Star and the parking structure. Jaggers backed up, killed the headlights. Someone had spray-painted the three monkeys on the wall – see no evil, hear no evil, speak no evil. The paint had dripped before it dried, lending the simian faces a demonic cast.

Dusk eased down the dial on the day. A few lights blinked on in buildings farther up the hill.

Candy propped herself against the wall by the rear door of the old cannery. She peeled back the wrapping on her Super-Fun CrazeyBerryz Icestik!

She could make a spectacle of herself with a Popsicle.

Setting one foot flat against the wall behind her, she arched her back away from the wall and twirled the ruby-red tip between her lips. She knew precisely what she looked like.

It was good to be her.

5:53. No cars. No pedestrians.

That whisper returned: *Can you still pull this off, Candy? After X left his stamp on you, are you sure you're the same? Or are you damaged goods?*

Yes, she was sure. No, she wasn't damaged goods.

She was a traffic stopper. A Hall & Oates maneater. The kind of calendar girl that made you want to freeze the month. She used to be all those things with her clothes on *or* off. So what if, thanks to Orphan X, her naked superpowers had dimmed? She was still irresistible.

5:57. No vehicles. No foot traffic.

The wind shifted, producing a whiff of fish from the walls of the old cannery. The berry ice inexplicably tasted like peach. Somewhere in the distance, someone was blaring a Salt-N-Pepa–Led Zeppelin mash-up. These post-Soviet states were so gloriously ass backward.

She licked her berry-peach ice and waited. Refat Setyeyiva, come on with your bad self and your fucked-up name.

The door creaked open.

At first he didn't see her. His scruffy face stayed bent down as he fumbled a file into a soft briefcase. He got two steps into the alley when she cleared her throat.

A soft, feminine melody.

He glanced over.

That stopped him.

He wasn't bearlike as so many former throwers were. His massive body was still shaped the right way, mass up top, tapered through the waist. She wondered if he'd given up the steroids entirely or if they made him look too damn good to quit.

He was staring at her, no doubt wondering some things of his own.

She was a mirage. He seemed afraid to blink lest she disappear.

She parted her mouth. Let the ice pop inch further past her orange lips. Let her tongue squirm into sight on the side.

He didn't notice the Škoda Fabia Combi rev to life behind him.

How could he?

His gaze stayed locked on her even as the car bore down, headlights dimmed. She tilted toward him and plucked the soft briefcase from his hand. At the last moment, Setyeyiva seemed to come back into his body. He whirled around as the car smashed into him, the brakes already chirping.

He flew. Landed. A bark of air left his lungs on impact.

He stared at her with uncomprehending eyes.

She licked up the Popsicle's shaft. Might as well give him a little morphine on his way out.

Jaggers rolled forward, crushing the big man. The car bounced up and down and up and down and then was in front of him, perfectly positioned to load the body. Jaggers popped the trunk and climbed out.

Candy dropped the ice pop and walked over, the briefcase swinging at her side.

She smirked at that whisper that had been haunting her of late. Damaged goods her ass.

The Škoda Fabia Combi had few advantages, but two of them happened to be generous hatch space and a loading sill a mere 611 millimeters off the ground. The roomy hatch was lined with plastic tarp, taped expertly around the sides.

Candy took the ankles, Jaggers the armpits. They huffed and they puffed and they swung the man in. The car had no sooner creaked down on its chassis than they heard a clacking of high heels behind them.

They turned to see one of the boardwalk girls teetering up the alley toward them, her baby giraffe legs constrained by a micromini banding her thighs together. She had a sweet almond-shaped face framed with straight raven-black hair. She might've been eighteen or a precocious fifteen – you never knew with these East Slavic types. She looked very concerned in a wholesome oh-my-gosh way that seemed at odds with her getup.

She said something in what sounded like Turkish – probably Crimean Tatar. Noting their expressions, she switched to Russian. *'Are you all right? Was there an accident?'*

'Yes,' Candy replied in Russian. *'But we're okay.'* She reached over quickly to shut the hatch, but Jaggers stopped her.

Candy looked at him. His button eyes peered back at her, showing no depth.

'No,' Candy said to him under her breath.

Jaggers said nothing but kept his hand on the underside of the hatch lid, holding it open.

The girl drew nearer. *'You're sure you're not hurt? Do you need me to call someone?'*

'No, no, we're fine,' Candy said. *'Thank you, though, sweetheart.'*

The girl stopped. They were alone in the alley, just the three of them cast in the slanting glow thrown from a window above. At some point in the past few minutes, night had come on in full.

'We could use a hand with the trunk,' Jaggers said. *'I think it got warped in the crash. We can't get it closed.'*

The girl looked confused. But she gave a one-shoulder shrug. *'Okay.'*

As she started toward them, Candy tried again to yank the rear door closed, but Jaggers held it firm.

And then it was too late.

The girl looked down, saw the tangled body held by the plastic lining, and opened her mouth. Jaggers sealed in her scream with a jaundiced hand, his fist jabbing twice at her neck. He dumped her into the cargo space on top of Setyeyiva's body and slammed the hatch lid.

Only now did Candy see the slim silver pen clenched in Jaggers's bloody hand.

The girl rattled against the closed hatch. Wet thrashing. A screech of breath.

The words hissed through Candy's teeth, cold with rage. 'She's still alive.'

'Not for long.'

Jaggers squatted, dropped the pen down a sewer drain, and rose wiping his hand on the thigh of his slacks. The rattling grew fainter and then stopped.

Candy punched him, a quick jab that snapped his head back on his stick neck. The pain seemed to have no effect. He dodged her cross, countering with a gut shot that doubled her over. Then he laid her low with a leg sweep. As she curled on the ground, sucking for air, he pressed himself on top of her, his slender fingers cinched not too tightly around her neck.

'She saw us.' Though he kept his voice low, he wore a grimace, and through his clenched teeth wafted the stink of his breath, stomach acid and rot.

She brought a knee up between his legs hard enough to jolt him a foot forward. But he didn't so much as grunt. He only rolled off her, climbed into the driver's seat, and waited. Candy rose and stood for a time in the dark alley, giving her breath time to even out. Then she walked around and got in.

They drove several blocks in silence. Jaggers pulled over by the body shop they had scouted the night before. Leaving the car running, he picked the padlock and slid the gate open. He drove through and into the garage.

Another benefit of Škoda Fabias: Crimea was lousy with them, like cockroaches, and every shop worth its salt was stocked with spare parts. As Jaggers pulled off the crumpled bumper, Candy took from Setyeyiva's briefcase his laptop as well as a hardware token cryptocard that generated a new randomized log-in code every sixty seconds. Sitting on a workbench with the laptop resting across her knees, she waited for the token numbers to flip, then punched in the code.

She and Jaggers slogged away quietly and in concert, Candy clicking on the keyboard while he mounted a new bumper and grille and hammered out creases in the hood. He worked with the quick, efficient movements of a rodent. They were making good headway, and the night was young, but they still had to deal with the bodies in the trunk.

She accessed the databases, finally locating what looked like the right one. Then she ran a search for 1-855-2-NOWHERE and waited for the data to load. The information came up.

'Goddamn it,' she said. 'God*damn* it.'

Jaggers looked up from his crouch at the bumper, where he was wielding a spray-paint gun. In the dim light, his dark eyes were holes in his face. A surgeon-like paint mask covered his nose and mouth, so his voice seemed to issue from the air itself.

'What?' it asked.

'Orphan X never parked the phone number here. It was a misdirect. He paid them a fee to open a dummy account.'

'Orphan Y can follow the money.'

Candy sneered. She'd been at this longer than Jaggers. 'Orphan X set up that account for us to find, you idiot.

Which means there will be no following the money. Not by Van Sciver, his übersoftware, or anyone or anything else.'

Jaggers returned to his work, misting a fine layer of silver across the crease in the hood. The news seemed to carry no weight for him. She wondered if he cared about anything.

'You killed that girl for nothing,' she said.

He didn't shift focus from his work. 'We killed Refat Setyeyiva for nothing.'

'Yeah, but that was the job.'

A line of silver paint settled across the hood, effacing the final flaw. 'How interesting that you see a distinction.'

He set down the spray gun and appraised the car, which looked as good as new. Then he retrieved his carry-on bag from the backseat and began to strip. He kicked off his shoes and tugged down his pants. He wore no underwear.

What she saw startled her.

Rather what she *didn't* see.

She'd heard of it before, of course. But it seemed like one of those bizarre conditions consigned to medical case studies and dusty journals. Not something that belonged out here in the real world.

He piled his bloody clothes on the concrete floor, spilled some oil on them, and lit them on fire. Then he looked up, naked, unashamed, and expressionless. 'I suggest you do the same.'

Her leather pants were clean, but her bustier sported a few smears from moving Setyeyiva. As Jaggers dressed in fresh clothes, she stripped off her shirt and threw it onto the small pyre.

She grabbed her encrypted satphone and walked outside, already dialing.

Standing beneath the firmament, she waited as it rang and rang. A click announced Van Sciver's presence on the line.

'HOW was your MEAL?'

'No nutritional content,' she said.

There was a slight delay as their conversation ping-ponged between various virtual telephone-switch destinations. 'Are there any inGREDients we might use to prepare a future meal?'

'No.'

She waited until it became clear that this was not a delay but a silence.

She'd visited Orphan Y at his undisclosed location only once, choppering in with a hood over her head. She pictured him there in his great room, lost in the flickering lights of the monitors, his very flesh seeming to crawl with the numbers pouring across the screens. It was as if he'd achieved singularity, given up his human form to become one with the data.

'Y?' she said. 'You there?'

'I WILL identify HIS NEXT RESERVATION. And I WILL SEND you two to DINE with HIM.'

The air soothed her bare, burn-ravaged back. She drew in a cool breath, tilted her face to the smog-smeared stars. Somewhere pots clanged and a car backfired and drunken young men yelled in the night.

She thought of a girl with raven hair bent over the open hatch of the car. Her almond-shaped face, sweet and simple. The blood spurting from her carotid.

'The man you stuck me with,' Candy said. 'My fellow diner. The guy's a psychopath.'

'YES,' came back the multitude of voices. 'But he's MY PSYCHOPATH.'

30

Someone's Idea of a Library

Two dogs, thirteen guards, two snipers, one doctor, and Dex.

In his room late that night, Evan considered his next move. He'd been building a mental blueprint of the facility, biding his time for the right moment to escape. Now that René had brought in more men, Evan wanted to know more. Not just about the men but about René. This inexhaustible supply of guards raised further questions. What was René really up to here? Had some of the potential escape routes been compromised?

Evan looked at the fireplace. Made up his mind. Crossing the room, he eased the sliding door open. Knocking out two of the security cameras meant he could move unseen by the balcony, fireplace, and desk.

From the balcony he gazed across at the barn. The big door was rolled back. Inside, two of the *narcos* practiced hand-to-hand on a wrestling mat laid down in front of the vehicles. They were skilled fighters, acquainted with martial arts. Throws and kicks and deflections. Several others rimmed the periphery, pounding the mat and shouting encouragement. This time around René had wisely hired not just gunmen but fighters familiar with the down-and-dirty.

Shivering against the cold, Evan stepped back into the bedroom but left the sliding glass door wide open. Climbing into bed, he pretended to toss and turn, landing himself just offscreen. Then he shoved a pillow under the covers at the periphery of the hidden camera's view where his shoulder might be. A chilly current kicked up, the open slider pulling a stream of air into the room.

He waited at the edge of the bed, staring over at the ceiling vent, straining his ears.

When the halogenated ether hissed through, he rolled over and buried his face in a pillow. He felt the draft across his back, the gas moving past him, filling the balcony, dissipating in the night air. He waited until the hissing stopped and then waited twenty minutes more. Breathing grew hard, the feather pillows trapping his breath. But he managed. Finally he lifted his face.

Awake.

He moved carefully around the foot of the bed and walked lightly into the bathroom, keeping to the strip of concrete next to the sink. With his toe he snared the edge of the trash-can liner. He fluffed it open, filled it with water, carried the bulging bag back into the bedroom and over to the hearth.

He poked a hole in the bottom of the liner and used the bursting bag as a watering can, flooding the cedar logs. They popped and hissed, giving off smoke that the chute suctioned up. The fire died down to a cherry glow, the logs disintegrating into ash.

Evan retrieved his hiking boots from where he'd placed them by the footboard and used them to stamp out the remaining embers. Then he moved them from his hands to his feet, lacing them up tightly. After waiting for the flue to cool, he pushed it open.

Wide enough to fit his shoulders. Barely.

Time for a recon mission.

Sitting on the fireplace, he leaned back and slid his head and torso through the flue. It was tight, the walls crowding in, the stink of wet ash clogging his throat. He wiggled up to a standing position.

Past the vent the chimney opened up a bit. That made it easy for him to shove his way up off the floor, using his forearms and the tread of his boots to push outward against the scorched brick. He moved in lurches, a few inches at a time.

Every foot or so, he'd stop and listen. He'd pulled a similar Santa ploy once in a chimney in the Czech Republic, squirming his way between floors to eavesdrop on a conversation. But given the thick walls of the old chalet, he had no luck hearing anything aside from his own breathing.

He made slow, painful progress. Grit caked his cheeks, crammed itself beneath his nails. The glow of his bedroom vanished underfoot, leaving him in absolute darkness. After a time he saw a spill of golden light from a room above. He wormed his way up toward the next floor.

His calves cramped, his thighs burning. He was unable to wipe off the sweat tickling his brow, so he blinked hard, contorting his face. He couldn't look up to gauge his progress because flakes of ash fell down into his eyes. But he sensed the light growing stronger, sweeping across his shoulders.

At last his hand made contact with a lip in the flue. After so many tentative climbing holds, the firm grip felt reassuring. He grabbed the lip with both hands, put the soles of his boots against the wall beneath, wedged his back against the opposite wall, and rested.

He wiped his forehead on his sleeves and then took stock.

He'd arrived at the edge of a shaft angled down to a fireplace on the fourth floor. The log holder below was stacked high with unlit cedar logs.

Before scouting the room he wanted to check what was above.

Gathering his strength, he pulled himself farther up the flue, put his boots on the lip he'd just been gripping, and strained to reach above him.

Two thick bars, coated with soot and welded into place, blocked the way up.

He stood there, balanced above the fourth floor in the guts of the building, breathing away his disappointment. There'd be no going up and out onto the roof, which would have afforded him an ideal vantage to pinpoint the locations of René's men. But all hopes for intel gathering weren't dashed; he could still make it down through the fireplace beneath him and into that fourth-floor room. And if there was one thing Jack had taught him, it was that there was useful information to be had everywhere.

He led with his arms, like going down a playground slide face-first. Halfway down the shaft, his grease-slicked hold failed and he tumbled into the fireplace, his shoulder smacking into the stack of cedar logs. A crooked, upside-down view told him the room was empty.

It was a study.

Careful not to upset the pyre of logs further, he eased his way out of the fireplace, emerging into the room. Using a towel slung over the stack of extra logs on the hearth, he wiped his hands and the soles of his boots.

Then he stepped tentatively onto an elaborate Pakistani rug. He checked behind him to make sure his boots left no track. His shirt and jeans remained filthy – he'd have to take care not to brush up against anything.

Brass sconces painted dim sprays of light on the walls. Dark bookshelves towered on either side of an imposing desk. An ergonomic chair sat cocked and waiting. Casting a glance over his shoulder at the closed door, Evan moved across the room. He pulled the chair out and checked the wall beneath the desk, confirming that the electrical outlets were indeed standard North American. Then he turned his focus to the file drawer. Its thick, shiny lock did not look factory-installed. There was no give when he tugged the handle.

The desk surface was spotless and bare, save a bouquet of pens and pencils sprouting from a leather cup and a pair of slender reading glasses resting on a desk mat. No letter opener.

Evan slid open the top drawer. Nothing inside but a few paper clips, a roll of Scotch tape, and a scattering of file tabs. The other drawers were empty.

The lack of personal items seemed in keeping with René's obsessive use of his DNA privacy spray. He went to great lengths to keep his identity hidden, to leave not a trace of himself behind. *I rent this life. What is mine is hidden away down a rabbit hole.* A necessity with which Evan was all too familiar.

He knew he was living on borrowed time by now – if they hadn't already figured out that he wasn't in his room, they would at any minute. He made the choice to keep looking. The key was finding something before they showed up. Something he could use.

He quickened his search. The trash can held only a balled-up junk-mail envelope. He uncrumpled it and checked the address label. It had been mailed to the Chalet Savoir Faire in Maine. *Maine.* Another piece of disinformation? He doubted it; no one would expect him to be snooping through trash cans on the fourth floor. He wadded up the envelope again and dropped it back into the bin.

As he rose, his face came level with the spectacles folded on the blotter. Something on one of the rectangular lenses caught his eye. He tilted his face to peer at it. A fingerprint-size smudge marked the glass.

Evan worked swiftly. After positioning the readers faceup on the mat, he snapped a pencil in half, then bent a paper clip open and used the tip to scrape the lead, letting graphite dust fall onto the lens. Once the dust coated the lens, he blew it gently off. Graphite particles held only where the oils of René's finger had touched the glass, forming two-thirds of a fingerprint.

Grabbing Scotch tape, Evan stripped a three-inch piece off the roll and pressed one end of the sticky side carefully over the print. The graphite dust clung to the tape, the fingerprint lifting away from the lens. Evan folded the tape over itself, sticky side to sticky side, sealing in the fingerprint to preserve it. Then he stripped off another short length of tape and adhered the fossilized print to the inside of his arm above the elbow, protected from friction and hidden from view.

Next he lifted the top drawer, pulling it off the tracks and setting it on the blotter. He felt in the space where the drawer had been in case René had taped the key on the underside of the wood. No luck. He tried the same with the drawers to the side. Nothing.

Stepping back, he assessed the dusty bookshelves. They were filled with venerable hardbacks stripped of their covers, the spines forming fashion-statement stripes of faded gray and olive green. It seemed more like someone's *idea* of a library than an actual library.

Evan's attention caught on a gap in the dust on the second shelf, a thin slot where one of the books had recently been removed. He walked over and plucked the book from the shelf, smiling at the title.

He cracked the cover of the Robert Louis Stevenson classic, and a key fell out, landing softly on the carpet. It fit the file drawer.

Crouched, he tugged the drawer open.

It was crammed with files, each tab featuring a different

name. He thumbed through the first one. Bank-account details. A Social Security number. The photograph paper-clipped to the back of the folder sent a prickle across the nape of his neck. It was a middle-aged man lying unconscious and naked on the bed downstairs.

The same bed Evan had slept in the past few nights.

Shaking off his discomfort, he continued to flip through the files. So many men and women had gone through René's operation before Evan. Every mini-dossier contained financial information. Clipped to each back cover was a photograph of a different naked, drugged victim positioned on the bed. He'd figured that René had run his scheme a time or two before, but seeing the crammed rows of file tabs, Evan grasped just how routine and efficient the process was. From what he could piece together, René had extorted over $300 million from these people.

The rear file tab had not a name but a question mark.

Evan pulled it free and opened it.

A printout of the katana sword on the auction Web site. His Privatbank AG account information. A fingerprint card. And a photograph of him sprawled unconscious across the mattress in his bedroom cell, just like those who had preceded him.

He studied the picture of himself, emotions moving in him like dark currents. Then he tore the photo and the fingerprint card into tiny bits and pushed them down a heating vent beneath the desk.

Behind him he heard the door creak open.

Manny shouted, 'I got him!'

Keeping his back turned, Evan rose. He gripped the broken pencil.

Footsteps pounded the hall.

'Turn around,' Manny said.

Evan did. 'It's about time,' he said.

Manny stood just inside the threshold, his less-lethal shotgun aimed not at Evan's face but at his crotch.

'Drop the pencil.'

Evan eyed the angle of the barrel and dropped the pencil.

Nando eased through the doorway, and then the fresh recruits poured past him and spread across the room's perimeter. Shotguns with neon stocks all around.

They waited.

Heavier footsteps announced Dex's approach. He broke through the ring and contemplated Evan, snake eyes peering through an expressionless mask. René entered a step behind him. He took in the open file drawer, anger lurking behind that plastic grin.

'I like a challenge,' he said. 'But you're testing my patience.'

Evan said, 'And you're testing mine.'

He stepped back until he felt the desk pressing against his hamstrings. René gave a nod to the men, who closed in on Evan from three sides, leading with their shotguns. Evan looked for any break or opportunity, but there would be none tonight.

Dex strode up to him, a needle flashing in his hand. A well-placed smack spun Evan into the desk, and he felt the pinch above his shoulder blade. Warmth spread beneath his skin, his muscles jellying. As he slipped to the floor, he caught a tilted glance of Dex peering down at him, his head cocked, his expression something between hunger and curiosity.

31

A Hard Man

Evan awoke naked on the floor of his bedroom, blinking into the harsh light of morning. His head throbbed. His mouth was chalky, his throat dryer than it had ever been. A single breath led to a coughing fit.

He started to rise when a ring of fire ignited around his neck.

His body slapped the floor, his muscles twitching against the rustic oak planks. He managed to fight one hand up to the blazing nerves of his throat and felt a metal band clamped into place.

A shock collar.

Behind him he heard Manny laugh. 'This is gonna make our job easier, *ése*. No more getting our arms all tired holding up the shotgun and shit.'

Evan pushed himself onto all fours, managed to get a wobbly foot down beneath him.

His neck caught fire once more, nerves burning up through his face. His chest struck the floor again. Convulsing, he couldn't tell if the shock was still running or if he was just feeling the aftereffects of the current sizzling through his skin.

When his vision unblurred, he watched Manny turning the transmitter over in his hand, admiring it. 'This thing is great.'

'Take it easy,' Nando said. 'René'll be *furioso* if you fry his brain.'

'It's not gonna fry his brain. People use it all the time.'

'For chimps in labs. At the *lower* setting.'

Manny grinned. 'Boss did say to put a little more *oomph* in it.'

Evan shoved himself up again, wiped drool from his lower

lip. He sneaked a glance at the inside of his arm, saw the tab of Scotch tape preserving René's fingerprint stuck there, hidden from view. 'No breakfast cart this morning?'

The next shock flipped him onto his side. Through the static he heard Manny laughing.

'Gimme that.' Nando wrestled the transmitter away. 'It's time for his exercise.'

Manny walked over and kicked Evan's feet. 'Hurry up and get dressed. Or I take back the transmitter.'

Evan trudged across the snow-dusted ground, scratching at his skin beneath the shock collar. The new guard in the tower watched him not with binoculars but through the scope of a dedicated marksman rifle. It wouldn't have the range of the sniper rifles in the mountains, but the right one in the right hands could be effective to six or even seven hundred meters. When Evan paused to identify the gun from its silhouette, the guard reached into his pocket.

Evan barely had time to wonder what he was doing before countless needle tips jabbed into his neck. He lost his legs again. Snow against his cheek, crusting the hollow of one eye. He lay there, panting for breath. There'd be no getting used to the shock level.

So the tower guard was also armed with a transmitter for Evan's collar. And God knew who else. Evan pulled himself up and staggered for the tree line, keeping his gaze low.

He'd thrown on multiple layers again. He felt bulky beneath two shirts and two sweaters, ballooning at the mid-section like Tweedledee.

Once he was hidden by the evergreens, he sat with his back to a tree and groped around the collar. Contact points rimmed the inside, metal prongs grouped in twos, the rounded tips jutting into his skin. His thumb found a notch near the back where the band snapped into place. No keyhole that he could discern. Perhaps the release was remote-controlled as well? The collar had little give; there'd be no moving the contact points off the skin. It was tight enough that swallowing was hard, like having a peach pit at the base of his throat that would not go down.

Rising, he hiked up the gradual slope of the northern face, wanting to get a better look at the entire valley. He crested a bulge in the mountainside and assessed his options. From this vantage it was clear that the western and eastern sides of the range were too steep to be traversed. Clifflike runs of shale would prevent any ascent while simultaneously leaving him exposed. He doubted that René had bothered to place snipers on those ends of the range. One shooter to the north and one to the south, aided by the eyes of the guard in the tower, could contain Evan in the valley.

Since the northern slope provided the best route to freedom, René had positioned the stronger sniper there. Which meant that when Evan made a break, he'd head up the opposite mountain. Wanting a better view of the southern rise, he hiked higher up the northern range now.

This was his last chance to recon.

He was leaving tonight.

Tomorrow René was planning to force him to empty out his bank account. Which was unacceptable for a host of reasons, not least of which were the ramifications of wiring money from his account without his own meticulous encryption procedures in place. Charles Van Sciver and an array of the most powerful search-software programs ever created were working around the clock for the faintest trace of the Nowhere Man to blip onto the radar. One click of the mouse would make Evan disposable to René and put Van Sciver onto his scent at the same time.

He was unwilling to deal with either complication.

Not with Alison Siegler and the boy out there waiting.

The thought sharpened his purpose, quickened his step. He fell into a rhythm, making decent time. The sun dominated a blue and cloudless sky, warming him enough to break a sweat despite the temperature. He stopped at intervals to eye the mountain across from him, mentally charting courses and backup courses, noting potential positions the sniper might take and the blind zones of those respective positions.

The Third Commandment: *Master your surroundings.*

He'd just started up again when a loud crack announced itself and a football-size chunk of bark flew out of the tree trunk to his side.

Evan halted. His breath wisped from his mouth once, twice.

He took a small step forward, and another rifle report sounded. Wood splintered overhead, and then a heavy bough rushed down, crashing a few feet in front of him.

He paused again, oriented upslope, trying to zero in on the sniper's position. He stepped to the left. This time he saw the muzzle flare an instant before the round kicked up dirt to the side of his boot.

The sniper was herding him down the slope toward the chalet.

Knowing he was clearly visible in the scope, Evan raised a hand: *Got it.*

Turning around, he started down the mountain.

He kept on in the direction the sniper had indicated, moving swiftly. Once he'd crossed a ripple in the mountainside, he knew he'd moved out of range of the scope. Rather than continuing down, he carved along the hillside, keeping to the dense trees. The pine air tingled in his mouth, his throat. At last he circled to the rear of the barn.

Bellying down behind the tree line, he peered through the trunks at the back door about fifty yards away. Two of the *narcos* patrolled the barn at intervals, the Dobermans trotting alongside. Evan watched and timed them.

In the tower beyond, the guard scanned the woods with his scope, holding his radio to his face with increasing frequency and agitation. A few minutes later, a contingent of three guards exited the barn and jogged into the forest to the north. Though it wasn't yet dusk, they wore night-vision goggles pushed up high on their foreheads in case the hunt went long.

Evan watched them go, then waited for the patrol to rotate one more time. When they passed, he broke cover and darted for the barn.

The first ten paces left him in full view of the tower, but the guard there stayed focused on the northern slope, rifle scope pressed to his face. Evan sprinted for the cover of the barn, at last falling under its shadow.

The rear door was unlocked. He cracked it, peering inside, wind whistling across the back of his neck. The G-Wagons and the Rolls were parked among a scattering of mechanic's tools. The gear lockers rimming the interior sported hefty padlocks. Though he could see no one, he heard the echo of voices somewhere inside.

Footsteps crunched the fresh snow along the adjacent side of the barn — the patrol returning. The breeze carried the sound of the dogs' panting, and then plumes of breath wisped around the corner a few feet off the ground.

Evan slid into the barn, eased the door closed.

The open space was broken only by a small box of an office that was little more than two thin walls and a flimsy door in the corner. Through the interior window, he spotted movement, so he hit the floor and lay still, breathing grease fumes.

Cold air drafted beneath the rear door, blowing against his face. He heard the patrol approaching and tensed in case the guards detoured inside. The sounds grew near, and then shadows dotted the gap beneath the door – broad blocks for the men's boots, flickering spots for the Dobermans' paws.

They passed.

Evan rolled behind the nearest G-Wagon, then rose to a crouch and peered through the vehicle's windows into the office. All he could make out now was a sturdy arm leaning against a cabinet, the back of the hand tattooed with a too-wide grin.

A voice carried over. 'What is he planning?'

It sounded like Nando.

He heard Despi answer from somewhere in the office. 'I don't know.'

Nando again. 'Will he wire the money tomorrow?'

'He won't tell me.'

'What does he tell you?'

'Nothing. He tells me nothing. He is a hard man.'

'Maybe you're not good enough. Maybe we need to replace you. With your sister.'

If Despi replied, Evan couldn't hear it. His eyes picked across the scattered gear, finally lighting on what he was looking for.

A car jack.

The one he'd spotted Samuel using two days earlier to prop up the Rolls-Royce.

When the handle was turned, the scissor jack cranked open into a diamond, but when closed it was relatively thin. Thin enough, he hoped, to hide beneath his bulky sweaters and smuggle back into his room. Given that Manny and Nando no longer came within twenty feet of him, he had a decent shot. He just had to sneak back to the woods, circle around, and then emerge casually from the tree line.

But first he had to get his hands on the jack. It rested in the open just beyond the hood of a Mercedes, three steps onto the wrestling mat.

If he made a move for it, he'd be briefly but completely exposed.

'We send a man by her apartment now and then, watch her watering her tomatoes on the balcony,' Nando was saying in the office. 'Beautiful hair, just like yours.'

Despi's reply was muffled by the walls.

Evan crept from cover. One step, setting his boot down silently, rolling from heel to toe. Another brought him onto the blue rubber mat. He leaned over, reaching for the jack. His fingertips had just reached the metal when the door flew open and Despi filled the frame, her face burning.

Dex and Nando remained behind her in the office, though their gazes were not yet lifted.

Despi stared at Evan, trying to process his being here.

Crouched over the jack, he stared back.

Her expression held a mix of dark emotions; it was unclear which would win out. Keeping his eyes locked on hers, Evan started to retreat behind the hood of the G-Wagon, moving out of Dex and Nando's view.

That's when he heard the rear door open behind him.

Claws scrabbled against the concrete floor. The Dobermans erupted in snarls. He was hidden between the two big SUVs, but not for long.

Despi remained unmoving as a statue in the doorway, her lips slightly parted, one hand still raised from when it had shoved open the door, her eyes flared wide. She blinked, swallowed hard.

He held up his hands and nodded at her: *Go ahead.*

The dogs' barks grew louder. On the far side of the G-Wagon, the *narcos* shouted in Spanish. He sensed movement behind Despi, Dex and Nando drawn toward the commotion.

Evan gestured at her more firmly: *Do it.*

She raised her arm. Pointed at him. It took two tries for her voice to work. 'Here! He's here!'

She'd done an admirable job conveying panic.

Nando knocked her aside, barreling past her, his heavy coat flicking high in his wake. Already he held the transmitter aloft, pinching the button with his thumb.

Evan registered barely a half thought – *Oh, fu* – and then the current surged into him, radiating through his head and torso.

Convulsing on the floor, he sensed the dogs' snapping jaws inches from his face. Confused, they barked and snarled; humans weren't supposed to twitch like that. As they strained their leads, their handlers leaned back to keep them from tearing into him.

A command rang across the concrete from the far side of the barn: '*Off.*'

The Dobermans waddled back a few steps and sat, panting around wide grins. Ropes of saliva necklaced the sleek, dark fur of their chests.

Evan rolled his head on the rubber mat, catching an upside-down view of René silhouetted in the opening made by the pushed-back barn door.

He said, 'You don't stop, do you?'

Evan made a noise intended to convey assent.

'No more walks for you. No more exercise. And no more time.'

'Until what?' Evan's words came out fuzzy.

'Until you wire me my money. Open of business tomorrow.' René continued in and stopped behind the Dobermans, stroking their heads. 'Good boys. Good, good boys.'

He fished treats from his pocket and rewarded them.

'Do you like dogs?' René asked Evan.

Evan coughed hoarsely into the mat.

'It's their loyalty that gets me,' René observed. 'Purer than love. You know the joke. Lock your dog and your wife in the trunk of your car for twenty-four hours. When you open it, which one is happy to see you?'

The Dobermans bared their teeth. Their marble eyes stayed locked on Evan, who'd managed to shove himself to a standing position, his hands on his knees. The skin of his neck prickled, angry and raw. Behind Nando, Despi caught his eye, her forehead twisted in anguish. He looked down quickly, not wanting to give away their rapport.

'Put him in his room,' René said to Dex. Then, as he breezed past Evan, 'Be showered in time for dinner.'

Evan shook his head, trying to clear the static. Too late he realized he was smirking.

René halted. His face reddened. 'Is something amusing, Evan?'

'No.'

'Why are you grinning?'

'Because I get it now.'

'Get what?' René waited, growing impatient. 'What do you think you get?'

Evan squared to him. 'I think you *want* to be a psychopath, René. But you're not. I think what you are is lonely. I think the only way you can get guests to your dinner table is by paying them or forcing them. I think you believe you can buy your way out of your misery, and that isn't amusing – it's profoundly fucking pathetic.'

René drew his head back, his chin doubling. His flush deepened, color seeping unevenly along the nipped-and-tucked lines of his face. Then his expression hardened, the vulnerability clamped behind a mask of controlled rage.

He walked across the barn, through the rolling door, and out into the blazing white. Evan was watching him fade into the lightly falling snow when another jolt of the collar cut his legs out from under him.

32

Ready

Evan sat cross-legged on the floor, his shoulders bowed. He hadn't gotten the car jack. Without the car jack, he couldn't break out of his room. If he couldn't break out of his room, he couldn't help Alison Siegler and the boy.

Evan was down to his last few hours.

He reminded himself how much he could get done in a few hours.

One way or another, he was getting out of this room. And out of this chalet. He would fight his way over the snowy peak of the mountain, leaving a trail of bright arterial blood in his wake.

A noise issued overhead, startling him from his thoughts. The hissing gas had come so much earlier than usual, the sun not yet kissing the western horizon. This was his punishment for laying René bare in the barn – to bed without dinner. René was done taking chances; he was going to knock Evan out and revive him at the deadline in a few hours to make the wire transfer.

Holding his breath, Evan rushed to the sliding glass door and threw it wide. He stepped outside, but the clean air quickly turned bitter, the gas being drawn through the open door. Rushing back inside, he lay on the bed and buried his face in a pillow.

His breathing grew heavy. A wave of grogginess came on. He fought to stay conscious. The hissing finally stopped, but he kept his face buried, waiting for the air to clear.

That's when he felt the vibration.

The RoamZone beneath the mattress. The boy calling him.

Another vibration signaled the second ring.

Evan lifted his face. He could still taste the halogenated ether riding the back of his throat.

Third ring.

He rolled off the bed, his kneecaps banging the floorboards. Shoved an arm beneath the mattress. Came out with the wrecked RoamZone.

The high-power-density lithium-ion battery was still going strong. The kid's number guttered across the cracked screen.

Just in time Evan thumbed the green icon and held the phone to his face. Somehow the circuit board held together. 'Hello?'

'It's me.' Same voice as before, but even more hushed.

The connection was bad, static fuzzing the line.

Evan swallowed hard. His head was swimming from the gas he'd inhaled, but he fought his thoughts back online. 'Are you okay?'

'I don't know. I'm trapped here. There's never enough food. I don't want this life. I didn't ask for it. I didn't ask for any of it.'

'What are they doing to you?'

'That's not even the worst part,' the boy said.

'What is?'

'I'm nothing here. *That's* the worst part.' His hushed voice held a kind of awe. 'No one cares. If you don't exist, then it doesn't matter, right?'

'No. That's not right. Look. Listen.' Evan blinked hard, rubbed his eyes, forging through the muddle in his head. 'Whatever's being done to you, it's wrong. It's not your fault. And you're not the only one.'

'I know it happens to other kids,' the boy said. 'I see it, even. But when it happens to you, it feels like you're the first person it's happened to in the whole world.'

'I know.' Evan felt emotion pressing at the back of his face. 'You're resourceful. Scrappy. Like I was.' The ether had loosened his inhibitions. He heard his words drawl, knew he was saying more than he should.

He was supposed to be the Nowhere Man, armored in his role as savior and hero, indomitable and distant and safe.

But right now he felt like none of those things.

The static grew to a roar, and for a moment Evan thought the call had dropped. But then the kid's voice came back in. '– can't talk about it.'

'Why not?'

'I'm scared to. It's not safe.' A wet breath.

Evan took a breath of his own. Held it. Then, 'Can you get out?'

'Nowhere to get to.'

'Find help?'

'No one can help me.'

'Can't you run away and go to the cops?'

'No. I need *you*.'

Locked on the third floor of a guarded chalet at the base of a snowy valley, Evan nodded. 'I'll get to you,' he said. 'I'm coming soon.'

In the silence he could hear the boy breathing across the phone.

Finally the kid said, 'I have to go now. I'll try 'n' call back if I can.'

'When you do,' Evan said, 'I'll be ready.'

33

The Inexpressible

Parking Level 3, submerged in a sea of crimson.

Evan is underwater, trapped inside his own locked-down body. His lips stitched shut. Drowning in Jack's blood.

Jack ripples across from him like some hard-bitten merman. His arm is raised. The fine hairs of his forearm waver like tendrils of seaweed. His finger points at Evan.

You.

Evan strains and struggles. His muscles bulge but cannot move. Paralyzed.

For the first time, he lifts his gaze to brave Jack's stare directly. Jack's eyes are not what Evan expects. They are filled not with accusation but with love.

Yet the finger still points.

And Evan realizes.

Not: You did this.

But: You hold the key.

Evan feels it roiling inside him, years of pent-up anguish and guilt and grief, an age-old whirlpool of despair. It is every feeling he had consigned to the depths of his gut, every unspoken word he has packed down his throat.

It reaches a vomit pitch, and he understands that it will no longer be denied.

Acid burns up his esophagus and claws crablike into the back of his mouth.

His lips strain at the sutures.

And then rip free.

It breaks through, a howl cracked out of the hidden core of himself, expressing the inexpressible.

It says, Help me.

34

What It Is You Do

Evan bolted awake, aware of a presence in the dark room.

He'd meant only to lie down for a moment after the boy's phone call, but the lingering effects of the sleeping gas must have put him out briefly.

Someone stood at the end of the bed.

Was he out of time?

He sat up, blinking rapidly to stimulate his night vision, the shock collar shifting painfully around his neck.

The form emerged from the darkness, curved and feminine beneath a thick bathrobe from the spa.

She parted her robe. Beneath it one arm clutched something to her stomach.

Drawing near, she set the object on the edge of the bed, out of view of the remaining surveillance camera.

The car jack.

'Make them pay,' Despi whispered.

He stared at the slender tool indenting the sheets.

'You were trying to get it,' she said. 'I don't know what for. But you have it now. So do what it is you do.'

'I can't take this. If he finds out –'

'He'll what? Hurt me?' She gave a quiet little laugh. 'Hurt me *more*?'

'You. Your family. You have too much to lose.'

'As do you,' she said. 'You have one hour until he comes for you.'

He felt it then, the swirling blackness at the heart

of himself, the inner whirlpool from his dream. 'Don't help me.'

'No. You don't get to tell me this. You don't get to decide.'

Evan stared at the car jack, wanting it desperately. For himself, yes. But even more for Alison Siegler, for the boy waiting for his help.

He said, 'But he'd kill you, your family. You can't take that risk.'

'*I* can't? Or *you* can't?'

He thought of Jack's eyes, conveying urgency and love. His finger pointing at Evan through the crimson sea. *You hold the key.*

'I can't,' he said. 'I can't be responsible for something that could hurt you.'

She gave a laugh that held no humor. 'We don't get to choose that. That's part of being human.'

He looked down at his hands, clenched loosely in his lap.

'You can't do it on your own,' Despi said.

She studied him, one eyebrow arched in an unspoken question. Her robe hung open, showing the slope of her divine belly – *Venus at the Bath*. She was waiting to knot the sash again and leave, either with the car jack or without.

He looked down at it there on the sheets. If he accepted it, he had to accept all the responsibility that came with it.

He looked back up at Despi.

He nodded.

35

Into the Snowy White

In a single shirt and sweater, Evan felt less bulky than on his previous excursions. He had to be for what he was about to do.

He stepped out onto the balcony. The moonless sky was black as pitch, broken only by flurries of snowflakes that swept through the welded bars. A trio of guards clustered around the fire outside the barn, warming their hands, Kalashnikovs resting at their sides. They did not look over.

He had a limited window of time out here in the dead of night. His gloveless hands already felt cold, and the more numb they got, the more useless they'd be.

Raising the scissor jack, he jammed it between two of the bars. Then he cranked the handle. The jack expanded, irising open with enough force to lift a four-thousand-pound car.

The bars bowed. Evan kept rotating the handle, leaning into the effort. The sounds of creaking metal intensified. The resistance grew stronger, his forearms straining. And then two of the bars gave way at the welded joints, popping free. One struck him lightly in the chest and clanged to the floor of the balcony. The other plummeted into the snowy white.

He shot a glance at the guards by the barn, but they were telling stories, focused on the flickering light of the fire, not the darkness beyond. Sticking his head through the gap, Evan looked down, but the fallen bar was lost to the white bank below, the thin black slot in the ground already being layered over.

Onward.

He squeezed his head and one leg through the hole, then drew his body carefully behind him. The bag of Doritos crinkled in his waistband, where he'd tucked them. The RoamZone phone bulged in his pocket, awaiting the kid's next call. Despite the extra baggage, Evan made it through the gap.

The bars provided a ready grip from the outside. The only problem was how cold they were, sticking to his palms. When he adjusted his grasp, he left some skin behind. He lowered himself down into a squat, his ass hanging in thin air, his heels cantilevered off the outside edge of the balcony.

He checked the guards, firmed his fists. Then he let his feet slide free, his legs dangling. For an instant his grip faltered, and he thought he was going to plummet two stories onto the open ground, landing in full view of the guards. But somehow he held on.

Bucking his legs, he swung himself out and away from the chalet and then back in. Another swing built momentum, and as he flew toward the building, he let himself drop. He landed off balance on the slick balcony below, his heels skidding out from beneath him. He hit the balcony flat on his back.

Manny was standing on the other side of the sliding glass door right in front of Evan, peering directly at him. Evan's inhale caught in his throat. Then he realized: Manny couldn't see him. The room lights were on, and he was using the glass door for a mirror as he buttoned his shirt.

Evan lay perfectly still. Snow fell on the side of his cheek. Two feet to the glass. Two feet more to Manny.

Manny's mouth twitched to the side as he finished with his shirt, and then he flashed his golden smile at himself and turned away to grab socks off the bed.

Evan rolled smoothly back over his shoulders and out of view.

The neighboring balcony was within reach. He jumped onto it from the railing. He came down awkwardly but at least didn't Charlie Brown the landing like last time.

The attached room looked empty. He checked the sliding glass door, found it locked.

Onto the next balcony, another graceless ballet leap through elegantly falling snow.

This slider opened under his touch.

He entered a dark bedroom that looked to be a match of his own. Moving swiftly, he crossed to the door, cracked it, and peered out. His vantage showed a clear shot up the hall to the stairwell.

Gliding the doorknob forward, he wheeled out, pivoting to check the blind length of hall to the hinge side of the door.

He found himself face-to-face with Nando.

36

A Real Fighter

Nando's arm was raised; he was in the middle of taking a bite from a PowerBar. His elbow pinned the butt of the AK-47 slung around his neck, keeping it aimed forward.

Before Evan could move on him, he dropped the protein bar and leapt back, raising the gun. *'¡Pare!* Right there. *Manos. ¡Manos!'*

Evan did not lift his hands. Nando's eyes darted, his Adam's apple jerking with each inhalation. But his grip looked firm.

'This is a predicament,' Evan said. 'You have your *cuerno de chivo* instead of the beanbag shotgun. I'm the item of value in this equation, not you. If you kill me, what will René say? After all his hard work?'

Sweat glossed Nando's face. He lowered the tip of the AK, aiming at Evan's thigh.

'Careful,' Evan said. 'You hit an artery, I bleed out. Neither of us wants that.'

Nando rolled his lips, swallowed. A notion glimmered in his eyes. 'Easy solution,' he said. Keeping his trigger hand on the weapon, he fished in his pocket and came out with the shock-collar transmitter. He was breathing even harder. Beneath the unhooked top buttons of his shirt, his chest was shiny with sweat. 'Now what do you have to say?'

'You've got the upper hand,' Evan said. 'But look at you – racing heart rate, nearly hyperventilating. Now look at me. Look at me closely. And ask yourself: Do I look scared?'

Nando wet his lips.

Evan said, 'The next question is, why not?'

Nando's fist tensed around the transmitter.

Nothing happened.

He pointed it at Evan, clicked several more times, the whites of his eyes pronounced.

Evan tilted his head back, exposing his chin. He'd taken the new trash-can liner from the bathroom, folded it over six times, and wedged it into place between the metal prods and his skin. The polyethylene plastic band was just thick enough to block the electric shock.

The transmitter slipped through Nando's fingers. He brought his hand around to the fore end of the AK.

But Evan was already airborne. His body coiled and exploded into a Superman punch, his right leg cycling forward and then pistoning back, whipping his right arm at Nando. His fist crashed across Nando's cheek, snapping the head to the side with a crackle of vertebrae. The *narco* collapsed in a puddle of limbs as if his spinal cord had been ripped out of him.

No sooner had Evan landed than he heard a door open behind him. He spun around to see Manny emerge two rooms down the hall.

'Shit,' Manny said. He leaned back through the doorway, returned hoisting a shotgun with a neon orange stock.

The sling of Nando's AK-47 was tangled around his body. There'd be no time to free the weapon. Evan swept up the handheld transmitter and ran for the stairs.

The *foomp* of a flexible baton round vibrated the air. Evan hunched, the beanbag glancing off his shoulder blade and decimating a wall sconce. Behind him he heard Manny jack the shotgun, chambering another round.

Evan slid onto the stairs, the next shot whistling over-head, punching straight through the drywall. The stairs hammered his back, his heels finally jarring into the first landing. Bouncing to his feet, he spun around the newel post and bounded down the next flight, nearly tripping as he spilled into the empty library of the ground floor.

Manny's shouts echoed through the stairwell. Various radios crackled to life elsewhere in the chalet. Heavy boots pounded the marble, the guards radiating outward in the building. Their first priority would be locking down the perimeter.

So Evan ran the opposite way, toward the heart of the chalet.

He passed a closet, a bathroom, nearing the vast living room. A boot squeaked in a room across the hall, and he spun through the opposite doorway, flattening himself to the wall just past the jamb. Gear clanked as the men stepped out into the hall. Evan was close enough to hear them breathing. A radio spit staticky Spanish – '¡Ven a recoger los perros!' – and the boots squeaked into action again, soles pounding away to the front of the chalet.

Evan eased out a breath through his teeth, studied the transmitter. He thumbed an offset red button on the side, and the collar released from his neck. He caught it before it could clatter to the floor, then dropped it and the transmitter into the base of a potted fern. Balling up the banded plastic bag that had protected his neck, he flung it into a corner.

Already he could hear the Dobermans' barks echoing off the hard surfaces of the foyer. Then came the scraping of claws against marble as they hurtled up the corridor.

Evan ran toward the dining room, hip-sliding across the table and banging through the swinging doors to the kitchen. No one was there.

His gaze swept the room. Knife block next to the wood-fired oven. Pantry door slightly ajar, showing a sliver of black at the seam. Pasta pot filled with water sitting cold on the stovetop of the center island. Hanging pot rack. The nearest counter held all order of serving supplies – cupcake liners, black cloth napkins, toothpicks, wads of cheesecloth, towers of fluted ramekins.

Rear swinging doors led to the ballroom, but the dogs would be up his back before he'd be able to get through. From the sound of it, they'd reached the living room already. Neither set of swinging doors featured locks; it would be impossible to barricade them against the dogs and do anything else.

Pounding paws tapped the parquet floor of the dining room. A crashing of chairs knocked aside.

There was no more time.

Evan shoved the pasta pot off the stove. It clanged loudly, water spilling out, slicking the tile floor. He leapt across the puddle and yanked open the pantry door, holding it before him, an angled shield.

The dogs exploded through the swinging doors, hitting the tile floor at a full gallop. Their paws scrabbled for purchase on the wet floor, their legs splaying, like fawns trying to gain footing on ice.

Their snarls dwindled to whines as they rotated into quarter turns, sliding across the wet tile, banging off the angled door, and ricocheting neatly into the pantry.

Evan slammed the door, trapping them inside.

Snatching a jar from the nearby counter, he flicked up a toothpick, wedged it into the keyhole in the pantry door-knob, and snapped off a splinter of wood, jamming the lock.

The dogs howled and scratched, but the door held. Already Evan could hear their handlers closing in, boots smashing through the wreckage of the dining-room chairs. They were steps away. He looked around. If he ran through the rear doors, he'd be an easy target in the bare expanse of the ballroom. The pantry was spoken for. The island provided scant cover.

There was nowhere to hide.

*

The two handlers burst through the doors and scanned the empty kitchen over the tops of their shotguns. The first man gestured at his partner to check the ballroom.

He waited, sweating, while his partner crept across and knuckled one of the swinging doors open. He turned back, shook his head. '*Nada*, Ángel.' Then he did a double take at the knife block, pointing at the empty slot. Both men's mouths firmed.

The dogs howled and scraped at the inside of the pantry door. Ángel walked over and jiggled the locked doorknob. Then he opened a cabinet next to the pantry and slid the key off the bottom shelf. He tried to insert it into the keyhole, but it wouldn't go.

Crouching, he studied the doorknob.

Taking his eyes off his partner.

Who was walking backward along the rear counter, his raised shotgun rotating between the sets of doors. He faced outward, sliding one hip along the marble ledge as he passed before the mouth of the wood-fired oven.

As he eased by, two arms appeared in the dark chamber of the oven behind him, reaching slowly through the bricked arch. A boning knife glinted in one fist.

The handler kept on unsuspectingly even as the hands crept forward on either side of his head.

The arms seized him in a lightning strike.

Evan braced the handler's head forward so the slicing motion of the blade wouldn't nick his own forearm once it passed across the throat.

It did not.

He crawled out of the dome of the oven, cradling the still-shuddering body. He kept the head tilted forward so the lungs wouldn't make a sucking sound through the slit and alert Ángel, who was still squatting by the pantry with his back turned. Sliding soundlessly off the counter, Evan lowered the corpse to the floor.

Ángel rose, frustrated. *'La pinche cosa está atascada.'*

He turned.

A moment of horror.

He shouted for help even as he raised the shotgun. Evan ducked behind the island before the shot, realizing too late that Ángel had wisely aimed not at him but at the pot rack hanging above.

The crash was thunderous. Pans pelted down over Evan's upraised arms, knocking the knife from his grasp. He spilled onto his back.

Ángel dove across the island, gliding on his substantial belly, soaring off the end at Evan, the butt of the shotgun jabbing at Evan's face. Evan barely had time to get his legs up. His boots embedded themselves in Ángel's stomach, and he went with the momentum, rotating into a backward somersault and catapulting Ángel off.

The guard smashed through the swinging doors into the ballroom.

Evan scrambled up and charged after him, kicking through the doors. The right one slammed into Ángel just as he got a hand on the shotgun. He rolled with the blow, coming onto his hands and knees as the shotgun skittered out of reach across the hardwood floor. He cast a longing glance after it, then rose to focus on Evan.

They circled each other. Ángel's foot position was solid, his base low. He kept his hands raised in a fighting position, palms turned in, unclenched, floating up around his face. A real fighter.

His attack options, however, were limited, since Evan had to be taken alive.

Evan had no such limitations.

Ángel led with a cross. Evan bladed his body, coming over the incoming arm with a *bil jee* finger jab to the eye. He deflected the punch, his firmed middle finger simultaneously jellying the guard's right eye.

Ángel grunted – more shock than pain – and reeled back, one hand rising to the socket. Evan pressed his advantage, driving forward with a punch, but the injured man proved surprisingly agile. He threw a parry into Evan's triceps, knocking him off balance, then slammed a palm heel to the outside of Evan's jaw. He let his hand slide past Evan's chin after the impact, stepping behind him and locking him in a sleeper choke.

The flurry was so quick that Evan barely registered the blur of Ángel's hands. There was no time to process it now; his carotid was cinched, and he was losing blood to the head. His canted face was angled at the chandelier overhead, resplendent enough to rival the one in the foyer. The dripping crystal teardrops, rainbowed with ambient light, blurred and smeared. Static dotted his vision. A few more seconds and he'd go out.

With everything he had, he stomped his heel down into Ángel's instep, a foot destruction targeting the proximal interphalangeal joint of the first metatarsal. The force of the impact shuddered Evan's bones right up his leg.

This one Ángel felt right away.

Gasping, he released Evan and hobbled back, his right foot bent behind him, raised gingerly off the floor. He skipped another few steps, his left leg propping him up. One hand floated before his wrecked eye. He might have been weeping. It was hard to tell. His good eye stayed locked on Evan's hands, tracking their every movement.

The Japanese master who had taught Evan hand-to-hand when he was a boy used to say, *If they're ready for a punch, go with a kick.*

Dum tek is the Cantonese name for the oblique kick, but Evan always preferred its street name: the schoolgirl.

He turned his hips, chambered his knee high to the side, and pistoned his heel down and forward into Ángel's left shin.

The ankle, bearing the guard's full weight, collapsed.

Ángel went down, arms flailing for balance. Evan hit him with a stiff jab to the throat, crushing his windpipe and hastening his fall.

As the dying guard thrashed about, guppying for air and slapping the hardwood, Evan walked over to the listing grand piano, the sole item in the deserted ballroom. It had been shoved to the far wall, a patina of dust coating the raised lid. Several of the strings had snapped. He picked out a good length and twisted the end loop free of the hitch pin, removing the wire.

Four feet of tempered high-carbon steel with good tensile strength.

Useful.

He coiled it into a coaster-size loop and stuffed it into his pocket.

Shouts and approaching footfalls carried through the corridors. The others had figured out the gambit and were finally abandoning their posts at the periphery to crash in on the center of the house.

This, too, fit Evan's plans.

Behind him Ángel bucked stiffly, his heels rattling against the floor, a diminishing drumroll.

Evan snatched up the fallen shotgun and sprinted from the ballroom.

37

More Animal Than Human

When Evan eased through the misted glass door into the spa area, he heard René's voice squawking through a radio: '– don't know where he is. Keep David locked down until –'

After throwing the dead bolt on the doors behind him, Evan peered around the corner and down the corridor of Jacuzzis and saunas that led to the lap pool fringed with artificial grass at the end. David leaned drunkenly against the last door in the row, slugging overproof Bacardi from the bottle as two *narcos* paced on the fake grass and conferred over their radios. One held a less-lethal shotgun, the other a Kalashnikov. The guy behind the *cuerno de chivo* was so hefty that rolls of fat bulged at the base of his neck. He wore a thin chinstrap beard and a gold pendant necklace with big diamond letters spelling out CALACA.

Skeleton.

These *narcos* were big on irony.

Evan set the stock against his shoulder, preparing for the turn. Taking a corner was both art and math. Jack used to call it 'cutting the pie.'

Before he could move, Calaca looked up, spotting Evan, and started as if he'd been stabbed. '*Marco, allá –*'

Shotgun raised, Evan whirled into the corridor and moved briskly toward them, letting the first round fly. It sailed inches past David's nose, striking Calaca's forehead with a dull thud. The fat man staggered back, heels of his hands pressed to his skull, and tumbled into the pool. The

AK-47 flew off his upflung arm, clattering onto the concrete across the water.

Marco swung his shotgun over, but Evan's next round blew it out of his hands, sending it skittering over toward the pool.

Evan never slowed.

David fell back against the glass wall of the Korean mist room as Evan hurtled past, closing on Marco and whipping the shotgun stock up, clipping the *narco* under the chin. Marco reeled back into a reverse flip, his rising feet knocking the shotgun from Evan's hands. Evan had an instant to marvel at just how badly he'd underestimated Marco's fighting skills before Marco rotated back around onto his feet. He bounced low to cushion his landing, snapping off a quick left at Evan's face, crushing his eye.

Evan blinked through the sting, his eye watering. Marco pressed his advantage, unleashing a flurry of punches. Caging his head with his forearms, Evan backpedaled in the narrow corridor, getting a little space as Marco hammered at him with bare-knuckle blasts. Finally he managed to shove Marco off, and they faced each other, panting. Beside them in the corridor, David recoiled into the wall as if hoping to transport himself straight through it.

Glancing over, Evan saw Calaca standing in the middle of the pool, having just regained his feet. He started to slosh toward his AK-47 at the far side of the pool.

Evan couldn't let him get to that weapon.

Evan's shotgun lay on the tile next to Marco's feet, the barrel pointed toward the pool. Evan dove for it, snatching it up and getting off a shot just before Marco drove a heel into his kidneys.

The beanbag round flew across the spa and smacked into Calaca's shoulder. The fat man went down again, gurgling water. Evan tried to bring the shotgun with him as he rolled onto his back, but Marco kicked it free. It glanced off Evan's cheek, then cracked off the thick glass enclosure of the rain shower.

Evan threw himself up onto his feet. Marco feinted at him a few times, trying to create a reaction opening, but Evan didn't take the bait.

Evan's lower back throbbed where he'd been kicked. His eye watered from the blow. Swelling pressed his cheek upward, a raw-numb tingling.

Marco was a much better fighter than Evan. If they kept this up, he'd take Evan apart piece by piece.

Evan had to land a single destruction blow quickly, take out a limb, and press on from there. He didn't dare glance at the pool, but he heard Calaca surface again. Soon enough the fat man would reach that Kalashnikov.

Marco's eyes ticked to Evan's swollen cheek, broadcasting his next move. His feet set, his shoulders swiveling as he shot out another jab. Evan threw a pencak silat double-hand glancing parry – *slap-slap* – to an arm trap, grabbing Marco's wrist and immobilizing the arm. With the heel of his hand, he shattered the elbow, blowing the arm out in the wrong direction. He tried to hold a chicken-wing control, but Marco flailed free, his broken arm dangling limply at his side.

Over in the pool, Calaca forged through the water, taking another unsteady step toward his AK-47. Evan had to slow him down again.

Marco bared his teeth, blinking sweat out of his eyes. Evan weighed the odds, knew he'd pay either way. Turning his back on Marco, he snatched up the shotgun and fired off another round at Calaca. The beanbag ricocheted off the fat-padded base of the man's skull, knocking him back underwater.

Evan braced himself, knowing that the strike would come, and sure enough, Marco's side kick hammered him into the wall. He heard himself grunt as if listening from afar. Marco's next kick was aimed not at Evan but at the shotgun, jamming Evan's finger in the trigger guard and sending the gun flying. It crashed off the wall barely a foot from David's face and fell to the tile.

Evan and Marco parted in the corridor, took some space. Marco cradled his broken arm across his stomach. Evan only had to watch his feet now. They circled each other, breathing hard. Marco set for a roundhouse, starting to throw his right leg. Evan thrust his lead foot forward into a jeet kune do oblique jam, striking Marco's inner thigh at the junction of his hip. The counterstrike caused a crazy stop-motion effect, halting the kick before it started, Marco's bent leg hinging away in reverse – a slammed door wobbling back from the frame.

Behind him Evan heard Calaca rise from the depths again, heard him paddle toward the AK. Evan let his eyes dart toward his dropped shotgun, but Marco moved swiftly, sweeping it across the slick tile with his instep. The gun plopped into a Jacuzzi.

Evan watched Calaca's thick hand grab the far lip of the pool and pull his body to the edge. There was nothing Evan could do now until he got through Marco.

Marco had only one move, and Evan waited for him to take it.

He kept his eyes on Marco's rear leg.

Again Marco tried for the roundhouse. This time Evan let it come. Ducking, he tucked his head behind his elbow and pointed the tip of his ulna at the incoming knee. It struck the patella precisely, shattering the kneecap. Marco screamed, skipping back on his good leg.

Evan had his first chance to square up. He got off a graceless shotokan front kick, a pure-force delivery of the ball of his foot to the middle of Marco's chest. Marco flew back, banging through the glass door behind him and into the sauna. He landed in a crumpled heap across the sauna by the cedar bench.

David remained flattened against the wall of the corridor like a piece of art, frozen, still clutching the Bacardi 151 bottle. Evan grabbed the rum from his hand and hurled it through the open door into the sauna. The bottle shattered against the heater, flame already chasing the high-proof spray. Fire rained down on Marco. He gave a shriek that sounded more animal than human.

Evan swung the sauna door shut, snatched a Jacuzzi net skimmer from its mount, and rammed it under the handle, seating the end against the opposite wall of the corridor. The door was pinned shut, Marco trapped inside.

Evan picked up Marco's shotgun and started toward the pool. Behind him the muffled screams in the sauna reached a pitch he felt in his bones.

Seemingly dazed, Calaca was still in the pool, hunched over the lip, straining to reach the AK-47, which remained just out of reach. Evan stepped onto the artificial turf, his boots crunching audibly. Calaca turned, and Evan hit him in the collarbone with a baton round, the impact punctuated by the splintering of the thin bone. To his credit, the guy kept his feet, but barely, sagging against the concrete edge. One beefy arm slapped the concrete behind him as he held his head and torso above the surface.

With wide eyes Calaca peered back over his meaty shoulder. Then he turned to grab again for his gun. His fingertips edged it farther away. Grunting against the pain, he drew back for another lunge.

Evan reached the paisley-shaped bar with its decorative Christmas lights arrayed across the surface. He smashed a few of the colorful oversize bulbs against the sustainably farmed rain-forest wood, then tore the string free.

'*Espera,*' Calaca said. He was shivering in the water, clinging to the concrete edge, his grooved skull glistening with droplets. '*Por favor —*'

Evan slung the string of broken lights over and into the pool.

The effect was half explosion, half sound effect, a massive *foomp* that knocked Calaca upright. His body jolted a few times and then sank below the surface. A moment later he bobbed up, floating on his back, arms in a Christlike spread, his gold necklace glittering in a tuft of chest hair that had escaped the collar.

Two dogs, eight guards, two snipers, one doctor, and Dex.

In the corridor David remained where Evan had left him, frozen against the wall, arms raised. In the barred sauna across the space, flames continued to crackle, but Marco's screams had ceased.

As Evan approached, David held out his hands, shrinking away. 'Please don't kill me. I'm a victim, too. I'm —'

Evan grabbed his jacket, ripping the slender remote free from the inner pocket, taking the fabric along with it. The force of the motion spun David around, and Evan kicked him into the Korean mist room. He vanished into a billowy sheet of white haze, landing with a satisfying crash.

Up the corridor a Kalashnikov coughed out a burst and pebbled glass flew into sight, raining across the tile.

René's men breaching the spa door.

Evan jogged back over the fake turf, upgrading his less-lethal shotgun to Calaca's AK-47. On the bar the tray of snacks was gone, replaced by a basket of apples. Evan pocketed two. One of the guard's heavy jackets was looped over the back of a lounge chair.

He grabbed it as he ran by, heading for the elevator.

The car was there and waiting, and he slid inside just as the cavalry spilled into view, weapons raised. Evan and René's men had a half second to stare at one another.

Evan gave a little shrug as the doors rolled shut.

The elevator whirred its way slowly to the basement.

Arming sweat off his brow, he aimed the barrel of the Kalashnikov between the bumpers, waiting for them to part. They did.

He had expected almost anything.

But not this.

38

A Bad Night's Work

Bags of blood.

Dangling from mounts inside glass-fronted medical refrigerator units, the shiny IV bags bulged like glossy red fillets.

There was medical equipment, too, complex elephantine machines with tangles of cords and smooth beige casings. Enough gurneys for a warfront triage center. And Dr Franklin sprawled across one of the mattresses, his jaws loose around a rubber strap, blinking languidly.

Evan threw the emergency stop lever, freezing the elevator, and stepped out into the basement. It seemed unreal, a warehouse of dream imagery. He stared through the refrigerator windows at the chilled bags, coded by date and donor name.

They hung like shiny fruits, an orchard of blood.

Evan stopped in his tracks in front of one of the blood-storage units. To his side rose a gleaming, chrome-plated industrial safe. Five feet tall, heavy-duty steel hinges, bolted to the floor.

Curious.

Beside the safe was a tall metal filing cabinet, one drawer slightly ajar. He flicked it the rest of the way out. Medical files, each tab with a 'patient' name. He snapped one up from the rack, flipped it open. A full medical workup of a girl listed as seventeen years old. Blood screening and analysis, pathogen reduction and purification, red-blood-cell and platelet count.

Franklin seemed barely to register Evan's approach. His skin had a gray, stoned pallor. Stubble fuzzed his cheeks and neck. A needle dangled from his left arm just below the cinched rubber strap, the tip still embedded in a swollen vein. Vials neatly lined a metal medical tray at his side.

Evan set the heavy coat on the neighboring mattress. 'What is all this?' he asked.

The doctor's chapped lips moved, but no sound came out.

Evan grabbed one of the vials. Fentanyl. He threw it across the room. That brought the life back into Franklin's eyes.

'What is all this?' he said again.

Franklin's slender hands spread open as if bestowing grace. 'This is René's secret garden.' He smiled. 'It's how he's fed.'

'Fed. He *transfuses* himself with this blood? For what?'

'Studies. There are studies . . .' Dr Franklin's gaze loosened, and he drifted off.

Evan cuffed him across the face.

The elevator shaft conveyed raised voices from above, distorted shouts and radio static.

Evan looked at all those bags, all those donor names. 'He kills these people?'

'No, no. Unless . . .' A smile flickered across Franklin's face, an inside joke. 'Unless there are accidents.'

His eyelids fluttered. Evan traced his dilated pupils to the ancient brick fireplace across the basement. Beneath the log holder, mounds of dark ash.

Only now did Evan feel the cold of the room seeping through his skin, sinking into his bones. Crossing the space on deadened legs, he dropped to his knees on the hard concrete before the fireplace. He swept a hand through the ash. Came up with a metal hoop the size of a silver dollar.

A gauge earring.

He thought about the black smoke he'd seen pouring from the chimney two days before.

Evan drew his hand through the heap one more time, let the ash sift between his fingers like sand. A dental bridge remained on his palm.

He wished now that he had killed David for helping lure the victims here.

It was not, however, too late for Franklin.

Half turning, Evan unleashed a volley of rounds at the refrigerator units, shattering the glass and ripping through the IV bags. Shards and red droplets filled the air, raining down on the concrete floor. He shot up the equipment next, riddling the oversize units, sending forth showers of sparks. Only the safe remained impervious, the bullets pinging off the chrome exterior.

From his languid recline, Franklin watched Evan approach.

A clanking echoed down from above, the guards up in the spa forcing open the elevator doors. Evan could hear René's men monkeying down the shaft.

He stood over Franklin, backlit by the dim glow of the shot-to-shit unit behind him, his shadow falling across the doctor's face. A drop clung to the lower lid of Franklin's left eye, but he didn't look sad. He looked relieved.

'Yes,' Franklin said with a wan smile. He swept an arm toward the sparking machines. 'It deserved it.' He blinked, and the tear gummed on his lashes. '*I* deserve it.'

Evan raised the AK.

The single report echoed around the concrete.

Across the room a series of thuds announced the men's landing on top of the elevator. From the sound of it, they had numbers. Evan had succeeded in drawing them here to the belly of the chalet.

He buttoned up the guard's heavy coat. Kicked over a

medical cart beneath one of the basement windows. Readied the slender remote in one hand, the Kalashnikov in the other.

He shot out the basement window, then hopped up on the cart and dove through the opening in the glass. As soon as he hit the snow, he clicked the remote, turning on the outdoor lights.

The chalet and grounds lit up like day.

A pair of approaching guards reeled back, clutching at their night-vision goggles, the sudden brightness scalding their retinas. The sniper on the northern slope behind his night-vision scope would likewise be blinded.

With the last of his bullets, Evan stitched a line of holes across the guards' critical mass, spilling them forward into the snow.

As he tossed the weapon aside, swept up a set of night-vision goggles, and bolted for tree cover at the base of the southern slope, he ran his mental tally.

Two dogs, six guards, two snipers, David, and Dex.

Not a bad night's work.

39

To the Brink

Snow flurried even under the canopy of pines. Evan worked a switchback beneath the trees of the southern slope, sticking to a furrow cut into the mountainside to keep his head low. He had a hitch in his step, and his ribs ached; all that fighting had taken a toll.

He didn't know the south sniper's position, so he paused again, snapping the night-vision goggles down over his eyes and peering across the crest. The NVGs cast everything in a green glow.

He swept his gaze up the hillside, caught a set of eyes glinting back at him.

He reeled away, banging against a boulder before realizing that the eyes belonged to a white-tailed deer. It stared dolefully at him across the night before bounding off with a twitch of its legs.

Evan crouched by the boulder, catching his breath and reaching back for the wilderness skills he'd learned as a young man. The three keys to survival: shelter, fire, water. He'd been taught how to pick a spot – high ground, cleared space – and to frame out a hut, shingling leaves over branches. But the current situation wouldn't allow for that yet. There would be only sporadic rest stops until he was out of the valley and across the range.

He was running on increasingly numb legs. Any stop could kill him. And yet if he got too cold, his body would lock up and he'd die of exposure. Which meant he had to balance himself on the razor's edge, running himself to the brink of freezing before pausing to reheat over a fire.

To the brink but not an inch further.

He drove on up the slope.

René surveyed the wreckage of the spa, his jaw tensing until he could feel knots at the corners. David stood behind him, an ice pack pressed against his pretty face where it had struck the pebble-studded bench inside the mist room.

One of René's men struggled to fish Calaca's corpse from the pool; another mopped blood from the tile. Manny was downstairs safing the lab, and René had dispatched Dex with the remaining three guards to follow Evan's tracks. The snow proved helpful, the footsteps clearly marked. A radioed update had informed René that Evan had backtracked a few times to obscure his trail but hadn't had enough time to pull it off convincingly.

Dex was good with footprints.

René rubbed his eyes until they burned.

David removed the ice pack and pressed gingerly at the bruise coming up on his forehead. 'Guy was like a *typhoon*,' he said. 'It was pretty insane.'

René opened his bloodshot eyes. His thumb and forefinger held dust from the foundation he'd dabbed over the spider veins on his nose earlier. The look he gave David must have held everything he was feeling, because David recoiled from it, blanching. Fear had stripped away the kid's seen-it-all veneer; he looked his age, not a day older.

David cleared his throat. 'I'll be upstairs.'

René said, 'You'll be right here until Manny gets back.'

For once David offered no pithy retort.

As if on cue, the elevator doors opened and Manny emerged. He ran a tongue across his gold teeth, one cheek quivering nervously beneath the eye. 'You're gonna want to see this, boss.'

René felt something inside him turn to ice.

Evan ducked under a half-snapped tree trunk, hurdled a snarl of branches, pressing up the face of the mountain. The crisp air charged his lungs, set them tingling. Though he'd made it halfway up the mountain, the final incline looked to be the steepest.

As he scrabbled up a cracked sheet of shale, his boots sent pebbles cascading behind him. He tumbled over the brink into a bed of decomposing needles. The sharp tips poked his palms as he shoved himself back up.

He paused to tie his boots even tighter but had trouble gripping the laces, his fingers fumbling around the cords.

Another few minutes and he'd be too cold to help himself.

Though the sun remained below the horizon, a curtain of dirty gray showed to the east, starting to rise across the black bowl of the sky. It was just light enough that he might risk a fire. Given the condition of his fingers, there wasn't a better choice. He stopped, panting, warring with himself.

I will get to you. He'd promised the kid.

And he pictured that yellow shipping bill floating away on the wind outside the holding house in Fullerton, the last record of Alison Siegler.

He had to heat his body just enough so it could keep driving forward.

He scanned his surroundings with the NVGs, looking for any sign of the sniper. Nothing.

Inside a ring of close-set trees, he cleared a small patch of ground. He gathered a few fallen branches. Melting snowflakes clung to the bark, so he used the piano wire to strip the wetness and expose the dry wood beneath. The wire pinched his pink hands. It was a sloppy, imprecise process, but it got the job done.

He coiled the piano wire back into a coaster-size loop. British secret-service agents used to hide Gigli surgical wire saws in their clothes during World War II, and Evan took a cue from them now. Yanking the padded insole out of his left boot, he slid the wire up toward the toe and then replaced the insole on top of it. As he laced up his boot again, he felt barely a bump beneath the ball of his foot.

Next he removed the packet of Doritos from his waistband. By now they were mostly crushed, but he selected a few of the bigger pieces and arrayed them on the ground. One of the lesser-known benefits of Doritos is that they're highly flammable.

With a fingernail he scraped a gob of pine pitch from the nearest trunk and smeared it across the crushed chip fragments to increase the combustibility. Then he tore two strips from the bottom of his undershirt and braided them into a rope, which he tied to either end of a not-too-thin stick to form a bow. His fingers were growing numb; had he waited a few minutes more, he'd have been unable to form the knots.

Now he sawed the rope back and forth rapidly across another stick held perpendicular, causing the stick to spin in the makeshift tinder. Before long he busted a coal, which he flicked into the bits of chips. A few steady breaths stoked it high enough to catch the humble heap of branches, and then a tiny fire flickered beneath his outheld hands, warming the palms.

Normally he'd bring water to a rolling boil before drinking it, but he didn't have anything to use as a pot, and besides, he trusted fresh-fallen snow. He warmed himself, chewed a bit of ice, then ate an apple. The whole time he kept his NVGs lowered, scanning the hillside and the valley below.

Life crept back into his face and arms.

Just a few minutes more and he'd be on his way.

The elevator doors opened on the blood-spattered basement. René emerged through the fog of his own disbelief, blinking to ensure that what he was seeing was in fact real.

Spoiled blood dripping from tattered IV bags.

Medical machinery reduced to wreckage.

Dr Franklin's fragmented head resting on the sodden sheets of the gurney.

The tangle of images knocked around inside him, sharp edges slicing beneath the skin, rising up his throat until he bellowed his rage at the ruined medical lab. It was a roar of rage, yes, but laced with pain.

He sensed David and Manny shrinking away behind him, backpedaling to the walls, giving him space.

René's chest heaved as he caught his breath. He'd relocated many times before, and he would relocate again. But this time he'd have to rebuild from scratch. New equipment. New doctor. New blood.

Amid the remnants of the once-glorious operation, the safe rose, gleaming and intact. René crossed to it, running a finger across a dimple in the chrome plating where a round had been repelled.

He said, 'Unlock it.'

Manny stepped forward, fumbling at his key ring.

'Are you sure?' David said. 'You swore you'd never –'

'Unlock it.'

Manny rammed the key home and turned the weighty dial. The lugs inside released with a clang, and the door parted from the frame on well-greased hinges.

Inside were several small glass vials and two filled syringes.

René removed a syringe, and Manny took a quick step back, as if what it contained was contagious, airborne.

It was not.

But it was scary enough to deter proximity.

René touched the pad of his thumb to the plunger. The power of the ages held in the span of his hand. He cleared the air from the syringe with a hint of pressure from his thumb.

Manny's radio crackled, one of the trackers calling in: '– *recogimos sus huellas. Quizá hay una fogata delante y* –'

Footprints and a campfire. They were closing in.

René snatched the radio from Manny's trembling hand and held it to his mouth. He regarded the gleaming tip of the needle. 'Bring him to me.'

Evan kicked snow over the ashes, stomping out the embers. Feeling had returned to his extremities, and he didn't want to risk lingering over the tiny flames any longer. Lowering his NVGs, he gave another spin, searching the mountainside.

A wink of reflected light caught his eye. Way up by the brink, ten or so klicks distant, a man lay prone on an outcropping of rock, angled slightly away.

The south sniper.

Evan's last obstacle.

The man swept the rifle slowly back and forth, scanning the hillside below.

As the scope moved to turn full circle, Evan dropped to the cold earth behind a tree trunk and lay still. He exhaled down into the collar of his jacket so his clouding breath wouldn't give him away.

When he risked a look again, he saw that the sniper had directed his attention to another stretch of the rise. Dawn was leaking through the valley, sending a glare off the new-fallen white.

If Evan could get across the swell of land beside him, he'd be out of sight, his path to the summit clear. Once he made it over the brink into the vast surrounding mountains, René's men would never catch him.

One more stretch of snow and he'd be free.

He checked the sniper again, but the man was still facing away.

All clear.

Evan bolted.

The uneven earth jarred his boots, the dense pines jolting back and forth, as much obstacle course as cover. He crested the rise and saw the ground slope away. He slid down on the soft-packed snow, dropping over the final swell, dipping from the south sniper's vantage.

He was beyond reach.

He'd made it.

He lay for a moment, catching his breath, enjoying the sight of the wide-open sky above. Then he shook snow from the cuffs of his pants and started to stand.

He'd just pulled himself up to full height when a wedge of tree trunk exploded two yards from his face as if hammered free with an ax. Before he could process what had happened, he heard the big-caliber signature boom across the valley.

For a moment his thoughts spun in freefall. It made no sense. The south sniper was lost to a fold of the mountain behind him. And the shot's trajectory was wrong.

He scrambled into motion, heading for the nearest tree line. A bullet kissed the top of his shoulder, fraying the thick coat and obliterating a branch. He juked left, a half-assed wide-receiver move, but already his legs were throbbing, his boots skidding on ice.

Another shot whipped overhead, annihilating a pinecone. Splinters rained down across his shoulders.

Any way he turned, he was in the crosshairs.

The pinecone was a message, sent from the base of the valley. An incredible shot.

With dawning dread Evan put it together.

The north sniper had moved out of position, coming across the range to pin him down from an unexpected angle. This man who had taken a pinecone off Evan's palm from five hundred meters.

And Evan was in the middle of an open patch, fully exposed. One wrong step and he'd be missing a limb.

He froze.

He could feel his heartbeat in the hollow of his throat.

He gritted his teeth.

Bowed his head.

Then he raised his arms, raised them high and wide so they'd be visible through a scope. He waited, his breaths jerking through his chest, steaming in the night air.

After a time he heard footsteps crunching through the snow behind him. The sound of reckoning.

The footsteps neared, but he didn't dare turn around, didn't dare move. Not until a kick to the kidneys knocked him to the ground. Dex stood over him, his head cocked with some sentiment that couldn't quite make it to his eyes. Two *narcos* flanked him, their AKs pointed at Evan's chest.

Dex's big hands swung at his sides, the tattoos flashing. Too-broad smile. Bloody scowl.

One painted mouth dipped into a cargo pocket. The fingers came out gripping the hinged-open shock collar. Wearily, Evan lifted his head from the snow to see the big hands nearing. His vision clouded.

Even so he could hear the collar clank shut around his neck.

40

People Who Deserve It

Evan's feet dragged lifelessly behind him, leaving ski tracks in the snow. The morning glare off the ground was piercing, forcing him to squint. His legs and arms throbbed from the cold. His head hung forward, hair latticing his eyes. A *narco* had him by either arm, Dex leading the merry little charge.

They hauled him into the barn and threw him onto the wrestling mat. Shuddering, he curled on the blue rubber. Only now did he allow himself to register the state of his body. The chill crept into his bruises, stung the ring of raw flesh around his neck. His head swam from the cold, from the exertion, from more kicks and punches than he could keep track of. He could no longer feel his nose or his lips. His ankles ached. His thighs burned, his calves were on fire, his breath growing more ragged by the second.

If he died here in this desolate valley, he'd be another in a long list of people who had failed Alison Siegler and the boy.

And yet how could he rescue them when he was in need of rescuing himself?

There was a lesson in that somewhere, of that he was sure, but he didn't know what. If Jack were alive, he'd summarize it neatly into something pithy – part koan, part fortune cookie. He'd put the situation into context, salvage it by turning it around on Evan, transform impotence into insight.

Evan stared at the circle of *narcos* penning him in and tried to convert his helplessness to rage, but the old tricks no longer worked. Not right now. He felt undressed, vulnerable.

Defeated.

He heard the barn door roll open. Footsteps.

He caught a whiff of familiar cologne. It smelled like a country club.

René's voice settled over him. 'Your plan didn't work out very well.'

'No,' Evan said. 'Doesn't seem to have.'

Two of the men patted him down roughly. One of them yanked the RoamZone from his pocket and handed it to René. With amusement René regarded the smashed screen and the cracked casing, bubbled from the fire. He laughed at the seemingly useless phone and tossed it back at Evan. With numb fingers Evan fumbled it into his pocket, then curled into himself again to try to generate warmth. The collar scraped into the tender flesh at the contact points.

René adjusted his eggplant-colored scarf. 'You look cold.'

Evan licked his cracked lips and tried not to shudder. Tried and failed. Finally he let his eyes roll up to take in the stout man once again. Manny stood behind him.

Evan drummed up a smile. 'The band's getting back together.'

'You'll find that your humor is going to evaporate quickly,' René said.

'I've seen what you do in that medical lab.' Evan's fingers moved to the scab in his arm. 'You stole my blood? When I was passed out?'

'You're too old,' René said. 'You're just the bank. The kids, they're the feast.'

Evan had to breathe a few times to get enough oxygen. 'Why do you want their blood?'

René took a moment to smooth down his hair. He adjusted

the thick fabric of his suit, skimming his hands over the lush lapels. 'Scientists at Cornell have been conducting the most fascinating research,' he said. 'They took old rats and young rats and stitched them together at the flanks. Literally combined their circulatory systems. You wouldn't believe what they discovered.'

'Try me.'

'The short version is that it reversed aging in the older rats. Turns out that bathing old stem cells in young blood has a rejuvenating effect. It enhances memory, strengthens skeletal muscle, hastens healing. Who would have thought that the fountain of youth was right there all along? A fountain inside our youth?' He paused, pleased, and studied Evan. 'Let me guess. You object vehemently. I've committed a moral atrocity that flies in the face of nature.'

'Antibiotics and skyscrapers fly in the face of nature,' Evan said. 'I don't give a shit about natural or unnatural. I care about who you're doing this to.'

'Oh, I just skim a little off the top. Like a mosquito. Besides, you're hardly one to object to hurting people.'

'I only hurt people who deserve it.'

René showed off his glorious caps. 'You are such a wonderfully pure thing. A self-made construct.'

Evan pushed himself up to sit on the mat. He still felt weak from the exposure, but his arms were tingling, the blood flow picking up again. 'The young rats. You didn't say what happens to them.'

'Well, that's the unfortunate part,' René said. 'They aged prematurely. Their muscles broke down, didn't heal the same way. Every benefit has a cost.'

'As long as you're not paying it, right?'

'That's right.'

'So you get David to lure kids here? And you siphon off

their blood? But it's not a perfect science, is it? Sometimes it goes bad.'

'Every advancement has its complications.'

'There's a difference between stealing and killing.'

'Not really,' René said. 'In one instance I steal blood. In the other I steal a different resource – the only resource not able to be replenished. Time. Killers are only thieves of a different stripe. They steal time – the time their victims would have had left to live. Ten years. Forty. They take it to enhance their own time. It's a trade, and it favors the bold. Just like those who can afford better medications, safer cars, who had the birthright luck not to be born in a flea-bitten Third World shack. That the kids I' – here he searched for a word – '*sip* from generally emerge unharmed is a testament to my magnanimity. There's nothing to stop me from taking *everything* every time.'

'Except your kind heart.'

'I don't *like* to do harm, you see. I'm just *willing* to.' René set his hands on his knees and leaned over Evan, and for the first time Evan considered just what a large man he was. 'However, given the mess you left in my basement? I'll *enjoy* what I'm going to do to you.' He stood up, clasped his hands. 'But we have so much to clean up first.'

Dex was suddenly behind Manny, relieving him of his Kalashnikov. There was a slight delay as Manny seemed to realize what had happened, and then his mouth stretched into a rictus of dread, a twitching oval lined with gold teeth. No words emerged.

'Xalbador, he speaks poor English, is that correct?' René asked, gesturing at one of the men who had dragged Evan through the snow.

Manny stared into the middle distance.

'Is that correct?' René repeated.

Manny managed a nod.

René flicked two fingers, and Xalbador stepped forward. A skinny kid in his early twenties, he hadn't yet thickened into manhood. A wide belt cinched his jeans, holding them up. The Santa Muerte tattoo on his neck was inked but only half colored, a few scabs still showing from the needle. With his wispy mustache and lupine cheeks, he was young and mean and had a lot to prove.

Manny would not look at him.

René said to Manny, 'Will you translate for me?'

Another tiny nod.

René cleared his throat. 'Tell him that given your failure, he will be succeeding you in your position.'

Manny's lips wobbled, his mustache bristling. He palmed his mouth, trying to still it.

'Tell him,' René said.

Dex sidled a step closer, set a hand on the ledge of Manny's shoulder.

Manny said, *'Dado mi fracaso, es posible que vas a tomar mi posición.'*

'Tell him that his primary – no, his *only* job – will be to watch our guest.' René stabbed a finger down at Evan on the mat.

Manny cleared his throat. *'Solamente . . . solamente tienes que echarle un ojo a nuestro huésped.'*

'Tell him you are hopeful for his success and wish him well.'

Manny's Adam's apple twitched. He turned to René. *'Por favor –'*

'You are hopeful for his success and wish him well.'

'Tengo la . . .'

René nodded encouragingly.

Manny licked his lips, his gold caps gleaming. His brow

glistened with sweat. *'Tengo la esperanza de . . . de tu éxito y . . . y . . . te deseo . . . deseo lo mejor.'*

René looked at Xalbador, who raised his AK-47 and put a tight grouping of bullets through Manny's chest.

Evan thought, *Two dogs, five guards, two snipers, David, and Dex.*

Xalbador dragged Manny's body out through the rear barn doors, leaving a path of blood across the concrete.

'Nice show,' Evan said.

'Don't worry,' René said. 'It's not over yet.'

Dex pushed open the door to the interior office and pulled Despi out by her hair.

41

No Ready Answer

Despi kicked and tried to shove herself away from Dex, but she was seismically overpowered. He carried her across the barn like a squirming lab rat and set her gently on her feet before René. Dex kept one hand clamped on the back of her neck.

Somehow Evan had managed to find his feet. Four guards ringed him. In case the Kalashnikovs weren't sufficient, each was armed with a transmitter for the shock collar.

Anyone could get in on the fun now.

René regarded Despi. 'Our guest used a car jack to aid in his non-escape,' he said. 'Any idea where he got it?'

Evan said, 'I stole it from the barn when I snuck in here yesterday.'

René kept his gaze steady on Despi. She writhed in Dex's grip, and then the muscles of his arm corded and she gave a yelp and stopped struggling.

'If you tell the truth,' René said, 'I won't hurt you.'

'I'd never take anything from her,' Evan said. 'I don't trust her. She's one of your employees.'

'Despi,' René said gently, 'I have cameras in the barn. Is this really a lie you want to stand behind?'

Slowly, she raised her eyes to meet René's. She gave the faintest shake of her head, the tips of her dark locks swaying.

'Did you give him the car jack?' René asked.

Her lips trembled. She nodded.

'Okay.' He stroked her chin. 'Okay.'

'Do you really have cameras in the barn?' she asked.

'No,' René said.

She bit her lower lip. 'You promised you wouldn't hurt me.'

'And I will honor that promise,' René said. 'Nothing will happen to you. In fact, nothing will happen here at all.'

She closed her eyes, freeing tears that slid down her olive skin.

René turned and started out.

Evan stayed tense.

'However.' René stopped, his back to her. 'One of the many benefits of money is that I can commission people anywhere in the world.'

Despi blanched.

Slowly, he turned. 'Say, in Rhodes. Athens.' He held out his hand, palm up. One of the *narcos* placed an iPad on it.

'No.' Despi shook her head. 'No, no, no.'

René hummed to himself as he tapped the screen. He held up the device for Despi. Evan couldn't see what it held, but he saw the glow reflected in Despi's eyes.

The impact on her was immediate. She took a half step back as if staggered by a punch. Her face shifted, hollowed out beneath the skin, her eyes sunken and glazed.

René swiped a finger across the screen, bringing up the next image.

She strangled a small noise in her throat. Her words came in a hoarse whisper: 'No. Not her, too.' She hunched over, her shoulders shuddering. She made sounds befitting war zones and hospital rooms.

Guilt flared up inside Evan, scouring his insides, threatening to consume him.

'Not a hair on *your* head will be touched. As promised. In fact, you're free to go.' René rested a hand on Despi's forearm. 'Dex will drop you at an airport of your choice with a full wallet. By helping my guest, you've earned your freedom. I hope it was worth it.'

Despi straightened back up. Her face was flushed, streaked with tears, but her gaze was fierce, unbroken.

René said, 'I'll even let you say good-bye to your friend before you depart.' He gestured toward the wrestling mat.

Despi's stare skewered René. For a moment he even seemed unsettled.

Then she started over to Evan. She looked broken from within, her limbs held at the wrong angles, her gait and carriage different, as if she were learning to walk inside a new body. René indicated for his men to give them some space.

Evan wasn't sure if she was going to strike him. If she wanted to, he would let her. Instead she embraced him, squeezing him hard, her face mashed to his chest.

He stroked her thick, thick hair. 'I'm sorry,' he whispered into her. 'I tried to warn you.'

He was shocked at the note of anger that had found its way into his voice. Fire crawled across his skin, matting his shirt to his back. Everything felt jumbled together inside him, trespasses past and present. He pictured Jack clutching at the ball of his shoulder, his hand gloved in blood. A little more pressure, a little more time and he might have lived. If Evan hadn't asked him to meet. If they'd chosen a different day, a different hour, a different parking structure. If Evan had been quicker on the draw. If he hadn't taken the car jack. If he'd thrown Despi out of his room.

The photographs René had shown Despi of her slain family would live inside her as surely as Evan's memories of Parking Level 3 lived inside him. He couldn't *undo* it for her. Not just her present anguish but the years of pain to come, dividends paid out over the decades.

She looked up at him with the same fierceness she'd shown

minutes before. 'You think my family would've been safe if I *hadn't* helped you? Don't be naïve.'

He hadn't thought anything could shock him right now, but there it was. 'Naïve?'

'You think you're at the controls just like René. But you couldn't control this.'

He felt his face loosening with emotion.

She said, 'Accepting that you need help like everyone else – it doesn't guarantee a good outcome. Nothing does.'

He had a hard time swallowing. 'Then why do it?'

She kissed him. Her tears, wet against his cheeks. She pulled away, held his face, her breath hot. 'I don't know how to live with this. With what I saw.'

'I know. I know that's how it feels.'

'How would you kill me? Right now?' Her voice held a note of pleading.

He looked at her brimming eyes. The wisp of hair caught in the corner of her mouth. Felt the warmth of her pressed against him, her fragile, human form.

For the first time, he had no answer.

Dex snapped a black hood over her head and yanked her out of Evan's arms. He dragged her to the Rolls-Royce, her legs stumbling to keep up. After cinching the hood and knotting it off, he opened the rear door, depositing her inside. He reversed out of the barn, the back of the majestic car kissing a snowbank outside, and drove off.

Evan felt a sting in his palms and unclenched his fists to see that his fingernails had indented the skin. He looked over at René. 'At one point the tables will be turned –'

'And . . . let me guess,' René said. 'You're going to kill me.'

'*Worse.*'

René must have read something in Evan's voice, because he blinked a few times. Regained his composure. Forced a smile.

Outside, a band of gold rode the horizon, tinting the caps of the snowbanks blue. René checked his watch. 'The markets are almost open. Are you ready to wire the money?'

Evan cleared his throat, spit a gob of blood on the pristine blue mat. 'No,' he said.

René gave a little nod and then breezed out, passing two of his men. 'Search him and bring him to the lab.'

42

Corners of His Mind

Straps bit into Evan's chest, stomach, and thighs, adhering him to the gurney. Hard leather restraints bound his ankles and wrists to the side rails. He fought to find a place inside himself that would protect him from what would come. SERE training had taught him to deal with stress, disorientation, torture. To this end he'd been maced, electrocuted, and drownproofed, his reactions observed and critiqued. He'd learned to find corners of his mind to retreat into. It never made the pain go away, but it allowed an extra layer between him and it, let him observe the agony from a slight remove. As with meditation, it was essential not to take his thoughts or sensations literally. He had to find the space around them. In the space there was relief.

From whatever René was readying over by the vault, Evan would be requiring a good deal of relief. Dex stood at René's side, but facing Evan. He held up his grinning hand, wore it over his mouth.

'I've tried to be reasonable,' René said, 'but I've never come across anyone as stubborn as you.' His back remained turned, his bowed shoulders rippling with some movement of his unseen hands. Daylight and frigid air streamed through the shattered basement window. 'I wanted this to be civilized but you refused and refused and refused. And so now.' He turned to face Evan, a syringe in hand. *This.*

In the course of his training, Evan had been injected with sodium pentothal and other 'truth serums.' He wondered if that was what René was up to here. A psychoactive medication would make him more pliable, more likely to be manipulated into sending the wire transfer and unleashing whatever came with it. But even as a kid, he'd found the drugs not to live up to their reputations.

Judging by Dex's tattooed grin and René's very real one, whatever that syringe held was something much worse.

'I can promise,' René said, as if reading Evan's mind, 'it's like nothing you've ever encountered.'

A fly buzzed over and landed on Evan's knuckles. He wiggled his fingers to scare it off. 'More sadistic research out of Cornell?'

'Out of Oxford, actually. You wouldn't believe what it cost for me to procure a few tiny vials of this.' Taking his time, René ambled closer to Evan. 'Like most experiments, it started with a simple question: What if you could make prison sentences for heinous crimes last *longer*?'

Evan's heart rate ticked up, pulsing in the side of his neck. 'Longer?'

'Longer than a lifetime.' René regarded the syringe with something like affection. 'There was a couple who kidnapped a four-year-old boy. They kept him in a closet, tortured and starved him for weeks, then beat him to death. Given the UK's disdain for capital punishment, the husband and wife were given a thirty-year sentence. Which seems woefully inadequate.'

Evan thought of the *Horizon Express*, plowing along at twenty-three knots, a white furrow in the deep blue sea, and Alison Siegler somewhere aboard in one of thirty-five hundred containers, closing the distance to a fate nobody deserved.

And he thought of the boy's voice over the phone line: *You should see how they keep us here. Like cattle, all lined up.*

'Yes,' he said. 'It does seem inadequate.'

'What if you could make someone serve a thousand-year sentence in eight hours? Ten lifetimes of purgatory crammed into the span of a single workday?'

The tip of the needle neared. Evan's fear mounted, threatened to overtake him.

'Can you imagine the horror?' René said, leaning in.

Evan struggled furiously against the straps, but they were designed for precisely this purpose. The needle slid into his arm.

René smiled. 'Don't worry,' he said. 'I'm just going to give you a single dr—'

Evan felt a slight pressure in his vein and then watched René's mouth continue to open more slowly than seemed conceivably possible, each millimeter taking an hour, two hours, and the end of the spoken word pulled out and out, stretched from a block of steel into a thin metal wire, a sound and a vibration, the endless tunnel of the *o* like a wormhole through the ages, and over the forever-gaping mouth René started to blink, but the movement of his eyelids was like the rise and fall of a lake's watermark across the seasons, limitless microseconds crammed between microseconds, the creased skin around his eyes rearranging infinitesimally, a universe of motion contained in a single blink until at last, after a day's grueling wait, Evan could see the thin blue veins etched in his closed lids and he knew it would be another day for them to open yet again, and the word was not yet completed, the wrinkled lips still closing the *o* into the *p* even as another sound overpowered the slow-motion hum of René's voice, a buzz slowed to its constituent audio parts, and Evan pulled his gaze to the source, but the shifting of his eyeballs felt like altering the course of a freight ship, ligaments and muscles flexing and tugging to recalibrate his view excruciatingly, until at last he fixed upon the bottle flying airborne over René, its hairlike bristles waving sluggishly on its metallic green thorax, its wings flapping so gradually that Evan could see the quality of light alter through the semitransparent wings that were embellished with intricate patterns to put any stained-glass window to shame, and the whole horrifying, unfettered, attenuated time, Evan's mind raced inside his skull at a real, frantic pace, alive and horror-filled, scrambling like a mouse trapped in a bowl of water, desperate, so desperate to get —

He jerked his head back into the pillow, a breath screeching through his lungs. His muscles had knotted from neck to calves, arching his body against the restraints. He turned his head to the side and vomited, warmth drooling across his cheek onto the sheets.

'I'll do it,' he said, in a voice so hoarse he didn't recognize it as his own. 'I'll wire the money.'

43

Unleash Hell

Evan sat before the monitor in the study on the fourth floor, his hands on the keyboard. The computer was brand-new; he'd watched Xalbador remove it from the box. That it was air-gapped, having never been hooked into the Internet, was helpful, but whatever cloaking and encryption software René had in place to hide the wire transfers would not be as impenetrable and untraceable as those Evan used. He'd learned at the elbows of the best technical security specialists in the world.

As had Van Sciver.

Van Sciver had a team of them in his employ now and more data-mining capabilities than René could possibly dream of.

Click a single button and unleash hell.

Maybe unleashing hell was the only shot Evan had left.

The heated vent above breathed warmth down his neck, making him break out in a sweat. Or was it fear, only now worming its way out through his skin? He'd spent so many years safe in obscurity, unseen and unexamined. Now the carefully positioned boulder he'd been hiding beneath was about to be rolled back, his life exposed to a blinding light.

He thought about the infinity he'd spent strapped to the gurney, an infinity that had lasted precisely two flaps of a blowfly's wings.

He looked over at René, a last-ditch effort. 'You don't want me to do this.'

René smiled, folded his hands. 'I don't?'

'The wrong people will come. You will not be happy.'

'I've done this a time or two,' René said. 'My procedures are completely secure.'

Evan said, 'You don't have any comprehension of what secure is.'

René snapped his fingers. With extreme caution Dex handed him a syringe. The clear, viscous liquid rippled inside. A single drop had nearly undone Evan. He couldn't imagine what horrors a full injection would bring.

Taking a deep breath, he keyed a series of pass codes into the Privatbank AG Web site. He paused. 'Once I click this button, I can't control what will happen.'

René jammed the needle into the side of Evan's neck. He brought his ruddy face close, sweat drops clinging to the points of his hair. He spoke through locked teeth. *'I am done negotiating.'*

Evan felt the twenty-one-gauge stainless-steel tube embedded in his neck. A half-inch movement of René's thumb and he'd be trapped in an eternity of suffering.

He felt something leak out of him. The last of what he had.

He closed his eyes. Tapped the mouse. The loading wheel spun, and then a whoosh indicated that the money had gone.

René eased the needle out of Evan's neck, and Evan allowed himself a quiet exhalation. He stared at the screen. WIRE SENT.

'What's coming won't be worth twenty-seven million dollars,' he said.

René turned to Dex. 'Put this animal back in its cage.'

Dex seized Evan, yanking him to his feet and shoving him toward the door.

'At last,' Evan said, 'we're calling things what they are.'

44

Celebration

René stood before the picture window of the master bed-room, hands clasped at the small of his back, watching snow flurry against the pane. It occurred to him that it was a pose suited to a Cassaroy. Regal and imposing, spine held straight enough to disguise that two-inch deviation. An artist could come along and paint an oil of him planted here victoriously, an oil that would have been worthy to hang alongside por-traits of Cassaroys past that sobered the grand halls of his childhood manor.

And yet.

He had a niggling sense that it wasn't time to rest on his laurels. He'd prevailed in the battle, sure, but there was a greater war to be won.

He felt a stirring, the sensation he got when he was closing in on a financial trail, readying for the kill. He closed his eyes, sensed the data shifting, so many bits and pieces, a pat-tern almost discernible just beneath the surface.

Behind him David stirred in the silk sheets, exhausted from the day's travails. 'Are you coming to bed?'

'Our guest is clearly not who I thought he was,' René said, watching the snow shape-shift outside. 'But I think he's something even bigger than I imagined.'

'What?'

'I don't know,' René said, finally turning. The rungs of David's stomach muscles stood out like something artificial, something poured from a mold. René was surprised by how little the sight aroused him. His office awaited. There were queries to be made, baited hooks to be tossed into the Deep Web. He walked past David, heading for the door. 'But I'm going to start digging.'

The women's bathroom in Mexico City International Airport smelled of disinfectant and Montezuma's revenge. Candy wet a wad of paper towels in the sink and retreated behind a stall door. She peeled off her shirt and bra, the fabric clinging to her burn scars, then gingerly patted her weeping back with the damp towels. She allowed herself to grit her teeth but did not make a noise.

Relief was relative.

The pain was so constant that she sometimes forgot it was there. But not after an eighteen-hour flight spent leaning against a scratchy polyester seat cover.

Sitting next to Jaggers had only added to the agony. She hated everything about him. His stink. His jaundiced skin that under the yellow glow of the reading light looked like dried papaya. How he sucked his teeth after eating instead of using a toothpick.

The way he'd killed a beautiful young fawn of a Tatar girl who'd only walked into the alley to see if they needed help.

That the mission had proved to be a dead end only added to Candy's frustration. They'd laid over in Amsterdam already and would now enter the U. S. from the south, a not-worth-noticing commuter flight from Mexico City to San Diego. She was willing to endure any amount of hellacious travel and the myriad discomforts that came with it as long as the journey held the faintest glimmer of hope for catching Orphan X. She'd forge through fire and brimstone to get a crack at his untarnished flesh.

That's why she hated return flights. They spelled failure.

She finished patting down her back and let the paper towels drop to the floor. Hanging her head, she eased a breath through her teeth. The air cooled the moist skin, a momentary break from the itching, the burn.

Putting her shirt back on would be unpleasant. Gathering her will, she stared at the bra wrapped around her clenched fist.

All her training, and here she was nearly vanquished by a 34D in a bathroom stall.

A boarding announcement for her flight echoed through the bathroom. She readied herself to finish dressing.

A vibration in her jeans caught her attention, the punk rendition of 'I'm Every Woman.'

Excitement licked up her spine.

She clicked TALK, held the phone to her cheek.

'I HAVE made YOUR next RESERVation.'

'Already?'

'You HAVE to EAT WHILE the meal IS HOT.'

'Gladly,' she said. 'How hot is this particular meal?'

'PIPING.'

The lick of excitement turned to a tremor.

'PARTICULARS to follow,' spoke the chorus, and then Van Sciver clicked off.

Grinning, Candy slid the phone back into her pocket. She pulled on her shirt and shoved through the stall door. On her way out of the bathroom, she dumped her bra in the trash.

After all, this called for a celebration.

45

A Different Kind of Ruckus

Hot water pounded the top of Evan's head, streaming down his shoulders. No matter how long he stayed in the shower, it seemed he could not get warm. His internal clock told him that it was a few hours past midnight. René seemed to be forgoing the sleeping gas, perhaps in honor of Evan's last night at Chalet Savoir Faire. Evan had been told that he would be hooded and driven away tomorrow, dropped off somewhere in the middle of nowhere so René would have plenty of time to clear out.

He had his doubts.

He figured René was waiting for the next business day to get a human confirmation from his own bank that the money had arrived and was free and clear. Then he would dispose of Evan.

For now Evan was back in his cage, and the cage had been made escapeproof. The bars on the balcony were rewelded and reinforced, the fireplace flue was bolted shut, and the front door had sprouted two more dead bolts. Evan had nowhere to go except into the shower, so here he was.

At last he got out and dried off using one of the bamboo-shoot-patterned towels. The shock collar seemed to be waterproof. The tape holding René's fingerprint had all but sealed to the underside of Evan's arm like a clear Band-Aid.

The plastic trash bag had been replaced in its spot near the toilet. The only person who'd seen him use it to thwart the collar was Nando, and he hadn't survived long enough to tell anyone. Evan tried to take solace in this shred of an advantage.

His clothes remained balled on the floor where he'd kicked them off. He'd been searched well, but René's men hadn't thought to check beneath the insole of his left boot, where he'd hidden the piano wire.

They'd transformed his room into a dungeon, and all he had was a trash-can liner and a loop of piano wire.

He reminded himself that despair was not a luxury in which he could indulge right now.

He dug the RoamZone out from the pocket of his dirty jeans and studied the cracked screen, wondering where the boy was and what he was going through right now. He recalled the boy's scared voice, his words distorted over a swollen lip: *So what? I get beat up all the time.* Evan looked at the four walls that held him. Being trapped was one thing. Being kept from helping a kid who needed him was nearly intolerable. *You should see how they keep us here. Like cattle, all lined up.*

And Alison Siegler. The *Horizon Express* would be nearing the locks of the Panama Canal by now, where her cries would be drowned out by the massive gates, the roaring culverts, the grinding machinery of the chambers. Every minute Evan was in René's hands brought her closer to her destination. She was eight days from delivery.

Frustration raged, a blade-winged bird beating inside Evan's chest. He forced himself to breathe evenly, to calm the bird, to focus.

He headed out of the bathroom and into the walk-in closet. He was just pulling on some clean clothes when he heard a rumbling from outside.

He rushed across the room and out onto the balcony, hard snow pelting him. The lights beneath the eaves bathed the front of the chalet in an alien glow that leaked around the corner. No one was in sight.

He heard the noise louder now, powerful engines roaring off the walls of the valley. Straining, he peered through the bars. The steel slats had been tripled, slicing his view into fissures.

The gravel road was blocked from view. He breathed and he waited.

At last an enormous moving truck edged into sight as it turned in to the circular cobblestone driveway and passed from his field of vision.

And then another.

Another.

The last parked with its rear still visible. Workers coalesced at the back of the truck around the rolling door. It rattled up on creaky tracks and banged, dislodging a shelf of ice from the roof.

Several of the men hopped inside, and a moment later an enormous flat item, sized like a barn door and ensconced in protective wooden crating, emerged. The workers lowered it from the truck, laboring under its weight, and staggered out of view toward the porch.

Evan realized now why René had chosen not to knock him out with halogenated ether. He wanted Evan to witness this.

Whatever *this* was.

The workers came back for another like-shaped object. Evan wondered just what the hell it was.

A few minutes later came a different kind of ruckus from deep inside the chalet.

Saws revving and power screwdrivers and the screech of rent metal.

Construction noises.

Evan returned to his room, put his ear to the sturdy front door, and listened for a while. After a time his legs grew sore, so he sat with his back to the door. An hour passed and then another, the clamor never subsiding. A few times he nodded off, but the sound was piercing and irregular enough to avert sleep.

The dread gathering in his stomach didn't help either.

He watched the first light of morning filter through the bars. It crept across the floor, inch by inch. It had just reached his toes when he heard the moving trucks rumble away.

A blissful moment of silence followed.

Then the electricity hit, flame erupting around his neck, shooting tendrils of heat through his jaw and down into his chest. The shock flattened him to the floorboards.

It continued, feeding Evan a steady current of pain. Somewhere beneath the static, he realized that these were the new procedures before anyone entered his room. René was taking no more chances.

Sure enough, a moment later the door swung open, shoving his body aside.

Dex reached down and gathered him up.

46

All the Honey

Dead on his feet, Evan stumbled along the corridor a few paces ahead of Dex, a collared dog being taken for a walk. Instead of a leash, Dex had only to hold the transmitter up. A tap of his finger would send Evan to the floor.

They passed the library and then the sunroom. Every step heightened Evan's curiosity. And his concern. What torture device had René built for him?

When they passed through the doorway into the ballroom, Evan was shocked into stillness. He gaped at the item that had been constructed in the dead center of the vast space.

A rectangular box the size of a cargo-shipping container, built of what seemed to be bullet-resistant glass, probably Lexan or another sturdy-as-hell thermoplastic polymer. A freestanding room, nearly seamless, save for a small vent in the back befitting a reptile terrarium.

A hatch resembling a bank vault's door had been cut into one end of the rectangle, swung ajar on massive industrial hinges. The heavy door looked to be a solid foot thick, as were the walls. Embedded below the steel-bar handle was an inset screen and a sensor panel the size of a Frisbee.

René stood proudly in front of the Lexan vault, his surviving guards lined up behind him like White House staff awaiting a new president. René nodded at the open door, and Dex prodded Evan forward.

As Dex shoved Evan across the threshold, his shoulder skimmed the frame. The corner sliced right through the fabric of his shirt, as sharp as the lasered edge of a carbon-steel plate.

Evan stood inside, the air compressing around him as Dex pushed the door closed. It clanked sonorously, and everything grew suddenly quiet.

Dex pressed his left hand to the Frisbee-size panel. The inside of the door featured a matching panel and screen, both of which now lit up. The panel displayed the outline of Dex's hand along with the network of veins running beneath the skin. A word glowed to life on the screen above: MATCH. Next, a series of commands populated the screen – LOCK, OPEN, DISABLE, RECODE. The LOCK button highlighted as Dex touched its counterpart outside, and lugs slotted into place, locking the door and sealing Evan inside.

No cords or wires were in evidence anywhere in the clear Lexan around the instrument panels; the system was run by an internal battery, a safeguard against the power's being cut.

René observed Evan studying the controls. 'The vein patterns beneath the surface of our skin are as unique as our fingerprints,' he said. 'This system uses infrared sensors to identify those patterns. Something about hemoglobin absorbing the light – it's all too clever for me to keep up with. What I do know is that you will never crack out of this box.'

'So this is where I live now?'

'No. I'm just testing it.'

'For what?'

René drew closer, facing Evan through the transparent door. 'Remember when you said I would not be happy after you sent that wire?' A sly grin. 'Well, I *am* happy.'

His voice, at a conversational pitch, came through clearly; the sensor panel also served the function of relaying their words through the foot-thick Lexan.

'You indicated that bad things would follow. You were

right. Bad for you. Good for me.' René leaned in even more, his mouth close enough to the door that his breath clouded the Lexan. 'I know who you are.'

A sudden cold seemed to fill the transparent box.

'Who am I?' Evan asked.

'Orphan X. The Nowhere Man.'

'You have me confused with someone else.'

'I was given all the buzzwords. A "richly funded covert-action program." "Neutralized tier-one targets." "CONUS and OCONUS operations."' René's forehead wrinkled or at least did its approximation of wrinkling. 'The last two sound like sexual acts. They mean what, precisely?'

'Google 'em.'

René smiled. 'I know we had a deal, but you've hardly shown consideration for our agreement. Killing my men, destroying my equipment. Why should I honor what you won't? Given what you did to my lab, I need even more funds to rebuild, to acquire new medical machinery, buy another doctor. All this time I've been focused on what you have. Little did I realize that *who you are* is more valuable.'

Evan asked, 'Who told you this about me?'

'I have my sources.'

'These sources,' Evan said. 'They found *you*.'

René wet his lips. 'I put out inquiries. Answers came back.'

'How did those answers come back?' Evan pressed.

'Through an e-mail associated with the bank account in which your money landed.'

'Your highly private account at the end of your highly encrypted trail of wire transfers?' Evan said. 'Wonder how they got that information?'

'No,' René said. 'I wonder how much they'll be willing to spend for you. I'm guessing it'll be a lot more than twenty-seven million.'

'I don't doubt it,' Evan said. 'Do you know who you're dealing with?'

'Not the initial party. But some of the others.'

Evan felt another plunge in the temperature of the Lexan vault. 'Others?'

'It seems you're a wanted commodity in many quarters. Once I received word of your . . . secret identity, I explored the market. My subsequent correspondents were willing to communicate through more traditional untraditional means. I managed to scare up a few more bidders.' René lifted a finger and tapped the glass in front of Evan's face. 'We're having an auction.'

'You might not want to stick your arm into that beehive.'

'But, Evan,' René said, already turning to leave, 'that's where all the honey is.'

47

Collision Avoidance

Evan stuck his head and torso into the fireplace like an auto mechanic, examining the new bolts studding the flue damper. It didn't give even a millimeter when he pounded it with the heels of his hand.

The Ninth Commandment dictated: *Always play offense.* But he was running out of moves fast.

He thought about what his last sortie had cost Despi. He could see the glow of René's iPad in her deep brown eyes, how her face had crumbled at the sight held up before her.

He hit the flue even harder, the ring echoing up the closed-off chamber beyond. He kept striking the metal plate, unleashing frustration and rage until his knuckles ached.

Jack came to him in a wisp of memory: *Good thinking, son. Damage the only weapons you got left.*

Evan stopped, breathing hard in the musk of the hearth, letting the throb in his hands subside.

A faint noise reached him, and at first he thought it had been conveyed from somewhere inside the building through the chimney itself. But no, it was more distant. He drew himself out and listened carefully.

A scraping sound. Not from the chalet but from outside.

He moved to the sliding glass door and stepped through into a blast of snow. It was late afternoon, the front edge of dusk made gloomier by bruise-colored clouds blotting out the sun. Squinting against the flakes, he peered through the dense bars toward the sound.

It took a few moments, but finally several figures came visible about halfway between the chalet and the barn, forms laboring in the whiteness. He could make out only their outlines, but eventually it became clear that they were using shovels, their blades scraping against the ice.

As the snowfall diminished, he noted four of them working away.

Not digging. Clearing a space.

He leaned closer, hands clenching the cold bars. The space, set a good distance from the buildings and any trees, looked to be about ten meters by ten meters.

It struck him what they were making, and suddenly even the bite of the air couldn't cool the electric surge of panic rolling through him.

He came inside, put his shoulders against the sliding glass door, and closed his eyes. Tilting his head back, he took a few deep breaths, trying to calm himself.

The hissing from the air vent caught him off guard. His eyes flew open, and he gulped in a mouthful before realizing what he'd done. Already he felt the haze climbing into his head, the weight gathering on his eyelids.

It was so much earlier than usual. René had been wise to vary the schedule, to make the gassing episodes unpredictable.

Stumbling to the bed, Evan barely had time to curse his lack of preparedness before passing out.

The vibration stirred him from a deep, dreamless sleep. He groped beneath his pillow, came out with the wrecked Roam-Zone. A familiar number flickered across the cracked screen and then vanished.

It took great effort to lift his head. 'Yuh?'

His mouth was bone dry, his tongue bitter, coated with a chemical aftertaste.

The same hushed voice came through the line, barely audible over the poor connection. 'Are you coming to get me?'

Evan sat up. With mounting frustration he looked at the new dead bolts, the welded cage of the balcony. He forced a swallow down his sandpaper throat. 'No, I'm . . .'

He was at a loss for how to complete the sentence.

'Why won't you?'

'I . . . I can't right now.'

Static flared up, and Evan prayed the line wouldn't cut out. How fragile his connection to the world, to what his life had been.

'*Try,*' the boy said. 'You have to try.'

'I did. I am.'

'The girl said you take care of people who need help,' the boy said. 'I should've known it was fake.'

'It's not fake,' Evan said. 'I'm not fake.'

Crackling on the line rendered the boy's response inaudible.

Evan made a fist, pressed it against his thigh. Hard. 'I just . . . I just don't know how to help you right now.'

'It's all lies and stories,' the boy said. 'No one saves anyone.'

Breathing in powdered sugar and sunscreen at the Veterans Day parade, Jack's warm hand resting on Evan's coat-hanger shoulder. Pavarotti's nine high Cs washing over them in the fire-warm study. The hard part is staying human. *The view from the window of a dormer room that was his and only his.*

'Yes. They do.' Evan couldn't remember the last time he'd gotten choked up. It felt bizarre, out of control.

In the silence he could hear the boy breathing across the phone.

'You'll forget me,' the boy finally said. 'Everyone does.'

'No. I won't.'

The voice grew even quieter, barely a whisper. 'You *have to* remember me.'

Heat burned beneath Evan's face. 'I will.'

The connection cut in and out, stealing the boy's words. ' . . . have to . . . be too late . . .'

As Evan strained to hear, a noise came from outside, a resonant thumping.

A sound he knew all too well.

He threw his legs over the side of the bed, willed himself to stand. His knees felt wobbly, his skull filled with concrete.

The noise grew louder, vibrating the walls, the floor beneath his feet, the flesh on his bones. He was unsure if the vise pinching his temples was a headache or just dread tightening its grasp on him.

'Listen,' he said into the phone. 'Hold up. Just . . . hang on.'

He dropped the RoamZone onto the bed and stumbled to the balcony. The frosty air hit him full force, but the snow had vanished, leaving the night as clear as glass.

Two glowing dots approached through the sky, one red, one green.

Collision-avoidance lights.

The helicopter banked and set down on the patch of cleared ground between the chalet and the barn. A door swung open, and a man emerged onto the makeshift helipad, a black hood tied over his head.

Bundled in a thick coat, Dex walked out to meet him. The Dobermans at his side barked and barked at the still-spinning blades. Dex untied the hood from around the man's head and tugged it off.

Even in the faint light, Evan recognized the man.

Tigran Sarkisian.

The Great White Sark.

An international private arms dealer.

In Spitak in 2005, operating as Orphan X, Evan had killed Sark's brothers, his grown son, and six of his cousins.

Sarkisian shrugged off the cold and ambled for the house, accompanied by one of René's *narcos*.

The helicopter lifted off. Through the slits in the steel, Evan watched it coast into the endless blackness to the west. As it grew more distant, the sound of its rotors oddly grew louder, amplified off the walls of the mountain range, coming at him in stereo.

Evan's stomach fell away as he realized that he was no longer listening to the first helicopter.

He swung his head back toward the barn.

There they were, the lights of the next approaching helo. A good distance behind were two more floating dots, one red, one green. And behind that chopper, two more lights, and then two more, and then two more. He let his eyes skim across the incoming flight path, an airborne highway a dozen helicopters deep, each holding someone eager to lay hands on the Nowhere Man.

Alarm cut straight through the fog of the drugs, his mind suddenly alert, his skin prickling.

He remembered the RoamZone on the bed, the live connection, the tendril of a lifeline connecting him to the boy. Running back inside, he snatched up the phone.

'Hello? I'm here. I'm here.'

He stared at the RoamZone, dead in his hand.

The kid had hung up.

48

Some Bizarre Mating Dance

'Our beautiful women were hung naked from crosses, you see, in Der-es-Zor. My mother was child, but she remember. She say they were glorious even in this horror. Proud and naked, long hair blowing like the mermaids.'

The Great White Sark paused to wet his lips. Evan sat on a folding chair inside the Lexan vault in the ballroom. Sark overcrowded a matching chair on the far side of the transparent door. Just two men having a conversation. He looked much worse than when Evan had seen him last, his grizzled stubble the color of frost, pouches hanging beneath his milky eyes. He was an old man now, well into his seventies, but the power contained in his bearlike body was still evident.

'I have reclaimed this atrocity for my own use.' His lips parted, showing pitted yellow teeth. 'The crucifixion. So painful you invented a word for it. Your word "excruciating," it comes from this. "Out of crucifying," it means.'

In his cold metal chair, Evan listened wearily. He had the gnawing sense of having traded roles, of finding himself in a situation befitting one of the people he'd devoted the past six years of his life to rescuing. Now *he* was the one captive and defenseless, ready to be sold to the highest bidder, just like Alison Siegler. The Lexan room was his own version of intermodular Container 78653-B812.

He'd received his visitors one after another, a newlywed outside the church, each potential buyer coming in to peruse the merchandise.

At some early-morning hour, Dex had roused him from bed with an electric shock to the neck and marched him downstairs to the ballroom. Dex had spread his left hand across the sensor panel to unlock the Lexan door, giving Evan a good view of the tattooed bloody scowl, a preview of things to come.

Security measures had changed. Dex now wore a handgun strapped to his wide belt. The other *narcos* had added pistols, too, in addition to their AKs. It was no longer just Evan they had to worry about. René had assembled a collection of the world's most lethal criminal masterminds, and even if he'd had his men strip-search all the buyers and transport them here blind and disoriented, beanbag shotguns were no longer gonna cut it.

'When I buy you,' Sark continued, bringing Evan back to the claustrophobic present, 'I will do this to you. Insert nails here.' He jabbed a too-long fingernail into the underside of his wrist. 'A weak spot between bones of forearm. Nail go in nice and smoothly. Your feet also must be nailed to relieve strain on wrists. This will allow you to hang longer from cross. People, they die from . . .' His hand circled the air, searching out a word. He muttered to himself before snapping his fingers. '*Asphyxiation.* The arms grow tired. The chest and lungs, they overextend. This is when I will add a footrest to help you.'

Pale light sheeted from the high-set windows, giving the ballroom the aura of a cathedral. Dex stood near the dilapidated piano, arms crossed, his shiny dome catching light, his face shadowed.

Xalbador guarded the room's entrance, the Kalashnikov slanted back over his shoulder, one thumb hooked behind a shiny gold rodeo belt buckle.

The four remaining *narcos* had shuttled the buyers back and forth all day, supervising them and giving curt directives, an armed bed-and-breakfast staff. The snipers, Evan figured, were still in the hills, providing just-in-case oversight.

Of the buyers who'd come to threaten him so far, he hadn't seen the party he dreaded most – Charles Van Sciver or one of his Orphan representatives. Not that the guests Evan *was* receiving were pleasant.

'I want to savor every drop of your pain,' Sark continued. 'No dying of shock, no quick-and-easy heart attack. Sepsis is my preference for you. It takes longest time, provides most agony. I want to keep you for *days*. My record is five.' He held up a callused hand, fingers spread, in case Evan needed a visual aid. 'But you are strong. This I remember.' Standing seemed to take Sark some effort, his joints arthritic. He tapped the Lexan between them almost fondly, his mouth splitting in a grin, showing those pitted teeth once again. 'I am hopeful you will do much better.'

Assim al-Hakeem entered the ballroom, the glare from the windows falling across his shoulders, seemingly adding more weight. He limped toward the provided chair outside the Lexan vault, one shoulder permanently shrugged. He'd suffered nerve damage from all the explosions.

In the summer of 2002, Evan had killed Assim's twin sister, triggering the car bomb she was transporting to a Fourth of July parade in Virginia Beach. The early detonation had scattered her and her Dodge Neon across Interstate 264.

Sadly, Assim had not been in the passenger seat. He'd been a busy boy that year, sending a natural-gas truck into a synagogue in Tunisia and engineering a bus bombing in Karachi. American-born, he and his sister moved easily between nations, renting themselves out at exorbitantly high rates. Though ostensibly Muslim, they were not ideologues; they were devoted only to their bank balances. It was rumored that they'd even provided services to the CIA in Colombia.

With great relief Assim lowered himself onto the chair. He licked his chapped lips, showing chipped front teeth.

'Hello, Nowhere Man.'

'Assim. You look tired.'

He sighed. 'All that traumatic brain injury. It's like football. After a while you can't even tell the difference between a hard hit and a concussion. There are lesions in my brain now, they tell me. I don't have many years left. I've got all the money in the world and no time to spend it.' He gave a sheepish laugh, lifted a tremulous finger. 'I have one thing to set right before I die. And I am willing to spend every cent I have amassed to that end.'

'I understand.'

'Do you? Do you understand what you've taken from me?' He leaned forward, elbows on knees, his jittering arms making his shoulders wobble. 'Do you understand what you do?'

'Yes. I do what you do. But for better reasons.'

'I don't think so. Ayisha and I, we were pure. We understood our jobs, our motives. We never wrapped ourselves in dogma or morality or became true believers of one stripe or another. We called it what it was.' He looked weary, so weary. His gaze grew loose, unfocused. 'She was beautiful.'

'Yes,' Evan said. 'She was.'

'I miss her every day. I was with her from conception. We grew together in the womb, two parts of one whole. It's like missing a limb – no, like missing half of my body.' His smile showed off the uneven edge of the broken teeth. 'I hope to teach you what that feels like. Missing half of your body and being alive to know it.'

He rose unsteadily.

Xalbador had to assist him on his way out.

*

The Widow Lakshminarayanan did not bother to sit on the provided chair. Thin and birdlike, she circled the Lexan vault, taking in Evan from every angle. Her sari, a luscious orange trimmed with gold and money green, swept the floor around her invisible feet. She seemed more an apparition than a human. Wiry gray hair framed her small, wrinkled face; though she was in her forties, she looked like a great-grandmother.

She'd aged preternaturally after Evan had dispatched her husband with a cell phone packed with C4. He'd been a counterfeiter and launderer of epic proportion, an equal-opportunity provider who'd cleaned for everyone from Punjabi cartel leaders to Muslim extremists. Despite being a financial and technological genius, Shankar Lakshminarayanan had been a gentle soul who eschewed violence. He left personnel and business disputes to his wife, who displayed no such reservations.

She was said to prefer straight razors.

In the background now, two of René's guards arranged folding chairs in rows on the stretch of hardwood before the Lexan vault, opening them and setting them down briskly. *Snap.* Clang. *Snap.* Clang.

The widow took another turn around the box, and Evan turned with her, keeping her in view. As she circled, he spun, like they were doing some bizarre mating dance.

The guards continued to set up for the coming auction. *Snap.* Clang. *Snap.* Clang. The quality of light had changed in the ballroom, afternoon fading into evening. With the exception of a single midday bathroom break, Evan had been inside these four Lexan walls since waking, breathing his own stale air. René had placed no restrictions on the buyers, and most of them had wanted to take their time with him.

It had been a parade of prior missions, a Dickensian

haunting, a *This Is Your Life* tour of Evan's past. The Nowhere Man, dragged from the shadows and placed on display inside a transparent box – it was his worst nightmare stretched along an exponential curve that grew steeper with every visitor. He'd seen foes from all around the globe. The daughter of a Serbian war criminal. The Fortune 500 father of a serial rapist he'd erased in an early pro bono mission as the Nowhere Man. A Hong Kongese gangster looking to preempt a future visit.

Everyone, it seemed, but the contingent that Evan feared most. Van Sciver and his happy band of repurposed Orphans.

Evan had stopped pivoting with the widow, but he could feel her predatory stare heating his back now, raising the hairs of his neck. Unease overtook him, and he spun on his heel.

She was clasping the wall behind him in a sort of embrace, scarecrow arms spread, bone-thin fingers clutching the Lexan. Her stare bored a hole right through him. Keeping her eyes locked to his, she licked the glass, leaving a smudge. Then licked it again.

At last she turned and walked out, Xalbador rushing to her side to steer her to her room.

Behind Evan the guards finished placing the last of the chairs. *Snap.* Clang. *Snap.* Clang.

He drew in a deep breath, wondering if his day was over at last.

A clopping of footsteps announced René's entrance. His suit, which looked to be a thick wool blend, bulged at the hip. It seemed even the master of the chalet was bearing a handgun beneath all that fine fabric. David hung on his arm, an ornament on display, with an e-cigarette wedged between his index and middle fingers. Evan wondered if they'd been in the parlor entertaining.

'We done?' Evan hadn't spoken in hours, and his voice came out husky.

'Not yet,' René said. 'We have one final party, and they're very eager to see you.'

Clasping his hands, he swiveled to the doorway.

Escorted by Xalbador and his AK-47, Candy McClure entered the room wearing a dark green halter dress, the dagger of the deep-cleavage neckline plunging down between her breasts to her belly button.

Orphan V, back from the dead.

Last he'd seen her, he'd locked her in a closet in the spillage of hydrofluoric acid, a little treat she'd intended for him. He'd heard her pounding on the door and screaming but had been massively outnumbered, busy ducking bullets and trying to get to a not-so-fair maiden in distress.

At Candy's side now was a dead leaf of a man, short and slight, with jaundiced skin and darting flat eyes. No doubt another Orphan.

David vaped off his e-cig, eyeing Candy. 'She is *spectacular*,' he said. 'Isn't she?'

Candy strode across the room on stiletto boots. She confronted Evan through the glass, legs spread, muscular thighs tensed.

She reached for the halter at the base of her neck, untied it, and let the top of the dress fall forward, exposing her torso.

Behind her, David gasped, one hand rising to cover his mouth. At first Evan didn't understand.

Then she turned.

Whorling scars covered her back and shoulders. Evan stared at the ridges and fissures with disbelief. The seam of disfigurement ran nearly perfectly down her sides; she looked like a doll pressed together from two different molds.

She swung back around, giving him her glorious front.

'Hello, X,' she said. 'We've been looking for you a long time.'

49

Flicker of Coldness

Candy moved toward Evan, lifting her arms to retie the halter at the base of her neck.

'I didn't know that happened to you,' Evan said. 'Not like that.'

She must have read something in his face, because he saw a flicker in her eyes, a softness shimmering through the gem-hard surface. But only for an instant.

'I'm not gonna waste time telling you what I'm gonna do to you,' she said. 'When the time comes, I'm just gonna *show* you.'

René said, 'You're that confident you'll win the auction?'

'It's not a matter of confidence,' Candy said. 'It's a matter of fact. Ain't that right, M?'

The sullen little man gave no indication that he'd heard her, but Xalbador read the shift in the air and hoisted his Kalashnikov to a low ready position. Dex moved around the perimeter of the ballroom, sidling into Orphan M's blind spot.

'You see,' Candy said, 'we're the only ones here with *unlimited* money.'

René laughed. He didn't realize that she was being literal, that as the head of the Orphan Program, Van Sciver could access money directly off the U. S. Treasury's printing presses.

'In that case,' René said, 'I wish you the best of luck.'

'Oh, we're not the buyer,' Candy said. 'We're the delivery

service. One of your conditions before we boarded your helicopter was that we leave all electronics behind. But one of our conditions is that you provide me a means to contact my buyer.'

'You're not in a position to set conditions.'

'I am not authorized to bid without providing confirmation for my buyer,' Candy said. 'Believe me. You don't want to leave this much money on the table.'

René pursed his lips. He seemed to be wrestling with himself. 'Dex,' he said at last, 'please bring Ms. V the encrypted satphone.'

'Because your encryption procedures worked out so well last time,' Evan said.

'They did,' René said. 'For me.'

Dex crossed the ballroom and placed a bulky phone in Candy's hand. She winked at him, then dialed. As it rang, she tapped her boot, a smart-ass show of impatience.

Abruptly, her expression hardened. 'Confirmed,' she said.

She listened for a time. Then she moved toward the Lexan door, wiggling the phone at Evan. 'Someone wants to say hi.'

One finger adorned with a metallic nail pressed the speaker button, and then a bizarre combination of voices poured forth. 'Hello, Evan. it SEEMS you have FINALLY dug YOURself a HOLE TOO deep to CLIMB out OF.'

Evan raised his eyebrows, an unspoken question for Candy. She read his face, gave a nod.

When Evan thought of him, he always pictured the burly kid he'd known back at the Pride House Group Home. Now he felt the flicker of coldness that used to move through his chest when, as the smallest boy in the pack, he caught the ruthless focus of Charles Van Sciver.

Evan cleared his throat. 'I'm not buried yet.'

'No. WE will be PAYing for that PRIVILEGE. I believe

V WANTS TO take some TIME with you FIRST. That WILL BE my GIFT to her. For HER devoted SERVICE.'

'It didn't have to go this way,' Evan said.

'IT IS WHAT it IS, and THAT'S ALL that it IS.' Van Sciver's old standby. And also, judging from the dial tone emanating from the phone, his sign-off.

Candy kept her gaze on Evan but held the phone behind her, raised over one shoulder. Orphan M came forward to claim it. He carried it back across to René.

'You'll have tonight to consider your finances,' René said. 'Bidding will begin in the morning.'

'Yeah,' Candy said, turning on one stiletto prong. 'We're not willing to take that risk.'

René's laugh was more like a stutter. 'You don't have a choice.'

Dex stiffened. Xalbador readjusted his grip on the AK.

Orphan M neared René and held out the phone. When René reached for it, M snatched David and spun him around, shoving the uncapped tip of a pen into his neck.

Immediately Xalbador's AK-47 was pressed into Candy's temple. Dex had his handgun drawn – a .45 auto – and aimed at Orphan M, but the little man was barely visible behind David. From the safety of the Lexan vault, Evan watched the standoff.

Calmly, Candy held up her hands, fluttered her fingers. 'Hear me out,' she said. 'I will offer you one hundred million dollars right now. We take him and we're gone.'

René's smile stretched across his tight face. 'Leaving me with a houseful of furious psychopaths.'

David's head was torqued back, his face flushed high at the cheekbones. 'René,' he said, his voice throaty and cramped. 'I want to go home now.'

All of his hipster cool had evaporated, and he looked like what he was: a college-age kid in over his head. The e-cigarette spun on the hardwood at his feet, and Evan couldn't help thinking the kid would never get the chance to graduate to Marlboros.

M's fist flexed, the pen indenting the skin above David's carotid. 'Consider the boy,' he said.

René's face shifted into something like disappointment. 'I have,' he said. He drew the handgun from his hip holster and shot David through the chest.

David's hands pressed over the wound as he slid from M's grasp onto the floor. He stared up at René, mouth wavering while his life poured out between his fingers.

'Dex, please show our high rollers to their room.' René holstered his gun. 'Bidding will begin in the morning,' he said again on his way out.

50

Making His Preparations

Night.

Evan crouched at the side of the bed in the surveillance camera's blind spot, making his preparations. He folded the plastic trash-can liner over itself again and again, forming a one-inch band of polyethylene. This time it would have to fit perfectly beneath the shock collar, hidden from view. He slid it between the contact points of the inner rim and his skin, then used his fingertips to tuck it in. If the slightest edge peeked up into view, his chance would be blown.

And he'd wind up crucified or skinned or razor-bladed to pieces.

And Alison Siegler would be delivered to the man who had purchased her from Hector Contrell like a piece of exercise equipment.

And the boy who'd called Evan would languish in his own private hell, trying the RoamZone again and again. And again and again getting no answer.

Still crouching, Evan retrieved the piano wire from where he'd stashed it beneath the boot insole and crossed to the distressed leather chair that was bolted to the floor.

He removed his socks and used them to wrap his hands, then slid the wire around one of the chair's wooden legs. He coiled either end of the wire around his padded hands and started sawing.

Even through the cotton, the wire bit into his palms, but he kept at it. After about five minutes, he'd made a few centimeters of progress. But it was enough to give him some leverage.

Firming his grip around the wire, he jammed it deep into the tiny notch and yanked down. It took three tries but at last a wedge of wood chipped off the leg.

He stopped to catch his breath and flex his aching hands. His feet were freezing, so he slid his socks back on.

Then he picked up the wedge of wood. Eight inches long, two wide, a few centimeters thick.

With some force he was able to break it in half over his knee.

Now he had two pieces that fit snugly in his fists when he curled his fingers around them.

Handles.

He looped either end of the piano wire around a chunk of wood, twisting it tight, testing it and testing it again until there was no give.

A garrote.

He wrapped it up tightly, slid it into his sock, and pulled down the leg of his jeans to cover the bulge.

Then he pulled the spare pair of high-top hiking boots into his lap, tugged free the laces, and fashioned them into a double-strand noose. This he stuffed in his front pocket on top of the RoamZone.

He'd have one shot at this and one shot only. If a single thing went wrong, he'd spend his last agonizing minutes staring into the face of Charles Van Sciver. But for now there was nothing more he could do.

He dressed for morning and lay back on the bed. He let go of the grueling events of the day, tuned out his fears for tomorrow. There was only the present moment, his body on the soft, soft mattress, the faint sigh of his breath. If this proved to be his last night, then he wanted to enjoy every second.

This time when the gas came, he welcomed it.

51

A Shout into the Abyss

For once it was nice not to pretend. Candy didn't have to act like Ben Jaggers's wife or his whore or his partner in photo-journalism. It was all out in the open. They were two deadly trained operatives, here to reclaim a government asset. And to permanently decommission him.

Unfortunately, she still had to share a room with Jaggers.

In other circumstances it might've been romantic. Crackling fireplace, homey quilts thrown over matching queen beds, snowflakes clinging to the windows – it was like a friggin' Viagra commercial.

She let her dress fall around her stiletto boots and stepped clear of it. Bending over, she unzipped her boots and tugged them off. She put on a pair of silk pajamas, the fabric a salve against her throbbing back.

Not surprisingly, Jaggers didn't bother to turn around. He sat on the bed facing the sliding glass door. From behind he looked frail and weak. His shoulders seemed bird-thin, and there was a slight hunch to his spine. He was the unlikeliest Orphan she'd ever encountered.

'What's your story?' she said.

He still did not turn around. 'What story?'

'How did you get here? Become an Orphan?'

'That information is classified. You know this.'

'No shit. But it's me and you in a snowed-in chalet in the middle of Godknowswhereistan, and we can't fuck because you're lacking the requisite hardware. So I figure a little conversation might help us while away the hours.'

At last he turned, but only enough to give her his profile. That drippy nose, the runny chin. He was a sight. 'If you continue to break protocol,' he said, 'I'll report you to Orphan Y.'

'Van Sciver,' she said, 'has bigger concerns.'

Now Jaggers faced her fully. Sitting on the mattress, he drew his knees to his chest. He looked scrawny, an embryonic vulture. And yet those eyes held his power. Flat and hard like river-smoothed stones, the eyes of a shark gliding effortlessly through the depths in search of prey. Those eyes told the truth, and the truth was that there was no story, no background to make sense of, because men like Ben Jaggers didn't make sense. They just *were*.

'As do we,' he said. 'We can't underestimate this man René. He's impressive.'

'You admire him.'

'I admire what he did in that ballroom, how he took the winning cards right out of our hands. It was an intel failure on our part. We should have known what the man values and does not value.'

'Maybe,' Candy said, 'he valued it all. He just valued some things over others.'

She studied his face, but it was like studying a dinner plate. She thought of him in that alley behind the old Crimean cannery, how when the girl had approached, he'd managed to shape his features into something human, into something requiring neighborly aid. *We could use a hand with the trunk. I think it got warped in the crash.* Candy pictured the girl's one-shouldered shrug. Jaggers's clawlike hand slapped over her mouth, the slim silver pen jabbing at her neck. The wet thrashing against the closed trunk. She'd been beautiful, that girl, and it was a sin to destroy something beautiful.

It struck Candy now that Jaggers had killed her not because it was prudent as he'd claimed but because he resented her beauty. He *envied* it. And he admired René not for the chess move of killing his young friend but for the ruthlessness of the act. To destroy something you cannot be is to embrace your darkest heart, to yield to an ungodly desire. It is to be hijacked by what you aren't rather than nourished by what you are.

Because what you are is nothing.

Van Sciver's mantra played in her head: *It is what it is, and that's all that it is.* She heard it differently this time, not as a hard-boiled directive but as a shout into the abyss. Maybe ultimately that's all they were, her and M and Y, untethered souls, parentless and brotherless, stripped of their humanity, forever echoing in the chasm.

What had she seen in Orphan X's eyes when she'd revealed her mutilated back? Remorse? Whatever it was, it was not what she'd expected. She'd devoted every waking minute to tracking him down, hellbent on staring him in the face. Whatever she'd been hoping for, it certainly hadn't been the glimmer of empathy she'd spied in his eyes. She hated him all the more for it. Didn't she?

Or had she seen in X a reflection of what she herself had felt since her flesh had been defaced? The weakness of human emotion.

Orphan M had said something.

Candy blinked. 'What?'

He glanced at his watch. 'I said it's time to make contact.'

Clearing her throat, she went into the bathroom, where she removed a contact-lens case from her toiletries bag. Leaning close to the mirror, she fingertipped a lens onto her right eyeball.

The contact was a spherical curve of liquid crystal cells that projected high-def images. Invisible to all but the user, the lens created a virtual display several feet from the face.

She fluttered her fingers, the metallic press-on nails catching the dim light. The radio-frequency identification-tagged fingernails allowed her to type in the air without a keyboard.

Before hooding Candy and Jaggers and loading them in the private jet, René's men had searched their luggage compulsively for any communication devices. They had no way of knowing that Candy had been wearing her phone.

She let her gaze loosen to focus on the floating display. It always took some time for the double-blind comms connection to initiate.

The cursor blinked red, red, then finally turned green.

Van Sciver's text scrolled before her face: HAVE YOU SECURED THE ASSET?

She lifted her fingers like a pianist and typed a reply text in thin air: POWER PLAY FAILED. WILL WIN HIM @ AUCTION TOMORROW.

She chewed her lip, waited nervously.

I'M UNWILLING TO TAKE THAT RISK.

OK. She took a deep breath, studied the bathroom walls.

WHERE AM I? DID U BACKTRACE SATPHONE CALL?

REMOTE LOCATION IN MAINE.

Maine didn't make sense given their travel time. To throw off their estimates, René's men must have flown them back and forth in the jet before loading them into the helicopters.

She waited, watched the blinking green cursor.

After a moment another text appeared: WE GOT THROUGH THE CRYPTOGRAPHIC CIPHERS ON HIS SATPHONE, BUT WE ONLY HAD TWO SATELLITES VISIBLE FOR THE GPS

TRILATERATION. WE'RE MAKING TIMING CORRECTIONS NOW, ZEROING IN ON PRECISE COORDINATES.

R U GOING 2 SEND A DRONE?

GETS TRICKY OVER U.S. SOIL.

She typed, WE LIVE 4 TRICKY.

I'M TAKING NO CHANCES, Van Sciver texted.

WHICH MEANS?

BOOTS ON THE GROUND.

She pursed her lips. A physical raid backed by numbers? Van Sciver didn't operate this way. Ever. It would take a different level of coordination, logistics, mission planning. Which meant time.

CAN U GET HERE BY MORNING? she typed.

IF NOT, he texted, YOU'D DAMN WELL BETTER STALL THE AUCTION.

COPY THAT.

THERE IS NO VERSION IN WHICH ORPHAN X EXITS THAT BUILDING UNTIL I ARRIVE. UNDERSTOOD?

She took a breath. UNDERSTOOD.

The cursor went from green to red. She lowered her hands. The display vanished, leaving her looking at her own reflection in the mirror.

Her conscience, long buried and atrophied from lack of use, rolled over from its sleep. She kicked it in the face and put it back down. It had no business being awake for what she was about to do.

52

Some Kind of Advantage

Despite the drugs Evan was awake and alert with the first light of dawn. He lay on his back. Waiting. He sensed the planks compressing in the hall before he heard them creak. Dex could put some serious weight down on a floor.

The dead bolts clanked open, one after another, and the hinges gave a soft complaint as the mahogany door swung inward. Evan rolled over, feigning sleep, his eyelids cracked enough to register Dex's massive shape entering the room.

His cinder-block fist raised the transmitter to aim at Evan, and Evan reacted appropriately, jolting awake, shuddering on the sheets, clawing at his shock collar. It was, he thought, a convincing performance.

He'd had plenty of practice.

Dex led him into the hall where Xalbador waited, less-lethal shotgun in hand.

Not a word was exchanged as Evan headed to the stairs and wound his way down.

Dead man walking.

When they reached the ground floor, Evan caught a whiff of espresso in the air, the distant murmur of chatter. The library was empty, but a few early risers had gathered in the sunroom – the guests being catered to, pampered like Sotheby's VIPs at a pre-auction reception. The Great White Sark held forth by the banquette, swapping war stories with the others. The Widow Lakshminarayanan sipped tea in a corner, sitting ramrod straight. Conversation ceased as Evan passed by, all those sets of eyes lifting to trace his path across the doorway.

Candy McClure and Orphan M were conspicuously absent. Even if Van Sciver chose to deploy Orphans in pairs these days, they were built to operate alone. Old habits were hard to break. It was tough to imagine them chewing biscotti with war criminals and drug lords.

Evan kept on. He sensed Xalbador's shotgun trained at the space between his shoulder blades. Dex kept several paces ahead of him, walking sideways to hold him in view, the pistol dwarfed by his hand. Their three-man procession was coming up on the ballroom now. Evan felt his skin tingle as it did before a mission kicked off. Not fear, no, nor even the stress of anticipation, but an overwhelming sense of his own aliveness. He hated to admit how much he loved this, especially given the horrors he would face if he failed.

His vision sharpened until he could make out the knuckle grooves on Dex's trigger finger. He sensed the cadence of Xalbador's footsteps, the vibrations through the marble floor. Reading the rhythm of the men's movements, he predicted and gauged and prepared.

The makeshift garrote stuffed in his sock pressed coolly into his flesh.

They turned the corner, their boots tapping the hardwood. The rows of empty chairs were set out neatly, as if in anticipation of a wedding service. The Lexan vault waited. They crossed the freshly polished spot on the floor where David had bled out.

Ten more steps.

Evan used the chirp of Xalbador's boots against the floor to measure the man's distance behind him. He slipped a hand into his pocket, digging for his bootlaces, curling his fingers around one side of the improvised noose.

Six more steps.

His muscles tensed. His cells sang. It would come down to instinct, timing, and luck.

Four.

The high-set windows threw Xalbador's shadow forward next to Evan. He flicked his eyes over, reading the dark outline, noting the shotgun's position. Letting his right hand dangle, he gripped his jeans at the thigh and gave a little tug, the pant leg riding up a few inches, putting the garrote within reach.

Dex cast a last glance back at Evan before pivoting, his hand starting to rise to the sensor panel beneath the big steel handle of the Lexan door.

Two steps.

One.

The fine hairs on Dex's arm glistened in the morning light. His big hand spread, that tattooed grimace growing even broader, the blood-dripping canines coming clear. Everything moved in slow motion, as if Evan were again living inside that single drop from René's syringe.

Dex's giant palm touched the panel.

The inset screen flared to life, reading the road map of veins beneath the skin.

MATCH.

The lugs released.

The foot-thick door swung open. Three inches. Six. A foot. Dex's hand was still raised, the flared fingers starting to retract.

Evan yanked the bootlace noose from his pocket. He stepped not for Dex but *past* him, lunging for the widening gap in the door. As he skimmed by Dex's shoulder, he lassoed the still-raised hand. Xalbador shouted, the shotgun aimed, but Evan had already put Dex between himself and the barrel.

Dex wheeled, disoriented by the fact that Evan was fleeing into the Lexan room instead of away from it. Dex was spinning in one direction, Evan in the other. With his free hand, Evan grabbed for the .45.

And missed.

For an instant he tumbled toward the Lexan vault, his left hand gripping the end of the bootlaces, his right flailing.

Then the slack came out of the laces.

The noose cinched around Dex's wrist. His arm snapped straight. Evan held on with everything he had.

His momentum carried him past the razor-sharp edge of the doorway, across the threshold, into the vault. He seized the inside door handle and slammed the bulky door shut as hard as he could.

It hammered Dex above the junction of his wrist, nearly cleaving the arm in two.

Dex's mouth stretched wide, his lips wavering. It was really strange to see a man scream and not make a sound.

Evan put all his weight against the handle, pinning Dex's arm. He'd released the noose, but the knot held, the laces embedded in the flesh at the base of Dex's hand a few inches below the massive wound.

Holding the blood in the veins.

Now he just had to remove the hand.

Keeping his grip on the door handle, Evan ripped the garrote free of his sock. Dex reared back, the weighty door swinging open, then smashing shut again on the hatchet wound of the wrist. His mouth spread in another silent roar, but by then Evan had already looped the piano wire around the arm, sinking it into the deepening gash above the wrist.

Gripping the roughly hewn wooden handles, Evan twisted the garrote. Ligaments snapped. The bones of the wrist started to separate from the base of the ulna and radius. It was grisly, hard-going work.

Evan sensed a blur of movement overhead, found himself

looking up into the barrel of the .45. He jerked his face to the side as Dex pulled the trigger, the percussion so loud that for a moment Evan thought the round had in fact penetrated his head.

But he heard it ping behind him – and then again and again, ricocheting endlessly around the small box. It seemed only a matter of time before the bullet would find him.

Evan was dangling from the garrote's handles, wrenching with all his might, yanking Dex against the door to hold it shut. Dex shoved himself back, trying to widen the gap and position himself for another shot.

And still the round pinged and pinged.

Xalbador gripped Dex around the midsection, fighting a tug-of-war over the mangled arm. Dex jammed the gun through the gap again, and Evan clustered both ends of the garrote in one hand and grabbed for the barrel with the other, forcing the bore to the side of his head.

The gun bucked powerfully – he felt the ache in the bones of his fingers – but didn't fire. He squeezed the slide assembly even tighter, keeping the pistol from cycling. As long as he held on, it wouldn't be able to eject the round it had already fired. Torquing his wrist, he managed to wrench the .45 free of Dex's grip. The pistol skittered across the Lexan floor behind him.

The first shot was still rocketing around the enclosure, whining and cracking off the walls. He felt the air move, the bullet riffling the hair on his head, missing by a whisper.

The world was nothing but the ringing aftermath of a struck bell; his head felt thick and dead, stuffed with rags. Dex reared back again, Xalbador yanking him, the door yawning wide. Evan's fists ached around the wooden handles. His boots slipped on the slick Lexan. Dex and Xalbador were going to rip him right out of the box.

He lost his feet, swinging around on his ass, pulled by the garrote toward the threshold. At the last minute, he threw a boot wide, wedging it against the doorframe, and hurled himself back.

The tendons snapped audibly. Evan toppled backward. The severed hand fell free, slapping the floor.

Dex and Xalbador cartwheeled away, Dex's stump flinging up, trailing crimson mist. Evan heard the bullet zing overhead and then silence – it must've flown out the open door. He scrambled forward, reaching for the metal handle and slamming the thick door.

Dex rolled on the floor, clutching his arm. Xalbador crawled out from beneath him, transmitter in hand, trying in vain to electrify Evan's shock collar.

Holding the door shut, Evan groped behind him for the severed hand. His fingers cupped Dex's. He gathered the hand in and slapped it against the sensor panel. It leaked blood, but the noose had held, still cinched around the base of the hand above the jagged line of the wrist.

The sensor whirred and processed. Had the bootlaces held enough blood in the hand for the sensor to read the vein pattern?

Xalbador was on his feet now.

The screen lit up.

READING.

READING.

In his peripheral vision, Evan sensed bodies pouring through the doorway, backup arriving.

Finally command buttons littered the screen – LOCK, OPEN, DISABLE, RECODE.

Evan thumbed RECODE.

Xalbador lunged for the handle.

Evan spread his own hand on the panel. The screen flashed

green, and the lugs engaged with a clang an instant before Xalbador curled his hands around the handle.

Xalbador tore at the steel bar, his flailing locks spattering sweat across the Lexan. He stopped flailing. His shoulders sank.

He and Evan stared at each other through the transparent door.

Behind Xalbador, Dex rose to his feet and aimed his muted screams at the elaborate chandelier. Bidders and guards sprinted into the ballroom, jostling and shouting and overturning chairs. At the head of the pack, René halted, the sole point of stillness in the room. His face was flushed in streaks along the lines of plastic surgeries past. A cold rage cemented his jaw.

He glared at Evan, locked safely inside the Lexan vault. Removing his transmitter from a pocket inside his suit jacket, he aimed it at Evan and squeezed.

Evan took a step back, picked up the .45, righted the folding chair, and sat.

René squeezed the transmitter again, then hurled it aside. He charged across to the vault and tugged on the handle, his thin hair cascading over his forehead. Then he stopped, sweeping his bangs back into place. 'So you've locked yourself in your own cell.' His voice, filtered through the panel, had a tinny quality. 'You think that gives you some kind of advantage?'

Evan leaned to pick up Dex's severed hand from the floor. The blood-dripping scowl inked on the skin was now augmented with the real thing.

The alligator skin below René's left eye twitched. A squiggle of a vein showed at his temple. 'We still have you trapped.' He coughed out a laugh that was equal parts fury and disbelief. 'How exactly do you see this ending?'

Evan lifted Dex's florid scowl. And placed it over his mouth.

53

Some Delicacies

Confusion and mayhem roiled through the ballroom, catching like a flame. Sark had someone by the lapel – a Somalian warlord? – his drawn-back fist restrained by one of the *narcos*. Dex staggered out leaving a jagged trail of blood, another *narco* at his side. Candy and Orphan M had appeared. They alone looked composed, leaning against the grand piano in the rear of the room, a nightclub act between sets. Candy caught Evan's eye.

And she grinned.

Behind her beautiful teeth, there was hunger.

René gestured frantically for the guards to get everyone under control.

Evan sat calmly on his chair watching the show.

As the commotion built to a crescendo, Xalbador swapped out his less-lethal shotgun for an AK-47. Standing on a chair, he swept the barrel across the crowd. *'¡Cállense!'* he shouted. 'Shut up!'

It took some prodding from the other *narcos*, but at last a version of order had been restored.

'I can sell him, box and all,' René said, addressing the crowd of bidders. 'You can buy him and starve him to death, like a lizard in a jar. Savor every minute.'

'This is not our agreement,' Sark said. 'I want it to be worse than this for him. I want access to his soft flesh.'

The Widow Lakshminarayanan made a throaty sound of agreement. The others voiced their displeasure.

'He has a gun,' the Somalian said.

'He's locked inside a bulletproof box,' René said.

'What if he –'

'If he so much as opens that door, he'll be looking straight down the barrel of an AK-47.'

Evan made eye contact with Candy in the back of the ballroom. Though he couldn't be sure from this distance, it seemed she was enjoying herself almost as much as he was. The clamor grew, and René waded into the group to make assurances.

A debate raged over what to do. No simple solution was forthcoming. Evan had taken René's biggest strength, his ingenuity, and turned it against him.

Lexan is bullet-resistant, impact-resistant, heat-resistant up to 212 degrees and cold-resistant down to 40 below. And that's at normal thickness. The vault walls were a solid foot deep. René had thought he was building Evan a cage.

But he'd made him a suit of armor.

Evan relaxed in his chair. He wouldn't be going anywhere anytime soon. And the customers were growing increasingly displeased.

'– sarin nerve gas through the rear vent,' the Serbian was recommending.

'How does that get him in hand?' Sark said. 'We must hire a crane. Drop this box from a great height and shatter him free.'

The Hong Kong gangster's translator was working overtime to keep his employer in the conversation. '– get the entire unit offshore on one of our crude-oil tankers. We can slide him off into the sea and watch him sink.'

A chorus of protests went up, the argument threatening to explode into violence. At last Assim pulled René aside. They quietly conducted a more serious discussion at the fringe of the chairs.

When they were done, René signaled to Xalbador, who quieted the scrum once again.

'We have a solution,' René said.

Sark's glaucomic eyes found a sudden focus. 'Which is?'

'Breaching the vault,' Assim said.

At this, Candy stepped forward, interested at last. M hung behind her, his eyes level with her shoulder, observing the scene quietly.

'Mr al-Hakeem and I were just discussing the risk of damaging the goods,' René said. 'We'd hate for the overpressure from the charge to pancake the Nowhere Man's vital organs.'

'Yes,' Sark said. 'That would be a shame.'

'Fortunately, I have quite a bit of experience,' Assim said.

'Blowing shit up,' Sark said. 'This is not breaching.'

Assim raised a shaking hand and smoothed his wispy mustache. 'Al-Mansoura, Yemen, 2010. Bucheli, Colombia, 2011. Gombe, Nigeria, 2012. Taji, Iraq, 2013.'

'What are these?'

'Prisons,' Candy said, her grin growing broader. 'Jails. Detention Facilities.' She turned to address the group. 'The good news is that this piece of shit has busted through perimeter walls, cells, and dungeons on three continents.'

'*Four,*' Assim said. 'Edmonton Max Security Institution.' A wan smile. 'Last month.'

René turned, casting his brown gaze at Evan. 'You have to get him out alive.'

'I could blast a sardine out of a tin without snapping a slender little bone. Believe me . . .' Assim smiled, showing his broken front teeth. 'I want him alive more than you do.'

'Do you have explosives on the premises?' Candy asked.

'Dex is being choppered out for medical attention as we

speak,' René said. 'My exceedingly discreet transport team will deliver whatever Mr al-Hakeem requires within a few hours.'

'Take your time.' Candy looked across at Evan and ran her tongue along her lips. 'Some delicacies are worth waiting for.'

WHERE R U?

EN ROUTE WITH THE TEAM. CONFIRMING COORDIN-ATES, BUT WE LOOK TO BE LESS THAN AN HOUR OUT.

VAULT ABOUT 2 B BREACHED. THEN AUCTION WILL COMMENCE.

STALL IT. WIN THE AUCTION. ORPHAN X IS NOT TO LEAVE PREMISES UNTIL I ARRIVE.

HURRY.

The air tasted recycled. Evan tucked the edges of the plastic trash liner into the shock collar, making sure the buffer hadn't slid out of place. He could hear his breaths off the Lexan walls, vibrating his eardrums, an inside-a-snare-drum effect. The folding chair pressed hard and cold into his lower back. The bidders milled about, their focus directed at him in passing, as if he were a fish tank in a crowded lobby. So many of his enemies were right in this very room. And yet they constituted only a fraction of those who wanted him dead.

With some fanfare the explosives arrived at last, a wooden shipping crate stickered with a hazmat logo and carted in by three *narcos*. Assim directed them to place the crate in the back of the ballroom behind the rows of folding chairs. His motor skills might have deteriorated, but at the sight of the explosives he snapped into his body differently, all simmering intensity and curt directives.

Again Candy and Evan locked eyes across the rows of

chairs. She pursed her lips. Let them pop open. A good-bye kiss.

This time Evan actually found himself smiling back.

After assessing the crate, Assim walked over to the Lexan vault and measured the door, a pencil protruding from his lips. He ignored Evan, focused only on the task. Then he walked back to the crate and ordered the men to unload it. They lifted out a spool of hundred-grain detonating cord. Thin plastic tubing packed with pentaerythritol tetranitrate, det cord explodes at four miles a second, giving the effect of simultaneous detonation. A linear precision cutting charge, it can be wrapped around a concrete pylon or contoured to any outline of choice, the best bet in the world of explosives to get that Wile E. Coyote-shaped-hole-in-a-wall effect. It is ideal for rock-carving work, building demolition, dock-pile removal.

But it is best for breaching.

Before Assim was done, it would knock the Lexan door off its hinges and Evan off his feet, leaving him exposed to a firing squad of AK-47s.

The explosives and gunpowder amassed in the ballroom could take out a small militia group.

Evan had a handgun.

To be precise, he had six bullets in a Kimber .45. Given what he was facing, it wasn't much of a weapon.

He heard Jack, perennial teacher and father, laughing at him from beyond the grave. *That Kimber's not your weapon.* You *are the weapon. And your finger's the safety.*

As a child, as an operator in high-threat zones, as an impostor in the ordinary-life world of Castle Heights, he moved alone. For as long as he could remember, loneliness had been his companion. But never had he felt as isolated as he did now, locked in a transparent box, surrounded by people competing for the right to slaughter him.

He wished Jack were here.

Over the years he felt Jack's absence acutely – as loss, as guilt, as remorse. But not like this.

Right now he missed Jack himself. Jack of the baseball-catcher build. Jack of the world-class squint, the well-grooved crow's-feet. Jack who always knew when to not say anything, when to just rest a hand on Evan's boy-skinny shoulder.

Evan had been unwilling to admit to himself what a toll the last week and a half had taken. But now the rawness overtook him, threatening to divert his focus. He snapped himself back into line, reminded himself where he was and what was at stake. He was in a shark cage circled by great whites; the last thing he could afford right now was a stroll down memory lane. Jack was dead. It was up to Evan and Evan alone.

The bidders had settled in to wait not so patiently on the folding chairs, quarreling or sitting sullenly. Candy McClure and Orphan M were the only two not in the room. Evan wondered what plans they were hatching in private. As much for show as for anything else, René kept one dedicated guard standing by the vault door, his AK trained on Evan. Back by the grand piano, Assim was on his knees, cutting precise lengths of det cord off the spool.

A ring of duct tape dangling from his mouth, Assim walked back to the Lexan vault again. With shaking hands he taped a length of det cord along the hinge side of the door. He used smaller strips to augment the main charge. When he was done, he stood back to admire his work.

For a moment he and Evan faced each other through the Lexan.

'Ready to get yanked through the looking glass?' Assim tapped the Lexan. 'We're minutes away.'

Evan felt his heart rate quicken, so he focused on his

breathing. Right now there was nothing to do but inhale and exhale, inhale and exhale.

Heading back down the aisle toward the staging point in the rear of the ballroom, Assim snapped his fingers. Two guards carried over a hefty olive green ammo can. They moved cautiously, setting down the metal box with extreme care. Assim unlatched the lid, smiled down at the contents. It took two men to lift out the initiation assembly. They did so gingerly. It was a factory-assembled unit, fifty feet of wasp yellow nonelectric shock tube wound around a coil, the blasting cap already crimped onto the end. Given that it was shock-sensitive, even a four-foot drop onto the hardwood could set it off.

The non-el shock tube, once unrolled and connected to the det cord, would function like a fuse. From a healthy standoff, Assim would flip a lever, propagating the firing impulse through the shock tube snaking across the ballroom floor to the vault door. A fraction of a second later, Evan would be lying on his back inside the blasted-open Lexan vault, bleeding from his ears.

Sensing that a climax was near, the bidders vacated their chairs, gathering around Assim.

René turned to Xalbador. 'Two of our guests are missing.'

One of the other *narcos* said, 'They're resting in their room until the auction starts.'

'Get them,' René said.

Xalbador nodded and started out.

René turned back to the room. 'Are we ready?'

Assim rose, his legs trembling from the exertion. He'd sweated through his shirt. 'Just have to connect the shock tube to the det cord.'

Sark elbowed his way through the cluster. 'What will you use to initiate?'

A faint whirring sound carried across the rows of empty chairs and then a loud clank. The bidders turned as one.

Evan lowered his palm from the inside panel, the vault door clicking open. He jabbed the door out, knocking the guard onto his ass, then swung it back to use as a shield. He peered from the slender gap, the Kimber .45 pointed.

'I have a suggestion,' he said.

54

Bad Dogs

From there it went fast.

Evan put his first bullet through Assim's shoulder, making the man tumble to the side and clearing the sight line to the initiation assembly.

The toppled guard unleashed the AK at Evan, but the swung-open slab of the door deflected his fire, the rounds whining off the angled Lexan.

René looked from Evan to Assim and back to Evan, his ruddy cheeks lighting with realization. Grabbing the Widow Lakshminarayanan's sari, he flung her in front of the initiation assembly to block Evan's angle.

Evan shot her through the back of the calf. She screeched and balled up as he'd hoped she would. The yellow shock tube and crimped blasting cap peeked into view above the crown of her head.

Evan fired and missed, the bullet blowing out one of the legs of the piano.

From the doorway Xalbador screamed orders at the remaining guards.

René backpedaled in the surging crowd, grabbing Sark's jacket from behind and pivoting them both, putting the man's girth between him and the explosives.

Evan fired at the assembly again, but the volley of bullets from the guard's AK drove the Lexan door into his arm, his shot sailing wide. The guard's flurry was punctuated with a click, the magazine finally run dry.

Over by the doorway, Xalbador picked up the slack, firing haphazardly. His rounds sprayed the Lexan wall, but Evan tuned him out.

He aimed the .45.

Two bullets left.

The bidders stampeded for the exits, bodies and kicked-over chairs flickering across his field of vision. The blasting cap strobed in and out of view.

Even in the mayhem, he found an inner calm. Inhale. Exhale. Wait for the space between heartbeats.

He let a final cool breath pass through his teeth.

With steady, even pressure, he pulled the trigger.

The bullet struck the cap at its union with the shock tube. The first explosion was instantaneous, the shock wave lifting Assim and the widow off the floor, their limbs spread, heads corkscrewing on broken necks.

Evan withdrew behind the door into the vault, rushing to swing the hefty door shut after him. He wasn't worried about the initial explosion. He was worried about what was coming.

The assembly was close enough to the giant spool of det cord to propogate into a bigger boom.

He didn't have to look up to know when it happened. The air told him. The molecules seemed to still as if drawing their breath, the stunned nanosecond of calm before the hurricane.

And then everything let go.

The blast hammered the vault door the remaining inches into the frame with enough force to knock Evan across the inside of the vault. He bowling-balled through the folding chair and racked up against the rear wall.

Bright orange flame lit the world around him – it was as though he'd flown into the sun. Heat pulsed through the Lexan walls, the ceiling, even the floor. He couldn't see anything, and for a moment he worried that he'd underestimated the charge, that he was going to bring the whole goddamned chalet down on top of him.

But a fresh wind suctioned off the flames and black smoke from all around him, the vault emerging from its sheath of fire. As the air started to clear, he looked up to see the massive chandelier plummeting down at him. By instinct he covered his head. The chandelier shattered across the transparent roof into a million brilliant pieces, each facet lit with a yellow lick of flame.

Bits of crystal tinkled across the hardwood. Bodies twitched. The entire rear wall of the chalet had blown out. Snow drifted in, swirling among the ash, settling across the piano and the corpses – a wartime tableau.

His ears didn't ring so much as scream. His head hummed.

The vault door had wobbled open again. Sprawled on his ass inside the Lexan box, Evan blinked, trying to draw the ballroom into full focus. The scene was biblical.

They lay dead. All of them. The chairs had slid to the walls, many of them still upright. Through the gaping hole where the wall had been, Evan heard the Dobermans somewhere outside, barking and barking, notes of terror mingled with their snarls.

With a groan he found his feet and lumbered out of the Lexan vault.

The air carried the scent of sap and snow and burned flesh. Across the ballroom Sark's charred body lay sprawled in a heap of others against the wall, his face and chest missing as if scooped out. He'd almost made it to the kitchen.

Impossibly, he wiggled.

Evan stared with incredulity. Sark heaved upward, and for a moment Evan thought he was going to sit up stiffly, a B-movie vampire rising from his coffin. But then René squirmed out from beneath the wrecked corpse. He staggered a few steps and leaned heavily against the wall.

Ash painted his forehead, and his cheeks looked raw. Evan stepped forward and raised the .45, and René swung his head heavily to face him.

The two men stared at each other across the churning air of the ballroom.

René lifted a hand, fingers splayed. 'Let's –'

Evan shot him in the chest.

René slammed against the wall. Something fell from his pocket, bouncing over the jumbled bodies before coming to rest on the floor.

A vial filled with a familiar viscous clear fluid.

René let out a cry, his fingers clutching his rib cage. Muted sobs shuddered his shoulders.

Then he straightened up. His hands fell away. In his palm a flattened slug.

Evan's head swam with impossibilities – René's vampiric experiments had made him *bulletproof*? But then logic kicked in. Images assembled slowly in his mind, the way René's jacket never wrinkled, how the fabric seemed to buckle rather than fold.

The *suit* was bulletproof.

Over the years Evan had heard of civilian clothing built with the same carbon nanotubes used in flexible body armor. And now he'd wasted his last bullet firing into an impenetrable navy plaid coat.

René coughed, doubling over and clutching his ribs. He glanced at the vast opening blown through the rear wall a few feet away. Grimacing, he forced himself upright.

Evan cast aside the empty Kimber and advanced on him.

Still holding his ribs, René hobbled for the hole.

Evan had only taken his first step when he heard

movement behind him. Xalbador stumbled through the rear doorway; the explosion had blasted him right across the threshold into the hall. He looked ragged, dragging one foot. Blood crusted his earlobes, and he was making unintelligible noises. The Kalashnikov dangled around his shoulder from its strap.

With an injured arm, he tried to tug the AK up to aim at Evan. The barrel lifted a few inches, firing into the floor past the tips of Xalbador's boots. He struggled to support the gun with his other hand, to raise it higher and bring Evan into the sights.

Evan halted in the middle of the ballroom, Xalbador behind him, René ahead. Xalbador managed to heft the gun closer to horizontal. The next burst chewed up the floorboards midway between him and Evan. The recoil knocked the AK from Xalbador's hands. He clawed at it, drawing it up again from the strap.

Instinct surged in Evan to go for René. But if he did, he'd be leaving himself exposed, and Xalbador looked to be seconds away from steadying the AK.

Wheezing, René reached the edge of the crumbled wall. He cast a panicked look back at Evan and then slipped outside.

Evan turned and ran for Xalbador. Sweat greased the *narco*'s face. Biting his lower lip, Xalbador struggled to fight the gun back into position. His damaged arms couldn't sustain the weight. As Evan closed in, the muzzle came up crooked, firing wildly to the side.

Evan kicked the gun free. Xalbador charged him, coming over the top of him, beating at his back with bony elbows. Evan held him low around the waist in a football tackle, Xalbador's big gold belt buckle grinding his cheek. Gathering his legs beneath him, Evan unhooked the belt and reared back. He kicked Xalbador's hip while tearing at the buckle, spinning the guard into an off-kilter 180, a string-pull top being launched.

Before Xalbador could reorient himself, Evan whipped the rodeo belt buckle at his face, clipping his chin. As Xalbador reeled back, Evan threaded the belt through the buckle, slung the makeshift noose over his head, and ripped him off his feet. Xalbador got a hand beneath the band of leather, his legs churning for traction.

Evan shot a glance at the blown-out back wall, his apprehension mounting. How many steps had René taken toward freedom by now? Twenty? Thirty?

Xalbador jackhammered himself back into Evan, and they tripped over a protruding floorboard, sprawling in opposite directions. Xalbador flung the belt off from around his head, but already Evan was on him, arm drawn back for the kill blow.

Electricity sparked at Evan's neck, the charge knocking him off Xalbador. He convulsed on the floor, fresh-fallen snow icing his cheek. Twitching, he clawed at the shock collar.

Xalbador sat up, aiming the transmitter at Evan, his finger depressing the button.

When the explosion had thrown Evan across the vault, the bunched trash liner must have pulled free from beneath one of the contact points. Pain radiated, grinding through his collarbones, his ribs, the base of his skull. He forced himself to focus through the static dancing across his eyes, willing his body to move. A moment later his legs listened, scissor-kicking him into a spin on the floor, one boot weakly striking Xalbador's arm. It was enough to dislodge the transmitter from Xalbador's grip.

The jolt in Evan's neck subsided. Snowflakes blew across his face, no salve for the burn circling his throat. Somewhere through the clouds of dust and ash, he registered the dogs' barks. They sounded louder.

Louder was not good.

Evan shoved himself onto all fours, crawling toward the AK-47, his knees and hands skidding on the snow-slick floorboards. Behind him he sensed Xalbador rising, stumbling the opposite way after the fallen transmitter. Evan pulled himself forward with one hand, using the other to try to stuff the trash liner back into place. He had to put Xalbador down and get after René.

Evan got one hand on the AK when the shock hit. The pain was blinding, blurring his vision. He rolled onto his back, dragging the gun across his chest.

Xalbador strode toward him, pointing the transmitter. The first shock electrocuted Evan's fingers, knocking his hand off the collar. The stinging intensified, lancing through his gums, searing his eye sockets. Evan dug deep through the pain, trying to get his brain to speak to his hands and make them obey.

He got them to clamp the gun. He could feel his mouth stretched Joker wide. His grip trembled, jogging the AK back and forth. Sweat drenched his face. Electricity crackled through his neck, a drumroll of needle points.

But he didn't let go.

Xalbador quickened his step, rushing for Evan.

Across the ballroom the Dobermans spilled through the wreckage of the outer wall, sleek shadows coated with snow. Their heads oriented toward Evan, noses twitching, bat ears spiked.

Evan told his hands to firm the weapon. He told his arms to raise it. The tip of the AK wagged back and forth. He willed it another inch upward as Xalbador neared.

The dogs' claws scrabbled across the wet floor.

Pain filled Evan's head, turning the air opaque. He tried to see through the soup, tried to aim at Xalbador's growing shape. His hands vibrated around the stock, the trigger.

Xalbador yelled, leaping for Evan.

Evan lanced bullets up his chest and tore the carotid right out of his neck. Xalbador landed in a heap at Evan's feet, the transmitter skidding across the floor.

The circle of flame around Evan's neck relented.

He hauled in a screeching breath, tasting oxygen for the first time in what seemed like days.

The Dobermans surged across the bodies toward Evan. For a second he considered shooting them so he could rush after René, but they were dogs and even bad dogs deserved the benefit of the doubt.

He dropped the AK, lunged for the transmitter. One of the Dobermans latched on to the cuff of his jeans, whipping his head back and forth. Evan kicked at him, twisting to grab the transmitter. The second dog landed on his chest. Evan barely had time to get an arm under the slender chin. Jaws snapped inches from his face, flecks of saliva spattering him. Even through the icy draft, he felt the heat of the dog's breath. The first dog tore at his cuff, rattling the heel of his boot against the floor.

The fangs brushed Evan's cheek. Holding off the jaws, he thumbed buttons on the transmitter blindly. At last he hit the red one, the shock collar unlatching from around his neck and sliding onto his chest.

Mustering what strength he could, he hurled the dog off. Snatching the open shock collar at the hinge, he wielded it like a weapon, the contact points aimed outward. The dog gathered himself and leapt. Evan jammed the collar into the dog's open mouth and hit the shock button on the transmitter.

The dog twisted in midair, a fish breaking water, its yelp carrying up to the high ceiling and bouncing down again. His paws barely touched the hardwood before he bolted out of the ballroom, galloping for the safety of the hall. Leaning forward, Evan jabbed the live collar to the top of the other dog's head, and the dog shot backward, releasing Evan's cuff.

He considered Evan for a moment, teeth bared, head cocked, so Evan leaned forward and shocked him again. The dog bayed his confusion and took off, following the fresh paw prints out of the ballroom.

Evan sat there for a moment, his elbows resting on his knees.

He allowed himself two breaths.

But there were still snipers in the hills, a guard in the watchtower, Candy McClure and Orphan M loose somewhere in the building, and René making his getaway.

Evan stood up.

He grabbed the AK first. One of the dead guards had a nice thick jacket, which Evan appropriated, along with the full magazine from his gun. Trudging over to the jumble of corpses by the kitchen, he plucked up the vial that had fallen from René's coat and regarded it in the light streaming through the back of the house.

Somewhere a helicopter started up, the sound of chopping rotors riding the breeze.

Pocketing the vial and readying the Kalashnikov, Evan stumbled through the demolished rear wall into the bracing winter day.

55

Almost There

BIG EXPLOSION AND FIREFIGHT DOWNSTAIRS.

HOLD HIM.

SOUNDS LIKE FALLUJAH DOWN THERE. WE HAVE NO WEAPONS.

GET SOME. PIN HIM DOWN.

COPY THAT. NEED BACKUP ASAP.

I'M BRINGING ALL THE BACKUP YOU'LL NEED.

ETA?

ALMOST THERE.

R WE CLEARED FOR KILL IF NECESSARY?

There was a pause, the longest pause Candy could remember Van Sciver ever taking. At last his text appeared.

YES.

The helicopter had lifted off by the time Evan ran around the corner of the chalet. On aggressive tilt, it forged into the eddies of snow. He aimed the AK, but the body of the helo had already vanished into the white, its lights out of reach. Panting, he watched until they, too, disappeared.

The guard in the watchtower was leaning over the railing, gazing at the wake of the helicopter through the scope of the rifle. Evan jogged up from the side, shouldering into the wooden supports, and fired directly up. The snow blunted his view, but he heard the wet thump of impact, and a moment later the rifle plummeted down from the heavens, lodging in the snowbank in front of him.

No dogs, no guards, no doctor, no David, no Dex.

Just two snipers in the hills.

And two Orphans in the house.

Evan stepped forward, snatched up the gun, and examined his haul.

An AR-10 in 7.62, clearly a designated marksman rifle. Evan could get almost seven hundred meters from it, but, given the snow, five hundred would be pushing it.

Not that he was complaining about the snow. Right now it was protecting him from the dedicated sniper rifles in the mountains; with a range up to fifteen hundred meters, they'd have a massive advantage once the air cleared.

Which it looked to be doing right now, the billows lessening in intensity, the snowfall growing more sparse by the minute.

A movement at the front door of the chalet hooked his attention – Candy and Orphan M spilling into view on the porch. Their heads tilted up, locking on Evan. They regarded one another across the distance.

He'd have no time to set up a shot on the rifle. They were beyond effective firing range of the AK-47, but Evan lifted it and gave them a greeting anyway. The rounds pulverized the stone porch, driving them back inside.

They'd have to regroup, scavenge weapons from the wreckage of the ballroom.

He'd better use the head start well.

Slinging the AR-10 over a shoulder, he jammed a new mag into the AK and bolted for the tree cover of the south slope. The snow thinned before his eyes, the gleam of the afternoon sun cutting through the haze.

At that instant something lasered into the ground a few feet from his boots, the spray peppering the right side of his body. A moment later a supersonic crack announced the shot.

Evan cut sharply. With a quick glance, he registered a glint of reflected light past the bulge two-thirds up the mountain, a fine long-distance overwatch position. The sound of another shot rolled across the valley, but he'd heard no impact, the round having sailed wider than the previous one. He dove over a fallen log, skidding into the safe embrace of the densely packed tree trunks, and sat, panting. He gave a moment of thanks for the south sniper's mediocrity; the north sniper would've tunneled a hole through Evan's rib cage.

He stood up, took stock of the weapons, and sprinted into the pines. He had to take out the south sniper and get over the brink before nightfall. Candy and M would be on his heels soon enough.

Rather than cut directly upslope as the sniper might anticipate, he sliced horizontally around the base of the woods to pop out on the far side of the bulge. It was slow going, his boots sinking into the snow, but he managed to hold a steady pace.

When he reached a ravine, he held several paces back from the last row of trees. Keeping to the shadows, he scanned the mountainside through the AR-10's scope. Greens and browns streaked together, and then he scanned past a spot of flesh.

He rotated the scope back.

Sure enough, the sniper was taking a position higher on the bulge, angling down onto the patch of pines directly up from where he'd last spotted Evan. The sniper crawled over an outcrop, at one point rising to full height.

The average man is one meter from crown to crotch, a useful measurement for optically determining distance to target. To gauge the sniper's position, Evan fitted him between the horizontal lines of the stadia. Five hundred meters out. The man pushed on upslope, diminishing another notch. Five twenty-five.

Evan consulted the range card taped to the butt stock. The laminated square of paper noted the specific ballistics for the hand load of the rifle. How much the bullet dropped per hundred yards. Range solutions. The exterior trajectory of the projectile.

Bracing the rifle on a flat patch of shale, he dialed an elevation into the scope to correct the aim for the ballistic arc at 525 meters. When he focused again, the sniper was gone.

Closing his right eye, Evan pressed his left to the rubber cup and sighted on a thicket of trees next to the outcrop.

Nothing. The guy had vanished.

A whip-poor-will called from the treetops, the agitated warble scoring Evan's mounting uneasiness.

He'd set up for an ambush. Not a firefight. Under close scrutiny he'd be visible through the patchwork of branches and leaves. But if he repositioned now, his movement could draw the sniper's eye.

The sniper had been focused eastward; he had no reason to search in Evan's direction. Unless something else had grabbed his focus. Something that had made him seek cover from anyone along the very sight line on which Evan had situated himself.

Very slowly, Evan shifted from his belly onto his side and peered down through the woods to the valley floor. Way below, a few slivers of the chalet were visible between the trunks. Something darted across one of the slim gaps, trailing blond hair.

Candy McClure. A moment later there was a second flash, lower to the ground.

The Orphans had drawn the sniper's attention. The shooter had reoriented to face this way.

Which meant that he was facing Evan.

Evan's stomach clenched. Rolling back into position, he placed his eye on the scope in time to see a muzzle flare between two of the tree trunks in the thicket. An instant later the shale at his side kicked up, rocks embedding in the trunks behind him forcefully enough to sway the tips of the pines overhead.

Twelve inches to the left and he'd be missing an arm. He had to squeeze off a shot fast before the sniper got off a second round.

Evan zeroed in on the afterglow of that muzzle flare in the shadows of the thicket. He aimed a hair to the right on the assumption that the sniper was right-handed and lying on the left side of the rifle.

He pulled the trigger.

He never saw the impact, but a pink haze drifted out from the darkness between the trunks.

Evan hopped to his feet and charged upslope.

The shots had announced his presence to Candy and M — and, worse, to the north sniper, who had proved himself to be a serious shooter. Evan had to get to the south sniper's rifle if he hoped to go head-to-head with him.

He figured the north sniper was already on the move, circling the rim of the valley, crashing through the woods to get within range. And Candy and M were no doubt moving up the mountain at him from below.

Driving up the incline, Evan pistoned between rocks, skimmed through trees, ignoring the pain that was firing the muscles of his legs. His bobbing torso felt exposed, hung out like a paper target. Wind whipped his ears, a whoosh to match the adrenaline surge in his veins. Every step seemed to take an eternity. And yet he hadn't drawn fire.

The outcrop loomed ahead. For a time it seemed his legs

were churning uselessly, bringing him no closer. At last the stone came within reach. Bracing for a bullet to the back, he hurled himself over the stone, rolling into the thicket of pines. He expected hard ground but landed on something soft and yielding.

The body of the south sniper.

Evan's shot had squarely hit the mark. It occurred to him that he'd never seen the sniper's face. And never would.

He rolled the body away from the big gun. A Sako TRG-42 in .338 Lapua Mag. A professional-grade platform, still set up for a shot. Evan swung into place next to it.

The crosshairs perfectly marked the spot on the shale where he'd been moments before. Tilting the gun downslope, he scanned across the treetops. Flickering in and out of cover, Candy charged up the mountain, Orphan M at her heels. They'd harvested AKs from the ballroom bloodbath.

Two quick shots and it would be down to Evan and the north sniper, squaring off in the snowy bowl of the valley.

Snugging his cheek to the stock, Evan led Candy slightly, the crosshairs marking the air inches in front of her face. She vanished behind a dense copse of pines, but he kept the rifle on its trajectory, timing her progress, waiting for a break in the trees.

It came, and he was ready for it.

Candy reared into the scope. His finger tightened on the trigger. The crosshairs found their mark.

An instant before he could fire, the air exploded around him. He heard the meaty smack beneath his ear, felt a wrecking ball strike his shoulder, and then all he saw were pine needles and branches blurring by. The earth rushed up to greet him. Dirt in his mouth. Splinters in his cheek. Ice in his ear.

And his own blood puddling on the ground beneath him.

56

Mostly Certain

He was alive. Of that he was mostly certain.

His body was shocked into paralysis. But he could move his eyes. He strained them, trying to piece together what had happened.

If he'd taken a .30-cal to the shoulder, he'd be dead or missing the limb. His hand lay in view in front of his eyes. He believed it was still attached to his body. The fingers were smooth and pale, slightly curled. Concentrating with everything he had, he made them twitch.

Okay, then. Still attached.

His pupils moved to the Lapua and then to the tree beside it. A football-size bite had been taken clean out of the trunk, the raw inner wood exposed. Bits of bark swirled in the air, ignoring gravity.

The north sniper had missed him by inches, the round sending a hunk of tree shrapnel smashing through Evan's shoulder.

Evan realized, almost secondarily, that he wasn't breathing. His throat felt snarled, the airway knotted. His stomach lurched a few times as if in anticipation of puking, and then his rib cage released and he drew in oxygen, a primordial sucking sound as though someone had punched holes straight through his lungs. For a time he gasped into the pine needles.

Blood spread out beneath him, sticky on his neck. The warmth reached his cheek. If he didn't stanch the bleeding – and fast – then this off-kilter view of the forest floor would be his final screen grab before he powered down.

Somehow he sat up, though he might have blacked out once or twice doing it. He found himself gaping down at his torn coat and the ball of his right shoulder, a scramble of pink flesh and shredded muscle. Shards of his clavicle glittered in the wreckage. Bright blood pumped through the wound at intervals, pushing rivulets down his arm and into the matted fabric. When the collarbone shattered, it must have lacerated the subclavian vein, causing a massive hemorrhage.

The damage was too close to his neck to tourniquet.

A wave of light-headedness passed through him, bringing with it the image of –

– *arterial blood soaking the shoulder of the blue flannel. Jack's hand, already wearing a glove of crimson, clamps the wound.*

Evan blinked his way back to the present, lifted his left hand, and clamped it over the wound.

He forced breath into his lungs, tried to wrestle his thoughts into place through the swamp of sensations engulfing him. He'd been trained for this, to strategize under extreme stress and pain, to shield the pilot light and keep it from being snuffed out.

Candy and Orphan M were still a good ways downslope with plenty of steep terrain to make up. Since he held high ground, they'd have to move slowly, cautiously. But the north sniper could be anywhere. And he knew precisely where Evan was.

'Draw back from the tree line.' He'd spoken the command, it seemed, rather than thinking it. It was the only way he could make his limbs move.

He scuttled backward, shoving with his heels, before realizing he wasn't standing up.

Rising without using his arms was difficult, but he managed. He withdrew into the thicket, nearly tripping over his boots. Both rifles were back in the clearing along with the AK, but he couldn't possibly operate them anyway. Blood snaked down his right arm, dripped from his fingertips.

The pain tasted of –

– *wet concrete, the humid air of Parking Level 3 pressing into his pores, the elevator lights casting a red glow and –*

– he fastened his left hand tighter over the wound, breathing –

– *the all-too-familiar tang of iron, the sickly sweet trace of cherry blossom, which –*

– he swore he smelled, but he knew he was here in a snow-layered valley in Maine, stumbling upslope and trying to tamp the blood back into his body. He wondered if it was possible to be in two places at once. Maybe that was what dying was, pulling up the net of time, events and places jumbling together and –

– *Jack is clutching his bloody shoulder –*

– as Evan was clutching his and –

– *Jack says, 'I'm already dead. It caught the brachial.'*

'You don't know that. You don't –'

'I know that.' He lifts a callused hand, lays it against Evan's cheek, perhaps for the first time ever.

Evan tripped, his knee plowing into a drift. He wobbled for a moment, leaning into the rise. The spill – so bright against the snow, a robin's red, red breast.

Shoving himself vertical again took several phases. His feet moved, somehow carrying him onward, upward. He pinballed off trees. They proliferated, an endless span of trunks splitting the earth like the bars of a cell.

At last he sensed an openness ahead, the woods giving over to a bare patch of blinding white. Through the last trees ahead, a stretch of uneven powder swept up to the summit fifteen or so meters above.

He had to make it.

The snow sucked at his boots. He yanked them free, fighting for balance. He would not go down. His teeth chattered. He couldn't feel his arm.

It occurred to him that he was going to die. And yet all he could see was the –

– paroxysm of pain racking Jack's body. Jack fights out the words. 'Listen to me. This is not your fault. I made the decision to meet you. I did. Go. Leave me. Go.'

Evan thinks he is choking, but then he feels the wet on his cheeks and realizes what is happening to his face. 'No,' he says. 'I won't go. I won't –'

Jack's good hand drops to his belt, and there is a clank, and then his service pistol is up between them. He aims it at Evan. 'Go.'

'You wouldn't.'

Jack's gaze is steady, focused. 'Have I ever lied to you?'

Evan stands up, stumbles back a step. It dawns on him that Jack's flannel shirt is still mopped around his hand. His fist tightens around it, moisture spreading between his fingers. Somewhere above them in the structure, tires screech. Boots pound concrete.

'Son,' Jack says gently. 'It's time to go.' He rotates the barrel beneath his own chin.

Backing up, Evan arms the tears from his face. He takes another step back, and another, and then finally he turns.

Running away, he hears the gunshot.

Jack's words echo in his head. It's time to go. It's –

– time to go.

'Goddamn it,' Evan said. 'Damn it. Damn it. Stupid fucking way to die.'

The blood-crusted fingers of his left hand had gone numb, making it harder to hold the seal on the slick flesh of his shoulder. He lost his center of gravity, tilting into a soft white bank. He tried to right himself, but the snow gave way beneath his weight, delivering him gently to the ground. His hand was too weak to hold back the blood anymore. The warm current trickled through his fingers. He breathed into the cold earth. Blinked ice crystals off his eyelashes.

Since Jack he had let no one into his life, and so there would be no one to miss him.

'Stupid,' he said.

He felt himself fading away, the Nowhere Man blurring into the whiteness. A lifetime spent blending in, leaving no traces. Which also meant leaving no mark. He'd built his armor, ring by ring, but now he felt himself crushed under the weight of it, sinking into oblivion. So this was how it would end? The proverbial whimper?

His entire body was shuddering. A more intense vibration near his hip differentiated itself, and it took him a moment to identify it.

The RoamZone.

The kid.

The ringing phone called his thoughts to Alison Siegler as well. It occurred to him that when he died, instead of the customary tunnel of light, he was going to see the *Horizon Express* steaming relentlessly for the Jacksonville Port Authority.

Evan squeezed his eyes shut.

Son. It's time to go.

He released his shoulder, the blood flowing freely now, and dug for the phone in his pocket. He lifted the battered RoamZone to his face. His hand, a uniform crimson. His knuckles, tacky against his cheek.

He thought of how he usually answered the phone – *Do you need my help?* – and wanted to laugh.

He said, 'I . . . I can't . . .'

The boy's voice, hushed and fierce. 'You forgot.'

'No. I didn't. I just can't . . .' A wave of pain swept away Evan's breath. He grimaced, bit his lip, waited for it to pass. 'I can't help you, okay? Can't . . . help you.' The ground tilted around him, a roller-coaster loop through space and time, and he was talking to the kid and to Alison Siegler, to Jack on the floor of Parking Level 3 and to himself, trapped hopelessly in a valley fifteen meters from the summit.

'I can't . . . help any of you . . . anymore . . .'

It's time to go.

Every breath brought pain. Evan said, 'There'll be . . . someone else . . .'

'No.' The boy's words faded in and out of static. 'It *has* to be you.'

Evan felt himself seeping into the cold ground.

Some long-buried part inside him split open, a flood of emotion sweeping him down, down, plunging him into deep, freezing waters. A tear cut through the snowflakes, crusting his cheek, a single warm track across his skin and –

– a straw-thin spray squirts between Jack's fingers –

– he was crying but felt something instead of sadness, something like liberation.

Time to go.

'. . . sorry,' he said. 'I'm sorry . . .'

The phone died. Evan tilted it to see the screen, his hand trembling violently. No bars left.

'. . . sorry,' he told the ground. 'I'm sorry . . .'

Go. Leave me. Go.

'Okay, Jack,' he said. 'Okay.'

He breathed wetly for a moment. Stared between the last tree trunks at that bare patch of earth just within reach ahead. The setting sun caught the rise of powder in all its creamy glory. Fifteen meters to the peak. He deserved at least that.

'I want to make it,' he told himself hoarsely. 'I want to see the top.'

He shoved the phone into his jacket pocket – this piece of the kid he would not let go of – and placed his hand back over his shoulder. His grip was still loose, so he used his chin to pin his hand more tightly over the wound. Somehow he wiggled to his knees. Leaning into a pine, he found his feet.

His first step broke him through the tree line. The sudden openness made his breath catch. The pain ebbed, draining out of him. As he forged up the unmarred blanket of white, the world came into vivid focus. The saw-toothed edges of snowflakes. The violet spill of the sunset through puffy clouds. The air, so fresh it stung his throat, telling him that right now, in this moment, he was still alive.

A golden glow limned the mountaintop. His last steps would carry him there.

At once the horizon seemed to bubble up in one spot, the bulge taking shape as a human form – someone coming over the peak from the far side. The figure stood atop the crest, backlit. Evan squinted into the light, noted the silhouette of the rifle held across the man's chest.

A .338 Lapua Mag.

The north sniper.

You deserve it, Evan told him, though the words didn't make it out. *You were better.*

He could no longer feel his legs. Now that he'd halted, he wouldn't be able to start up again. He stared wistfully at the apex just a few strides away.

His blistered lips moved. 'At least I tried,' he said.

The sniper's features were cloaked in black. He raised the rifle.

Evan felt a deep thrumming in his bones and the blissful release of having no options left.

He could stop fighting.

The scope glinted in the day's dying light, and Evan sensed the crack of a shot.

He pitched forward, holding his eyes on the brim of the valley. He wanted his last view to be of the summit.

The thrumming turned to thunder, the beating of giant wings. The sniper was jerking around as if yanked by strings, laced through with bullets. A strange calm descended over Evan as he grasped what this was: a dying fantasy played out in his mind's eye.

Well, then he might as well enjoy it.

The thunder took on a rhythm, the whomping of some great beast. And then a Black Hawk broke majestically over the wall of the valley, sunlight gleaming off the blades. A door gunner leaned out over the skid, peering down over a machine gun, assessing his work.

Jack.

Of course. What better than Jack Johns as Evan's archangel and a Black Hawk to bear him into the sweet hereafter?

The machine gun unleashed overhead, razing the pines behind Evan, and he understood that Imaginary Jack was protecting him, driving Candy McClure and Orphan M back into the woods, pushing them downslope and away.

Evan was safe now. He was beyond harm.

The helo set down, the rotor wash ruffling Evan's hair, his clothes. He smiled into the fever dream.

Jack hopped down and tromped over to Evan, the sun winking into sight behind his head. He'd aged. He'd be in his seventies by now but looked a hale sixty.

Evan knew that he was beyond a dying fantasy, that he was dead and gone, riding the last random neuron firings through his expired brain.

Two more men leapt from the Black Hawk and jogged

over, a stretcher bouncing between them. Jack shouted over his shoulder, 'Get him out of here!'

The men sped up, wading through the snow.

Jack set his hands on his knees and grimaced down at Evan. 'What are you doing lying there?'

'. . . dying.'

Jack's face warred between concern and anger. 'You gave that asshole a wide-open shot. Where's your gun?'

'. . . back in woods . . . couldn't fire anymore . . . right arm . . . no good . . .'

Jack's square head snapped down, assessing Evan. 'Nothing wrong with the left one,' he said.

Evan peered up at the brilliant violet sky, grinning.

Jack. That was Jack.

The medics finally arrived, bulled Jack aside, and swept Evan up. They jostled him back toward the Black Hawk on the stretcher, Jack jogging alongside them. Evan caught an upward view of Jack and could see that concern was winning out now.

As they loaded Evan into the chopper, the RoamZone fell out of Evan's coat pocket. He twisted and grabbed for it, crying out, but the noise of the rotors swept away his words.

'What?' Jack shouted. 'What's wrong?'

They slid Evan into the belly of the Black Hawk. He kicked and reached. Jack followed him in, the shattered phone in his hand. 'This? You want *this*?'

Evan nodded.

Jack looked from the busted casing and shattered screen to Evan, his forehead furrowed. 'Okay.'

Evan grabbed the phone, squeezed it tight. A needle pricked his arm. His stomach swooned as they lifted up. The cold, cold air breezed through the open door.

Jack was shouting into a headset: '– blood units ready,

throw the saline in the freezer, and get a trauma surgeon there. *Now.*'

They banked high above the valley, and Evan peered down at the dollhouse of the chalet, spirals of smoke still rising from the blown-out wall.

Jack: 'I don't care how hard it is. You don't get me someone in time, I will land this helo on your skull. Understand?'

Movement below caught Evan's eye. A caravan of black SUVs blazed up the gravel road, sweeping onto the cobblestone driveway, doors flying open, men spilling out.

Breaking from the tree line, two dots sprinted to meet them.

Evan felt himself going out, and he blinked hard, fighting to stay conscious.

A figure broke from the pack of men, waiting to receive Candy McClure and Orphan M. The man was dressed differently from the others, wearing some kind of cloak. He paused, turning skyward to glare at the Black Hawk as it hung overhead. His hood was raised, his face shadowed, but Evan knew right away who it was.

Van Sciver.

The Black Hawk banked again, the view swept away, replaced by the endless scroll of the sky.

Evan shut his eyes, and this time they didn't open.

57

A Very Persuasive Call

Pain.

Horizontal.

Drifting along as if in a canoe.

Evan's throat — sandpaper and rust.

His hand cramped around the RoamZone.

Needle jammed in his arm, saline bag clutched in Jack's blocky fist.

Fluorescent lights floated overhead.

An empty corridor led to another empty corridor.

Doors.

A warehouse interior.

Arranged in the middle of the blank space, lit like a movie set, a full operating theater.

Bizarre.

As out of place as René's basement lab.

The afterlife was weird.

A doctor in blue scrubs ran over. 'Who is he?'

Jack's disembodied voice, gruffer than usual. 'John Doe.'

'Who are you?'

'John Doe Sr.'

Thumb on eyelid.

Flare of penlight.

Latex fingers on the side of his neck.

A nurse called over, 'Can someone please tell me what the saline is doing in the freezer?'

Jack waved her off.

Trauma shears zippering open the coat.

Fabric peeling wetly back from Evan's wound.

'Jesus,' the doctor said. 'Um . . .'

Jack: 'Speak.'

'Look, I got a very persuasive call from the 202 area code telling me to get to this location. I want to help, believe me, but I'm an anesthesiologist –'

'An *anesthesiologist*? For the love of Mary.'

'He needs a vein graft into the damaged subclavian vein. That requires a trauma surgeon.'

'I *asked* for a trauma surgeon.'

'Guess how many of *those* there are in Piscataquis County? Your guys, they finally tracked one down, but . . . um, the weather, the roads – she's still two hours out. I'm just a place-holder till she gets here. But . . .'

'Get the words to come out faster.'

'Look. I'm sorry. He's not gonna make it that long. He's not gonna make it.'

Jack's face bunched up.

Evan tried to make a noise, but nothing happened.

The lights wobbled in and out.

'Okay.' Jack tilted his forehead into the span of his palm. When he looked up, his eyes were different.

'Kill him,' Jack said.

58

Cold

Cold.

59

Reborn

Lights fuzzed into existence.

Cabin. Soft bed. Jack sitting bedside.

'You have been,' Jack said theatrically, 'reborn.'

'You look old,' Evan said, and drifted into the beckoning darkness.

60

The Only Person Worse Than Us

Fade in on a new day.

Evan's shoulder pulsed beneath the bandages. Jack remained in that bedside chair, same clothes, more scruff. The cabin smelled of wet cedar and coffee.

Seemed like a sorry-ass excuse for the Elysian Fields.

Was it real?

'Quit whining and get your ass up,' Jack said. 'We got work to do.'

Yeah, Evan thought. *It's real.*

'What's . . . date?' Evan's throat clutched, sending him into a coughing fit.

Jack said, 'October twenty-seventh.'

Three days. That gave Evan three days to get to Alison Siegler before she got to Jacksonville.

He was still coughing. Jack handed him a glass of water. Evan took a sip, felt the coolness glide all the way down his parched throat into his stomach.

The cabin was one big room. Worn leather books lined a bookshelf, ordered by descending height. A water-filled heavy bag hung from one of the ceiling beams. A kettle perched on a stovetop, centered on the heating coil. Not a crumb, not a speck of dust in sight. Jack lived here, all right.

Evan set the glass down. Grimacing, he reached out with his left hand and poked Jack's chest. Solid.

'You're supposed to be dead,' he said.

'Later,' Jack said.

'I thought it was a dying vision. A deus ex machina in the form of a Black Hawk. My trusted mentor at the helm.' Evan had put more bite into 'trusted mentor' than he'd intended.

'We wouldn't have seen you if you hadn't broken out onto that open patch of the mountain.'

'How'd you get my vicinity?'

'We got there after the explosion at the chalet, did a sweep below the outside brink of the valley. We were scanning the mountainsides with a parabolic mike, picked up the audio signature of your murmuring. You were . . .'

'What?'

'You were apologizing.'

. . . sorry. I'm sorry . . .

The boy had saved Evan's life, then, not vice versa.

Evan would repay the favor soon enough.

If the kid hadn't called, if Evan hadn't answered, Jack's crew wouldn't have zeroed in on him. If he hadn't broken tree cover to stagger for the summit, he wouldn't have been spotted. The last ounce of what he had to give was the ounce that had saved his life.

A burning intensified on Evan's leg. He flipped back the sheets. A red scar seamed the inside of his calf. They'd harvested a saphenous vein?

He said, 'How am I . . . ?'

'We took you offline,' Jack said. 'Suspended animation.'

Evan waited.

'The doc induced hypothermia. Drained your blood, flushed your system with cold saline.'

'My veins?'

'Internal organs, heart, brain – everything. We took you down to fifty degrees. The colder the cells are, the less oxygen they need. We had to slow down your chemical reactions, keep your brain from realizing it wasn't getting any oxygen.'

'You making this up?'

'Nah. They been playing with it behind the fence for years now. They call it emergency preservation and resuscitation.'

'It's been tested?'

'On pigs.' At this, Jack allowed a gleam of amusement to cross his eyes.

'Survivability rate?'

'Seven percent.'

Evan swallowed.

'Oh, come on,' Jack said. 'Best odds you've had your whole damn life.' He looked away quickly, but not before Evan saw his blue eyes moisten. 'You were dead for two hours and thirteen minutes. The trauma surgeon finally showed up.'

'What'd she do?'

'After taking my head off? She performed the graft. Then we packed you in hot-water bladders to bring you back to body temperature, rapid-infused you with warmed blood products, kick-started you with a defib. You're Frankenstein's monster. "The fallen angel."'

'Where's my phone?'

Jack looked concerned at that; he must have read the emotion on Evan's face. Sliding open the nightstand drawer, he pulled out the beat-up RoamZone and tossed it onto the sheets. 'You okay?'

'Do I fucking *look* okay, Jack?'

'I know we have a lot to talk about.'

'You think?'

Jack glanced away, his jaw shifting.

'I can't believe it's Thursday.' Evan tried to sit up, with mixed results. His vision spotted, and then the spots bled together. He lay back down. 'I've never been out four days.'

'You've never been dead before.'

'Right. Unlike you.'

Snowflakes plastered the window.

'Where am I?'

'Alleghenies.'

'Am I free to leave?'

'What?' Color came up beneath Jack's cheeks. 'Of course you're free to leave. What do you think this is?'

'I don't know. What is this?'

'This is me saving your ass.'

'Well, you haven't exactly been forthcoming these past *eight years.* So forgive me if the issue of trust is in question.'

Jack let that one ring off the walls for a moment. He templed his fingers, looked down at them. 'I have a fake driver's license for you, cash, all that. You're free to leave as soon as you're rested up. I'll take you wherever you want to go.'

'Where's the nearest road?'

'Four-point-three klicks downslope.' He rasped a hand across his chin. 'You gonna hitchhike out of here, Evan? In the shape you're in? That'd show me, all right.'

Evan bit his lip hard, let his thoughts boil. His head throbbed, but he pretended he didn't notice. 'How'd you get onto me?' he finally asked.

'*I* didn't. Van Sciver locked on after the money wire. I keep an eye on Van Sciver. Once word went out wide on the auction –'

'You're watching him?'

'Mostly unsuccessfully. For years now. As he tries to watch me. Shadow games.'

'You're not sanctioned.'

'Nope. I'm as dead and gone as you are.' That half smirk. 'But I've still got friends in low places.'

'Have you seen Van Sciver face-to-face?'

'No. This is the closest we've come.' Jack reached into

the drawer, came out with a time-stamped satellite image zoomed in on the chalet.

Evan stared at it incredulously. 'You still have access to birds?'

'Depends who you ask.'

The grainy photo captured Van Sciver's face pointed up at the sky, nothing more than a dark oval beneath the raised hood of the cloak – the precise moment Evan remembered before blacking out. SUVs spotted the driveway around Van Sciver, a frenzy of beetles.

Evan stared at the blurry form. 'The hell's he wearing?'

'A Faraday-cage cloak. The metallized fabric blocks RF signals, X-rays, thermal imaging – even blocks him from drones.'

'He looks like Gandalf.'

'You know how he is. Trinkets and paranoia – they're like catnip to him. He's the only person worse than us.'

Evan's head suddenly felt quite heavy. 'You're supposed to be dead.'

'Later, Evan.'

Evan was too weak to argue. 'What did you get on René?'

'René?'

'The guy who took me. Who held the auction.'

'Everyone dispersed after your rescue –'

'It was an escape.'

Jack showed his palms. 'Okay. After your *escape* they didn't find much at the chalet. Auto-erase features were remote-initiated on the hard drives, so all those surveillance cams? They proved worthless.'

'How are you getting this intel if you're off the grid?'

'Three decades in the shadow service, I still got plenty of baited lines on the inside.'

Evan shifted on the bed, and his right shoulder let him

know about it. 'What about the stuff he left behind? There was a lot of shit in that chalet.'

'I talked to one of my hooks at the Bureau. The investigation is young, but he said everything in that chalet was pretty well end-stopped. Rare paintings, weird medical crap, advanced weaponry – there's plenty to run down, but it'll take time. Black market, dubious provenance, cash payments, blah, blah, blah. I'm sure something'll yield, but you know how it is backtracing through the black markets. Like digging a hole with your face.'

Evan pictured René waving around that clear cylindrical bottle, misting the DNA privacy spray over every surface he touched. The empty drawers in the study. *What is mine is hidden away down a rabbit hole.*

'How'd he pay for the place?' Evan asked.

'The money trail looks like a spiderweb. Ball bearings –'

'– within ball bearings,' Evan said with him.

Jack seemed amused. Evan was not. His neck was having trouble supporting his head.

'Every payment wired in from a different shell corp,' Jack said. 'He's got elaborate encryptions for movement between entities –'

'Van Sciver cracked his encryption.' The words came drowsily. Evan wondered what kinds of painkillers were in his system. There were too many questions spinning through his head for him to grab hold of.

Three days to get to Alison Siegler. Right now the *Horizon Express* would be doglegging around the eastern tip of Cuba, turning back for the mainland. And God only knew where the boy was.

Jack spoke, pulling Evan from his thoughts: 'With the resources Van Sciver has at his disposal, he can crack anything.'

'Not anything,' Evan said. 'He got through René's wire encryptions. But never mine.'

'The point is — this wack-job René? The guy's Teflon.' Jack shook his head. 'We have no idea who he is. He's a ghost.'

Evan moved his right arm, felt the muscle scream.

'Don't,' Jack said. 'What are you doing?'

Evan's fingertips found the tape plastered to the inside of his left arm. Weakly, he peeled it free. His skin tugged up, a thousand tiny pinches. He held the length of tape to the light.

Trapped inside, René's fingerprint.

Jack peeled it from the pad of Evan's thumb.

At last Evan let his head tilt back onto the pillow. It felt like drifting into a cloud. 'You're welcome,' he mumbled, and fell asleep.

61

To Do Harm

Evan woke up sometime in the night. Darkness crowded the windows, making the cabin feel small and inconsequential, a box drifting through outer space. At the square of the kitchen table, Jack slumped in a chair, breathing heavily, his sleeping face uplit with the dancing glow of a screen saver.

As quietly as he could, Evan slipped from the sheets. His shoulder ached with each movement, but the pain was surprisingly manageable. He walked silently across the floorboards. His muscles felt tight, his lower back complaining about the bedridden hours.

Easing into the bathroom, he tugged the pull-chain light. His unshaven face glowered back at him from the mirror. He'd seen more attractive sights.

It took some doing to reach the string at the back of the hospital gown, but he managed, letting the fabric rustle forward off his arms and puddle on the floor. Biting his lip, he loosed the adhesive dressing taped across his shoulder, letting it hinge open. A gnarled patch of flesh capped the deltoid. A horizontal scar ran above the clavicle, an accent mark Mohawked with sutures. The bone looked passable, probably restraightened with the help of a metal rod.

His vision spotted, and he leaned against the sink to regain his balance. Another week or so and he'd be well enough to leave. But he didn't have a week.

He had to get to the boy, as promised.

To Alison Siegler.

And then to René.

Evan's hair was knotted, gummed with sap. His face had been wiped clean, but streaks of dried blood still marked the side of his neck, the edge of his temple. He smelled of sweat and dirt.

Lowering himself into the empty tub, he let the water trickle warm. A fresh razor rested on the cake of soap. He shaved carefully in the semidarkness, then used a washcloth to bathe himself. The lather filled the tiny bathroom with familiar scents, bergamot and saddle soap, lemon and musk — the smell of Jack. It brought Evan back to the two-story farmhouse of his childhood. His dormer bedroom looking across a blanket of oak trees. Strider, their Rhodesian ridgeback, lapping table scraps from Evan's twelve-year-old hand beneath the table. *The hard part is keeping you human.* Jack's foot ticking along to *La Fille du Régiment*. Nine high C's. Towering bookshelves and mallard green walls. Photograph of Jack's long-dead wife in its tarnished silver frame. Parking Level 3. Blue flannel. The tang of iron and cherry blossoms. *Have I ever lied to you?*

Have I ever lied to you?

Yes.

You have.

Evan shut off the faucet. With effort he hoisted himself up, stepped free of the bathtub, and managed to towel himself mostly dry. Leaving the dirty hospital gown, he exited the bathroom, crept across the room, and sat on the bed.

The cabinet of the nightstand held medical supplies. He spread them on the sheets. Tugged out a fresh square of gauze and tore the package with his teeth. The medical tape gave him trouble.

Behind him at the table, Jack was awake. Evan didn't know how he knew. He just did.

Jack's voice ghosted over his shoulder. 'Can I help you?'

'No,' Evan said.

Evan awakened the next morning to an empty cabin. He felt less groggy. After dressing in some of Jack's clothes that he found in the closet, he went over to the stretch of counter that passed for a kitchen and made himself oatmeal. He was still stirring the bowl when Jack stepped in from outside, snapping down the stubby antenna of a satphone.

'René Peter Cassaroy,' Jack said.

'That's quite a name.'

Jack flicked his head at a stack of printouts on the kitchen table. 'He's got quite a lineage.' He ducked out of his scarf, slung it on the coatrack. 'He's in the wind.'

Evan crossed to the table, flipped through the reports, all of them stamped CLASSIFIED. Most were from the FBI, which looked to be running point on the investigation. Evan suspected that the IRS docs would prove most valuable. A few scanned crime-scene photos had been printed out as well. The barn. The basement lab. The erupted ballroom. It seemed from another lifetime.

'The fingerprint cracked things open, sped up the investigation. The Bureau is piecing together a RICO case on top of murder, kidnapping – the usual suspects. Cassaroy paid top dollar to rent gunmen from the Sinaloa Cartel, as you know. A few young men and women have gone missing from the neighboring counties, and there are some bizarre assault claims floating around as well. The agents found similar groupings of disappearances and complaints near the last several mansions Cassaroy rented – Albuquerque, Cabo San Lucas, Brussels.' Jack tugged off his jacket, heaped it atop the rack. 'They've got meticulously maintained financial and medical files for the victims, helicopter flight logs, and a dead disreputable hematologist – Dr Franklin? But no René Peter Cassaroy. He's vanished.'

Evan sat down with his oatmeal over the stack of print-outs. 'I'll find him.'

'If you do, Van Sciver will be waiting. Like you said, he's already shown he can track René. He cracked his encryption once, he'll do it again.' Jack shook off his boots. 'He'll spring a trap on you.'

'I'll spring a trap on his trap.'

Jack settled into the chair opposite. He always sat still so as to limit any information given up by nonverbal tells. As a kid Evan had learned the same from him and from an inter-rogation specialist who'd rapped his knuckles with a metal file every time he made a hand gesture. He and Jack faced each other now, paralyzed grand masters contemplating their next move.

'How did you get out of that parking structure?' Evan asked.

'I stumbled from the rear stairwell right after you. I had a man in the area. He picked me up half dead, got me to an old friend at Walter Reed. I woke up stitched back together.'

Evan struggled to get his head around it. Jack must have had a Smoke Contingency also, a plan to disappear. Stashed papers and hidden accounts and a cabin in the Alleghenies. Eight years. *Eight years.*

'So those men I killed that night,' Evan said. 'The men who shot you – they were Van Sciver's men?'

'Yes.'

'How many are there?'

Jack looked at him blankly.

'Orphans,' Evan said.

'From what I can glean, only a half dozen or so left under Van Sciver's control,' Jack said. 'It's hard to get a precise count because, you know. Orphans.'

'Van Sciver's hunting down those of us who got out. Those of us who were deemed higher risk.'

'He's hunting some more than others,' Jack said pointedly.

'They're neutralizing us.'

'I know,' Jack said. 'I been working sub rosa, helping the ones who need it most.'

'You always knew. Even way back when, before you met me in that parking structure. You sent me the fake assignment to kill Van Sciver because you knew I'd refuse and go to ground. You knew I'd never kill one of my own. It was a play.'

Jack broke the mannequin standoff, rubbing his eyes. 'It was more complicated than that. Van Sciver was tasked with killing you. If you'd found out, you would've destroyed everyone in your path.'

'Yes.'

'The directive came from the highest level. You would have tried to kill your way right up the chain.'

'Yes.'

'You would have died. Even you, Evan.'

'I would have died for the truth instead of running from a lie. That's what you did to me. Eight years I've been running from that goddamned parking lot –'

'Eight years you've been alive.'

'That's all that matters to you?'

'*Yes!*' Jack brought his fist down on the table, making the bowl jump. 'That's all that matters to me.'

'I thought I killed you. I forced you to break cover to meet me.'

'I told you it wasn't your fault. I told you it was *my* choice to meet you. I told you –'

'It doesn't matter what you said. It matters what *happened*.'

'I knew you'd never run. Not as long as you thought I was

alive. At some point you'd stick your head up, make contact with me, and they would get you.'

'Like you did now?'

'I found out you were in trouble. And I moved heaven and earth to get to you. You're still a son to me. Look at me. You're still my son.'

'Do you have any idea what I've lived with?'

'How about what *I* bear?' Jack said. 'Taking you from that foster home. Stripping you of . . . human warmth. Putting you in harm's way to do harm. I dragged you into all this. I wanted you to get out. I wanted you to have a chance.'

'At what?'

'At a *life*!' Jack flared a hand angrily around the cabin. 'That isn't *this*. A wife. Maybe even kids. I tried to free you. I didn't think you'd scurry right back to it, Assassin for the People.' He tapped his palm on the table, a judge's gavel. 'That is what you do now, isn't it? Freelance jobs? For others, people who can't –'

'You've been keeping tabs on me?'

'From afar,' Jack said. 'I couldn't let you go. I could never let you go. I know you can't see it this way right now, but it was a sacrifice, what I did.'

'A sacrifice.'

Jack firmed at Evan's tone. 'You've never been a father.'

Evan felt the pulse fluttering his neck. 'A father? You weren't my father. I wasn't a son to you. I was a *weapon*. You shaped me into what you needed and used me until I was used up.'

Jack stiffened. The skin around his eyes shifted, and for an awful moment Evan thought he might cry.

Jack cleared his throat. 'You know that's not true. However angry you are, you know that's not true.'

'I have been paying penance,' Evan said. 'For the blood on my hands. Including yours.'

Jack sagged back in his chair. 'I couldn't risk losing you, Evan. Not after I lost Clara.'

'You swore. You swore you'd never lie to me. It was the one thing I could count on. The one solid thing I could trust in the world. You don't know what my first twelve years were like. In that home – in *all* the homes. You . . . you were the one thing I could ever count on.'

'I'm sorry.'

'Fuck you.' Evan stood and stuffed the stack of printouts inside his jacket. He grabbed the cash and the fake license and walked out.

For a long time, Jack sat in his chair, staring at the empty seat across from him.

His breathing grew harder.

He raised a hand and pressed it over his mouth. Tears forded his knuckles, spotting the rough wood of the table.

He did not make a sound.

62

That Gnawing Feeling

The boy's phone number, a 301 area code, was branded on Evan's brain. It had guttered across the cracked screen of the RoamZone only a few times, but he'd committed it to memory. He turned the ten digits over now in his head. As familiar as a remnant from a dream.

Bouncing along the bitter interstate in the passenger seat of the semi he'd hitched a ride with, he snatched a pen from the cup holder and jotted down the number on the back of his hand. He stared at the scrawled digits. That same feeling gnawed at him again, that he'd seen the number before.

'You all right, bud?' the trucker asked, exhaling the smell of Red Man tobacco.

'Fine, thanks.'

'Where do you want I should drop you?'

A sign flashed overhead as they crossed Baltimore city limits.

'Anywhere's fine.'

'You from around here?'

'I guess I am.'

'Well,' the trucker said, 'welcome home.'

Evan hopped out at the next gas station. He found a pay phone at the side, right between the bathrooms.

He called the only person left on the planet he could trust to deliver what he needed.

It rang three times before the gruff voice answered. 'Crazy Daisy's Flowers. Something for every occasion.'

Evan said, 'I need a backpack cutting torch, an H&K MP5SD, a compressed-air grappling hook strong enough to take the weight of a jungle penetrator, and a skiff with two hundred-and-fifty-horsepower engines to meet me in Daytona Beach by tomorrow at noon. I'll tell you a location. I don't want to see any faces. Just the stuff waiting at a pier.'

There was a long pause.

'This,' Tommy Stojack said, 'can be arranged.'

'Good.'

'Anything else?'

'Yeah.' Evan smirked. 'Advil.'

'You going full Somali pirate on me?'

'I assure you,' Evan said, 'it's for a good cause.'

'Good cause or not, you're gonna have sticker shock. I have to work it cross-country. Plus, you know, discretion. I got a hook at Camp Blanding, he's our people. Something like this, I can't just use some clown-for-hire. After all, you never know who's who in the zoo.'

'Just tell me the price. And I'll pay it.'

Evan hung up.

Now, on to the boy.

He hauled up the tattered Yellow Pages dangling from a security cord and searched out the nearest cybercafé. There was one a few miles away – *$4/hr! Terminals clean-wiped after every logout! We accept Bitcoin!* Cabs were scarce, so he hoofed it, walking fast enough to stave off the cold. The chill crept into his shoulder, and he had to remind himself not to hunch to favor it. The tendon, muscles, and skin had to stretch in order to heal properly.

At last he stepped into the java-scented shop, peeled a hundred off the roll Jack had set aside for him, and requested a workstation and a universal phone charger. He plugged the

RoamZone into a desktop outlet, fired up the computer, and ran a quick search.

Reverse-phone-number directories proliferated. He found a free one and keyed in the kid's number. Sandwiched between various pop-up ads was the result:

No record of this number exists.

Evan stared at the screen, his discomfort growing.

One workstation over, two teenage girls laughed at a YouTube video, all gleaming white teeth and vanilla-scented hair spray.

Evan called up a second directory, keyed in the number again, and waited as the loading bar filled.

Number last used in 1996.

He stared at the screen, his stomach roiling. How the hell had the boy called him from a line that had been retired twenty years ago?

The previously associated address was available provided he endure a fifteen-second car commercial. His fingers drummed the desktop as he waited through a jingle promising o-percent APR for seventy-two months.

That gnawing feeling made some more headway, chewing through his assumptions.

He glanced nervously over at the RoamZone plugged into the outlet by the mouse pad. No lights, no bars, no indication that it was charging. Slowly, he reached across, picked up the shattered case. He unplugged the charger, plugged it in again.

Nothing happened.

The phone wasn't just out of juice. It was completely smashed, an untenable mess of broken glass, fragmented circuit board, and obliterated SIM card.

It had never worked.

Not since René had crushed it underfoot that first morning Evan had woken up in the chalet.

In the harsh light of the Baltimore day, it seemed painfully obvious. A phone that withstood a Godzilla stomping, that never ran out of juice, that magically got reception in a far-flung valley under a snow-thickened sky. Evan thought about how the gas had poured through the heating vent, tipping him into a drugged stupor. The blood-loss hallucinations he'd experienced at the end as he staggered for the summit.

The unconscious pulling strings, opening trapdoors, spinning its webs.

Of course.

A sheen of sweat covered Evan's body.

On the computer the car commercial ended, the link to the address springing up. Dazed, he dropped the ruined RoamZone into the blue recycle bucket under the desk and swung his attention back to the monitor. He felt drunk with disbelief. His hand reached for the mouse, clicked the link.

An instant before the fresh screen came up, the truth dawned on him, setting his skin tingling. He knew what it would show even before it loaded.

An East Baltimore address.

He knew it well.

63

The People No One Wants

The battered row house leaned against its neighbors, the whole lot of them tall and narrow and crooked, drunkards staggering arm in arm from a bar. The flaking paint was a different shade of green now. Same front window that the pack of kids used to peer through when the Mystery Man made his mysterious appearances. Same basketball courts across with the same chain-link fence surrounding the same cracked asphalt. Same handball walls layered with new graffiti.

The Lafayette Courts projects that used to loom in the background were long gone, replaced with a health clinic. Satellite dishes perched pigeonlike on balconies and rooftops. A licensed marijuana dispensary now squatted on the plot that once housed the apartment building that had gone up in smoke when Jalilah's nana dozed off smoking a blunt.

Evan turned back to the dilapidated row house. Bumblebee hazard tape crisscrossed the front door, orange cones lining the sidewalk in front. Bulldozers and backhoes lingered in the wings, construction workers chewing sandwiches, shooting the shit. Flyers fluttered from telephone poles, announcing that the building was slated for demolition.

The street had been blocked off, a crowd gathered at the sawhorses as crowds did in East Baltimore. The same faces on different bodies. Crack-ravaged cheeks. Coyote eyes. Elaborate press-on nails. A few industrious souls rolled coolers across the chipped concrete, selling bottled water and Doritos to the spectators for a buck a pop. Dinner and a show.

Evan walked over to a worker crouched near a spool of cable.

'Mind if I take a closer look?'

'Not safe, pal. The boom's kicking off in a half hour. Don't wanna get your hair blown back, ya feel me?'

'I feel you.'

The worker swept an arm at the piano-key row of façades. 'I wish we could take down the whole lot of them. You wouldn't believe what a shithole the place was.'

'What was it?'

'Housing for the elderly – and I use the term loosely. "Housing," that is. My cousin had his mother-in-law here, said it was worse than the dog pound. Asbestos in the ceiling, mold in the drywall, rats beneath the floorboards. Used to be some kind of facility for retards and before that a foster home for boys.'

'I'd heard something about that.'

'All the people no one wants. They cram 'em in, let 'em rot. It's a crime, really. Not that anyone gives a shit to do anything about it.'

Evan stared at that front window, saw his own twelve-year-old face pressed against the pane with all the others. Danny and Jamal and Andre. Tyrell, who caught shit because his sister was a whore. Ramón, so skinny his hips could barely hold up his stolen Cavariccis.

'Look, man, I'm sorry, but you gotta clear out before my supervisor comes over.'

Evan nodded and withdrew.

He circled the block, cut through the glass-strewn alley next to Mr Wong's ancient dry cleaner, where they used to loot the dish of Tootsie Pops every chance they got. The back of the row house appeared at the alley's end.

In his memory the rear slat fence towered overhead, a castle wall. Now it came up to his chest. Resting his hands on the top, he looked down onto the stamp of crumbling concrete that passed for a backyard. When he hopped over, his shoulder was none too happy about it.

Hazard tape blocked the back windows and door. The kitchen pane had been shattered, shards poking up from the frame like teeth. He peered through the mouth. Explosive charges had been placed on the walls and ceiling to make the building implode. It would collapse in on itself like so many of the lives lived here.

Carefully, Evan pulled himself through and climbed down off the sink. Piles of beer cans. A heap of stained blankets. Cigarette butts worming up from a pickle-jar lid. The place had been abandoned for a time, no doubt in preparation for the demolition. But the bones were the same.

There was the ghost of the kitchen table where plates slopped with generic, no-brand mac and cheese had conveyor-belted across the days and nights, a neon orange blur.

I'm trapped here. There's never enough food.

Here the counter edge Danny shoved Andre into, earning him seven stitches across the forehead.

I don't want this life. I didn't ask for it. I didn't ask for any of it.

And across in the living room, the spot where Papa Z reclined in his armchair, remote in hand, Coors nestled in his crotch.

No one cares. If you don't exist, then it doesn't matter, right?

Evan walked over and stepped on the floorboards two feet inside the threshold. Sure enough, they gave off a creak.

He and the boys had done a lot of sneaking in and out of the Pride House Group Home.

Staring at the ragged carpet of the living room, Evan saw a specter of the scene that had played out between these walls so many years ago: the Mystery Man talking to Papa Z about the boys, weighing pros and cons, a chef at a butcher counter. And Evan and the boys spying from down the hall, elbowing and whispering and wondering what the hell it all meant.

In the hall the det cord wrapping an exposed beam in the mold-eaten drywall was a few inches off the stress point. Probably wouldn't make much of a difference. Next to the gaping hole, the wallpaper seam bubbled out. Evan grabbed a lifted tab and peeled it away, revealing a dagger of the old wallpaper, an awful plaid pattern that Tyrell had christened White Man Pants. Evan stared a moment, the memory vibrating his cells.

Then on down the hall to the bedroom he'd lived in for two and a half years, a submarine-berthing area crammed with bodies. Closing his eyes, he pictured the bunk beds lined side to side like livestock pens.

You should see how they keep us here. Like cattle, all lined up.

He stepped inside the room. It smelled the same – rot, dust, desperation. He crossed to where his mattress used to lie on the floor. The other foster kids would trample him half inadvertently when they hopped out of their bunks. He looked at the ceiling, found the crack that forked into a lightning bolt. The one he'd gaze up at in the dark like it was some kind of wishing star and wonder who he was.

Where are you from?

I don't know. I don't remember.

Do you have a family? Parents?

I don't . . . I don't know. It's been so long.

Machinery revved up outside. A jackhammer screamed

into asphalt. Gears clanked, a bulldozer lurching forward, blade lifted like a metal claw.

Will you help me? Will you?

Evan had sworn a promise to his twelve-year-old self: *I'll get to you.* Here he was. But what did he want?

The echo of the voice came again: *You* have to *remember me.*

He walked to the doorframe. Carved into the wood with Papa Z's trusty pocketknife were the boys' height markers. The undertaking had lasted one summer month, until it became clear that given turnover and growth spurts, the notches would chew up the entire jamb.

Evan ran the pads of his fingers over the nicks and the carved initials next to them.

There at the top, the highest by a good six inches, were three letters: CVS.

Charles Van Sciver.

Then Ramón. The others descended in a cluster, the initials overlapping, turning the wood into a crosshatched mess.

Way down at the bottom, as far below the scrum as Van Sciver's was above, there was a solitary notch.

It has *to be you.*

Evan had to crouch.

There it was, the *E* still holding on after the years, though the initial of his original surname had long been effaced.

How small he'd been. He'd known it back then, of course, but he'd never let himself recognize it. He'd been too busy scrapping and fighting for his life, for his sanity, for a way out. He had neither size nor strength, so he'd had to rely on grit and tenacity. Only these he could control. Everything else he had to ball up and cram down deep inside himself.

It has *to be you.*

329

That nick, set apart so far below, made it undeniable. His vulnerability. His powerlessness. His loneliness.

What had he hoped for back then? What kind of future had he dreamed of when he'd stared up at the lightning-fork crack in the ceiling? Had it been visions of Wilson Combat 1911 pistols and encrypted virtual private-network tunnels and trauma surgeries to patch himself back together? Drinking vodka at his counter, sharing each night with a wall of herbs and a city view? Sleeping inside a penthouse prison cell of his own making?

He'd been desperate enough to grab the first ticket out. Had he stayed behind, he'd be in prison by now, long dead, or jackaled out from the streets or drugs. Jack Johns had saved his life as surely as when he'd swooped in on that Black Hawk. And yet Evan hadn't looked back since climbing into Jack's dark sedan as a scared twelve-year-old kid. Hadn't reconsidered whether the tooth-and-claw skills that had gotten him out of East Baltimore were still the best ones to carry him forward. When he'd driven off with Jack, the world had yawned open to him like a summer day, but a part of him had been put on pause, as stalled as a stuck DVD.

He fought his way back to that scared little kid, pried open the rusty hatches, and looked at what was locked inside. It was hard to acknowledge, harder yet to feel.

And yet crouching here in a slant of afternoon light filtered through a filthy window, he felt it.

This part he wasn't very good at.

It has *to be you.*

He wiped his mouth. His throat felt parched, his voice husky. 'Okay,' he said. 'I see you.'

On his way out, he adjusted the charge wrapping the beam in the hall.

Standing in the crowd a few minutes later, another

anonymous body jockeying for position behind the saw-horses, he watched the building crumble. A slow-motion cascade, all that rot and mold collapsing inward until nothing remained but a heap and a cloud.

You have to come.

I got here, he thought. *I promised I would.*

One moment he was in the heat of the crowd. The next he was gone.

This part he was good at.

64

The Slender Man

The slender man always got excited as the hour neared. All the cues for arousal were there. The big cranes, the smell of diesel, the containers lined up like giant dominoes.

It meant that soon he would claim his prize.

Entering JAXPORT, he felt like one of Pavlov's dogs, salivating at the bell. His heartbeat quickened as he took in the sights, breathed the muggy wet of the St. Johns River, which crept by in the background as dark and lazy as lava. He was perspiring through his dress shirt.

His Town Car purred along the roadway. He sat in the back, a bottle of champagne icing in a bucket. It was a celebration sixteen days in the making. Resting on the seat next to him were a set of fleece-lined wrist cuffs and a ball gag. Also, a chilled bottle of Fiji. Hector Contrell would have arranged nourishment for the journey, but the slender man found that they generally arrived parched.

His bodyguard and driver, Donnell, knew not to speak, not to say anything that might break the spell of this magical time.

The drive up, you see, even this was part of the foreplay.

Donnell turned off the main road to a rear cargo zone, the designated area where a series of under-the-table payments had determined that intermodular Container 78653-B812 would be set down. That was the beauty of it. Most everyone who worked at a port took bribes. No one had any idea what the container held.

It was there waiting, placed alone on an apron of asphalt.

Donnell got out first, his coat jacket shifting around his bulk, pulled tight across the holster.

The slender man emerged and took a moment there in the midnight silence. He tilted his head back and drew in a deep breath of fresh air. It was a starless night, the sky an impenetrable sheet of black, save for the moon, which beamed with an intensity that reminded him of the comic-book illustrations of his youth.

He recalled the photographs of her from the online catalog and reminded himself to lower his expectations. They didn't always arrive in the best shape. But once they were cleaned and rested, they were usually restored to their previous condition, good for several months. Even then he could most often fetch a decent price selling them used. For people with lower standards, there was still value to be extracted.

The slender man nodded at Donnell, who produced a key, moved forward, and fussed with the massive cargo-door lock. Then he swung out the leverage handles, the lock rods clanking in their holds. He stepped back, a magician revealing the prestige. After so much planning, the theatrics were essential. Nothing could shatter the mood.

As the doors creaked open, Donnell eased farther back out of the sight line and stood beside the slender man, leaning against the driver's door with his hands folded.

This was the slender man's favorite part, when he let them out of the dark box they'd been living in for weeks. He was their keeper, their owner, their God.

But this time something was different.

The inside, it wasn't pitch-black.

A rod of light dropped from the roof of the container unit. Had Contrell installed a light for her journey?

The slender man blinked but could make out nothing in the darkness beyond. It looked like a spotlight on a stage. The aesthetics rather suited him.

'Don't be shy, my love,' he said. 'Step forward.'

A rustling issued from the shadows, a form emerging.

She was bigger than he would have thought. Broad-shouldered.

She was also a he.

And the 'he' was holding what appeared to be a nine-millimeter submachine gun of German design.

The slender man felt his throat clutch when he realized that the light on the ceiling wasn't a spotlight at all. It was the golden light of the moon, shining through a hole that had been cut in the top of Container 78653-B812.

In the gleam of the muzzle flare, he saw the actual Ms. Siegler crouched in the back corner of the container behind the man, hair matted down across her eyes.

Beside him Donnell danced a little jig, the rounds jerking his limbs this way and that.

There came a moment of silence, a curl of cordite rising from the muzzle, during which the slender man grappled with the fact that the carefully curated mood was in fact shattered.

He tried to say something, but the sound he forced through his dry throat was an inhuman croak. He'd never known that terror could feel like this, a physical sensation running through every vein, inhabiting every cell, threatening to explode from the core of you straight through your skin.

The silence stretched out longer yet as the barrel drifted casually to face him, the bore waxing into a full moon to match the one above.

And then he sensed his body flying back against the side

of the Town Car, the safety glass of the windows cascading around him, and he tried to make out the face of the man behind the weapon that was tearing him to shreds.

The face was nothing but a silhouette, as black as the darkness that surged up and claimed him.

65

Fragile Little Bond

The cab swept into the porte cochere, delivering Evan to Castle Heights. He spilled out of the car, raw from pain and two days of grueling travel, his bedraggled appearance undercutting the grand entrance. When he reached for the heavy glass door to the lobby, a dagger of pain shot across his ribs. He lowered his arm and staggered a half step to the side, nearly colliding with Ida Rosenbaum of 6G.

The wizened woman, crusted with makeup and built like a fire hydrant, glowered up at him. 'Careless, aren't you?'

'Sorry, ma'am. I'm just . . .'

'You're just what?'

He tried to let his right arm hang normally. 'Just a little jet-lagged.'

'Jet-lagged? Had a rough business trip, did you?'

He ducked his head to hide the band of skin on his neck that still bore scabs from the shock collar. 'You could say that.'

'My Herb, may he rest in peace, worked his fingers to the bone and never complained a day in his life. We knew what hardship was, our generation.'

'Yes, ma'am.'

'We weren't kvetchers.'

'No, ma'am.'

She clutched her purse to her jacket, a shade of red not found in nature. He realized she was waiting for him to open the lobby door for her. To avoid doing a close-quarters pirouette, he had to reach for the handle with his right hand.

He braced himself, opened the door through the fireworks exploding inside his shoulder, and smiled with gritted teeth. With a waft of rose water, she passed beneath his arm. And with great relief, he released the door and stepped into the cool air of the lobby.

'Evan Smoak!'

As he pivoted at the sound of the raspy voice, Peter collided into him with a hug. Wincing, Evan patted his back.

The boy wore true-blue jeans with a toy gun and holster on one hip and a lasso on the other. A shoved-back cowboy hat completed the John Wayne vibe.

'You like my Halloween costume?'

Evan gave a nod, shuffle-stepping for the elevator. He needed to get upstairs and peel off the dressings before he bled through. 'Can't beat the classics.'

When he looked up, Mia stood right there, holding an empty pillowcase. 'Hi, Evan.'

'No costume for you?'

'This *is* my costume.' She flared her arms theatrically. 'It's called "Single Mom Without the Time-Management Skills to Comb Her Hair."'

He caught himself noticing the birthmark kissing her temple, the way her curly chestnut hair fell across her shoulders, and reined in his focus.

Elevator. Upstairs. Now.

'Haven't seen you in a while,' Mia said. 'What mysterious things have you been up to?'

'Too mysterious to recount,' Evan said.

She took him in more closely, her forehead twisting with concern.

Peter tugged at Mia's sleeve. 'Can he come over for dinner tonight instead of Ted?'

Ted?

'Can he? Mom – can he?'

Mia colored. 'No, honey.' Then, to Evan, 'He's a . . . friend.'

Evan gave another nod, took another step toward the safety of the elevator doors.

'Then can he go trick-or-treating with us?'

'Peter, I'm sure Mr Smoak has better –'

'I'm gonna shoot horse thieves and bad guys. You should totally come.'

The toy gun was out of the holster, and Evan was staring at it, a hard edge of discomfort rising inside him, something he was unaccustomed to feeling in the floral-scented lobby of Castle Heights. 'I can't –'

'What did you dress up as when *you* were a kid?'

'I didn't . . . I didn't really celebrate Halloween.'

'Why not?'

Evan was eight hours from his last dose of Advil, the pain starting to cramp his peripheral vision. '*Don't* aim that gun at me.'

His voice startled all three of them.

Peter lowered the toy gun. 'You don't have to be mean.'

'I wasn't being mean.'

'Yes,' Peter said. 'You were.'

Mia slung an arm over Peter's shoulder. 'C'mon, sweetheart. Let's get you some candy.'

They withdrew. Evan stood a moment before turning to the elevators.

By the time he got upstairs, the headache had crept down into his neck, meeting the fiery nerve lines shooting up from his shoulder. He went straight to the kitchen, tugged open the freezer drawer of his Sub-Zero, and assessed his options. A single bottle of Stolichnaya Elit remained. Triple-distilled, the vodka was purified through a freeze-filtration process that dropped its temperature to zero degrees to eliminate the impurities. He wasn't sure his arm could inflict the abuse he generally put a martini shaker through, so he poured two fingers over ice, palmed a trio of Advil, and took a sip.

As crisp as it was clear. It struck him that his vodka indulgence was something like a purification ceremony. After all the blood and filth he'd waded through, he didn't drink to numb his senses. He drank to try to cleanse himself from the inside out.

He pressed the frozen bottle to his shoulder. It stung. He let it.

Leaning on the poured concrete of the center island, he glanced across at his vertical garden, the wall textured with herbs and plants. The mint was taking over, as it did. This wall, the sole splash of green amid the metals and grays, was his one stab at living with life. The attempt struck him as poignant and pathetic at the same time.

I wanted you to get out. I wanted you to have a chance.

At what?

At a life! That isn't this.

He pushed away Jack's voice, exhaled through clenched teeth.

Whatever Jack had hoped for him couldn't be worth as much as the sight of Alison Siegler being tended to by paramedics. Her shoulders had been hunched and she'd started at the touch of the paramedics, but when she rose to walk to the ambulance, she'd stood tall, unbroken. Evan had been across the St. Johns River by then, watching from an unlit pier on the opposite bank.

He took another sip, let the Stoli blaze a path through his insides. After the past couple weeks, he couldn't get his muscles to believe that it was safe to relax. The alarm was set, the front door barred, the windows armored. Even the walls here had been upgraded – half-inch residential Sheetrock replaced with five and eight-tenths commercial-grade, which provided better sound attenuation and more structural rigidity in the event that someone tried to breach the place. He considered how much of his life he'd spent bricking himself in.

A wife. Maybe even kids. I tried to free you. I didn't think you'd scurry right back to it.

What else did he know? For his entire adult life, he'd been one of those rough men standing ready in the night to visit violence on those who would do harm. A sentry willing to go up against the Hector Contrells and René Cassaroys, the Assim al-Hakeems and Tigran Sarkisians. If not him, then who? Maybe now that he'd been freed from the guilt of killing Jack, he'd be freed from seeking endless absolution for his sins. Freed from being the Nowhere Man.

Which meant he could be someone.

Someone real.

He thought of Mia and Peter out in the neighborhood right now, going door-to-door, collecting Kit Kats and M&M's.

He downed the last of the vodka, studied the empty glass, trying to ratchet himself back to reality.

He had to get a new RoamZone up and running in the event Anna Rezian had found the next client requiring his help. He owed her, and he owed whoever would call.

Plus, René was out there. Which meant Evan still had a job to do. As Evan sat here waxing philosophical over an empty tumbler, René was no doubt already laying the foundations for his next operation, another kidnapping, the next gruesome medical lab. If Evan wanted to finish René, he'd have to beat the FBI to him while dodging Van Sciver and his attack-dog Orphans.

He owed as much to Despi. She'd brought him a tire jack, and her entire family had been slaughtered for it. *I don't know how to live with this,* she'd told him. *With what I saw.*

René was a devourer of lives. Evan couldn't let him continue, not with the wreckage he'd leave in his wake.

And yet . . . that birthmark, a kiss on Mia's temple. Peter's charcoal eyes, his croaky voice.

Evan washed the glass and then made his way down the hall, passing the empty brackets where the new katana was supposed to hang. Over the past few days, he'd learned to remove his bandages and undress with minimal pain.

Standing naked at the threshold of the shower, he flashed back to that bathroom at the chalet. The floor sloping to a drain. Bar of soap and a folded towel. Prison toilet, trash-can liner to the side.

Of their own accord, his fingers had moved to his scabbed neck.

He ducked into the warm stream. The first hit of water always stung the collarbone, but the burn quickly abated. He breathed hard, reminded himself that he was home.

He was, he realized, barely holding it together. His weight tugged him to the side, the wall cool against his ribs. He let the hot water beat against his crown.

At some point autopilot clicked on, the rituals of survival keeping him in motion. He got out, toweled off, rebandaged. In his bedroom he confronted the dresser, glaring at the bottom drawer with its false compartment bearing the bloodstained flannel – Jack's very own Shroud of Turin.

Evan carried Jack's shirt up the hall and across the great room to the free-standing fireplace, set it atop the pyre of cedar logs, and watched it burn. The coordinates by which he had charted the past eight years, up in smoke. As matter turned to air, he recognized that his own misguided sorrow and guilt had coalesced in the stiff fabric, as much a part of the shirt as the dried blood staining it. Even after no trace of the flannel remained, he found himself standing before the flames.

Returning to the bedroom, he pulled an unworn pair of dark jeans from the stack of duplicates. One drawer up were the fresh V-necked gray T-shirts, also neatly folded, also identical. A hinged wooden box in the closet held four Victorinox watch fobs still in the package. He took one out, clipped it to his first belt loop on the left side.

What did it say about him that he was so easily put back together? He'd long thought that it was a positive attribute, a testament to his durability, but now it felt artificial, unhuman. He was rebuildable, a snap-together Lego toy. His well-stocked drawers reminded him of the mac-and-cheese meals of his childhood, an assembly-belt existence from as far back as he could remember. And as far ahead as he could see. One mission would bleed into the next until the inevitable. If not Van Sciver, someone else. Evan would get older. His reflexes would get slower. Sooner or later he'd be a half-second too slow. Would he have balanced the books by then? And even if he had, would it make a difference?

Not a train of thought an assassin should engage in.

Exhaustion descended over him, a heavy cloud. That was it, then. He was tired. A good night's sleep would purge his brain of this existential nonsense.

Heading back to the bathroom, he stepped through the hidden door in the water-beaded shower and into the Vault. A Hardigg Storm Case by the weapon lockers held a neat row of replacement RoamZone phones, each nestled in black foam. He plucked one out, slotting in a new SIM card, then dropped into the chair before the bank of monitors burdening the sheet-metal desk. A few clicks and he'd switched the phone service to a company in Bahrain.

He turned on the RoamZone – no messages from Anna Rezian's referral – and plugged it into the desktop charger.

An impulse grabbed him. With flying fingers he called up Castle Heights' internal-security feeds, then zeroed in on the lens positioned by the twelfth-floor elevator. He rewound at 3x, the digital footage herky-jerky.

There.

A few minutes ago, the camera had captured Mia walking backward with a man down the hall, reversing into the elevator, the doors zippering shut behind them. She'd gone to meet him in the lobby. That seemed noteworthy.

Evan clicked PLAY, let the doors part, freeze-framed on the man.

Ted.

The guy looked pleasant enough. Rumpled hair, work-casual clothes, black Chuck Taylors throwing in a dash of cool. A Web designer or an advertising exec, maybe. He'd know how to barbecue. CrossFit gym membership, vacations to Maui. A peaceful, ordinary existence, work and play and time to reflect.

He thought of Mia's smile and wondered how dinner was going downstairs.

With Ted.

The RoamZone perched in its charger, awaiting the next call from the next client. Evan stared at it with enmity. It wasn't just a phone. It was a collar and chain. For an instant he let himself imagine what it would be like to be free of it.

Plucked fresh from the living wall, basil, sage, and tomatoes sizzled atop the cooking eggs. With a dip of his wrist, Evan folded the omelet, completing the half circle, and then slid it onto a plate.

He'd woken early, meditated, and stretched. He couldn't yet hang from the pull-up bar with his full weight, but if he tugged at it with his right hand, he could lengthen out the muscles of the arm. He'd required the jungle penetrator to bear him up the side of the *Horizon Express*, the cable attached to the grappling hook reeling him in on the deployed seat like a hooked fish.

At the store this morning, he'd stocked up on the basics — eggs, cheese, vodka. Now he sat, ate, and enjoyed the view of Downtown twelve miles to the east. The high-rises thrust up abruptly, a compact little skyline fit for a snow globe.

He made his way to the Vault, cocked back in his chair at his L-shaped desk, and reread every last word of the print-outs he'd taken from Jack's cabin. They contained the starting points of the investigation into René Cassaroy, the trails the FBI was currently running down. The crime-scene photographs taken at the chalet seemed less useful, capturing the aftermath of the bizarre events. Bullet-riddled basement lab. Barn with two G-Wagons and a blue wrestling mat. Files spread across the Pakistani rug of the fourth-floor study, each one sporting a bright yellow evidence and property tag.

Evan set the papers to the side. It made no sense for him to follow the same tracks the FBI was. They had more resources and would be too far ahead. The question was, what did he know that the FBI didn't?

He started with René's escape. Jack had mentioned that the Bureau was looking into helicopter flight logs, so either the agents were on René's heels already or he'd covered his tracks. René didn't have to go in any one specified direction, which made it harder to —

Evan stopped, excitement pulsing in his chest.

Dex.

Severed hand, lifted out by helicopter.

His destination would have been set. A hospital. Not just *a* hospital – a hospital with a department of surgery and a helipad.

The FBI had no idea what had gone down in the ballroom, so they wouldn't know to search for a patient missing a hand.

A quick Google spin gave Evan only three contenders within a helicopter tank's distance of Chalet Savoir Faire.

To the databases. Whenever Evan did break-ins from his computers in the Vault, he went through a string of anonymous proxies, remote services that allowed him to go in with one IP address and come out with another. He routed through Shanghai, then Johannesburg, bounced between a triptych of Scandinavian countries, then popped through Colombia and Moldova for good measure.

He was ready to attack. Most hospitals relied on the Epic medical-records system, which Evan knew well. In no time he'd jimmied a few virtual back doors.

The second hospital rang the cherries. A six-foot-five male, 290 pounds, with a severed left hand had been admitted at 1:47 P.M. on Sunday, October 23. Name given: Jonathan Dough.

Heh.

The record noted that the patient did not – or would not – speak. He'd been seen immediately by a vascular surgeon and taken directly to the OR. He'd checked out early the next morning against medical advice. Payment had been made in cash.

Evan scanned the discharge forms. Most of the personal information had been left blank. But there at the bottom, a phone number was given.

Why would Dex, a mute, have a cell phone?

Already Evan was reaching for his RoamZone.

He dialed. It rang. And again.

A click as someone picked up. A heavy breath came across the receiver.

'René Cassaroy,' Evan said.

'You found the Easter egg I asked Dex to hide for you. I'm glad. I've been waiting for your call.'

It took Evan a moment to adjust to the sound of that voice again, especially here within the walls of his own place. He realized he was on his feet, pacing around the Vault. 'Why's that?' he asked.

'I wanted to talk to you. Set a few things straight.'

'There's nothing you can say that will change what's coming.'

'That's where I tend to think ahead. You see, given what I know of you, I thought you stood a reasonable chance of getting out of that valley alive. I don't know how you did it, but count me impressed. I've never had the opportunity to . . . *behold* a specimen like you.'

'I'm planning to give you another chance. To behold me.'

'That's what I assumed. Which is why I took out an insurance policy.'

'Which is what?'

'Despi.'

Evan stopped pacing.

'You thought you were clever knocking out a few of my surveillance cameras. But did you really think we couldn't regulate you in that room? We had full audio. You should've heard yourself, pathetic and delusional, babbling into a broken phone, talking to . . . talking to *whom*? Who were you talking to like your life depended on it?'

'Myself.'

'I guess you were.' René laughed. 'But my favorite listening came from the snippets we picked up of your conversations with Despi. The woeful tale of her kidnapping. How we kept a loving eye on her parents, her sister. We listened to you two form your fragile little bond. I know you care about her. I know you'd be upset if any harm came to her.'

Evan was gripping the phone too hard, the tension radiating up into his right shoulder, fanning the flames. 'Yes,' he said. 'I would.'

'We have men in Despi's vicinity, watching her just as they did her sister, her parents. You're familiar with the work they did there?'

'I am.'

'She'll be left alone if you leave me alone,' René said. 'So decide if your need for revenge is worth her life. You've failed her once already.' The brief pause was underscored by the faint hum of the connection. 'If I get the tiniest indication that you're within a hundred miles of me, I will have her gutted.'

'What makes you think I'll give you the tiniest indication?' Evan said, and cut the line.

66

Banged Up in All the Right Ways

'How'd it go? The Somali-pirate routine?' Tommy Stojack ambled across the cave of his armorer shop, passing warped speedloaders, cutting torches, a stray crate of antitank grenades with Cyrillic lettering on the shipping label. He reached into a jumble of ARES pistol frames stacked like chicken bones atop a Pelican case. Each frame was a forging of aluminum – basically a solid piece of metal shaped like a gun.

Evan said, 'It went just fine.'

'You rescue the princess, slay the dragon?'

'Something like that. I came to settle the bill.'

Evan handed Tommy a thick roll of hundred-dollar bills. Tommy hefted it, as if gauging its weight, then smiled his gap-toothed smile and tapped the roll into his shirt pocket.

Evan looked at the aluminum forging. 'You said you had the upgrades for me?'

Tommy crossed his arms, mock annoyed. '"Hey, Tommy, by the way, thanks for producing a cutting torch, a suppressed subgun, and a skiff for me out of thin air from ten states away on twenty-four hours' notice."'

'Right,' Evan said. 'Thank you.'

Tommy jabbed at Evan with a forefinger that had been blown off at the second knuckle. '"And a grappling fucking hook."'

'And a grappling fucking hook.'

'"And how have you been, Tommy?"' he said, circling his hand in a prompt.

Evan said, 'How *have* you been?'

Tommy shrugged, dropped the shit-slinging routine. 'Nothing but high-speed, low-drag antics here. This new broad I'm seeing, she wanted me to try yoga. I told her I wasn't in touch with my inner vagina enough, ya know?' He raised that stub of a forefinger. 'Then I tried that shit. And I realized. I'm not in touch with my inner fuckin' SEAL enough.'

'It's that hard?' Evan asked.

Tommy dug through the mound of ARES frames, grabbed one in particular. He'd machined out the interior, drilling the pivot points for the fire-control group. Pistol frame in hand, he limped back toward his workbench. 'Those skinny bitches, they can balance on a pinkie finger for longer than I can stand up anymore.'

'So you're doing yoga now?'

'Hay-ell no. But I will tell you. Yoga pants? Best invention of the past hundred years. Let's just say downward dog gives me upward dog. But even that ain't worth it.'

Tommy half tilted, half fell into his rolling chair. Though he never talked about where or how he'd served, he had enough hearing loss, blown-out joints, and surgical scars for Evan to know he'd been a tip-of-the-spear operator. He was banged up in all the right ways. Now he worked as a contract armorer for various government-sanctioned black groups, specializing in procurement and R&D. Or at least that's what Evan had gleaned. Their conversations had always been light on proper nouns.

Tommy's shop, a desert-baked building rearing up from the sand in off-the-Strip Vegas, looked like an auto shop from the outside. Few people knew its location, and fewer yet had earned the right to visit. Tommy kept a surveillance camera at the door, which he'd unplugged when Evan called on him.

Tommy took a swig of black coffee across a lower lip packed with Skoal Wintergreen. 'I got no interest in working out no more. Makes no sense at this point. Spend what? Two hours a day? They say exercising can add seven years onto the end of your life. But I figure those seven years are about what you get if you add up all the hours you'd spend sweating your sorry ass on a treadmill. So I figure, why not skip all that misery, live out the good days, and hit the dirt when it's time?'

He rolled the chair away from the ammo and over to his smoking station, an ashtray made from a ship's battered porthole. A Camel Wide lipped out from the edge. He pulled on the cigarette, then dropped it into a red keg cup filled with water.

A kick of his combat boots set him shooting back across the floor toward Evan. Even as he glided, he popped a new slide assembly onto the aluminum frame. 'Don't get me wrong. I don't wanna slow down. You know me – Animal from the Muppets is my spirit animal.' He leaned over the pistol at his bench, adding the extras. 'But man, I'll tell ya, more and more I feel like I been shot at and missed and shit at and hit.' He paused to flex his remaining nine fingers, working out a cramp.

Evan thought of Assim with his hand tremors and unsteady gait, the physical toll of a lifetime of rough play. Was this what was in store for them all? A hard end to a hard life?

I wanted you to get out. I wanted you to have a chance.

It was nearly impossible for Evan to recalibrate to the fact that Jack was still alive, that when he heard Jack's voice in his head, it was not from beyond the grave.

Tommy had said something.

Evan snapped to. 'What?'

'You lose your holster, too?'

'Yeah. I need a Kydex high-guard.'

'I know what you use.' Tommy scooped the wad of long-cut tobacco from his lip, thumbed it into an empty Red Bull can, washed out his mouth with more java sludge. 'How'd you misplace your gear? Got held up by a troop of Girl Scouts?'

'It's a long story.'

'Ain't they all.'

Tommy handed over the new 1911. Eight in the mag, one in the spout. High-profile straight-eight sights. Low ambidextrous thumb safety, since Evan preferred to shoot southpaw. Aggressive front-frame checkering. Extended barrel, threaded for a suppressor. Beavertail grip safety so it wouldn't fire if not in hand. Matte black to disappear in shadow.

It wasn't merely sterilized – it had never *had* a serial number.

A ghost weapon that, like Evan, did not exist.

Evan hefted the ARES. 'It's lighter.'

'Bet yer ass it's lighter,' Tommy said. 'Thing practically floats. But everything else is as lined out as the steel Wilsons I used to make you.' His biker mustache shifted above his grin. 'It's just *homemade*.'

Evan handed him another wad of hundreds and stood.

'Hold up, hoss.' Tommy slipped the cash into his shirt pocket. 'When have I ever let you leave without test-driving a new gun?' He chinned at the sand-filled steel pipe slanted downward next to the cutting torch. 'Eyes-and-ears are in the bin.'

Evan donned protective gear and then fired a full mag down the mouth of the pipe. The gun, tuned with throat-ramp work, fed smoothly.

When Evan turned around, Tommy had tugged out his earplugs, one cheek gathering to the side in a fan of wrinkles.

'You okay?' Evan asked.

'Tinnitus. From all the . . .' Tommy waved a hand by his head. 'I live with it nonstop, pretty much. I think of it as a reminder of all the shit I've done. Jiminy Cricket in there, making sure I don't forget a red second of it.' His smile was bittersweet. 'Every year I feel like I'm hangin' on to a little less. And *for* a little less. You know?'

Evan clicked the ARES into his Kydex holster. 'I know,' he said.

67

What Was Missing

CraftFirst Poster Restoration would have been a sweatshop if everyone weren't so well paid. Rows and rows of foreign workers toiling over screw presses and wet tables, spraying surfactants and dabbing at one-sheets with needle-thin paintbrushes. The operation, located at the back of an industrial park in Northridge, made money in a variety of ways. The woman at the helm specialized in bringing rare posters and documents back to their original form. She also happened to be the finest forger Evan had encountered.

He had spent the past week poring over the investigation documents and pounding the databases, looking for any buried thread that might lead to René Cassaroy. Chasing down leads in the IRS documents, he'd uncovered a host of addresses on various continents. Many forwarded on to additional addresses in Croatia, Togo, the Republic of Maldives, and other nations lacking extradition treaties with the U.S. Evan had plenty such addresses himself, some no more than an office front set up to throw trackers off course. To get beyond the long arm of the FBI, René had probably retreated to one of these countries, but which one was anyone's guess. Evan could spend a lifetime trekking around the globe, knocking on doors, staking out P.O. boxes, and talking to shady middlemen – unless he produced a concrete lead.

Which was why he was here.

Way across the floor, Melinda Truong balanced atop a

ladder, reaching for a box at the top of a rise of industrial shelving. A sea of male workers milled nervously at the base of the ladder, calling up to her with gentle admonitions and offers of help. As she grabbed the box, one hip swung wide in a balance-beam correction, her waist-long black hair flinging wide like a flicked horse tail.

A collective gasp went up. The building itself seemed to hold its breath. Melinda righted herself and hopped down the ladder, her neon Nikes striking every other rung. At the bottom she presented the open box of X-Acto blades to an assistant and then scolded her workers in Vietnamese for doubting her.

'Now, get to work. I don't pay you to worry.'

Nodding respectfully, they hurried back to their workstations. They were all half terrified of her and half in love with her.

For good reason.

Dusting her hands, she noticed Evan threading his way through the tables toward her and grinned.

'And here I thought you'd forgotten all about me,' she said, reaching up to take his face in her hands.

'Impossible.'

On tiptoes, she kissed both of his cheeks, cheating to catch the edge of his lips. 'What do you need, darling? Another driver's license? Death certificate? Fresh passport for that getaway you're gonna take me on to Turks and Caicos?'

'I need your brain,' he said.

She crossed her arms. An Olympos double-action airbrush dangled from her hip. She'd padded the futuristic grip with pink tape to ensure that no one borrowed it. As the only woman in the building, she color-coded all her tools.

'My brain? I don't know whether to be flattered or insulted.'

'Flattered. It's a magnificent brain.'

She noticed one of her conservators sponging roughly at a Polish poster of *Rebecca* and smacked his shoulder. *'Careful! She's been through a lot, that poor girl. Show her some care. Handle her gently, like a lover.'* Taking Evan by the arm, she snapped back to English: 'I feel sorry for Mihn's wife. In bed she must feel like hamburger meat.'

She walked as she talked, casting an eagle eye across the workstations.

'I'm trying to find a man,' he said.

'Me, too.' A sideways glance. 'Okay, okay. Let's find *your* man. It'll bring some excitement to my life.'

'I doubt your life lacks excitement.'

'Let me cook you dinner sometime, and you can find out.'

'Deal. But for now –'

'But for now, a man.'

'Yes. I believe he's left the country. He's off the radar, and he's been careful to cover all the usual bases. I was in his house briefly. It was filled with luxury items, some rare. I'm hoping I can track him through unusual purchases he's made.'

'Why that approach?'

'Because,' Evan said, 'that's how he tracked me.'

'No, no, no!' She paused by a giant plywood worktable, lifting the padded earphone free of a painter's head to shout in his ear. *'Use* Bestine *to remove the tape adhesive residue.'*

She let the headphone snap back to the man's skull and kept on. 'So you'd like to track down which purchase?'

'He had an original Monet.'

'How could you tell it wasn't a fake?'

'I'm pretty sure.'

'If *I* made it, you wouldn't be able to tell.'

'I'm assuming you didn't make it.'

She gave a demure tilt of her chin. Proceed.

'It was of water lilies —'

'Of course,' she said. 'It's always water lilies with him. How many water lilies can a guy paint?'

'He didn't just do water lilies.'

'Right. Haystacks. Lotsa haystacks.' She sighed. 'Give me a *Metropolis* poster from the thirties any day. Have you seen the Boris Karloff *Frankenstein*? It just went at auction for —'

'Can you track a Monet like that?'

'Evan, the guy painted hundreds of them. Plus the forgeries — only *Starry Night*'s been knocked off more. Even if you *knew* it was real, how could you tell which water-lily painting it was? They all look like . . . well, like water lilies.'

From his jacket Evan pulled the printouts of the crime-scene pictures and fanned through them. But no dining-room shot of the Monet had magically appeared since he'd last perused the stack.

She read his face. 'I'm sorry. Was there anything else you saw in the house that you could track?'

'Lexan.'

'What?'

'Bullet-resistant polycarbonate resin acquired on the black market.'

She screwed up her face. 'Good luck there.'

He shuffled the printouts. Files on a Pakistani rug. Punctured IV bags draining onto the basement floor. The barn interior, two Mercedes Geländewagens and a wrestling mat.

He stopped. Stared at the last photo. Not what was in it but what was missing.

Melinda's tiny hand gripped his elbow. 'What?'

'A vintage Rolls.'

Evan had seen Dex drive away with it when he'd taken Despi. But it had never reappeared. René needed his toys. As his operation at the chalet drew to a close, he'd have wanted to get the car clear of the location, ready to meet him at his next stop. What had he said at the dinner table? *You could take silk sheets and caviar and inject them directly into my veins.* His obsession with luxury might be the thing that exposed him.

'What model was it?' Melinda asked.

'A Phantom.'

'That,' she said, 'might prove useful.'

Evan stared at the photo taken outside the barn. The edge of the picture captured the bank of shoveled snow that rimmed the vehicle path. It was indented with dozens of notches made by the G-Wagons when they'd backed up for their three-point turns. Evan focused on a particular imprint in the icy rise. Another bumper mark, much lower, studded with the rectangular outline of a license-plate frame. But he knew there had been no license plate on the Rolls. As he squinted at the shape, Melinda leaned over him, her breath smelling of Juicy Fruit.

'What?' she asked.

'The license-plate indentation in the snow here. I don't remember it having –'

'We'll look at that in a minute,' she said. 'Right now tell me – the Phantom. Was it a I, II, III, IV?'

'How can you tell?'

'I can't. But come.' She steered him between two wet tables, the mist from a retrofitted insecticide sprayer moistening their cheeks. 'Quan? *Quan?*'

A man in the far corner raised an arm hesitantly. Melinda beelined for him. He stood at attention as they approached. Covering his vast table, sandwiched between Mylar sheets, were sales brochures for vintage automobiles.

'You deal in car brochures?' Evan said.

'You'd be surprised,' Melinda said. 'This Bugatti one here? It's worth nearly three hundred grand.' She looked at Quan. *'You need to help him identify a type of Rolls-Royce Phantom.'*

She started to translate between the men, but Evan stepped in with badly accented Vietnamese. *'It had big fenders that swooped up over the front wheels. Swept-back pillars so the wind-shield was on a tilt. And it had those things over the rear tires —'*

'Fender skirts? With rivets?'

'Yes.'

'The Brits, they call them "spats." Close-coupled body style?'

'I don't know what that means.'

'Was the passenger compartment somewhat short? Did it look . . . zoomy?'

'Yes.'

'Like this?' Quan tapped the Mylar covering an old Rolls brochure.

'Not exactly.'

Quan bent over, rummaging beneath his stool, and came up with a coffee-table book. Flipping through the pages. *'This?'*

'No.'

'This?'

'Too big.'

'This?'

'Yes!'

'It's a Phantom III.' He smiled, showing crooked teeth. *'Goldfinger's car!'*

'How many were made?'

Quan consulted the book. *'Seven hundred twenty-seven chassis. Less with the body you describe.'*

'That's a lotta haystacks,' Evan said to Melinda.

Already she'd clamped his hand in hers, yanking him along hard enough to put a sting in his shoulder. Before he could thank Quan, he'd been whisked down a back hall and into a dark-walled photography room with blacked-out windows. The most private space in the building, it was generally reserved for illicit document work. Melinda stopped by a desk, snapped her fingers impatiently.

It took a moment for him to catch her meaning, and then he handed her the printout of the photo taken outside the barn. She slid it beneath an AmScope binocular microscope, the enlarged image coming up on the connected computer. Twisting her long hair in a knot, she flipped it over her shoulder and leaned to the wide eyepiece mounted on a boom arm. She studied the license-plate indentation in the snow. Evan did the same on the mirroring monitor.

'It looks like two stacked curves,' he said.

'Those aren't curves. They're *B*'s. A big one perched on top of a smaller one.'

'I don't get it.'

She snapped off the specialty bulbs illuminating the grainy picture and rotated to another computer, typing carefully on the keyboard so as to preserve her perfect nails.

The search engine swiftly brought up a logo: *Bonhams & Butterfields.*

Evan said, 'You're amazing.'

'You ain't seen nuthin' yet.' A search field led to a database for collectors, which led to —

'Five Phantom IIIs have been sold at Bonhams since it consolidated with Butterfields in 2002,' she said. 'Three were bought by an Abu Dhabi sheikh. One by that Ukrainian tennis player whose name I always screw up.'

'And the fifth?'

She pointed. The screen read, *'Anonymous buyer.'*

'There's your boy,' she said.

'Does he have to register with them to put in a bid? Can you track him?'

'Auction houses are extremely discreet when buyers desire privacy. So no, I can't track the buyer. However . . .' Her cheeks dimpled. She looked pleased with herself, a cat ready to be petted. 'I can track the car.'

For the first time, Evan allowed excitement into his voice. 'The car.'

'The chassis number, to be precise. It has to be registered when moved between countries. There are duties to be paid, taxes, all sorts of annoying bureaucratic paperwork.'

'I can take it from here.'

'Let me. We traffic in fine things. It's what we do.'

'How do I repay you?'

She leaned to swing her rope of hair off her elegant neck and tapped her cheek.

He kissed it.

'I'll be in touch by day's end. Check your e-mail.' She rose, smoothed the wrinkles from her yoga pants, and dismissed him with a wave. 'Now, go on. Some of us have work to do.'

68

Object Permanence

Evan hesitated outside the door of 12B. He and Mia had an understanding that he was to keep his distance from her and Peter. Mia didn't know precisely what sorts of jobs Evan did. But she'd learned enough to know that he wasn't safe to be around.

He reached for the doorbell, but his finger stopped shy of the mark.

What if she got angry?

What if she told him to leave?

What if Ted was there, whipping up an organic meal, expounding on the virtues of CrossFit?

Evan glared at his finger, wavering in midair. Given everything he'd endured in his life, how absurd that pushing a doorbell made him nervous.

He rang.

After a long pause, he heard footsteps. 'Damn it. Hang on. Hang on.' The door flung wide. She wore a bathrobe, soaked through, her wet hair dripping around her shoulders. One hand gripped a pink razor. 'Oh,' she said, cinching her bathrobe tighter. 'I thought you were the pizza guy.' She looked at her razor, then hid it behind her back. 'Um. Awkward.'

'Sorry to bother you. I know I'm not supposed to . . .'

'It's okay. It's good to see you. I mean, if I weren't in the middle of a shower and didn't have a Gillette Venus razor hidden behind my back.'

'It's still there?'

She checked behind her. 'Yup. Evidently I was hoping you hadn't developed object permanence yet.'

'I've got it down pat. I do struggle with stranger anxiety, though.'

'Okay.' She bit her lower lip. 'I'm all out of witty repartee and getting shivery. Can we move this along?'

'I just wanted to apologize to Peter. For the lobby last week when I was . . . short with him.'

'He's in his room. He snuck his Halloween candy in there, so enter at your own risk. I'll be drying myself off and pretending not to eavesdrop through the heating vent.'

'Deal.'

She vanished up the hall, and he walked over to Peter's door. It had been a long time since he'd been down here. The Batman stickers remained, as well as the skull-and-crossbones KEEP OUT! sign, but the Kobe Bryant poster had been replaced with one of Steph Curry.

The door was slightly ajar, and Evan knuckled it open. Peter started, diving to cover up the sea of dumped-out candy. He craned to look over his shoulder. 'Evan Smoak?' Rolling out of his emergency belly flop, he pulled a Snickers Mini from a fold in his pajama top and started shoveling candy back into the pillowcase frantically. 'Don't tell Mom.' His mouth was full, the words distorted.

'I wouldn't be shocked if she knows already.'

Chocolate smudged his cheek. His lips were raspberry blue. He chewed and swallowed. 'Why do you think she knows?'

'Because your mom knows everything.'

'Why don't you visit anymore?'

Evan resisted the urge to scratch at the remnants of the scabs on his neck. 'Like we talked about, your mom and I thought it'd be better if –'

362

'I still think it's dumb.'

'I understand that. Look, I just wanted to –'

Hopped up on candy bars, Peter leapt to his feet, ran to his desk, and began frenetically coloring in a *Star Wars* drawing. 'Did you know butterflies taste with their feet?'

'I did not.'

'What do you want to wear in your coffin?'

'A wetsuit.'

'Do frogs have penises?'

'Not the ones I've met. Listen – Peter? Look at me. I wanted to say that I'm sorry.'

He looked genuinely puzzled. 'For what?'

'For how I was in the lobby. You're right. I acted mean.'

'Oh. I forgot about that already. That was like *years* ago.' He set down his crayon, now worn to a nub, and looked at Evan. 'Friends don't make a big deal over stuff like that,' he said.

Evan had to clear his throat before he could respond. 'Okay,' he said.

'I hope you can come back sometime.'

'Me, too.'

Peter turned back to his coloring book, and Evan slipped out into the hall.

He was feeling better every day. Just this morning he'd teased the sutures out of his shoulder with stitch scissors and needle-nose tweezers. He'd regained decent mobility with his right arm, though he had to be cautious about how far and how fast he pushed it. Oddly, his calf was bothering him more today, the nerve line like a twisting strand of barbed wire.

He stopped in the living room to take in the place. Drying laundry covered the couch. Jazz played softly down the hall somewhere, early Miles Davis. The air smelled of vanilla candles and hot chocolate and dish detergent. The kitchen trash can overflowed.

A real home in all its messy glory.

The Post-it stuck to the wall by the kitchen pass-through was more faded than when he'd seen it last. Written in Mia's scrawl: *'Treat yourself as if you were someone who you are responsible for helping.'* She posted these life lessons, lifted from a favorite book, around the condo for Peter to read.

This one in particular had always given Evan pause. When he'd been trapped in that chalet, he'd been his own client for the first time, the one in need of rescuing. He wondered if he deserved the same happiness that he wished for the people he helped.

Mia surprised him. 'How'd you do with the Duke of Sugarbuzz?'

'He was . . . inquisitive.'

'Did he ask you if frogs have penises?'

'He did.'

Mia toweled her hair some more. *'Do* frogs have penises?'

'I don't believe they do.'

Watching her laugh, he felt something tug at him.

'What?' she said.

'Nothing.'

She bit her lower lip. Studied him. And yet she hadn't asked him to sit.

'I'd better go,' he said. 'Before you bust out that Gillette Venus razor again.'

'We wouldn't want that.'

He started out.

He was at the door when she said, 'I can't help but think that in some other life . . .'

He turned.

She looked at her nails, over his shoulder, everywhere but

at him. 'Where I'm not a DA and you're not a . . . whatever you are.'

He nodded.

'But it's not safe for Peter,' she said. 'I could never put him at risk.'

'No,' Evan said. 'Never.'

'I wish it were different,' she said.

'Me, too.'

'Good-bye, Evan Smoak.'

'Good-bye, Mia Hall.'

69

No Extradition

Before turning in for the night, Evan entered the Vault and logged in to the.nowhere.man@gmail.com.

A single e-mail waited for him from Melinda Truong.

'A Rolls-Royce Phantom III 1936 sports limousine with a Hooper body, Saoutchik chrome trim, and a chassis number of 9AZ161 passed through the Port of Rijeka on Friday, October 28. You're welcome. You can repay me by taking me to dinner. Or to Turks and Caicos. xoxo mt'

Evan cracked his knuckles, studied the screen.

Rijeka.

In Croatia.

One of the countries that has no extradition treaty with the U.S.

Evan reached for the IRS printouts, covered with his notes. On the backs of the pages, he'd scrawled all the addresses he'd turned up while trying to chart the sprawling map of René's financials.

In 2008 one of René's attorneys had taken receipt of a quarterly distribution from a now-extinct umbrella corporation at a condo address in Zagreb. The building, a mere two-hour drive east of the port.

Evan crossed the Vault and spun the dial on his floor safe. Lifting the steel hatch, he reached inside for one of his passports.

70

The Slightest Misstep

It had been hell.

Not just weathering Van Sciver's quiet rage. But being stuck with Ben Jaggers. And stuck with him Candy was, until the job was done.

As if she needed another motivation to reduce Orphan X to ash.

She sat in the driver's seat of a Passat wagon that had been advertised as 'family-size.' She mostly liked it for its trunk space.

To avoid Jaggers's stink, she breathed through her mouth, but then she got worried about all that funk getting into her lungs, and so she went back to breathing through her nose and suffering silently.

Croatia was amazing. More specifically, Croatian *men* were amazing. Tall and broad, full heads of lush dark hair, light eyes and golden skin – like Olympic athletes, the whole lot of them. And they proclaimed their love so readily. On the first night, on the first meeting. Of course, Candy got that a lot, but she got it more in Croatia.

When she wasn't stuck with Ben Jaggers.

Watching a luxury condo complex on a city-center street crowded with exhaust-belching buses.

In a fucking Passat.

Van Sciver – or, more precisely, Van Sciver's room of supercomputers – had unearthed René's location fairly quickly after the chalet combustion. A hub of five major freeways, Zagreb is a confusion of bypasses and congestion.

An ideal location for René to slip in and out of. Plenty of avenues for escape. But also plenty of stakeout spots like the one Candy and Jaggers had pinned down for the past week, parked off a major artery among a crowded lineup of other vehicles.

Why couldn't it have been Split with its view of the sparkling Adriatic or Dubrovnik with stone city walls and hills of lavender? But no, here she was in the Detroit of Croatia, stuck in a Volkswagen with that yellow bastard.

A group of Croatian men dressed in soccer uniforms hopped off a bus ahead of them, joking and shoving one another. Forked triceps and cleft chins. She felt taunted, a cat in an aquarium.

'Are you watching the building?'

'Mmm-hmm,' Candy said, flicking her eyes back across the four lanes of traffic to the high-security condo complex. She resumed watching people trickle through the front gate.

Fat woman with stroller. Silver-haired captain of industry. Three schoolgirls in fetching plaid skirts.

René had already had his daily morning outing, a trip to a bakery for a croissant and juice and to the drugstore for God knew what. Dex never left his side, his remaining hand shoved in his trench-coat pocket, a lumbering gumshoe with a thyroid condition.

Now they were back in the condo, a baited trap, and Candy had nothing to do but ogle soccer players, endure Jaggers, and wait for Evan to show up.

Under cover of night, Jaggers had managed to get several hidden surveillance cameras up around the building's perimeter, streaming into the laptop that rested on the console between them. It was available for close-ups and replays, but over the past days they'd seen few customers worth a second look.

Her phone sounded, Shakira's 'Hips Don't Lie.' She'd chosen the new ringtone mostly to annoy Jaggers, though he seemed annoyingly unannoyable.

He just sat in the passenger seat, as still as a frozen rat, an elaborate GPS unit resting across his stick-thin thighs.

She picked up.

'STATUS upDATE?'

'In clear view of restaurant. Still no sign of the expected party.'

'LIGHTNING BUG is ON StandBY. AwaitING coordinates.'

For obvious reasons Van Sciver had to keep the drone out of the air for as long as possible. Which meant no sky surveillance. Once Candy and M confirmed Orphan X's precise location, they'd input it into the handheld GPS unit, an unmanned armed aerial vehicle would flash above the thick clouds, and Zeus would hurl a thunderbolt from the heavens. There'd be no collateral damage. No *non*collateral damage either, if you thought about it.

If you killed the Nowhere Man, did anyone really die?

The targeted zap would get blamed on Hamas or Israel or some shit – that was up to Van Sciver to figure out. He was delighted to have a shot off U.S. soil and wasn't going to miss his chance. One of the joys of operating OCONUS was that there was no hue and cry over ROEs and constitutional rights and court precedents. There was a guy one moment and a crater the next and then everyone standing around with their hands in their pockets, shrugging.

The GPS unit in Orphan M's lap mapped the street and the surrounding buildings, drilling down coordinates using not degrees but minutes and seconds, which were accurate to 1/3600 of a degree, precise enough to guide a missile through a doughnut. The thing even accounted for minute tectonic crustal movement, Jaggers had informed her fetishistically. She'd told him that that sounded like a medical condition.

Candy focused again on her call with Van Sciver. 'I was still hoping to have a more leisurely meal with the diner,' she said.

They'd been over this.

'The COORDINATES,' the collection of anonymous voices said. 'And then DESSERT.'

The line cut out.

Evan sat in the bay window of the boutique hotel overlooking the crowded Zagreb city center, an open laptop resting on the cushion beside him. He had a clean sight line to the third floor of the condo building across the street where René Cassaroy was bedded down. Dex was there as well, in a connecting condo. Evan was still recovering full use of his right arm, but Dex was missing a hand, so he figured that put them no more uneven than they'd been before. At least Evan still had two opposable thumbs. He hoped to put them to good use.

He'd have to be extremely cautious in his approach to ensure that no communication went out to the men watching Despi. The slightest misstep could trigger a text or a call, and she'd be dispensed of as proficiently as her parents and sister had been.

Evan could understand why René had chosen to hide here. Several prominent businessmen and ministers lived in the complex, which was riddled with security cameras.

Logging on to the Internet, Evan accessed an untraceable account at Hashkiller and set its 131-billion-password dictionary to work. Within minutes he was on the luxury condo building's network. He found the security camera system next, matching the name to the decals on the building's main fence. Hashkiller made short work of that, and then a hundred-plus internal and external camera feeds appeared.

He picked the lenses along the route he was planning to take and then opened up the camera-control links. First he slewed the pan-tilt zoom lens above the front gate to face the sun. The image turned a uniform white. The neighboring ones he aimed directly at streetlights to the same effect.

The cameras in the interior east stairwell didn't have the same operability, so he turned off their auto-irising and then directed them to stop down. The pictures went black.

In case René had hacked into the security cameras on his own floor, a likely precaution, Evan took a single frame of valid video from each one, duplicated it 50 million times, and injected the gapless IP feed back into the video storage server. This created a spoof of each camera's normal scene, showing forever-empty corridors. Snapping the laptop shut, he stood, stretched out his shoulder, and headed for the door.

It was time.

71

Vaporized

Candy cracked her window to get a little fresh air and leaned away, not wanting to get sucked into the black hole of Jaggers's charisma void. He sat motionless in the passenger seat, his hands on the GPS unit as if about to embark on a game of Super Mario.

She monitored the residents and visitors entering the condo building's front gate.

Old woman with a purse dog. Hipster with sleeve tattoos and a slouch beanie cap. Ladies who lunched in pink pantsuits and glittering pearls.

'Halya Bardakçi,' she murmured.

Though she stared straight ahead, she sensed Orphan M's head dart over. 'What?'

'That was her name. The girl you killed in the alley outside Sevastopol.'

He picked up the laptop and reviewed footage. 'How do you know?'

Candy kept her eyes on the luxury complex.

Elderly couple. Teenage girl with bad eye shadow. A diplomat's wife who resembled a drag queen.

'I read the news story,' Candy said. 'She was just a down-on-her-luck kid.'

Bushy-mustached businessman. Swarthy janitor. Strapping college girl.

'Why does that matter?' Jaggers asked.

'Because, you dickless fuck,' Candy said, 'she could've been us.'

Jaggers jolted in his seat, and for an instant she thought he might strike her. But his eyes remained glued to the laptop. He'd screen-captured the image of the hipster who'd entered the building earlier and zoomed in on the face, barely visible beneath the beanie cap.

'Fuck,' Candy said.

'Make sure that he's inside René's condo,' Jaggers said. 'And ascertain which room. I'll ready the coordinates. The last thing we need is him getting away singed.'

Candy grabbed her phone and hopped out of the car.

Jaggers called after her, 'And V?'

She leaned back in.

'If you worried more about surveillance and less about a dead Crimean whore, we could've sizzled him at the front gate.'

She slammed the door harder than necessary and jogged for the building.

The Need raged and gnashed inside him. Without his infusions of young blood, René could already chart his deterioration. Achy joints, flagging energy, and that chalky residue always in his mouth. The taste of aging.

As soon as they coaxed the Nowhere Man out of hiding, Dex would put an end to him and they could set about rebuilding a new medical lab and acquiring new product.

Rising from his midday nap, René shuffled from the king-size bed toward the makeup counter of the bathroom suite. The windows were Lexan, of course, but to deter surveillance he kept the curtains drawn and the lights off. Just across the tile floor of the interior hall, the connecting door to Dex's condo was in clear view. It was closed for privacy, though given all the cameras they'd installed throughout the rooms, privacy was hardly an issue. When Dex wasn't at René's side, he kept watch on every inch of René's quarters from a collection of monitors next door, ready to alert their Greek freelancers at the first sign of anything out of the ordinary. It would take the tap of an iPad, no more, and hired knives would close in on Despi and carve her to pieces.

Dex had plans for Evan after that. He'd made multiple contingencies for how to eliminate him once he appeared. Disguised gunports in the common walls. Autolocking double-cylinder dead bolts on the solid-core front door to block egress. Vents wired up for gas just as in the chalet.

René braced himself for a look in the mirror. Despite the low light conditions, he winced at the sight. It was getting harder and harder to produce his confected self. Thinning hair swirled up from his pate. The bags under his eyes had grown bags beneath them, a landslide of bruise-colored flesh. His jowls held the weight of the world.

He began the process of putting himself together.

Cover-up filling in the crow's-feet. Concealer and color corrector. Fish oil and zinc, calcium and vitamin E. No need for Cialis, not holed up here, but he'd upped his Lexapro in an attempt to filter out some of the gray from the Zagreb pollution. He was just reaching for his Rogaine when his hand brushed across a heap of silken fabric on the dim counter.

A scarf?

He lifted it. Two slender pieces that came apart. Each was a skin-colored tube of fabric covered with elaborate patterns.

Fake sleeve tattoos.

He let them slip to the shag carpeting. His eyes lifted to the mirror.

Barely visible in the dimness at the back of the room was the outline of a face.

A man sitting on the upholstered settee, swallowed by the shadows.

René forced a smile. 'Evan,' he said, loud enough for the surveillance equipment to pick up. 'I knew you'd find me.'

René let his eyes tick over to that connecting door across the tile, checking to see if any movement interrupted the seam of light across the bottom. He pictured Dex readying the halogenated ether. The Greek henchmen moving on Despi. The door opening and Dex filling the frame. Given that Dex was down to one hand, it would take him so much longer to do to Evan what needed to be done.

The outline of the face stared back at him, a featureless mask. René stayed upright in his chair, staring at the reflection in the mirror.

'The thing is,' René said, listening for the hiss to come through the vents, 'this situation is more complicated than you've accounted for.'

Something crashed into the mirror, leaving a red streak, and landed with a slap on the counter. Pill bottles skittered across the surface, bouncing on the floor.

René shrieked.

He stared down at the enormous hand resting on top of the jumble of knocked-over beauty products.

Tattooed across it, an eerie, too-wide smile.

His rolling eyes found the connecting door. For a moment he felt an irrational stab of hope – there were Dex's size-eighteen boots shadowing the gap beneath. Then the darkness spread and spread, seeping beneath the door, creeping across the tile.

He felt his insides wither, his heart drop down the bottomless pit of his stomach.

Still, it seemed, the Nowhere Man had not moved.

René's throat seized up, too dry to speak. He croaked out the words. 'You can have your money back.'

'I don't want my money back,' the voice said.

'What do you want?'

'Someone once told me, if you control time, you control *everything.*'

The dark form rose and approached.

Too terrified to turn around, René stayed locked in his chair facing the mirror.

A hand drifted forward into a fall of light. It clutched a syringe filled with a viscous clear fluid.

René's mouth wobbled open as the needle slid into his neck.

Still the face remained lost to darkness.

René's last thought before the thumb depressed the plunger was of the double-cylinder dead bolts on the front door, trapping him in.

And then time stopped moving, sealing him inside it like a bug in amber.

Her cell phone held at the ready, Candy leaned against the door to René's condo, straining to listen for movement inside. A single text to Orphan M and Van Sciver would make it rain.

The neighboring door creaked open. Just as she realized that it might belong to a connected condo, a streak of movement flew at her. She braced herself for a strike, but it didn't come. Instead she was wrapped up, her arms locked to her sides, and then unfurled, a swing dancer who'd lost her lead.

A face blurred by as he spun her. She recognized his eyes. For an instant she let him lead.

Not that she had a choice.

And then she was free, tumbling across the threshold of the adjacent condo, the door slamming shut behind her.

She slipped on something slick, slammed onto the floor, and came up sticky.

She knew that smell.

She lunged for the door but knew all too well what she'd find. The double-cylinder dead bolts had autolocked. And she didn't have a key.

Her cell phone was missing, plucked cleanly from her hand. She thought of Orphan M below, waiting for her texted command.

There was little she could do now but brace for the drone missile.

Orphan M held his cell phone in one hand, the GPS unit in the other, staring from screen to screen. He did not allow his knee to bounce with impatience.

At last a text arrived.

HE'S LOOSE. I HAVE HIM PINNED ON GROUND FLOOR. JAM LOCK ON FRONT GATE + I'LL HERD HIM THERE.

Orphan M input the front-gate coordinates for the drone and then tossed the GPS unit on the seat, leapt from the Volkswagen, and Froggered across four lanes to the complex, dodging grilles and blaring horns.

He reached the tall metal gate, readying his pick set. He slid a slender diamond pick into the keyhole and snapped it off.

There'd be no getting through that gate now.

He sprinted back through traffic, nearly getting pancaked by a bus, and flung himself into the Passat before the next barrage of traffic swept by.

The GPS handheld unit rested on the dashboard, not where he'd left it on the seat. Puzzled, he picked it up, turned it over. The battery lid was slightly loose, one of the screws lifted a few millimeters from the plastic.

He stared at it uncomprehendingly even as the reality dawned on him.

The batteries had been taken out and put back in.

Which erased the previous coordinates.

And reset the unit to its own position.

His body went cold, and he realized that it wasn't cold he was experiencing – it was a full-body panic sweat. His head lifted.

Standing motionless in the sea of movement on the sidewalk across the street was Orphan X. He touched the imaginary brim of his beanie cap, gave a little nod.

M had time only to lift his eyes to the roof of the car before the Volkswagen vaporized.

72

The Old Stories

Despi stepped out onto the balcony of her family apartment to water the tomato plants vining through the rails. Wherever her sister lived, she'd always insisted on growing her own tomatoes just like their mother did. Now only Despi was left to maintain the family tradition.

Sunset was heartbreaking here and lately even more so. Violets and oranges shimmering off the sparkling Mediterranean, another day finding its ultimate beauty as it was extinguished. Only a slice of the sea was visible between the surrounding apartments, but her father had always said that a slice was enough to feel blessed, to feel assured of your place in the world.

How she missed him. How she missed them all.

She stepped inside through the breeze-swept curtain and set down the watering can.

Evan stood in her living room.

Her mouth moved, but no sound came out.

He removed a heavy-looking white envelope from his back pocket.

'What is that?'

'Pictures of the men who killed your family,' he said. 'Who were watching you.'

'I was being watched?'

'You were.'

'What do the pictures . . . show?'

'Corpses,' he said.

She swallowed.

'Where did you . . . How did you find them?'

'I found their names in a condo in Zagreb,' he said. 'Where I caught up to René.'

'He's dead?' she asked.

'Worse.'

She noticed that she was wringing her hands in her dress, and she made herself stop. She gestured at the envelope. 'What am I supposed to do with those?'

He said nothing.

'I don't want those. I don't want to see them.'

He stuffed the envelope back into his pocket. 'I didn't think you would. But I don't always know what people want.'

She looked at the watering can. 'I have nothing left. How am I supposed to rebuild a life?'

She'd seen him in a shock collar. She'd seen him beaten by men. She'd seen him on his knees. This was the first time she'd seen him powerless.

'I can't help you with that,' he said.

'Right,' she said. 'You're only good at destroying things.'

She put her face in her hands and wept. When she looked back up, he was gone.

'I'm sorry,' she said, though there was no one to hear it.

No matter how many times Evan had been to the Parthenon, it never ceased to take his breath away. The rocky outcrop thrusting above Athens, the ruined temple thrusting up even above that. Veins of mica and pyrite running through the marble, lending it a golden tinge. The perfection of the design, as precise as anything designed by computer. The ancient Greeks had even slimmed the Doric columns at the tops, an optical illusion to make it look as though the heavy roof were bowing the supports.

Evan came around a block of scaffolding and spotted him from behind, sitting at a tiny café table in the shade of a food-stand umbrella, sipping from a demitasse.

Leave it to Jack to find espresso in an ancient citadel.

Perspiration spotted Jack's shirt between the shoulder blades. Evan walked up from behind. As he drew near, Jack set down his demitasse.

'Evan,' he said without turning around.

Evan sank into the chair opposite him.

'Thanks for coming,' Evan said.

Jack nodded.

Two German kids ran by, tiny fists gripping bottles of Fanta Limon. Evan waited for their laughter to fade away and then said, 'I thought maybe we could start over.'

'Okay,' Jack said.

'You said you don't understand why I still do what I do after I left the Program. Why I didn't just disappear, lie on a beach somewhere, sip umbrella drinks.'

'Not my precise phrasing.'

'But the gist.'

'Yes.'

Evan struggled to find the words. 'For as long as I can remember, I've been out in the cold, nose up to the glass, looking in. I may not get to come inside, Jack. But I'm sure as hell not gonna let the wolves in at everyone else. No. That's one thing I'm good for.'

Jack looked heartbroken. He studied Evan. 'You don't owe anything, son. For what I tasked you to do. It's on me. You've got nothing to atone for.'

'I pulled the trigger, Jack,' Evan said. 'Every last time.'

For a few minutes, they sat and listened to the wind rush around the ancient stone. Jack pinched the crinkled skin beneath his eyes. When he looked back up, his gaze was clear.

'People talk about starting over,' he said. 'But you can't start over. All you can do is change direction.'

'Maybe we could do that,' Evan said.

Jack gave his non-smile, that slight bunching of his right cheek that said he was pleased. He tilted his face to the Mediterranean sun. 'Funny that we're meeting here in the shadow of the gods. Destiny ringing from the stones. The old stories.' He blinked a few times and suddenly looked much older. 'Can we break it?'

'What?' Evan asked.

'The cycle.'

'I don't know.'

Jack looked across at him. 'Are you willing to try?'

Evan said, 'Yes.'

Jack drained the last of his espresso, set down the glass, and stood up. Backlit, he looked down at Evan. 'Would you like to take a walk?'

Evan rose to join him.

73

Resolute

Anna Rezian looked nothing like the wrecked sparrow of a girl Evan had seen just a few months ago. She stood in a circle of girls on the high-school quad, laughing and sharing pictures on her iPhone. Her hair had mostly grown back, covering the patches she'd plucked out.

Sitting in his idling F-150 pickup, Evan watched her through a rise of chain-link fence. He didn't generally go near a client once he'd completed his mission, but he wanted to see her, wanted to be reminded of the good in the world.

A brief article had appeared online this morning. An American expat had been discovered in a high-end luxury condo in Zagreb along with a dead body. He'd been in terrible shape. The story had carried a single photo of the police leading him out.

The man looked to be in his nineties, his strawlike hair gone white, his loose skin bagging around his face, his joints angled arthritically. He hadn't yet recovered his capacity for speech, and one of the physicians remarked that he didn't know what the man could have encountered to have aged him so violently.

No one had any idea what had happened behind the gate of the high-end complex or whether it was related to the nearby street explosion that had claimed a life a week ago.

The school bell rang, the sound crisp in the November breeze. Evan drew in a breath of fresh air and watched Anna walk to class with a friend.

Maybe she wouldn't bother finding the next client to pass on Nowhere Man's number to. The next client who would find ⬛next client who would find the next. Evan found himself ⬛ering if Anna might just let it go and move on with her life.

⬛ wondering.

Hoping.

For the first time since he'd built the compound, Charles Van Sciver powered down the monitors. One wall at a time until all three had gone dark, his eternal horseshoe dimmed at last. The warmth of the screens vibrated the air, the afterglow of something just killed.

The act was largely symbolic. The computing power still churned in the banks of servers behind the concrete wall, and he could reignite the monitors at a moment's notice. But sometimes symbolic was good.

Sometimes you needed to drench yourself in darkness.

In the darkness his thoughts and desires clarified. In the darkness the path ahead was illuminated.

It was time to leave the foxhole.

He prepared himself. Then reached for the telephone.

One of three heavy black phones rang on the Resolute desk. Fashioned from the timbers of the British frigate that was its namesake, the desk had been gifted to the United States by Queen Victoria. American seamen had saved the ship after it had been frozen in Arctic ice, and the desk had pinned down the oval carpet ever since.

The seal on this carpet was rendered in bas-relief like Truman's, the cut pile trimmed to different lengths to delineate the eagle and stars. It was monochromatic, shadows within shadows.

A handsome man in his fifties excused himself from the assembly on the couch, crossed to the desk, and answered.

This was the only call on which Van Sciver didn't dare use his anonymizing voiceware. 'We lost him, Mr President.'

The handsome man pouched his lips and paused. If there was one thing he'd learned in office, it was the value of a two-second pause before responding. 'Get him back in play.'

He leaned to hang up, but Van Sciver's voice came through, so he moved the phone back to his face.

'Next time,' Van Sciver said, 'I'll handle it personally.'

The president allowed another two-second pause.

Then hung up.

74

Overlord of Everything and Nothing

It was hard to pick up the trace of sun-dried raisin in the vodka, but it was there, lingering behind the aftertaste. Handcrafted in small batches, Dash organic vodka was distilled seven times, filtered through coconut shells, and then micro-oxygenated until it was smoother than velvet.

Sitting on his black suede couch, Evan sipped it now, looking past the slit in the floor that housed his retractable flat-screen TV and focusing on the view beyond.

Los Angeles, a constellation of nearly 4 million lights. All of them seemed to be on display tonight. Checkering the neighboring apartments, running up and down the high-rises of Downtown, headlighting the cars Tetris-ing their way through the gridlocked streets below.

And Evan floating twenty-one stories up, observing it all with his glass of vodka, an overlord of everything and nothing.

Alone.

The congestion on the streets looked thicker than usual, and he realized: It was Thanksgiving.

He thought of Anna Rezian, her life back in motion. The RoamZone bulged in his pocket, charged and ready to go. What would next week bring? And the week after? How many more Hector Contrells would he face? How many seedy doorsteps would he darken, steeling himself for whatever atrocities waited inside? How long had he been stuck here inside this fortress-prison, inside this trope, this story?

He thought about breaking out of the narrative, about time moving along and – for once – him moving along with it. Unclicking that pause button and stepping into life with all its ordinary wonders and concerns.

You can't start over.

The drink had lost some of its charm.

All you can do is change direction.

And then Evan was up and walking. Through the door, up the corridor to the elevator, riding down nine floors. He moved briskly to 12B, tapped on the door before he could convince himself not to.

He sensed a shadow at the peephole, and then the door pulled open, a trace of lemongrass presaging Mia's appearance in the gap. From behind her, soft lighting and the smells of a laden table.

'Evan, it's –'

'If I stopped it all, would you consider letting me in?'

She stood in the doorway, confused. 'I – Wait – *What?* You'd do that? For me?'

'No,' he said. 'For me.'

She blinked at him. Peter leaned forward from his chair onto his elbows, his face poking into view, angled above a still-steaming bowl of mashed potatoes.

'That's what you're saying?' she asked. 'That you're willing to stop it all?'

He stared at her, feeling the pull of a thousand buried instincts as they fought their way to the surface. He opened his mouth to reply.

In his pocket the RoamZone vibrated.

Time decelerated, his senses on overdrive. Ahead, a room glowing with warmth, a table set with cheer. Behind, the cool of the dark hallway lifting the hairs on his neck. The phone in his pocket, calling him to duty.

It had taken so much to get him here, to the threshold. He couldn't bring himself to retreat from the door, to tear himself away.

He dug for the phone, lifted it to his ear, spoke the words. 'Do you need my help?'

A draft from the hall blew in, snuffed out the yellow and orange candles on the table. Black smoke spiraled up from the wicks. Mia searched his face, as if looking for something she could no longer find.

Through a staticky connection came a single syllable: 'Yes.'

It took a split second for Evan to recognize the voice.

It was Jack's.

Keeping the phone pressed to his face, Evan dipped his head apologetically and backed away from the light.

Acknowledgments

Last year, *Orphan X* introduced Evan Smoak to the world. It is no small feat in this day and age to bring a new character to readers, and I would like to thank the exceptional crew at Minotaur Books for doing it so beautifully. Andrew Martin, Hannah Braaten, Hector DeJean, Jennifer Enderlin, Paul Hochman, Kelley Ragland, Sally Richardson, Martin Quinn – Evan and I look forward to working with you for many years to come.

I must also acknowledge Rowland White at Michael Joseph/Penguin Group UK, as well as Izzie Coburn and the sales team, Ellie Hughes, Lee Motley, Matt Waterson, and their counterparts in Australia and New Zealand, for an equally astounding job.

And my reps, the best in the business:

- Lisa Erbach Vance, Aaron Priest, John Richmond, and Melissa Edwards of the Aaron Priest Agency
- Caspian Dennis of the Abner Stein Agency
- Trevor Astbury, Rob Kenneally, Peter Micelli, and Michelle Weiner of Creative Artists Agency
- Stephen F. Breimer of Bloom, Hergott, Diemer et al, and Marc H. Glick of Glick & Weintraub

And Evan's circle of consultants:

- Geoffrey Baehr, the brain
- Billy S____, the muscle
- Brian Shiers, the fighter

- Michael Borohovski (cofounder and CTO of Tin-foil Security), the intrusion engineer
- Melissa Hurwitz and Bret Nelson, the M.D.s
- Philip Eisner, the wordsmith
- Eddie Gonzalez, the translator of street slang
- Maureen Sugden, the (finest) copyeditor
- Bob Mosier, the automobile virtuoso
- Tore Saso, the banking expert
- Dana Kaye, the publicist (who fought Evan's every effort to stay off the grid)

All errors are mine. These folks don't make mistakes.

I'm also compelled to thank readers, booksellers, and librarians for embracing Evan Smoak the way you have. You make it all worthwhile.

And my family – Delinah, Rose, Natalie, my parents, my sister, and Simba and Cairo. I'm blessed to have you.